LAFAYETTE

This Book is a Gift of:

FRIENDS OF THE
LAFAYETTE LIBRARY

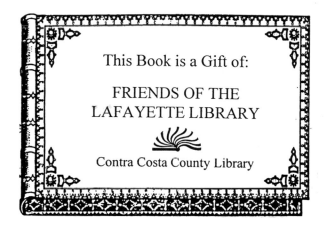

Contra Costa County Library

# Summer's End

# Summer's End

## KATHLEEN GILLES SEIDEL

WITHDRAWN

CONTRA COSTA COUNTY LIBRARY

# B

## BEELER LARGE PRINT

Hampton, New Hampshire, 1999

3 1901 02988 6241

**Library of Congress Cataloging in Publication Data**
Seidel, Kathleen Gilles.
   Summer's end / Kathleen Gilles Seidel.
      p.   cm.
   ISBN 1-57490-245-8 (alk.paper)
   1. Large type books. I. Title.

PS3569.E5136 S86 1999
   813'.54—dc21                              99-057819

Copyright © 1999 by Kathleen Gilles Seidel.
All rights reserved. No part of this book may be reproduced in any
manner whatsoever without written permission from the original
publisher, except in the case of brief quotations embodied in
critical articles and reviews. Please contact
HarperCollins Publishers, 10 East 53ʳᵈ Street, New York, NY 10022

Published in Large Print by arrangement with
HarperCollins Publishers, Inc.

BEELER LARGE  PRINT
is published by
Thomas T. Beeler, *Publisher*
Post Office Box 659
Hampton Falls, New Hampshire  03844

Typeset in 16 point Times New Roman type,
Printed on acid-free paper and bound by
Sheridan Books in Chelsea, Michigan.

*The first time we spoke on the phone, Nancy Fallone thought, "I'm either going to really like this person, or she's going to drive me nuts." How lucky she was—both came true. So in memory of countless carpools, a million sit-ups, and one red quilt, Nancy, this one is for you.*

# CHAPTER 1

"YOU WON'T REMEMBER ME," HE SAID. "WE BARELY spoke."

The voice on the other end of the phone was correct. Gwen Wells did not know who Hal Legend was. Apparently they had been at the same community dinner the evening before. He had gotten her phone number and was now calling to ask her to dinner.

He was asking her on a date.

Gwen had been on dates before, but the last one had been with a young midshipman who had subsequently made her a wife, mother, and now a widow. Surely the rules that had applied to dating in those days no longer applied.

But Gwen had a thirty-year-old daughter, Holly, who was a single lawyer in New York City, and Gwen knew enough about Holly's life to know how one went about dating a stranger.

Yes, she would love to get together with Hal Legend. (Holly always accepted first dates.) But it needed to be lunch. (*Keep it short* was Holly's rule.) No, no, he didn't need directions to her house. She would drive herself, she would meet him there. (*Have your own escape route.*)

"You're making this too easy for me," he said. "I was prepared to go to a great deal of trouble to see you."

And there was something in the way he said "you," something quiet and deep, that Gwen had not heard from a man in a very long time.

Three days later Gwen admitted to herself that she was

1

nervous about this date. She, usually well-focused, clear-sighted, and self-directed, was nervous.

She couldn't believe it. She was never nervous. She worried about her kids, of course, but who didn't? That wasn't the same as being nervous. Why was she even going? She was fifty-eight years old, for heaven's sake. All those rules about dating that she had picked up from Holly—it wasn't as if Holly had sat down and taught them to her. It had never occurred to either one of them that she would need them.

So why was she going? *I'm old enough to be a grandmother. Grandmothers do not go out on dates.*

In point of fact, she was not a grandmother, something which she forced herself to remember. *But that's only because neither Holly nor Jack are married. I'm old enough and that's what counts.*

She looked at her neat gold-banded watch. She was ready, and there were twenty minutes before she needed to leave. What should she do in those twenty minutes?

This was not like her. She did not fluster easily. She was Mrs. Poised and Reliable, Mrs. Organized and Predictable, the lady with the tidy closets and neat drawers. The Queen of the Unchipped Manicures. The commanding officer's wife, the one responsible for all the other wives when the boat was out at sea. Can't understand the notice from the bank? Don't know if you should get the car repaired? Too many wine bottles in your friend's weekly trash? You called Mrs. Wells. She could be counted on to sort out everything.

In those days an officer's fitness report always included an evaluation of his wife because the wives had had responsibilities too. Being an officer's wife was a job, and Gwen had been good at hers. Very good. Her husband would have never become admiral if she hadn't

2

been.

But that was over now. Her manicures were still unchipped, her closets were still neat, she was still trim and blonde, but she wasn't Mrs. C.O. anymore. Mrs. Admiral Wells was Gwen, out on her own, actually going on a date. She wished Holly or Jack were here. This would all be easier if one of her kids were coming with her. They were great. Everyone always liked them.

She stopped herself. She was not dependent on her children. She was not going to hide behind them. In fact, she was going to make a rule for herself. If she actually made it to this date, she was not going to talk about her children, and if she got a set of grandchildren between now and then, she wouldn't talk about them either.

She forced herself to wait another ten of the remaining twenty minutes and then drove to the restaurant. It was in the suburbs, across from Tysons Corner, one of the biggest malls in the Washington, D.C., area. Parking was easy. Too easy. Now she was twelve minutes early.

Some people were always falling further and further behind in life. She was getting further and further ahead. It would be nice if that were a cosmic metaphor, but it probably wasn't. She was just twelve minutes early for her first date in more than three decades.

This was stupid; this fretting was not like her. She pulled her keys out of the ignition and swept up her purse. She was going inside. So what if she was early?

The winter sunlight was thin, but it glittered off the low mounds of ice-crusted snow at the edges of the parking lot. Gwen pulled the restaurant door open. It was dark inside, and for a moment she could see only shapes. A man was rising, moving toward her.

3

Apparently he—if this was indeed the correct 'he'—had arrived even earlier. She pulled off her gloves and slipped them into her purse. Her eyes were adjusting to the light. She could see colors, now details.

He was a tall man with a full head of silvering hair and alert grayish eyes. The bones of his face were good, the slight squareness of his jaw balanced by the high cheekbones. He was a handsome man, but there was nothing overly arranged about his hair or dress. She liked that. She didn't like vain men.

She put out her hand. "You should have told me that you were the one who knew all the songs."

She had noticed him the other evening. How could she not have?

The dinner had been held at a historic mill, a high, round wooden building with exposed joists and stone floors. Someone had brought song sheets, and a small group—a nice mix of all ages—had enjoyed singing. But there were only four songs on the sheet, and they wanted to sing more. Someone suggested "Clementine" and "On Top of Old Smoky" after that. Then there was a pause; no one could think of another song. People started to stir as if they were going to leave the circle. Gwen was disappointed. She would have liked to sing more.

Then a man—this man—spoke. "Why don't we see if we can make it through 'Shine on, Harvest Moon'?"

Gwen knew only the chorus, or at least that's what she thought, but with this man prompting, she remembered more of the verses than she thought she did.

Each time the group finished a song, they looked at him, and he always had a suggestion for another: cowboy songs, Broadway tunes, Scout camp songs,

4

good songs, songs that were fun to sing. And whenever the group started to flounder, everyone singing lines from different verses, he got them back on track; he knew the right words.

"It really made the evening wonderful," she said to him now. "Singing can be such fun even if you aren't good at it."

"We had time to sing only because you got the buffet line moving."

It took her a moment to remember. Oh, that business with the extension cord.

The dinner at the mill had been a buffet, and the line had quickly grown quite long. It was easy to see why. The buffet tables had been pushed against the wall so that people could serve themselves only from one side. If they were moved out, the line could split in two.

But there was an extension cord, the caterers said. If the tables were pulled away from the wall, people might trip on the extension cord. "I'll stand on it," Gwen had proposed. This was the sort of problem admirals "wives" were expected to solve. "That will keep people from getting themselves tangled up."

So Gwen had spent the first part of the evening planted on a heavy safety-orange extension cord. No wonder Hal Legend had noticed her. She had been a human traffic cone.

"It was so silly," she said to him now, "to have anything on a buffet table that needed electricity. Or at least they should have brought a roll of duct tape to tape down the cord."

Her son, Jack, would have had a roll of duct tape in his truck. Jack never went anywhere without duct tape. But she was, she reminded herself, not going to talk about her children.

5

Hal nodded, agreeing with her either about the duct tape or the electricity or both, but he didn't say which. Clearly he had the sense to know that there was nothing more to be said on this topic. "They have a coat check. May I take yours?"

He was raising his hands, obviously planning on helping her with her coat. So she turned slightly and let him lift it off her shoulders.

He was tall. She wasn't used to tall men. Her husband, John, had been five-foot-nine, and many of his fellow submariners barely met the military's minimum-height requirements. A tall man spent too much of his tour on a sub ducking his head and twisting his shoulders. As a submariner's wife, Gwen had grown to admire short men. Many of them, teased through their childhoods, had grown up with steady courage and a fierce sense of service. They seemed denser, tighter, tougher than less efficiently built men.

But Hal Legend was tall. She knew nothing about tall men.

He checked her coat, and a minute later they were seated, the business of taking menus and refusing drinks occupying them for a few moments. Gwen had already decided she would get a Caesar salad. She glanced at the menu, making sure that one was listed. Then she set it aside and leaned forward.

"I didn't let myself call Barbara Hutchens"—the Hutchenses had been the ones, he had told her, who had brought him to the dinner—"to find out about you. So I am ignorant. Does knowing a lot of songs sum you up completely, or is there more?"

"No, the songs pretty much cover it. I am a music professor, and I specialize in folk songs of all different cultures."

A professor? She was a navy wife. What different worlds. "So you could have had us singing in Sanskrit?"

"Perhaps not Sanskrit, but certainly Serbo-Croatian."

She asked him about his work. Why folk songs?

"I like the energy of popular culture," he said. "I like learning about a society through the words its people sing."

That sounded good, but Gwen wasn't sure she really understood. "For example?"

He gave several. Political assumptions, religious practices, economic principles, everything about a society he was able to connect with the songs. She mentioned some of the songs she herself loved, and he had something to say about each of them, things so interesting that she knew that she would never again hear or sing the song without thinking those thoughts.

Her unease, her nervousness, was gone. She enjoyed listening to him talk. It was interesting. No, it was more than interesting. She could feel herself leaning forward, ignoring her salad. It was exhilarating. He had such insight into large issues. It was as if he were an eagle, soaring over the earth, seeing all, the trees, the lakes, the mountains, and understanding all.

A submarine speeds through dark waters, beneath everything, seeing nothing.

There was a lightness about Hal that her husband had not had. John had been an intense man, keenly focused, hungry to act. His admiral's stars had forced him to become wise, had forced him out of single-mindedness and into reflection, but the discipline had not come naturally or easily to him. Hal was different. He wore his wisdom lightly, the rightful crown to his years.

And suddenly all of this seemed right, this meeting a man when you were fifty-eight. At fifty-eight you no

7

longer met the midshipmen and the graduate students; you met the admirals, the professors, the men who had become the Arthurs and the Merlins and the Solomons. Those men, the ones who were truly confident and kingly, they were no more interested in pretty lassies than you were in bright-faced lads.

Gwen let the conversation drift toward more personal matters. Hal was a widower. He lived in Iowa, teaching at a small college there, but he was spending the spring semester in Washington teaching at Georgetown University. "I needed to get away for a while. I was living exactly as I had when Eleanor was alive. I had changed nothing. I couldn't think what to change. Everything seemed right, but empty."

His wife had died suddenly from a drug-resistant infection, a sore throat that had become pneumonia. "It was very surprising for us all," he said.

Gwen knew about that kind of "surprise." Her husband had also died suddenly. He had been driving home and had stopped to help a young mother with a flat tire. A drunk driver had careened off the road, killing John but not the woman or her two small children.

Hal winced at the story.

It had been four years. Gwen had done her mourning. She was as at peace as a person could be. "John was in the service. He had always expected that he might have to die for others . . . although admirals sitting behind desks usually aren't the ones who have to do it."

"I don't imagine they are," Hal agreed.

It would be easy, Gwen suspected, for the conversation to drift back to the general; they could talk about the military, about ideals of service, and so on. "Do you have children?" she asked.

He had three. His older daughter was a lawyer. She ran a legal-aid clinic. His son was a linguistic professor in California, specializing in dying Indian languages. "Some of these languages are down to their last two or three speakers, and those people are pretty old. Ian and his students are frantically trying to learn what they can."

Both his son and daughter were married with children. Phoebe, the daughter, had four children, and Ian, the son, had three.

"You said you had three children," Gwen said. "Your other daughter—is she married?"

"Amy? No, she's not."

Something pricked at Gwen. "Amy? Is that her name? Amy Legend? That's funny. She must have the same name as that figure skater then."

"Actually, she is that figure skater."

Gwen had been lifting her fork. She stopped, staring at him. Then she laid her fork back down.

Amy Legend? His daughter was Amy Legend?

Amy Legend had won an Olympic gold medal. She had been on the cover of *People* magazine. America loved her. She was a star, a celebrity. "Amy Legend is your daughter?"

He nodded. "We're very proud of her."

"Amy Legend? The Olympic champion Amy Legend?"

"Yes."

She was having lunch with Amy Legend's father? "Why didn't you say so earlier?"

"It seemed pretty clear that you didn't want us to talk about our children."

He was perceptive. Completely wrong—who wouldn't want to talk about Amy Legend?—but

9

perceptive. "That was before I knew that she was one of yours."

Amy Legend had been a lovely child, a golden-haired little sprite so pretty that she almost didn't seem real. When she was with her family at a restaurant or in line with her mother at the post office, people turned and watched her. Her features were delicate, her eyes darkly lashed.

Of course, at age four she had no idea that she was a little package of winsome grace. She cared only about her hair. She had short hair, and she wanted long hair. Oh, how she wanted long hair. She hungered for it, she craved it, she pretended she had it. She would loop a petticoat around her head and imagine that the white nylon was hair swishing and billowing. She would clamp a towel to her scalp and toss her head so the terry cloth would flick over her shoulders and cascade down her back. She cut pictures out of magazines with her little plastic scissors, pictures of hair, flowing tresses that curled and gleamed.

"Long hair is too hard to take care of," her mother told her, "and trust me, love, you look better in short hair."

Amy Legend was twenty-six now. She was wealthy, she was famous, and her mother was dead. She could have worn her hair however she wanted. But her mother turned out to be right after all—she did look better in short hair. "You wouldn't look *bad* if you let your hair grow," various stylists had told her, "but you certainly took better with it this length."

So hers was still short. It was beautifully cut in a soft, feathery style. Now honey blonde, it glowed with carefully placed golden highlights. It was great hair . . .

10

but it wasn't long.

"What was it like?" Gwen asked. "Raising such a gifted child? You read all about how much is involved, the driving and the traveling and the money. It's such a commitment." She had always been glad that her two children had been all-around types, good at a lot of things, not overwhelmingly talented at any one.

"Financially it was extraordinary, just unbelievably expensive," Hal admitted. "But Eleanor had some family money, so we never had to make any difficult choices, and once she turned professional, she paid us back completely even though we had not expected it."

"What about the rest of it, the logistics and all? Did it take over your lives?"

"No. She's a lot younger than Phoebe and Ian, and I am afraid we focused more on them. We had a little-kid household when they were little kids; we were about teenagers when the two of them were teenagers. Amy just had to go along. Plus, Phoebe and Ian—especially Ian—were very bright in the ways that a college community recognizes, and Amy's abilities were foreign to us. Then suddenly one day there were reporters in the driveway, wanting to talk about her."

The Legend family loved to read. Their high-ceilinged, turn-of-the-century brick house in Iowa was full of books. There were books piled on nightstands, on the breakfront in the dining room, on the top of the piano in the front hall. There were books at the foot of the stairs waiting to be carried upstairs, books at the top of the stairs waiting to be carried downstairs.

Eleanor—the family's mother—always had a book with her. She read while waiting to pick the kids up at

11

piano lessons, she read while eating her lunch, while waiting for a pot of soup to come to a simmer. Amy's older sister and brother, Phoebe and Ian, were readers too. They took books to the grocery store and leaned against the base of the coin-operated riding horse, reading while their mother pushed a cart through the aisles.

But Amy, lovely little Amy, was different. She did not like to read. When she was at the grocery store, she went to the cosmetic aisle and looked at the nail polish and lipstick. In good weather she played outside, turning cartwheels, dancing with her shadow, flipping herself down from the limbs of trees. In bad weather she roamed the house, restless, wanting to be entertained. Her brother and sister didn't need to be entertained. They could take a book and disappear for hours. They could play Monopoly for most of a day. Not Amy. She was a little hummingbird, always in motion.

The year she was seven winter came hard. Day followed day of freezing, sleeting rain. The skies were low and gray, the sidewalks were icy. The rest of the family loved it. They built fires in all the fireplaces, made popcorn balls, piled chamber music on the turntable, and reread their favorite books.

Amy could watch the firelight for ten minutes. Then she was out of her chair, rummaging through her mother's closet, trying on all her shoes and scarves, but Eleanor had little interest in clothes; her closet had few glittering treasures. Amy sneaked into her older sister's room and played with her makeup, streaking harsh lines of blue across her eyelids. But Phoebe didn't have much makeup. In desperation Eleanor flipped on the television. "Here, Amy, I think you might like this."

It was the Olympics, a preview of the ladies figure

12

skating competition.

Amy didn't like television. She didn't like to sit, doing nothing, but within moments she was mesmerized—the spins, the jumps, the flashing blades, and the costumes, oh, the gorgeous costumes, the glittering sequins, the chiffon skirts that floated and swirled, the soft feathers. She was breathless. Longing swelled inside her, a balloon stretching and growing until it was tight and hard.

"I have to do that. Oh, Mother, Daddy, *please*, I just have to."

Eleanor had no sympathy for her youngest child's obsession with glamour and affectation. She was English, a brisk, practical, self-assured woman. She liked the ballet, but figure skating? It was so . . . so middlebrow.

But anything that would keep Amy occupied during bad weather was worth doing. She called the college's hockey rink about skating lessons.

Oh, yes, an assistant coach's wife had been a figure skater. She'd be happy to give Amy a few lessons.

Amy went to her first lesson. The next day she took her skates to school. Eleanor assumed that she was taking them for show and tell, and Amy did indeed show them to everyone. After school, instead of going home, she bent her head into the biting wind and trudged to the rink. She put on her skates and went out on the ice, skating straight into the middle of a hockey practice.

The coach instantly blew his whistle. This fragile-looking child in her loosely tied skates was in genuine peril. But he knew nothing about little girls; it never occurred to him to ask why she was there. He told her that the team would be off the ice in fifteen minutes, and

13

as they were leaving, he motioned to one of his huge, shin-guarded, shoulder-padded players to go tie her little white skates for her.

She had been mesmerized by the players' speed. That's what she wanted to do, to go that fast, to fly like that. She stepped out onto the rough ice and started to skate. The coach forgot about her, and after the team had cleared out of the locker room, he flipped off the lights with only the briefest glance over his shoulder. Amy went on skating in the dusky half-light. She wasn't even thinking about costumes anymore. She wanted to skate.

An hour later the Zamboni man came to resurface the ice for the evening open session. And of course he was very surprised to see her. *Do your parents know you are here? Do you have permission to do this*? Any of those questions Amy would have answered honestly.

But he worded his question unthinkingly. "Are you supposed to be here?" he asked.

"Yes," Amy answered, and she was telling the truth. "I am supposed to be here."

"What was she like as a child?" Gwen asked. "I've seen pictures of her. She was lovely."

"Yes, she was," Hal nodded. "She was also obedient, very obedient. Until she started skating, she was dragged along everywhere, to Phoebe's and Ian's piano recitals and science fairs, and she always behaved well, probably better than a little kid should have. But most good skaters do have very obedient personalities. For years and years they have to do exactly what they are told, when they are told, and a lot of it is pretty tedious. They have to want to obey their coaches. It always surprises me that so much creativity can come out of

14

these very well-behaved people, and I'm still not sure that I know what makes Amy tick. When she's around the family, she always seems quiet and cooperative, just like when she was little."

"You don't accomplish what she was by being quiet and cooperative."

"No, you don't," Hal agreed. "There's clearly this big chunk of her that I don't know at all."

Amy could not wait a whole week for her next lesson. Please please *please*, could she have another one now? She would do anything, *anything*.

Her parents sat down and talked to her. As long as she worked hard, they said, she could skate all she wanted.

Worked hard? What were they talking about? Book reports, math problems, that was work. This was skating.

She could walk to the rink, so she went every day after school. She watched the hockey practices, she watched the Zamboni man, and she skated. She skated endlessly, forever. She never got tired of it.

She had no idea if she was any good. She didn't care, she just loved it so much. She even read a book that spring—a pictoral biography of Peggy Fleming.

Then one afternoon during the last week of school she came home from the rink to find her duffel bag laid out on her bed. She stared at it. It was heavy green canvas with a zipper and a single handle.

Duffel bags. That meant Minnesota, packing to go to Minnesota. Her family had a cabin on a lake in the northern part of the state, and that's where they spent the summer, the whole summer. Their cabin was in the middle of a forest, miles and miles from any town, and even that town was too small to have a rink. She would have to go the whole summer without skating. She couldn't do it. She just couldn't.

But she had to. No one gave her a choice.

"This is going to make me sound like a horrible snob," Hal was saying, "but we didn't have a lot in common with the other skating families. It wasn't merely that they were obsessed with their children's lives to an extent that seemed very unhealthy to us, but their notions of success were so limited. All they could think about was winning competitions and making money."

Gwen could easily understand how a person's vision could get "limited" to that, especially if you didn't have the family money Hal said his wife had had. "What were your definitions of success?"

"Creating beauty. Expressing the music. I think if we helped Amy at all, it was managing to instill that in her. If she did something lovely, if she made the audience feel something, then she had succeeded regardless of what scores she got."

Amy's ethereal childhood beauty stayed with her. Her mother came from an aristocratic background—three hundred years of privileged men marrying the prettiest girls they could find. That heritage showed in Amy. She remained lovely. Her arms, legs, and neck were willowy and graceful; her strength came in long, clean lines rather than in bunchy knots of muscle. Her torso was lean and compact, and her back was the most flexible her pediatrician had ever seen.

"She needs to be with someone better than me," her coach said. "There's nothing in Iowa for her." The coach recommended a training facility in Delaware. A

16

number of families who lived close to the training center took in boarders to help meet their own children's expenses. The local schools were used to giving the young skaters plenty of release time, or tutors could easily be found for those who wanted to be taught at home.

Eleanor had gone to boarding school; sending a child from home was not strange to her. Amy herself loved the idea. This was her dream, to skate all the time, to train with the best.

The rink was one place where she was always special. She would be bent over her skates, lacing them up, and she would hear the coaches, the other parents, whispering her name in the way that teachers had always whispered Phoebe's and Ian's names. She liked that. At home she felt like an afterthought, Amy the Afterthought. On the ice she was someone else. She was the one people thought about first.

Not in Delaware. Not at the training center there. She wasn't the best anymore. At first she didn't even seem very good.

Her talent was footwork. She could skip across the ice, her feet dancing in dazzling patterns, her blades slicing and crossing as lightly as if she were in ballet shoes. She could do sequences that even the senior girls couldn't. But she couldn't jump.

That's what mattered, the jumps. That's what everyone talked about, that's how the girls sorted themselves out, by who could do which jumps. Girls there younger than Amy had double axels, one even had a triple salchow. Amy's footwork didn't matter. You had to be able to jump.

The year she was thirteen, she qualified for the national junior tournaments. She placed twelfth. The next year she came in seventeenth.

Seventeenth. Worse than the year before. And she had skated a good, clean program. There was no way she could have skated any better. This was worse than if she had skated badly, much worse. What do you do when your best isn't good enough?

Almost unable to speak, she called her parents as soon as the results were posted. "This doesn't make sense anymore." She was in tears. "You're spending all this money, and nothing's happening. I'm not getting any better. I think I should come home."

Sometimes girls had to quit because of money; their parents couldn't afford their training anymore. They would simply disappear, and everyone would have to guess where they were, why they had gone.

But no one would have to guess about why Amy left. They would all know. She wasn't good enough. She had failed.

She knew what her parents would say. She should finish the year, the money didn't matter, the important thing was not to be a quitter. *I'm not a quitter,* her heart shrieked. *No one works harder than me. I'm just not good enough. I'll never get these stupid jumps.*

She couldn't go back to Delaware, not as seventeenth place, not as Amy the Afterthought. "Your flight is this afternoon, isn't it?" her father asked. "Do you want us to meet you in Delaware?"

"It won't do any good." She was still crying. "Nothing will help."

"It may not help you," he said firmly, "but it will help us, make us feel that we are doing something. I have an eight A.M. class tomorrow morning. I can't cancel it, but the minute it's over, I'll be on my way."

Her parents hadn't seen her skate in more than a year.

18

They rarely came to tournaments, and Amy didn't really expect them to. They were so different from all the other skating families. Nonetheless, by the time she got back to Delaware after the tournament, she heard that her father had called the front office. Her coaches were rearranging ice time, and the next morning he was there, a tall, lean man with thick, dark hair. She supposed he had flown to Philadelphia and rented a car there.

"Amy's a very nice little skater," she heard her coach say to him. "She has such wonderfully long arms and legs, her line is so lovely, and she carries herself so well. We have developed a very aristocratic look for her."

Amy didn't want to be a "very nice little skater." She wanted to be the best. She wanted to win.

"Let me watch her skate," her father said.

He stood at the boards, resting lightly on his elbows, his hands linked. He was wearing a tweed jacket, a pale blue shirt, and a navy blue knitted tie. It was strange to see a father at practice. Figure skating was a world of mothers. Even in the family she lived with, none of them saw the father very much. He worked two jobs to pay for his daughter's training.

The air in the rink was thin, the light pale and artificial with a meat locker chill. Amy skated her short program for her father, then her long program. When she came back to the boards, his expression was gentle, but she couldn't tell what he was thinking.

He touched her face. "You are so very lovely."

People said that to her all the time, how lucky she was to be pretty. "That's not enough, Dad."

"I know. Now tell me, who chose your music?" he asked.

"The coaches."

19

"What about this 'aristocratic' look that you are supposed to have?"

"I think it has to do with my not being any good at the jumps."

He smiled. "Is that what 'aristocratic' means? Not being able to jump?"

"They talk about elegance, coolness, serenity, things like that."

"Well, sweetheart, I'm willing to bet that these people here don't know any aristocrats, which gives you and me a leg up because we do."

"We do?" She was confused for a moment. "Oh, you mean Mother?"

Mother's grandfather had been an earl, and when she wrote letters to her own mother, she addressed the envelopes to "Lady Phoebe Cooke." Amy didn't really know what that meant—Mother never seemed to think it important—but it did sound aristocratic.

"Now, do you really think you should try to skate like your mother?" her father asked.

Amy's laugh was a little thin and watery, but it was a laugh. "No." All the other skating mothers drove gleamingly clean cars and dressed carefully, even when they came to watch the earliest morning practice, they wore makeup and their blouses were neatly ironed. Her own mother drove a battered station wagon. Her jewelry was all inherited—strange Art Deco pieces which she wore without much thought of how they looked with her clothes. Amy couldn't imagine trying to skate like her.

"So let's lose this 'aristocratic look,' " Amy's father said. "Your mother may be an aristocrat, but you are a red-blooded, bouncy American kid. Now, let me watch some of these other girls so I know what I am looking at."

Amy slipped her skate guards on and came around to sit with him in the bleachers. For the next hour they watched her friends. She knew some of their programs almost as well as she knew her own. She told her father what to watch for.

"Now, watch the height she gets on her jumps . . . see how tight she is in her rotations . . how clean her landing is."

"Amy, please," he said, "stop talking about the jumps. I'm tired of hearing about jumps."

"But the jumps are everything, Dad. They're what counts."

He motioned her to be quiet.

She couldn't remember when they had ever sat like this, just the two of them. The family often watched slides on Sunday evening, and if Phoebe or Ian wanted to work the projector, then Dad would pull her into his lap because she was the littlest, the only one who was still cuddly. But if Phoebe or Ian needed help with the projector, he would have to move her off his lap and go help the older one.

He wasn't liking what he was seeing on the ice. Amy could tell that. His lips were tight, and his head was pulled back, his neck angling sharply away from his shoulders and spine. She had seen him like that before—when she was little and would be struggling with her spelling words or trying to read something aloud. He would glance at Mother, and Mother would lift her hand—*this is Amy,* the hand would seem to be saying, *there's nothing we can do about it. She's not like the others.*

At the end of the session, he sat quietly for a moment, looking down at his hands, his lips tight. Then he spoke. "Why do you want to quit?"

21

This was a test. Amy knew that instantly. There was a right answer.

And she had no idea what it was. "Because I'm not good enough?"

He shook his head. "No. We have no idea how good you are. Every one of these girls is exactly alike. They are little robots. Your coach is very controlling. Do you know what I mean by that?"

Sort of. "But, Dad, she's the coach. We have to do what she says."

"No, you don't. You have to *listen* to what she says. You have to try it, give it your best shot, but if it doesn't work for you, you don't have to do it." He lifted his arm around her shoulders. "You know that your mother doesn't really enjoy watching you skate. Do you know why?"

Amy looked down at her hands. Of course she knew why. She wasn't Phoebe or Ian, she wasn't smart like Phoebe and Ian. That's what counted to her parents, being smart, not being able to skate. But Dad wouldn't say that. It was true, but no one would say it. "She'd rather be watching ballet." That seemed like a safe answer.

"There's some element of truth in that," he admitted, "but the important thing is that she doesn't feel like she's watching you." His voice was gentle. "It seems as if it's someone else out there. And I think, as usual, she's right. I don't know as much about figure skating as perhaps I should, but I do know a thing or two about performance."

Amy looked at him blankly. Oh, he was a music professor. That's what he was talking about, musical performances.

"The one thing that separates the great musicians

22

from the very good ones is not technique; they all have that. The great musicians love every note that they play, they become the piece of music. That's not happening when you skate. It's closest to happening with the girl in the blue. I almost have a sense of her personality, of who she is when she skates."

The girl in the blue was the two-time junior National champion. "Did you see how many triples she has in her program?"

A look of impatience flashed across her father's face. "No, I didn't. Amy, you're obsessed with these jumps. It's all you can think about. All that matters to you is the thing that you're worst at. Let's concentrate on what you're good at. Now, what is your favorite piece of music?"

Another test. Her favorite piece of music. She wasn't prepared. She knew that she ought to name something from the classics, Liszt or Brahms or someone like that. He would approve of that, but for the life of her, she couldn't think of anything.

She blurted out the name of a song currently playing on the radio. Then hated herself. Why had she said something so dopey? Now he was going to think that she was stupid.

Although of course he already knew that.

But his expression didn't change. His voice was even. "Fine. Let's get a tape of it."

"For a program? But it has lyrics. We can't use things with lyrics."

"Then we will rerecord it."

He stayed for three days, and for the first time in the two and a half years Amy had been there, she felt like she had the full attention of her coach and the choreographer.

He borrowed a pair of skates and came out on the ice.

"I didn't know you could skate, Dad."

"By the standards of everyone around here, I'm sure I can't," he answered. "But I played hockey constantly as a kid. As soon as the farm ponds froze, that's what we did."

"I didn't know that."

"You didn't?" He shook his head. "That's what got me the Rhodes scholarship, being able to play hockey— you had to be athletic as well as smart. If I hadn't skated, I wouldn't have gone to Oxford and I wouldn't have met your mother and then where would you be?"

Amy shrugged. This was weird, her not knowing that he could skate when skating was her whole life.

But ice hockey was nothing like competitive figure skating, and she resisted his ideas at first. He didn't understand how important the jumps were. "But, Dad," she kept saying, "the judges look for those jumps."

All the other families knew about the jumps. It was starting to make her mad. The other families came to watch competitions; some mothers were at every practice, every single one. She understood that her family wasn't like that, that they were different, but Dad had no business acting like he knew what he was talking about. He didn't.

He must have sensed her mood. He stopped and gathered up her hands in his, pulling her close. "I know you don't agree with me, but could you humor me for a bit? The minute I'm gone, you can go back to doing it the old way."

She could feel the tweed of his jacket along her forearms. The tweed was made of twists of blue and green, and the suede patches at the elbow were a soft brown. His hands were slender for a man's, but they

24

were warm.

He and Ian had learned calculus together. It had been during her last year at home. Ian, who seemed to be able to learn languages faster than Amy could read English, was actually having trouble in a subject. "Well, it won't hurt me," their father had laughed, and night after night they sat in the book-filled living room, moaning and making faces. But Ian had gotten an A.

Now her father—her father who had skated during his own childhood—was here, helping her.

She wanted to believe him, she really did. She didn't want to be mad, not when he had gone to so much trouble to get here, but what did he know about the sport? She looked over her shoulder at her coach.

That was a mistake. She knew it the instant that she did it. She was saying to him that her coach's opinion mattered more to her than his did.

Well, maybe it did.

Surprisingly the coach supported him. "Pretend that you're a professional, in an ice show," she suggested. "In an ice show you don't have to worry about judges."

No one had ever talked to Amy about a professional career. The best girls were already getting flowers from the ice shows and the management agencies, but not Amy.

"Can you think like that?" Her father's voice was gentle.

"Yes."

She was the most important element of the program, he said. Not the music, not the costume, not even the jumps, but she herself. He preached sincerity, absolute sincerity. "Do you love that move? You can't do it if you don't love it. No one will believe in you unless you believe in yourself." He talked about emotion and

25

getting the audience to feel what she was feeling. "Reach out to them."

And above all, she had to be herself. "Maybe it would be easier, even better, if you were a jumper, but you aren't. Pretending to be won't work."

He helped her understand that she liked the Top 40 tune because it was so cheerful, so full of bouncy anticipation. The first evening he found a piano and started playing a rough medley of three medieval German folk songs. Amy instantly fell in love with the songs. Hal played and replayed them, trying all sorts of different arrangements. Amy listened and listened.

After an hour he stopped playing. "You have a marvelous ear," he said, shaking his head. "I don't know why I hadn't noticed it before. I thought Ian was the only one of you who had it."

All her life she had heard that Ian was so good at languages because he had a nearly genius-level ability to remember and recreate a sound. It was strange, it was incomprehensible, to hear her ear compared to his.

They made a tape of the German songs, and the next morning they took everything they had worked on the day before and put it to the new music. Then he rearranged the music so the jumps made sense. She came to understand what she had hated about jumps was that they never seemed to have anything to do with the music. But now her music seemed to be lifting her and turning her on its own.

"What makes a jump work?" her father asked. "What makes you go around? What are the physics involved?"

Physics? Amy knew nothing about physics. Ian was the one who understood physics, not her.

Dad talked to the coaches. They gave him articles to read. "The latest research on jumps," he said to Amy

26

afterward, "argues for importance of upper body strength, and that can be improved."

So Amy started lifting weights.

She hated it. How she hated it. Skating was about speed and beauty and emotion, about lifting an arm and extending a leg and knowing, feeling, the beauty of the line. Lifting weights was drudgery, a job, and she hated it.

There were no short cuts; there was little satisfaction. She couldn't let her muscles become bulky, so she didn't have the challenge of seeing how much she could lift. She instead faced endless repetitions. It didn't matter which tapes she listened to or who else was in the room to talk to; lifting weights was always hateful, and she had never hated anything about practice before.

But she did it.

Her jumps were never as strong as some of the other girls'—they never would be—but they grew better, and she worked on her landings until they became feather-soft. If the jumps themselves were slow and low, that grew to seem right because she was like a feather, floating easily, effortlessly.

It turned out that the more her father talked to her coaches and the other staff at the training center, the less he thought of them. He asked her which two junior skaters she enjoyed watching the most. "I don't care about who is winning, not at this level. Simply tell me who you can't take your eyes off of."

She thought for a while. It was hard. At competitions you just thought about who was going to win. "There are these two guys—Henry Carroll and Tommy Sargent—I do love to watch them. Henry blazes across the ice, he has such power, and Tommy, he's little and he always seems so funny. He makes me laugh even when he's skating."

Her father seemed to like the sound of that. "Then let's look into who they train with."

"But, Dad, they never win."

"And I think that's in their favor. It's the little robots that are winning the Juniors."

Henry and Tommy were in Colorado, not at the big facility in Colorado Springs, but at a smaller rink in Denver, where they trained with a man named Oliver Young. Family finances had forced Oliver out of amateur competition before he had made a name for himself; he had skated in ice shows for several years and was now starting to coach. He was interested primarily in boy skaters; Amy would be the only girl at the Junior Olympic level.

"Will that bother you?" her father asked her.

"No." She had never gotten very close to the other girls in Delaware, even the ones she lived with; their rink was too competitive for friendships.

She moved to Colorado in the fall. Oliver agreed with her father. His philosophy was yes, you had to get all the basics, and yes, you had to lift weights, but in the end you had to learn to skate like yourself, and the next winter, the year Amy was fifteen, with a program full of dazzling footwork she won the Junior tournament. From seventeenth place to first in one year.

The girls in her old skating club tingled with frustration. They had thought Amy had left Delaware because she wasn't good enough. So why had she won? They were better skaters, they kept saying to themselves over and over, and it was true. But they were not better performers, and there was nothing that they could do about it. Amy's musicality—that she seemed to hear more in a piece of music than anyone else—and her

28

capacity to project herself, to make people feel what she was feeling, both of those were simply God-given talents, which Oliver Young recognized and fostered.

She went on lifting weights. Day after day, and she never liked it any better, never found it any more satisfying. Her family still made her come to Minnesota for a few weeks every summer, and she took empty sacks with her, filling them with sand for the numbing routine.

She came in ninth her first year in the Senior Tournament. Officials at the United States Figure Skating Association noticed her and arranged for her to enter a small international competition in Vienna. Such invitations were usually limited to the top seven or eight skaters, and the mothers of girls who had finished ahead of Amy at the Nationals were incensed. Why was Miss Amy Legend suddenly the USFSA's little pet? Their daughters deserved the organization's support, not Amy.

But those girls were the little robots, and at this level technique was no longer enough.

Amy's confidence increased. The next year she came in sixth, then third. Now the ice shows, the agents, and the management companies were sending her flowers, and the USFSA was determined to give her more international experience. She sparkled on the ice, skating with glowing warmth, and the year she was nineteen, she became National Champion. It was an Olympic year, and the USFSA named her to the Olympic team.

Nineteen was a good age. Ladies' figure skating had not yet gone the way of gymnastics, a sport dominated by tiny school girls whose rigorous training schedules had delayed their physical development. They were superb athletes, but they had little celebrity value. Only other schoolgirls were interested in them.

But the general public could identify with a young woman almost in her twenties. People loved reading about Amy during the weeks before the Olympics. She was so pretty, she dressed so delightfully. She was a little shy, looking up and out at the world from beneath her bangs as the Princess of Wales had once done. The media made much of her music professor father and how the music majors at Lipton College in Lipton, Iowa, performed and recorded all her music for her. They took pictures of her mother's grand ancestral homes in England and Ireland even though in some cases her mother had never laid eyes on the place.

Yet there were those who wanted to find fault. People who paid no attention to figure skating at any other time were suddenly experts, announcing that footwork could never win the Olympics. "She may be the most watchable skater of the circuit," proclaimed the network's skating pundit, "but her jumps aren't up to international standards."

"I think the American public is going to be in for a big disappointment," announced a male former pairs champion. "Amy Legend is not going to win the Olympics. She can't."

He was wrong.

The top women skaters usually don't go to the opening ceremonies of the Olympics. Theirs is one of the last competitions, so any skater who comes to the opening has an extra week of sitting around in a cramped dorm, eating institutional food and waiting for inadequate ice time.

But Amy had been watching the opening ceremonies since she turned seven. There was no way she was going to miss this one, no matter what it did to her training schedule.

"Let her go," her new advisers at the sports management agency told her coaches. "She'll get some great camera time."

Both Amy's parents had been involved in the selection of her management team. "No one on earth," her father had said, "can see through smooth talk faster than your mother. She'll have no patience for any of these people. If we find someone she can tolerate for twenty minutes, you'll have a person you can trust with your life."

These new advisers were telling her that medals weren't enough. "The American public has to love you," they said.

"And exactly how do I go about getting them to do that?" she laughed.

"By being yourself."

Be *yourself.* She was the only girl hearing that. The other top amateur girls were being "packaged"—that was the word they kept hearing, "packaging." Andrea was to be feisty; JillAnn was to be sweet. It put too much pressure on them, knowing that they were supposed to be sweet or feisty all the time.

No one ever spoke to Amy about a "package," and at first she assumed it was because she was hopeless, such a gooey blob of nothingness that she couldn't be scooped up into a container.

But her training partner, Tommy, tiny, wise, and witty, knew better. No one was talking to him about packaging either. "We're the real thing, Amy, you and me. Even Henry"—technically Henry was a better skater than either of them, but then he was a better skater than anyone on earth—"doesn't have it. We do."

31

Henry and Tommy had signed with the same agency. Henry was favored to win the men's gold while Tommy knew that he would be lucky to come in third. "You'll come into your own as a professional," the agents and managers kept telling him. "Don't worry."

All three of them went to the opening of the Olympics, and Amy had a wonderful time during that first week when they weren't competing. She had never played any team sport, and she suddenly found that she liked being on a team. She went to as many skating events as she could. Looking wide-eyed and pretty in her red, white, and blue team sweats, she cheered for all the other American skaters. She got a mad crush on one of the American hockey players, but fortunately for his concentration she never had the nerve to tell him about it.

She was third after the short program. She and Oliver had hoped to be in second place at that point, but with jumps like hers it was no surprise that she was not.

Then in that day between the short and long programs the Olympics stopped being fun. Tommy and Henry were skating in the men's final that evening, but all Amy could think of was her own fate—how large the gap was between her and the other two girls and how solid their jumps were. And then a worse thought took over—how very few tenths of a point separated her from the fourth-place finisher. The skating community might not expect her to get a medal, but the American public did. They believed in fairy stories. She was pretty, therefore she would win the gold.

*It doesn't work that way. There's no magic, no guarantees. It's just me and my skates.*

Henry won. Now all the people who were saying that Amy couldn't win were talking of 1976, when Dorothy

Hamill and John Curry, two skaters trained by the same coach, had won the women's and men's golds. Amy and Henry could repeat that. Oliver would become the Carlo Fassi of his generation.

It was too much.

So she fell. On the easiest of the triples, the plain old toe loop. A little overrotation. Tilting in the air. Fighting for the loading. Not being able to hold it, and she was on the ice. Her chance for the gold was gone.

So it was over. All those years of lifting weights— they had been a waste. Now it was all pointless.

She scrambled to her feet and caught up with the music. She wasn't going to think about the weights. Just as she had been watching the opening ceremonies for twelve years, so she had been watching people compete for twelve years, and long ago she had made a pledge to herself. *If I fall on a big night, I will not mind. I may have to stop competing, but then I can start performing. The judges may hate me, but I can make the audience love me. I will skate for them.*

She opened her arms in a swirling, embracing, almost triumphant motion, gathering in the audience. *I'm here for you now. It's too late for those people sitting at rink-side with their little computerized scoring machines. They've given up an me. But you haven't. You will love me . . . love me . . . love me.*

And they did.

The young Chinese woman in second place gasped in weary relief when she saw Amy fall. She turned her back to the monitors, knowing that she didn't have to worry about Amy anymore. She was to skate next, and so she was at the boards, taking her skate guards off when Amy's scores flashed up. She had not seen Amy's performance, and she was staggered by the numbers.

Amy had fallen; how could she be getting these scores?

So that skater, rattled and tense, fell too. Only she went on trying to compete. She could compete, but she could not perform. Amy was now in second place.

The German skater who had begun the evening in first place skated last, and she knew exactly what she needed to do—skate cleanly. She did not have to add any extra jumps, she did not have to take any risks. All she had to do was not fall down.

And that's how she skated, like someone who was determined not to fall down. And she didn't fall. But her skating was leaden and lifeless. Her artistic-impression scores were weak.

The judges try to be fair, but they also have to think about what is good for the sport. And there was no doubt after this evening's gutsy performance that the delicious little Amy Legend, even if she couldn't jump, was very good for the sport.

Amy had won because she had made a mistake, because she had forgiven herself for making a mistake.

After they hung the gold medal around her neck and played "The Star-Spangled Banner," she did all the fun things that Olympic medalists get to do. She carried the flag at the closing ceremony. She sat beside Mickey Mouse on a float at the Disneyland parade. A warmly smiling grandfatherly butler opened the door to the White House, and when the Olympians gathered for their picture in the East Room, a press aide made sure that she was the one standing next to the president.

She taped some commercials, toured with the other Olympic skaters, posed for a poster, made a television special, toured some more. Designers started lending her clothes. And everyone seemed to love her.

But she still had to lift weights.

Gwen and Hal stayed at the restaurant until four o'clock. That night she wrote him a proper note, thanking him for lunch, inviting him to her house for dinner. He called within five minutes of getting the note. He'd love to see her again. He couldn't wait. They shared that dinner, then an evening at the theater, followed by an afternoon drive through the wintry countryside and phone calls every evening.

Neither one of them could believe what was happening. They had never expected anything like this.

Hal was a scholar. He gathered information; he collected every variant verse of a song. But for the first time in his life, he seemed to have enough information immediately. From the moment he had seen this quiet, elegant woman alerting people not to trip on the extension cord, he had known enough.

They had grown up in surprisingly similar homes, Gwen in Maryland, Hal in Wisconsin. Their parents were educated with values and incomes that were comfortably middle-class. They readily admitted that had they met as teenagers, they would not have been drawn to each other. Early in their lives both of them had wanted adventure; they had wanted to be married to someone different from themselves. Gwen had chosen John and the itinerant life of the military while Hal had married Eleanor, aristocratic, earthy, unconventional. But with those long, satisfying marriages behind them, they were now ready for similarity, for ease and comfort.

Gwen knew that while Hal was not the man she would have chosen to begin her life with, he could well be the man with whom she would choose to conclude it.

35

# CHAPTER 2

AMY ADORED BEING PROFESSIONAL. SHE LOVED performing for a crowd without worrying about judges. She enjoyed the easy camaraderie among the dozen or so top skaters as they met up for tours, shows, or professional competitions. She liked getting dressed up and having her picture taken. She felt good about the charity work she did, passing out awards at the Special Olympics, opening blood banks, serving as honorary chairperson of countless benefits. She had yet to be caught in any major mistakes. She had not been arrested for drinking and driving—because she rarely did either—and none of her charities had ever been exposed as mismanaged frauds—because none of them were. Although it had been almost seven years since her Olympics, no other American female skater had challenged her place in the public's affections.

She lived in Denver. She, Tommy, and Henry continued to train with Oliver. They had built their own rink with saunas and whirlpools, a ballet studio, and—of course—a weight room. Their year followed a predictable pattern. Professional competitions began in October; most of December was turned over to the holiday shows. In January and February they either went overseas or worked on television specials. Spring was reserved for the big multi-city tours. During the summer and early fall they created all the programs they would need for the next year. In between they taped commercials, squeezed in appearances in other people's television specials, attended banquets, made speeches, gave interviews, signed autographs, and did their charity work.

Henry and Tommy were both gay, as were her coach, her costume designer, and her choreographer. In fact, when Amy had been an amateur, she sometimes had felt that the only time she met men who weren't gay was when she went home and saw her father, brother, and brother-in-law.

But as a professional she met different people— promoters, sponsors, advertising executives, businessmen, sound engineers, and lighting technicians—and some of these men liked her in ways that Henry, Tommy, and Oliver did not.

Such men would come to her practices and wait for her at rink-side with her water and her skate bag. They would have decided where to go to dinner and would have figured out how to get there. They would make sure all the arrangements were right at the rink and at the hotel. They would take care of her. She liked that.

And they would want only one thing in return—to be a part of her success. The weak ones simply wanted their share of the attention. They always managed to position themselves so that no picture was taken of her without them in it. They would want to sit in on every interview with her. They would want the interviewer to speak to them too. They needed people to believe that they were as interesting as she was, as important as she was.

The strong ones didn't care about attention; they wanted power. Amy was the staircase on which they would build their own careers. They would manage her, produce her shows, handle her investments. They would try to isolate her from her current coach, manager, financial adviser.

Both were bad for her career. "Amy, please," her agent had said to her two years ago, "could you please

37

go on this tour and not fall in love?"

"What do you mean, not fall in love?" she had laughed. "Falling in love isn't anything I can control, is it?"

"In your case, Amy, yes, yes, it is."

And of course he was right. She hadn't been truly in love with any of these men; she had simply loved being in love. So she had quit.

But she missed it. It was fun to fall in love.

Hal and Gwen both knew that Hal was in Washington only for the spring. He was committed to spending the summer at his family's cabin in Minnesota—"it's one of the organizing principles of our family life, summer in Minnesota"—and in the fall he would be back in Iowa.

But they were not the sort of people who allowed circumstances to decide their fate. Gwen had moved every three years of her married life; she could move again. She liked change. And if they found themselves unsure by the time Hal had to leave, they could write, visit, call, e-mail each other until they were sure.

But privately, within their hearts, each was already sure. Hal had first thought of her as Athena, the cool, dispassionate goddess of wisdom. Now he knew she was Vestia, the protector of the hearth and home. Her own home was ordered, graceful, and filled with light. He could see how a man, after months in the dark, tight spaces of a submarine, would be lured and then soothed by the quiet warmth of her world.

Hal had fallen in love with Eleanor because she seemed so unlike the nice Midwestern girls he had grown up with. Her strength of spirit, her will, her independence, her sexual permissiveness, seemed almost masculine to him, and he had been mesmerized.

38

But he was wiser now and knew that such spirit, will, and independence could also come in a more conventionally feminine form. And the sexual permissiveness—which had riveted him at age twenty-two—attracted him less now. He knew that it came with drawbacks.

He had to return to Iowa for a weekend in late April. "Why don't you come with me?" he said to Gwen. "You can look around the place, meet Phoebe."

Phoebe was his older daughter, the child of his who had been the closest to their mother. Gwen too had a daughter. Holly was her older child, and while Gwen did not love her daughter more than her son, she was closer to Holly.

And she had to wonder—if she had died before John and John was getting to know someone in the way that she was getting to know Hal, how would Holly have felt?

"You think *what*?" Phoebe stared at her husband.

"I think they are going to get married." Giles Smith spoke mildly as always. He was a big, shaggy sort of man with a silky reddish-brown beard. He seemed soft and approachable, almost a teddy bear, but his eyes were alert and intelligent. Sometimes his gaze was steady; sometimes it was in motion, flicking from one person to the next, taking in everything that was happening, understanding it all. "The senior recitals are the most public thing the music department does all year. Your father's going to have thought long and hard about bringing someone all the way from Washington for this particular weekend."

Earlier in the day Phoebe had gotten a call from her father. When he had taken a leave of absence to go to

39

Washington, D.C., for the spring semester, he had always said he would return to Iowa for the recitals of the senior music majors. Today he had called to say he would be bringing with him this Gwen person.

"But they've only known each other three months," Phoebe protested. "They can't be thinking about getting married."

"They aren't exactly kids. They have to know their own minds by now."

Dad marrying again? Phoebe couldn't imagine it. Someone else living in the house with him, working in Mother's kitchen—it seemed impossible. Dad caring about someone, really loving her? Phoebe felt as if she didn't know him.

She, Giles, and their four children lived in Iowa City, which was about twenty miles away from the smaller town of Lipton, where Phoebe had grown up and where her father still lived. Both Phoebe and Giles were lawyers. Giles was general counsel for the University of Iowa, a job that he loved. It was tough and exciting, combining public relations, damage control, and the law, and he was shrewd enough to exploit the misleading mildness of his appearance and manner.

Phoebe herself was in legal aid, working part-time, running a legal-services clinic staffed by law students from the university. She didn't love her work as Giles did his; the law probably wasn't her calling in life, but she certainly did believe that what she did was important. It was work that needed to be done.

Doing the right thing mattered to Phoebe. She was conscientious and orderly, both at work and at home. She typed the carpool schedules and did up the soccer phone tree. She negotiated between the group of parents who wanted an elaborate graduation ceremony for the

40

kindergartners and those who wanted to serve cupcakes and juice and be done with it. She talked sense into the people who thought that the fifth-grade Valentine's party should include boy-girl dancing. She silently, tactfully got yearbooks into the hands of kids whose parents couldn't afford them. Everyone who knew her admired her, but in truth, she was too busy to have close friends.

Of course, with her mother only twenty miles away, she hadn't needed close friends.

"But Mother's only been dead for a year. What can Dad be thinking of?"

"It's almost been a year and a half," Giles said gently. "She died in November."

Phoebe knew when her mother had died. She knew it to the minute.

She had been pregnant with Thomas, her fourth child, when her mother died.

That's what she kept thinking about during those days at her mother's bedside. Things like this weren't supposed to happen when you were pregnant. You were supposed to be worrying about your baby, not about your mother.

It had started with a sore throat. Phoebe had seen her on Sunday, and Eleanor had mentioned feeling raspy. But Eleanor was stalwart about illness, she made little of her discomfort, and Phoebe forgot about it. Tuesday morning she called her parents about something else, and she could tell that her father was concerned.

She had him put her mother back on the line. "Are you turning into the sort of old lady whose daughter has to take her to the doctor?" Phoebe did not think of her mother as old.

41

"I hate doctors," Eleanor groused. "They make you wait forever."

Eleanor was not a complainer. She really must not feel well. "I think you ought to go, Mother. I can come over this afternoon if you want." Phoebe wasn't joking anymore.

"Don't be silly. The weather looks horrible. There's supposed to be ice tomorrow. There's no point in you driving twenty miles through an ice storm just so you can wait forever too."

"But that's tomorrow. You should go today."

"I shall. I shall."

Eleanor went to the doctor. He gave her an antibiotic. She should have felt better in twenty-four hours. She didn't.

The ice storm came as predicted. A thin layer of cold air had settled near the ground, but the clouds were warmer. So when the rain fell late Wednesday, it froze as it landed, glazing everything with a glittering icy sheath.

Thursday morning Eleanor was admitted to the hospital with pneumonia. "We can monitor the antibiotics better here," the doctor said.

Phoebe went to see her mother immediately. She drove a big Ford station wagon, and its weight and good tires kept her on the road, but other cars were sliding into ditches, getting stuck at the bottoms of hills. Sharp rays of sunlight glittered off the ice-encased power lines and the twisted points of the barbed-wire fences. The piles of unraked leaves had frozen into stiff mats, and tree limbs hung dangerously low, burdened by the weight of the ice.

Phoebe ached for the green woods of Minnesota, where the needles from the tamarack trees rustled underfoot all summer long.

Her mother did not get better.

On Friday she and Giles decided that the whole family should spend the weekend in Lipton. It would be safer, more convenient. "I'm sure Mother will be out of the hospital by Monday, Tuesday at the latest," she said.

Phoebe was making a deal with God. *If we skip all our weekend activities, if Ellie misses the movie with her friends, if Alex doesn't go to tae kwan do, and if Claire misses tumbling, and Giles and I don't go to the Reynolds lecture Sunday afternoon, then Mother will be well on Monday.*

That wasn't the kind of God Phoebe believed in, but she didn't know what else to do to make her mother well.

And the deal wasn't working. Saturday morning a nurse who had known her since childhood took her aside, putting her hand on her arm. "I think you should call Ian and Amy. Have them come."

Have them come? That was a crazy idea. Ian lived in California. Amy was God knew where. Phoebe looked down at the nurse's hand. Her nails were trimmed and polished clear. Her watch was practical, with big numbers and a long second hand that moved in little ticks. Phoebe watched it hop past the twelve toward the one.

"Phoebe? Really, you should call."

Phoebe kept looking at the watch. "Dr. Morgan said as soon as they find the right antibiotic then everything will—"

"And that's true. If they find the right drug, she'll be out of the hospital early next week, but Phoebe, call them anyway, tell them to come."

*No, I can't. If they come, it means Mother is dying. If*

43

*they don't come, it means she is not.*

"Do it, Phoebe. Don't make your father have to decide to call them."

Phoebe took a breath. She could deal with that. Her mother wasn't dying, she was just helping her father. She was the oldest, she had always been the helpful one. She walked down to the pay phone.

She would call Ian first. She knew how to manage him. She never told him what to do. She would tell him what was happening, and he would do the right thing. He always did as long as someone else didn't tell him to do it. That's when he got difficult. He already knew that Mother was in the hospital. He wouldn't press her with too many questions.

Amy would be a different matter. Phoebe had no idea where she was. She supposedly lived in Denver, but she was never there. She was always off skating in shows, taping commercials, or making personal appearances. A long time ago she had given the family an emergency number to use if they ever needed to reach her. Phoebe didn't know if the number was good anymore. Or even if she had it with her.

But she did. It was there in her little address book under Amy's name. Phoebe dialed. An answering service picked up immediately. Yes, they took messages for Miss Legend.

*Miss Legend?* Phoebe had never heard anyone call Amy that. "This is her sister. I need to get a message to her. Our mother is ill. She should come home."

"I'll page someone right away," the operator promised. Phoebe went back to her mother's room.

The room was full of flowers, but they were all carnations. The ice storm must have kept the town's one florist from getting the usual weekly delivery, and they had to fill all the orders with carnations.

Phoebe hated carnations. They were stiff, angular, and scentless. They never seemed like real flowers to her. She couldn't imagine them actually growing in a field.

Her father was at her mother's bedside. Phoebe spoke softly. "You need to have something to eat, Dad. Ellie made some sandwiches this morning." Just as Phoebe had been her mother's first daughter, thirteen-year-old Ellie was Phoebe's first daughter, helpful and conscientious.

If anyone but his granddaughter had made the sandwiches, Hal would have no doubt refused them. But he was a good grandparent. He took the sandwiches.

Phoebe sank into his chair and touched her mother on the cheek. Eleanor turned her head. She nodded faintly, she recognized Phoebe, but she was too sick to care.

*Get well, Mother. I'm having a baby this spring. You have to get well.*

What did she remember most? The books, she supposed. C.S. Lewis. *Alice in Wonderland. Winnie the Pooh.* The British ones. Mother had given her the editions she had read as a child, wonderful volumes, some of them leather-bound with color plates. The American books—*Little Women,* the Oz books, the Little House books—the two of them had discovered together.

Phoebe fumbled for the nightstand, almost knocking over the little aqua plastic water pitcher. There was a pile of books there. She picked up one, any one, and she cracked it open to a page, any page. She started to read aloud to her mother, just as her mother had once read aloud to her.

She went on and on, she didn't know how long, she

didn't know what she was reading, but this was what she and her mother had always shared, books. This was what they would share now. Her father came back into the room. He put his hand on her shoulder for a moment. She went on reading. She knew that he understood.

Then the door eased open again. A hospital aide bent over her shoulder. "Ms. Legend, you have a phone call. It's someone representing your sister."

Her father took the book from her, and Phoebe slipped out into the hall. She picked up the phone at the nurses' station. The voice on the other end was male; he sounded young, identifying himself as the administrative assistant to someone Phoebe had never heard of. He listened as she repeated the message.

"You do know that Amy is in Holland, don't you?" he said.

Phoebe hadn't known that. People in Holland loved Amy. The tulip growers' association had named some fabulous, disease-resistant blossom after her. It seemed strange that they would honor an American like that. Surely Holland had skaters of its own.

"I don't care where she is. I need a number to reach her."

"I don't know that I can do that." His voice had a self-important little whine to it. "We will handle communications with her. When our clients are on tour, our job is to protect them from distractions."

Distractions? Was that what this was? A distraction from Amy's tour?

He was someone's assistant; she wasn't going to listen to this from someone's assistant. "Is there someone else I can talk to?" She couldn't remember who he had said his boss was.

"There's no need. I will relay—"

Phoebe leaned her forehead against the wall. The painted cinder block was cool, rough. Her rings were tight, and her clothes didn't fit right anymore. She felt sweaty and fat. She was tired. She wanted to lie down, she wanted to go to sleep, she wanted all of this to go away. *I'm pregnant. I want someone to take care of me.* "Would one of you idiots please tell my sister that our mother is dying?"

They did, but not soon enough. Someone decided to wait until her performance in Holland was over. As a result Eleanor Legend died while Amy's plane was circling O'Hare.

The day she died, the ice melted, but its weight had already pulled down tree limbs. The darkening spots of winter kill were already spreading on the shrubs. Hedges that had been full and green last summer would have twiggy patches this spring, and the gardeners would have to thrust their hands deep into the bushes, searching for the heart of the dry, dead branches.

Phoebe knew what her mother would want: a traditional funeral and a traditional burial, followed by a gathering in their home. "They should have had it at home," Eleanor used to say when a funeral reception was held in the church fellowship hall. "It's a lot of work, but that's the point. It gives you something to do."

Her father was planning the funeral, and Phoebe knew without anyone saying anything that she was in charge of planning the reception. She was in charge of everything at the house. She was the oldest. It was her job to take charge.

They were all staying in the family home, she, Giles,

and their three children, Ian, his wife Joyce, and their three children too. Friends and neighbors were bringing in food, but someone had to decide what to eat when. And that someone was naturally Phoebe. She was the oldest; that's what the oldest daughter does.

So she was in the kitchen, taking chicken off the bone, when Amy arrived. She had to rinse and dry her hands before her sister could hug her.

"Are you okay?" Amy whispered into her hair.

Was she okay? A flash of irritation shot through her. What kind of question was that? She was four months pregnant, and her mother had just died. "I'm fine."

Amy stepped back. For a moment it seemed that her eyes were asking the question again. *Are you really*?

But Phoebe kept her lips tight. She wasn't answering. She couldn't.

Amy looked pretty, her light, glowing hair curling delicately around her ears. She was already in black, slender wool trousers and a long sweater whose cowl collar brushed against the perfect line of her jaw, the black making her skin look porcelain fragile. Everything she had on fit her perfectly. Her sweater didn't catch and wrinkle across her hips; her slacks were hemmed slightly longer in back than in front so that the cuffs fell gracefully along the line of her shoe. It was always like that. Amy's clothes were always softer, better cut, better fitting, more detailed than anyone else's. When she wore a suit, the buttons on the sleeves were never the ornamental detailing that they were on Phoebe's suits. They were working-buttons with button loops or button holes that were bound on the lining side of the jacket and hand-worked on the outside. Last year she had worn a taupe-and-black-checked blouse, and whenever one of the front button holes crossed the check line, the designer had changed thread color. Sometimes it seemed as if Amy's clothes were a beautiful armor, as if she wore such exquisite clothes to protect her . . . although Phoebe couldn't imagine from what.

Amy truly had been a beautiful child, and it seemed that every time the family had her out of the house, the whole world would gather around to gush. Ten years older, Phoebe had been at her most awkward ages—twelve, thirteen, fourteen—just when Amy had been attracting the most attention. Phoebe had hated it. *Shut up*, she would want to scream. *You're not saying anything that we haven't heard a million times. So what if she's pretty?*

They shouldn't have been ten years apart. Fifteen or five would have been better. At eighteen Phoebe might have been proud of a beautiful three-year-old sister. At eight she might not have noticed. But at thirteen it had hurt.

Although what business did Phoebe have complaining? How far apart in age were her two daughters, Ellie and Claire? Nine years. And, yes, little Claire was prettier than Ellie.

Amy spoke. "Should I put my stuff in my room, or are any of the kids in there?"

*Why are you asking me? Mother's the one who decides who sleeps where, not me.* "The kids are in the attic. Your room is free."

Amy picked up her bag; it was small, the size of a gym bag.

That's probably what it was. Apparently she had gone straight from the arena to the airport, not even stopping at the hotel. "Is this a good time for me to take a quick shower?"

"We do have a lot to do."

49

How nasty that sounded. She hadn't meant it—she didn't begrudge Amy the opportunity to shower—but before she could take it back, Amy had already set her bag back down. "I can wait. It's no problem."

"Not if you flew first-class," Ian's wife Joyce said from the other side of the kitchen. "I don't suppose you feel so grubby when you fly first-class."

She made it sound like Amy had done something wrong by flying first-class. Amy didn't answer. "What can I do to help?" she asked Phoebe.

Phoebe thought for a moment. "Make up some frosting. Just a butter cream will do. Mother usually keeps two or three boxes of powdered sugar in the pantry."

Again she heard herself. *Keeps,* she had said. *Mother keeps.* The word should be *kept.*

*You didn't know, did you, Mother, when you bought that powdered sugar, that we would be using it for your funeral.*

It took Amy awhile to find the powdered sugar. Then it turned out she didn't have a clue how to make frosting.

She didn't know how to clean broccoli, she had no idea how to take the Cuisinart apart, and, most frustrating to Phoebe, she didn't know where anything was in the kitchen.

How could she not know? She had lived here, hadn't she? Mother hadn't rearranged anything. "It's where it always is," Phoebe would snap. That didn't help Amy, and it made Phoebe feel like a shrew.

And the whole time Amy looked great, standing up so effortlessly straight, a white butcher-block apron knotted neatly around her slender frame. She had indeed brought virtually nothing with her. So who did she

50

borrow clothes from? Ellie. That's whose jeans fit Amy, a thirteen-year-old's. It didn't seem fair.

After dinner that night Giles and Phoebe were in the library going over lists, trying to be sure that they had done everything, notified everyone. The door was open, but Amy knocked softly, waiting for permission to enter.

"What can we do for you?" Giles asked pleasantly. He and Amy had always gotten along very well. It had seemed odd because, as far as Phoebe could tell, they didn't have a thing in common.

"I was thinking about Thursday." Thursday was the day of the funeral, but only Dad had the courage to use that word. The rest of them simply talked about Thursday. "I wondered if you knew what you were going to wear, Phoebe."

Clothes. Only Amy would be thinking about clothes at a time like this. "I haven't had a moment to think about it."

Amy's lips tightened, and for a moment Phoebe thought she looked hurt. Phoebe supposed that she had sounded a little sharp, but Amy's obsession with clothes had always been such a nuisance. "Amy, you will have ten minutes to dress," Mother had said countless times. "Whatever you have on at the end of ten minutes, you will wear even if it is nothing but your underpants." It had been the only way to get Amy out of the house.

But an instant later Amy's expression was as composed as ever. "I'm asking a friend in New York to express a dress or a suit in. You said your clothes weren't fitting because of the baby. Can I have something sent for you too?"

"That's an interesting thought," Giles said. He turned

51

to Phoebe. "Do you need something?"

Actually Phoebe had thought about what she was going to wear, and her options were not good. This was her fourth child. She was already showing. The skirt to her black suit was straight; she would never be able to get into it. She could loop a rubber band through the waist-band button hole of her tweed skirt and wear that with her black blazer, but it would not look right, and Mother had always worn all black to funerals.

Phoebe cared about her appearance exactly the wrong amount. A person should either be like her sister-in-law Joyce and never care, or be like Amy and care all the time. But Phoebe generally cared only one or two Saturday nights a month, just enough to make herself unhappy at those times, but not enough to make her do something about it.

"Then let's take Amy up on this very nice offer," Giles said. He had read her expression. He knew she had nothing to wear; he also knew that she was planning on saying no. "It will be one less thing for you to worry about."

"I suppose it would be." Phoebe couldn't believe how grudging her voice sounded. *What's wrong with me? Why can't I be gracious?*

"What about Ellie and Claire, and Alex too, for that matter?" Amy asked. "My friend probably doesn't have much opportunity to buy children's clothes, and I'm sure he would love it."

He? Only Amy would know men who would love the chance to buy children's clothes.

"That's not necessary." Phoebe struggled to sound more pleasant. "They can wear their Sunday school clothes. The girls' dresses aren't black, but—"

"Oh, let's go for it," Giles interrupted. "At least for

the girls. It's going to be a horrible day. Maybe everyone will feel a little better in new clothes."

Giles was not the sort of man who had an opinion on every little thing. He spoke about something only when he truly cared about it. So Phoebe nodded and said that the girls would probably like new dresses. "But not Alex." He was six. "He would throw himself in the river before he would wear new clothes."

Fifteen minutes later, she heard Amy making the same offer to Ian.

"You're getting clothes sent from New York?" Ian asked. "Isn't that a little extravagant?"

There was an instant of silence. "It probably does seem that way," Amy answered.

"Well"—Ian's voice was brisk—"I'll certainly speak to Joyce about it, but I imagine they brought whatever they will need."

As Phoebe could have predicted, Joyce spurned Amy's offer. She was a social worker, working through the California schools with the Native American Indian population. She posed as quite the earth mother, making wonderful breads and rich, fragrant soups. She wore fading turtlenecks and long peasant skirts with her hair in a single braid down her back.

"I'm fine. You know me, I never worry about what other people think." Joyce always made a big point of that, how she was such a free spirit. "And we never pick out Maggie's clothes for her." Maggie was Joyce and Ian's teenager. "We respect her right to have her own taste."

The clothes came late Wednesday afternoon, and Phoebe had to admit that hers and Ellie's were perfect.

53

Hers was a downy black cashmere finished with a satin collar and cuffs. It wasn't a maternity dress, but the bodice had row after row of little tucks that gradually released just below the waist. It fit beautifully and felt like heaven.

"I have never looked this good in my whole life," she said, as she looked at herself in the mirror.

"That kind of collar does work well on us," Amy agreed. "I told Hank that we look alike, and he—"

"We don't look alike," Phoebe protested. Amy had always been the pretty one.

"Of course we do. Our coloring is different, and I primp a whole lot more, but our bone structure is nearly the same."

Phoebe looked back at herself. With this collar caressing her jaw, yes, for the first time she could see that she looked a little like Amy.

More important to her than her own dress was her daughter's. Ellie was not finding thirteen an easy age, and she would have joined her brother in the river rather than wear a dress that called attention to herself. Phoebe had asked Amy to tell her friend that. Whoever he was, he had understood perfectly. Ellie's dress was black challis with a dropped waist and a skirt of knife pleats. A double row of black buttons was the only trim. It was so quiet that even Ellie couldn't imagine making a fool of herself in it.

"What 'bout me, Mommy?" chirped four-year-old Claire. "What me?"

They were all out in the wide upstairs hall, looking in the full-length mirror. Amy went back into her small bedroom at the front of the house to unpack Claire's dress. She came out, gesturing to Phoebe. "Hank's let us down," she said softly. "I'm afraid Claire's dress is over the top."

That was putting it mildly. The little dress was an ornate Victorian fantasy. The skirt alone had a black crinoline, a flounced underskirt, and a lightly ruched overskirt. The seams at the waistband, the cuffs, and the throat were corded. Why anyone would manufacture such a dress in a size 4T was beyond Phoebe. She couldn't imagine anyone ever thinking it appropriate for a child.

"Pretty." Claire patted the black fabric as if it were a stuffed lamb. "Pretty. *Mine.*"

Claire was currently the youngest of three children, soon to be supplanted by another baby. "Mine" was an important word in her vocabulary. She held up her arms, wanting someone to take her shirt off her. Phoebe stripped her down to her little cotton underpants. Amy dropped the dress over her head, did up the buttons, and tied the sash.

"She looks like a little doll, Mom," Ellie said.

She did indeed. Claire had Amy's childhood coloring; she was blonde with very fair skin. The black of the dress made her look as if she was made of alabaster.

"If I'd been allowed to wear a dress like that when I was four," Amy sighed, "I would probably be a nuclear physicist today."

Phoebe looked up. Amy had pronounced "nuclear" properly, saying "nu-cle-ar" rather than "nuk-u-lar" as did most of the world. That seemed surprising.

She turned back to Claire, who was now dancing and spinning in front of the mirror. The dress was billowing around her. Phoebe wasn't sure what to do. The idea of wearing such a dress to a Midwestern college-town funeral was absurd. But Claire clearly adored it.

She sighed. "I don't know what to do."

Amy spoke. "If we care what people think of us, then we don't let her wear it. But if we care about what she thinks of herself, then we do."

Phoebe stiffened. That was Mother. Mother would have said something like that. Who would have ever thought that she would hear her mother's voice coming from her sister's lips?

And Mother never cared what people thought of her. "Then we let her wear it."

Joyce protested Claire's dress the most. "It's so inappropriate for a child," she fussed.

Joyce herself was in a plain black business suit with an oxford cloth blouse. Without any accessories she looked unfinished and ill at ease. Joyce and Ian didn't go to church, so their girls didn't have Sunday dresses. Fourteen-year-old Maggie was in a much laundered black cotton skirt and white shirt which made her look more schoolgirlish than her younger cousin Ellie, and Phoebe suspected that Maggie would make Ellie pay for that. Emily, Joyce and Ian's four-year-old, was in her father's arms sobbing because she didn't have a dress like Claire's.

Ian had the nerve to suggest that Claire not be allowed to wear her dress. "Emily is so upset that it's going to make the day difficult for everyone."

"It's Mother's funeral," Phoebe said tightly. "The day is going to be difficult whatever a pair of four-year-olds wear. You had your chance. Amy offered to get clothes for Joyce and Maggie and Emily."

"We didn't think she was going to make such a production out of it."

"You didn't think *Amy* was going to make a production out of something? For God's sake, Ian, how

56

long have you known her?"

They had never bickered like this before. It was because Mother wasn't there. With Mother around there had never been anything to bicker about. If she had approved of the dress, Ian would have never questioned it. If she had sniffed at it, Phoebe would have never allowed Claire to wear it.

They were on their own.

The church was full, and it was a big church, built in the days when people went to church every Sunday. All of Eleanor and Hal's friends came as well as most of the administration. Many of Phoebe and Giles's friends from Iowa City came too. Ian's high school friends and their parents came. It made a difference, all those people coming, showing that they cared.

Amy had no friends there. In fact, Phoebe hadn't even thought about Amy having friends until she saw the altar flowers—dozens and dozens—no, there were probably hundreds of them—of tulips of such a very dark purple that they seemed black. Their pale green stems arched under the weight of the dark blossoms and fell in graceful curves over the white marble urns.

Amy's friends had had them shipped directly from a grower in Holland. They were the most extraordinary flowers anyone had ever seen; they were unique, assertive, even majestic. Mother would have loved them.

And now, a year and a half after Mother's funeral, Dad was bringing another woman home.

Phoebe had understood why he had decided to take a leave of absence for the spring semester. "It's been a year," he had said. "I'm still living exactly as I was

57

when your mother was alive. I need to get away for a while, force myself to develop some new routines."

Who would have thought that the new routines would include another woman?

Dad said that Phoebe and Giles would like her, this Gwen person, that she was organized and feminine.

"Feminine?" Phoebe demanded of Giles. "Since when did Dad ever care about that?" Her mother had not been remotely feminine, and to Phoebe the word smelled of frivolity and girlishness.

She called her brother to tell him that Gwen was coming to Iowa.

"We could have anticipated this," Ian said heavily. "We should have expected that women of a certain age would be all over him. It should not be a surprise."

Phoebe shifted the phone to her other car. What crap that was. Ian had been just as surprised as she. But he liked to think he could anticipate everything. If you could anticipate something, you could control it, and Ian liked that.

Getting along with Ian and Joyce had been difficult this year. Phoebe wanted to badger him, startle him. *This is serious, Ian. Giles said they might get married.*

Married . . . another woman in Mother's house, taking Mother's place in the duplicate bridge club, using Mother's heavy silver trays, coming up to the lake in Mother's place.

It didn't bear thinking of.

Hal's house was rented for the semester. Phoebe urged him to bring Gwen to stay in Iowa City.

"Thank you for offering," he said. "But you know how crazy things get." The weekend of the senior music majors' recitals was crammed with department receptions and parties hosted by parents who wanted to meet favorite professors. "We probably need to stay in town. Everyone's offered to put us up, but I think we'll just stay in the Holiday Inn. Can you meet us there?"

The Holiday Inn in Lipton was a Holidome. The rooms ran around a central indoor courtyard that had a swimming pool, a ping-pong table, and little redwood terraces separated by planters. Phoebe called her father's room, but no one answered. "They are probably waiting for us in the bar."

"The bar here is pretty dark," Giles said. "Your father is likely to be at one of the tables by the pool."

Phoebe turned, and the moment she did, she saw her father walking toward them, smiling, his hands outstretched.

He led them toward the pool. At a glass-topped table sat a woman who stood as they approached. She had smooth blonde hair cut to her chin. She was slender without seeming fragile.

"Phoebe." Her voice was low and melodic. Her handshake was firm, her eyes were direct. She wasn't shy.

She was wearing lemon-colored silk, a pleated skirt with a scoop-necked shell under a crepe blazer. The silk and the crepe were exactly the same color, and there was not a single suitcase wrinkle in the silk. She had pearl earrings and a pearl bracelet. Her nails were polished a very pale rose. There was no telling how old she was.

Phoebe couldn't imagine her at the lake.

They all sat down. Gwen's spine barely touched the chair; her shoulders were back but relaxed. That's how Amy always sat. Phoebe forced herself to sit up straighter. Hal signaled for the waitress.

59

"Hal has told me that you're both lawyers," Gwen said pleasantly. "My daughter Holly is a lawyer. She works for Brand, Whitfield in New York."

Brand, Whitfield. Phoebe knew all about Brand, Whitfield. It was big; it was important; it was white. Their clients were bigger and whiter still. She loathed firms like that. That's why she was in legal services; she wanted everyone, not just the rich and the white, to have a voice and to have legal protection.

"Your daughter must work hard," Giles said to Gwen.

"She does. What about you, Phoebe?" Gwen was speaking to her. "Are you able to keep your hours part-time?"

Phoebe didn't want to answer. Gwen was too well groomed, too poised, too glossy. Phoebe didn't like her.

*You should be sitting here, Mother.*

But of course if her mother had been alive, they wouldn't be here. Mother hated places like this, the plants artificial, the air all chlorine-scented and stuffy.

"Of course she can't," Hal answered. "Our society does take advantage of women who want to work part-time. Many of them work far more than they are paid for."

Her father had answered for her. Phoebe felt herself flush. Ian and Amy were the ones who were supposed to cause problems, not her. She was the oldest, the helpful one, the one Mother and Dad could rely on.

"It's my own fault," she said. *Just think of her as someone you're meeting at a party, as someone you might never see again.* "I could say no."

"What are your cases like?" Gwen asked.

Phoebe answered, and then they moved on to talking about children. Gwen made the conversation easy. When it was over, when they were getting up to go to

60

the recital, Phoebe realized that Gwen had said nothing about herself.

That had never happened with Mother. Mother had always been the center of attention. She hadn't demanded it; she hadn't forced herself on people. She simply had been so interesting. Everyone who met her wanted to know more about her. She had such wonderful stories of growing up in Hong Kong and Bermuda, of staying with her parents in lavish hotels in Monte Carlo, using only room service because they were out of cash, waiting for money to be wired from home.

*Mother, please . . . when are you coming back?*

A person did not get to be general counsel of a large public university by being full of hot air. Even to his own wife Giles Smith did not puff off opinions or predictions unless he was very confident. And indeed, shortly after returning to Washington following the senior recitals, Hal Legend called his children to say that he and Gwen Wells were getting married.

# CHAPTER 3

JACK WELLS, GWEN'S SON, HEARD THIS NEWS IN Kentucky. When he was working, Jack wore a beeper clipped to the waistband of his frequently muddy jeans. He didn't often see his mother's phone number flash across the beeper's little screen—she rarely disturbed him in the middle of the day—so whenever she did beep him, he went directly to his truck and called her on his mobile phone.

Jack had his own business, moving houses. He didn't

move families and their belongings; instead he moved the actual houses, jacking them up onto flatbed trucks and sending them down the highway.

His organized, methodical sister had been skeptical about this latest enterprise of his. "Jack, you do everything at the last minute. You can't run a client-based business like that. You'll drive all your customers insane."

She had a point. He wasn't one to rush out and attend to every little detail months ahead of time. He had learned that about himself when he had owned a hardware store in Wyoming, which was what he had been doing before Kentucky. He wasn't lazy; he simply liked doing things at the last minute. He could focus better, think more clearly when things had to be done immediately. He became more resourceful, he made better decisions. One way to create such urgency was to fight fires—before he had had the hardware store in Wyoming, he had been on a county fire-fighting force in Virginia—another was to procrastinate.

He soon learned that there was still another—signing contracts with a tight deadline. He had built this business on his willingness to work fast. If clients wanted number-every-nail, historic-preservation-quality work, if they wanted perfection, they went to someone else. But if they just wanted the thing done and done fast, if they themselves had already procrastinated far too long, they went to Jack Wells. Jobs that seemed impossible to everyone else always sounded like a lot of fun to him.

So it was not usual that Jack had a fair bit to do today. All the permits, the police escort, everything involved in moving a mid-nineteenth-century farmhouse across three Kentucky counties, were set up for day after tomorrow, and the house wasn't close to being ready. People would have to be working nearly around the clock to stabilize the house, jack it up, get it on the wheels.

They were right on schedule.

"Hi, Mom. It's me. What's up?"

"Lovely things. Hal and I have decided to get married."

"Whoa, doggies . . ." Jack shifted the phone to his other ear. "You're getting married?"

"Yes."

He shook his head. He had just gotten his mind wrapped around the fact that his mother was dating. Now she was marching down the aisle. He had always figured that was how he himself would get married. He'd meet somebody who would set off the right bells, and three days later they'd be married. He didn't know when it would happen—he was twenty-eight already— but he certainly hadn't expected that his mother would get to it first. On the other hand, her life had been pretty calm and orderly for the last few years, and even though she never picked the newspaper off the front porch without combing her hair first, she liked having a fair bit of mess and noise swirling around her. What was the point of being a lighthouse on a perfectly smooth, sandy shore?

"That sounds like good news," he said. "I mean, if you aren't pregnant. You aren't having to get married, are you?"

"No, Jack." His mother's laugh was soft. She was used to his sense of humor. "I don't have to get married."

"That's a relief. So when is all this happening?"

"We don't know yet. Sometime soon. Before June.

63

Hal has a summer place in Minnesota, and he likes to get there in June."

"A summer place? You're marrying into a family with a summer place?"

Military families didn't have summer places. They couldn't afford to.

She laughed again. "Actually, a cabin would probably be a better description. I think it's on the primitive side. Hal says I'm to urge you and Holly to come up for a while."

"We will be there. In fact, we think it's really cool that you're going to be Amy Legend's wicked stepmother."

"That's less funny, Jack."

"Holly and I think it is."

That had been weird, finding out that not only was their mother dating, but she was dating Amy Legend's father. Jack had never had any dealings with celebrities. He had always assumed that it would be pretty tedious. You would be wildly curious about them, but wouldn't know what questions were all right to ask, while they wouldn't know a thing about you and probably were very happy with that state of affairs.

Oh, well, that was a bridge that didn't have to be crossed yet. Mom had already said that Hal apparently saw his famous daughter less than she would have expected.

They talked a bit more. Jack told her to tell him the minute she set a date and then slid the phone into its cradle, but instead of going back to work, he stayed in the truck.

His sister would call within seconds. He knew that. It was absolutely guaranteed. If he didn't answer, she would beep him and beep him and beep him until he

64

called her back, which would end up taking more time than if he just waited.

He turned on the radio, and as if by cue, the phone rang.

He picked it up. "You must have auto-redial," he said pleasantly.

"Of course I do," Holly snapped.

Jack picked up this morning's 7-Eleven coffee cup and unrolled the window to dump out the rest of the coffee. His sister was going to be okay about this. She wasn't afraid of change any more than he was. She just needed to let off steam.

Holly lived in New York City and worked at one of those killer eighty-hour-a-week law firms. She was doing great there, but whenever she mentioned a man with any warmth and Jack thought that maybe she was finally getting something that might someday resemble a personal life, he would find out that this man was happily married and much senior to her, a mentor, not a boyfriend.

And for about the four hundred millionth time in his adult life, Jack thought that Holly would have made one hell of an admiral.

The navy had been their dad's life, and he had wanted Jack, his only son, to follow in his footsteps, something that said only son had considered exclusively in his nightmares.

A military career and Jack would not have been good companions. At best his career would have been very short; more likely his mom and sister would have been baking cookies and visiting him in the brig. He probably would have done well enough during battle. He had, after all, loved fighting fires. There was nothing like being inside a burning building to get you focused.

There was no time to think, to ponder options; you had to rely on your training and your instincts. You made your decisions in a heartbeat and then you acted. You couldn't look back, couldn't question yourself.

But the United States did not conduct its foreign policy with any regard for Jack Wells's mental health. The country seemed to like keeping its soldiers and sailors out of battle, and the rest of a military career Jack was not cut out for. He hated routine; he couldn't stand following pointless rules; he wasn't organized; he wasn't punctual. He had little or no respect for people who sat behind desks and told people who weren't behind desks what to do. The only thing worse than taking orders from a person behind a desk was *being* the person behind the desk. Jack had learned that at the hardware store in Wyoming.

His sister, on the other hand, was organized and punctual; she knew how to set goals and meet them. She could do the same thing day after day; she could sit behind a desk for hours on end; she could return phone calls. To Holly there was no such thing as a "pointless rule." She would have overcome whatever obstacles she encountered at the Naval Academy; she would have been the one that the armed forces trotted out every time Congress debated the role of women in the military.

But it had never occurred to their father to encourage his daughter to join the navy.

*Big mistake, Dad. One of your biggest. You had one kid who could have made you proud.*

At the moment Holly was thinking about Mom. "What does she think she's doing?" she demanded. "Why do they need to get married? Why doesn't she just live with him for a while?"

"Live with him, Holly?" Jack crumpled up the 7-

Eleven cup. "Remember who you're talking about. This is our mother, Mrs. Admiral. Admirals' wives don't run around living with people."

"If they want to keep their dependent benefits, they do," Holly shot back.

Oh. He couldn't argue with that. Their father had died while on active duty; Mom's benefits had kept her extremely comfortable. But she would have thought through all that. She was one of the most sensible people that he knew. Holly, God love her, was sometimes too sensible, but Mom was usually right on target. "Maybe she's got an eye on his grandchildren. She'd take grandchildren over a prescription card any day."

"Oh, come on, Jack. That has nothing to do with it."

Jack was not so sure. "She's going to be okay, Holly."

"But she's moving to Iowa."

"So? What's wrong with Iowa? Think of all the crappy places we've lived. Iowa's not going to be a problem for her."

"I know," Holly sighed. She was done letting off steam. "I'm sure Iowa will be fine. I'm just being hysterical because we've never met him, because we don't know what's going on."

No. Holly was being hysterical because *she* didn't know what was going on. She was an older sister, and older sisters like knowing what's going on, they *need* it. Jack, on the other hand, was a younger brother, and he was quite used to never knowing a thing.

But he did know something. If their mother really was throwing herself into a dark hole in the middle of an Iowa cornfield, Jack would build himself a ladder and crawl in after her.

It really hadn't been so bad when Dad was out at sea. Mom had always made things fun. Every day was different. Sometimes they had "backward" days, eating hamburgers and creamed corn for breakfast, scrambled eggs for dinner. They had picnics all the time, even in the winter. "Indoor picnics" Mom would call them, and they would eat all over the house, on her bed, in the bathroom. They did lots of projects, making a periscope out of a gift-wrap tube and little mirrors, building landscapes out of papier mâché and plaster of paris, really neat, fun things that you didn't have to clean up every night.

Then the C.O.'s wife would call. The boat was coming in. Mom would come down to school and get Holly and Jack out even if his class was in the middle of a spelling test. There'd be this whole little parade of mothers coming into school to get their kids because the boat was coming in. The office would be full of people waiting to sign out. The moms would be all dressed up and pretty. Jack could smell their perfume. They had put it on because the boat was coming in.

"Oh, just go, just go," the principal would finally laugh. She understood. The boat was coming in.

There would be a ton of kids down at the water, racing up and down the long concrete pier, pointing and shouting at the white seagulls. "Don't fall in," the moms would call out. "Be careful." But they would be laughing, not really worrying. What could go wrong? The boat was coming in.

It would be a little speck at first. Then it would grow bigger and bigger until he could see the enlisted men on deck, waving frantically. Huge ropes would be tossed onto the pier, and metal gangplanks would clang into place. Men would pour off the boat, and everyone

68

would be laughing and shrieking. Holly and Mom would be on their toes, looking and looking, and then suddenly Dad would be hugging Mom, lifting her off her feet, and then he would scoop up Holly and him. He was so strong that he could lift them both at the same time.

Jack would be bubbling over. Dad was home. There was so much to show him—how he had learned to ride his bike with no hands, how much stronger his pitching arm had gotten. Look, look at this, at how far he could throw, how fast he could ran, and how much he'd grown, see that mark on the door, that was how tall he had been, but now, *now,* look at him now.

"Remember," Mom would caution as they drove down to the pier, "Dad will be tired. It will take him a few days to get adjusted to a regular schedule."

But Jack couldn't wait. "Do you want to see my new bat, Dad? You aren't too tired to see a bat, are you?"

And Dad always said, no, of course, he wasn't too tired. What had put that idea into Jack's head? He'd never be too tired for his kids.

Holly always did what Mom said. She took gymnastics, and even if she had been doing some new trick in the front yard every minute of every day for the last week, she didn't pop out of the car and do it for Dad as Jack would have. She waited a couple days and kind of eased into it. It was like she was pretending she hadn't learned the trick while Dad was gone, that she was doing it for the first time now that he was home.

And maybe because Dad didn't know anything about gymnastics and he did know all about the things Jack did, he never seemed to criticize Holly as he did Jack.

"I'm surprised that your coach doesn't drill you on the fundamentals more," Dad would say. "It's

69

Buckman, isn't it? I'll talk to him."

But Jack's coach was *Mrs.* Buckman. Lieutenant Buckman had formed the team, but he was out at sea now. Mrs. Buckman was really nice and all, but she didn't know much about baseball.

Things like that happened all the time around here. Dads would come home and make all these great plans, and just as everything got started, they would ship out again, and the moms would have to take over.

The family had a routine when Dad was home, dinner at the same time every night, Mom and Dad sitting at the table afterward talking well into the evening. There were no spur-of-the-moment outings, no long drives to feed the ducks. "Dad's so glad to be home, Jack. He doesn't want to go out."

They couldn't leave half-finished projects all over when Dad was home. Dad was used to life on a submarine where everything had to be kept in order. Jack couldn't bolt his breakfast on Saturday morning and grab his bike and spend the day with his friends. "Dad wants to be with you, Jack."

Then why the hell didn't he just stay home?

Even after he made admiral, even when he could have stayed home, he looked for every excuse to get back out to sea.

And now all these years later Mom was marrying again. "How's the date setting going?" he asked the next time he spoke to her. "Just name a time, and I'll be there."

"I know that." Her voice was soft, full of affection. "We're trying to find a date when all the kids can come. What does your calendar look like for late May or early June?"

"It doesn't matter. I will come anytime."

"That's what your sister said."

"She did?" Jack was surprised. To get Holly to take any time away from that precious law firm usually required a couple of sticks of good black-powder dynamite and a forklift. "Good for her. Then this should be easy. Just get the other guys to say what works for them, and Holly and I will show up."

Getting the "other guys" to say what worked for them did not prove so easy.

Phoebe, Hal's oldest daughter, wanted the wedding to be in Iowa where she currently lived. Iowa was home. Her father should get married there.

"But Iowa's not *our* home," Jack pointed out to Holly. Gwen was relaying the details of the family negotiations to Holly, who was then passing them along to him. "We've never heard of the place."

Then it turned out that Ian, Hal's son, didn't think Iowa was such a good idea. He lived in California, and it was hard to fly to Iowa from California, there were never any direct flights at the times you wanted, and it was expensive. Flying coast to coast was often cheaper. Washington, where Gwen was living, would suit his family better. They could take the kids to see the sights.

"I don't know these people," Jack reflected, "but I'm willing to bet that the brother doesn't want it in Iowa because then the big sister gets to be in charge."

"Big sisters are always in charge," Holly reminded him. "And we shouldn't be smug about being easygoing and flexible. Can you imagine how difficult we would seem if Aunt Barbara and Valerie were involved in planning this?"

Aunt Barbara was their mother's younger sister. Valerie was her daughter, their cousin.

"But that's the point," Jack returned. "Aunt Barbara and Valerie aren't involved. Mother's too smart for that. She told them from the get-go that they could come, but that they had no say in the particulars. What about Miss Amy?" Jack kept expecting to hear more about the family celebrity. "Where does she want the wedding to be?"

"I don't know," Holly answered. "Her name never comes up."

"That's weird." Jack would have thought that everything would revolve around her because she was famous. Apparently not.

Then there was a question of the date. Ian's and Phoebe's spring calendars were packed with soccer playoffs, the Cub Scout Blue and Gold banquet, the middle-school production of *Brigadoon,* the swim team barbecue.

Jack was now completely out of patience. "They're being worse than Aunt Barbara would have been. What's important here? A kid's soccer team or two people getting married?"

"It's a *travel* soccer team," Holly answered. Neither of them had a clue what a travel soccer team was. "Listen, Jack." Her voice grew stern. "Mom says we need to remember that they aren't military. They aren't used to change like we are. We're to go along. Mom wants us to be cool about this, so we're going to be cool about it. Do you hear?"

Jack's foot started to tap. He heard. He heard it now; he had heard it before. Holly was sounding just as she had when their father would come home after a long tour at sea. *Mom wants us to be quiet. Remember, men on a submarine live on an eighteen-hour day, six hours on watch, twelve off. Don't do everything at once, Jack.*

72

*It's going to take Dad awhile to get used to daylight.*

Hal and Gwen finally gave up. There would be no family wedding. Jack and Holly were invited, welcomed, encouraged—"Hey, I know an order when I hear one," Jack said—to come to the Legends' summer place in Minnesota for as long as they could. That would be a much better place for everyone to get to know each other.

Hal and Gwen were going to go off by themselves and get married. "We want to be alone," Gwen assured her kids. "When all is said and done, that's what this is about, the two of us. So we're going to Niagara Falls."

"Niagara Falls? *Niagara Falls?*" Phoebe was shocked. "Since when has Dad wanted to go to a place like Niagara Falls?"

Her family summered in the woods of northern Minnesota. They had traveled to Europe; they had been to India and New Zealand. But ordinary American tourist spots—Disneyworld, the Great Smokies, Atlantic City—they never went to places like that.

"I think it's sweet," her husband answered.

Jack wasn't buying this "we want to be alone" business for one minute. "This is nuts," he groused to Holly. "She wants us there. I know it."

"What Mother wants, Jack, is for things to be peaceful. She wants all of us little kiddies to like one another."

Jack rubbed a hand across the back of his neck. Nothing he had heard about Phoebe or Ian Legend had made them sound the least bit likable. "This isn't the Brady Bunch, Holly. We're not going to have to start

73

sharing bedrooms. Mother wants us at her wedding. I'm sure of it."

Jack was a person of strong instincts. Time and again during his adolescence his parents had bemoaned his tendency to act on impulse. "For God's sake, Jack, didn't you *think?*" And the answer was no, he hadn't.

But he wasn't an adolescent anymore, and he knew himself. Thinking was useful when he was figuring out *how* to do something. But when deciding whether or not to do it in the first place, thinking only got him in trouble. When something was right, he knew it in his gut.

He let his instincts run his life. If a beam felt right to him, he crawled across it. If he felt good about a person, he hired him. But if he felt the least pause, the slightest fluttering about something, whether it was a ladder or a piece of fruit or a business opportunity, he walked away from it.

So when Jack said he was sure of something, he was very sure. And he acted. Three days before his mother's wedding he changed the oil in his truck, checked the air in his tires, and called his sister. "We're going. I'm on my way. I'll pick you up tomorrow night."

While Holly Wells was prepared to drop everything and go to her mother's wedding, she was not about to drive across New York state. "Do you have any idea how long that would take?" she demanded of her brother.

Probably not as long as she thought it would. He did drive pretty fast. "Then fly to Buffalo," he suggested. "I'll get you at the airport."

He was waiting when her plane landed.

"So what did Mother say about us coming?" she asked him. "Was she thrilled?"

74

"I didn't tell her. I thought it would be fun to surprise her."

"Jack!" Holly stopped dead. Other passengers had to check their step, move around her. "You didn't talk to her? You didn't set up a place to meet? What if we miss them? What if we've come all this way and then we're not able to find them?"

"Oh, we'll find them." Jack was confident. "You worry too much."

When Holly traveled, all hotel rooms were reserved and guaranteed, the hours for tourist attractions were researched and noted. She left nothing to chance. Jack was the exact opposite. He had great faith that things would work out, and what irritated Holly, what seemed wildly unfair to her, was that they generally did work out for him.

And indeed, just as they were entering the bustling lobby of the hotel where they knew their mother was staying, just as Holly was trying to decide whether she should plant herself at the door and send Jack on a scouting party or vice versa, she heard a shriek of delight—

"Holly! Jack! You're here!"

## CHAPTER

GWEN WAS THRILLED. THERE WAS NO DOUBT ABOUT IT. Her children had come to her wedding. Now everything was perfect.

"Whenever I think about my first wedding, when I married your father," she said at lunch afterward, "it always seems so odd that the two of you weren't there. How could I have been doing something that important without my babies?"

Jack eyed how little was left in the second bottle of champagne. He looked up at Hal. "Did you understand what she just said?"

"I did," Hal answered. "I don't think it reflects particularly well on my intellect, but I did."

Jack liked Hal. He seemed like a straightforward, good-natured man, much more flexible than Jack's father had ever been. To Jack's dad, the world had been full of things to be fixed and problems to be solved, whereas Hal saw things to be thought about and issues to be understood. Jack supposed that if he had to follow one of them into battle, he would have chosen his father's quickness, but for just about everything else, he suspected that he was going to prefer Hal.

They were now talking about Hal's cabin in Minnesota. When Jack had heard the word "primitive," he had asked Hal exactly what that meant . . . not that he cared, but he imagined that his sister would.

Indeed she did. "Wait a minute . . ." Holly was staring at Hal. "What do you mean, no bathrooms?"

"Oh, we have a propane tank," Hal said pleasantly, "so there's a stove and a refrigerator. And lights, we have gas lights. They're—"

"Could we get back to the part about bathrooms? Do you mean you don't have indoor toilets?" She sounded horrified.

"I suppose that technically they're indoors"—Hal's voice was as mild as could be, but Jack suspected that Hal was enjoying this; if Jack were in Hal's shoes, he would be—"but you do have to go outdoors to get back indoors."

Holly was speechless. Holly was never speechless.

"You went to Girl Scout camp," Jack reminded her.

76

"They must have had latrines there."

"I went to Girl Scout camp almost twenty years ago," she answered. "I am not exactly a back-to-nature person these days." She turned to Hal. "How is it that you don't have electricity? I thought the R.E.A. took care of all these isolated places ages ago."

Hal shook his head. "I don't think any of us on the lake want electricity. It's probably reverse snobbism in some way, to show how disdainful we are of modern conveniences."

"So that's why you don't put in a generator?" Jack asked. He had already priced gas-powered generators with every intention of giving one to his mother as a wedding gift.

Across the table his mother was looking at him, listening. She gave her head a quick shake. She knew what he was planning and was telling him not to do it.

"I wasn't going to put in a nuclear reactor, Mom," he protested.

"One just never knows with you, Jack," she answered.

Ha looked puzzled, interested, but Holly waved her hand, encouraging him to ignore them. "I still don't understand," she said. "How do you shower?"

"You don't," he said pleasantly.

"You don't shower and you have to use a latrine?" Holly did not look happy.

"What did I ever do"—Gwen threw up her perfectly manicured hands—"to deserve such a prissy child? You'll be fine, Holly. You take baths in the lake."

"Holly is never fine," Jack pointed out, but he scooted his chair toward hers and put his arm around her shoulders as he spoke, "if she is more than three steps from a fax machine."

"Then bring a fax machine," Hal suggested. "It won't work. We have no phone lines, we have no electricity, but if it will make you feel better, by all means bring one."

As soon as Holly got back to New York City, she bought her mother a state-of-the-art cellular phone that could be recharged in the car. Gwen sent it back. "It's very sweet of you, but Hal says that even cellular phones don't work at the lake. It's too far from a transmitting tower."

"But cell phones work everywhere," Holly fussed at Jack. She was talking on her cordless phone; he was on his car phone. "Even backpackers take their cell phones with them."

Jack shook his head. Holly knew the strangest damn people. "We aren't babies, Holly. We don't need to speak to our mother every minute. She'll call us when she goes into town for groceries."

That proved to be most unsatisfying. Gwen was in town only during the middle of the day, and so most of the time she would end up talking to Holly's secretary and Jack's answering machine. It drove them nuts. They would call each other and fret. "Apparently we are babies," Jack concluded.

Jack was going to stay in Minnesota for as long as his mother needed him. Apparently Hal's kids stayed for nearly a month.

"Don't they have jobs?" Holly marveled. "How do they get so much time off?"

Jack was wondering how he himself was going to get so much time off. Sure, he was the boss, but that only made it worse. He could hardly expect his people to work hard when he wasn't. But his crew chief Pete had recently lost a grandmother whose house had proved to be worth a startling amount of money. As her only grandchild, Pete had inherited it all, and he was, Jack knew, looking for a business of his own.

"What about this one?" Jack asked.

Pete stared at him. "You're not thinking of selling, are you? Things are going great."

It was true; the business had done well. Jack had a comfortable cushion in the payroll account, a tidy profit at the end of the year, and a waiting list of clients. That was the problem.

Starting a new business was terrific. In a new business everything was a crisis from one minute to the next. It was almost as good as fighting fires. But the routine of running a successful business—that wasn't for Jack. He had learned that about himself during his stint as a Wyoming hardware guy. Clearly what he needed to do was start businesses that would fail. He probably would have enjoyed that a whole lot, having a corporation that blew up in the sky and rained flaming pieces of metal all over Australia, but so far he was not succeeding in this pursuit of failure. The hardware store had left him with a big clump of cash that he hadn't known what to do with, and now it looked like this business was going to do the same damn thing.

But Pete seemed to think success was a burden he could live with. They shook hands, agreed to hire someone to fix a price, and do the thing as quickly as possible. Jack hoped to get all the paperwork done before he disappeared to Camp Nowhere, but in the end he found that he was going to have to delay his departure by a couple of days.

"It's just as well that you're coming a bit later," his mother told him on one of the rare occasions when they were speaking to each other. "This way Phoebe and Ian will arrive before you. I think they feel quite territorial about this place. It might be hard for them to come and find you already settled in."

Jack really and truly did not give a shit about Phoebe's and Ian's territorial urges. "Why's it so important to them? Is it really that great?"

"It's incredibly beautiful, and you have to remember that they have been coming here their entire lives."

"Okay." Jack knew that having moved so much, he and Holly and Mom weren't as attached to any one place as a lot of other people were. "But don't they go nuts being so isolated?" The nearest phone was fifteen miles away over such lousy roads that it took almost a half hour to get there.

"Actually"—she lowered her voice—"that's what they like about it. I think that the isolation makes them feel more like a family."

"That's weird." Jack couldn't imagine anything that would make Mom, Holly, and himself feel like more— or less—of a family.

"Maybe I'm wrong," she said, although they both knew that she wasn't likely to be. "I trust you won't say anything about it."

"Lord, no." Jack was starting to think that he might be better off if he didn't say anything about anything to Hal's children.

Two days later Holly reported receiving a call from Phoebe Legend, Hal's older daughter. "She said that it is cooler than we might expect, so bring sweaters and something warm to sleep in, but there's plenty of rain gear up there. Don't worry about packing that."

Jack didn't worry about the things he was supposed

to worry about; he certainly didn't worry about packing. "What did she sound like?"

"Polite. She was polite, I was polite, that was it."

"You're good at that."

"Thanks. I also got a message from Mother, but I'm not sure I got it right. It said I was to be sure that you didn't bring a generator."

"A generator? Me?" he protested. "Now, why would she ever think that I would do a thing like that?"

"I don't know," Holly sighed. "I'm not completely sure what it is, but don't bring one, okay? She doesn't want you to."

"Okay."

Tommy was already on the ice when Amy came out to the boards and slipped off her skate guards. Technical people were milling around; a group of schoolgirls were sitting in a tight Duster on the bleachers, having gotten permission to watch practice, but Tommy and Amy were the only skaters.

That wasn't unusual. Henry Carroll, Tommy Sargent, and Amy Legend, Oliver Young's three skaters, were widely known for the length and diligence of their warm-ups and cool-downs. They were always the last ones on the ice to take their sweaters off, the last ones to start practicing their jumps, their routines. They never stretched until their muscles were warm; they never finished for the day without stretching again. Even when practice time was as limited as it often was during the big tours, they never shortened their warm-ups. They were fastidious about it.

And none of them had ever had a serious injury.

Amy waved to the schoolgirls—she would sign autographs for them later—and caught up with Tommy.

81

This early into the warm-up, they could still talk.

"How's Mark?" she asked.

"Lousy."

They were in Canada, having come to guest-star in Canadian skater Mark Widemann's television special. Of their threesome, only Amy and Tommy were there. Henry had not been invited because he and Mark were alike as skaters, muscular, powerful, technically precise, only Henry was better, and Mark would have been an idiot to have Henry come overshadow him on his own special. Everyone, including Henry himself, understood that. But Mark was having problems with his ankle. Like so many skaters he took too many chances with his training routines.

Amy and Tommy went on, warming up. The first ten minutes were always the hardest for Amy. After that her body took over, but until then self-discipline was the only motivation. Fortunately Henry and Tommy felt the same, and the three of them flogged each other through their opening drills.

Henry and Tommy were her closest friends on the skating circuit. Almost none of the women she had grown up competing against were still skating at her level, and because women's skating had by now become like gymnastics, with very young girls dominating the amateur competitions, Amy had little in common with the new skaters. She, Henry, and Tommy had by far the most sophisticated management in the skating world; the three of them spent their off-ice time reading reports from charitable foundations and studying business deals while the other skaters were playing ping-pong or flipping through catalogues. Often accompanied by a personal assistant, they were still the ones the media was the most interested in. While they would have hated the idea that they had become unapproachable stars, even "everyone-please-love-me" Amy had to admit that they didn't spend much time with the new kids.

The three of them balanced each other, and the balance seemed essential to each individual career. Henry was still determinedly competitive; he kept them all skating their best. Tommy was the witty showman; he kept them from taking themselves too seriously. Amy was all warmth and sentiment; she reminded them why they were doing this. Henry was the muscle, Tommy the brain, Amy the heart—together, Tommy often joked, they made one fine human being.

Their warm-up routine was a little history of learning to skate. They would begin with front crossovers, then back crossovers. They ran through all the single jumps, doing them in the order that they had learned them, then all the doubles, and finally whatever triples they were doing at the moment.

Both Tommy and Amy were into their doubles when Amy noticed Gretchen, their personal assistant, at the boards, motioning to them. Amy caught Tommy's attention, and the two of them skated over to Gretchen.

"It's off," Gretchen said immediately. "The taping's been canceled. Mark's ankle is worse. He may need surgery."

Tommy whistled. "That's hard luck."

But it wasn't all luck. Tommy and Amy knew that. Of course, either one of them could catch a rut wrong and be injured—it could happen in the next sixty seconds—but it was a whole lot less likely to happen to them than to anyone else.

"So are we free to go?" Amy asked.

"It's not going to be announced until ten, so it would probably look better if you didn't start packing until then."

"What's next?" Tommy asked.

None of them ever paid any attention to what they were scheduled to do next. Once they consented to do something, they deliberately forgot about it, letting Gretchen and everyone else worry about the details, while they focused entirely on what they were doing at the moment.

"Your break was next." For three weeks every summer Oliver insisted that they not set foot on the ice, that as much as possible they not think about skating. It restored their bodies, he said, and allowed their subconscious minds to work more creatively. "So Oliver says you should just add another week to that."

If all the schoolgirls hadn't been watching, Amy would have made a face. None of them liked their break. Living so completely in the present, they never made any plans for their breaks and ended up moping around Denver for three weeks. The result was positive; when it was over, they were full of ideas and desperately eager to skate, but the break itself wasn't as much fun as it should have been.

Henry and Tommy usually visited their families, but Amy's family was at the lake during July and she didn't like it there.

"You know," Tommy said to her, "you ought to go see your family."

"You say that every year." Tommy was appalled at how little time she spent with her family. But his family was always very happy to arrange their schedule around his, to come see him wherever he might be.

"I know what you're thinking," he said. "That Henry's and my families treat us like the gods that we are not because we pay all their bills, and your family treats you like the little sister that you are, but you should still go. Your father just got remarried, and you haven't met his wife."

That was unanswerable. Even if she only went for a day, she should go. "But there are no showers up there, Tommy. And it's boring. There's nothing to do but swim and pick blueberries. There's no TV, there's no newspapers, and you always have to worry about wasting the batteries in the radio. You would hate it."

"I am not proposing that *I* go," he returned. "Just you. And we do stuff we hate all the time. Every single day there's something we hate, but we do it anyway. There's no reason why you can't leave this afternoon or tomorrow. You can fly straight from here."

"I can't do that." She was resigned to the fact that she should go. But not right this minute. "I don't have any of the right clothes."

"Is there anyone on earth who could buy an entirely new wardrobe more quickly than you?"

That was an exaggeration, but Amy was an extremely experienced shopper, and Toronto had some fine stores. "Even if I do get some new clothes, I can't get in touch with them. There's no way to let them know that I'm coming, what flight I am on, all that."

"Then don't let them know. Just show up. Rent a car at the airport and drive yourself there. You're a grown woman. You can do that."

"No, I can't." When it came to Amy's family, she was most emphatically *not* a grown woman. "You just said it. I am the little sister. Little sisters don't rent cars and drive themselves anywhere."

"That's if they want to go on being the little sister their whole lives."

"You haven't met Phoebe and Ian. Being the little

sister is the only option."

Gretchen was listening to this without much interest. She had heard it all before. "If you really want to go, Amy, I'll figure out some way to notify your family."

"There're no phones there."

Gretchen waved a hand. Phones, schmones. Like many skaters, Henry, Tommy, and Amy did not have particularly good problem-solving skills. She did. That's what they paid her for. "You finish on the ice, and I'll see what I can do."

Twenty minutes later, she reported back. The receptionist of the area Chamber of Commerce had a teenage son, and yes, of course he would be happy to drive out to this lake with a message for Amy's family. "I don't suppose you know the fire number of your cabin, do you?" Gretchen asked. "That's apparently what they use instead of addresses."

Gretchen now knew more about navigation in the region than Amy did. "I'm clueless."

"That's okay. She says he'll find it."

So. Amy was going to the lake. And Amy did not like the lake. She hoisted her skate bag by the strap and hung it over Tommy's shoulder. If he was making her do this, he could at least work a bit.

He hooked his thumb through the strap. "You can call me every day. I'll listen to you moan."

"There're no phones up there, Tommy. Remember?"

"Oh."

They started walking to the exit, where a car would be waiting to take them back to the skaters' hotel. "How can there be no phones?" he asked. "Everyone has phones."

"There just aren't."

Knowing that both Mom and Holly would, at best, scalp him if he disobeyed, Jack didn't include a generator when he packed his truck. He was sorry. It wasn't that he cared whether or not he had electricity, but he had no idea what he was going to do with himself at this lake. Water sports weren't his thing, and he wasn't any good at lazing around doing nothing—but a couple of two-hundred-foot boxes of Romex wire would liven up anyone's day.

He was driving up from Kentucky. Hal had suggested that he could fly to Minneapolis and then change for a little commuter flight that would take him to a one-room airport within an hour of the lake. But Jack preferred to drive. He liked to drive, and as his sister frequently pointed out, he was an American male—he didn't feel complete without a set of car keys in his pocket.

Holly decided to skip the commuter plane too. He would pick her at the Minneapolis-St. Paul airport, and they would drive the rest of the way together. The lake was about five hours north of the Twin Cities.

He arrived in plenty of time—owing in part to the fact that Iowa State Highway patrol were not showing their cheery little faces along their stretch of Interstate 80. He spent the morning poking around the Twin Cities—there was a great salvage place in St. Paul called the Ax Man. Just after lunch he went out to the airport and parked in the short-term lot. He didn't usually pay higher rates to save himself a few steps, but Holly could get herself out of an airport faster than anyone he knew. She was always one of the first people off the plane, and she never checked her luggage.

But today a good thirty people disembarked before her, and when she did finally get off, she had only her attaché case with her. Jack stepped forward and hugged her.

"You checked your luggage?" He was surprised. She hated standing around waiting at baggage claim.

"Did I ever." She grabbed the placket of his shirt and turned him around. "Look who came with me." Her voice was suddenly all bright and chirpy. Holly was not a bright and chirpy person. "It's Nick."

Nick? Who was Nick? Jack looked at the person standing at her elbow. It was a kid, fifteen, sixteen. He was short with a wrestler's compact build. His jaw was square, his forehead narrow, giving him a belligerent, bulldoggish look. He had on black jeans and a white T-shirt. A portable CD player was clipped to his belt, and a thin black cord snaked up to the headphones that were looped around his neck. Jack had no idea who he was.

"You remember Nicky, don't you?" Holly's elbow ground into his ribs.

No, he didn't. They had a cousin named Nicky—actually, he was their first cousin once removed since he was Aunt Barbara's grandson, Cousin Valerie's son—but this wasn't him. Nicky was a little kid.

But who else would it be? Jack stared at him. "You're Nicky?"

"Yo, man." The kid stuck up his thumb. His nails were bitten off, and there were little lines of red across the top of each nail bed.

"We had such a pleasant flight together," Holly said sweetly.

Holly wasn't a sweet person either. Jack didn't dare look at her. "So are you visiting in Minneapolis?" he asked Nick. "Are we dropping you somewhere?"

"Oh, no," said Holly. "He's coming to the lake with us. Isn't that nice?"

No, no, it wasn't. Not in the least.

"My presence is not entirely voluntary." Nick's voice was bitingly sarcastic.

"Things were decided at the last minute," Holly said, "so there was no way to get in touch with you, Jack. You seemed to have turned your car phone off, and someone else is answering your pager."

He had turned his beeper over to Pete along with the rest of the business. But he had been on the road for only a day and a half. This must have been a very last-minute plan.

And if there hadn't been any way to get in touch with him, then there wouldn't have been any way to reach Planet Wilderness. "Does Mom know he's coming?"

"We hope." Holly's voice lilted upward, drawing out the last word. Clearly she had written, telegrammed, Fed-Exed, hired a sky-writing plane, done everything she could to warn their mother, but when Valerie and Aunt Barbara collapsed, there wasn't much else other people could do.

One of the absolute low points of Holly's and Jack's pre-adolescence had been when their cousin Valerie, then sixteen, had come to live with them while waiting out a pregnancy.

The plan was for the baby to be given up for adoption, and Gwen, who knew her divorced younger sister very well, had urged and urged Barbara, Valerie's mother, not to come for the baby's birth. But Barbara came. Both she and Valerie saw the baby, and they had wept themselves into taking the child home, thus giving them a chance to continue all of their tantrums and power struggles over the rearing of a child. Whenever they reached the end of their rope, they dumped Nicky on Gwen.

"He's not as awful as he looks," Holly said softly.

Nick had pulled his headphones back over his ears and drifted over to the newspaper machines.

"Why didn't you just say no?" Jack demanded.

"Because I knew Mother would expect me to say yes."

She had a point there. The only thing that irritated Jack about his mother was that she never told her younger sister to go hang herself. He groaned. They were doomed. "What's the story?"

"He was picked up shoplifting—"

"Shoplifting? Oh, lovely."

"—and all Barbara and Valerie could think of to do with him was ship him off to Mother."

"I don't suppose it occurred to either of them that Mom deserves a chance to get settled into this marriage before she has to take on their problems?"

Holly didn't answer that. There was no reason to. "The therapist they talked to said that Nick needed a good male role model."

"Oh, this is really nice. Hal has been in the family for four and a half weeks now, and we're already expecting him to be a good male role model for Nicky."

"They were thinking about you."

"Me?" Jack stared at her. "Me? No way. I'm no role model."

"You're better than anything else he's got."

That was probably true. Jack looked at Nicky again. In the flat, harsh airport light his skin was sallow and blotchy. What an unpromising-looking individual. "What's he going to do at this place?"

"What are any of us going to do?"

She had another point. She sure was right a lot. That's why she should have been an admiral. Admirals ought to be right most of the time. The world would probably be a better place if they were.

"Well, it's not going to get any better by waiting," he sighed. At least not at short-term parking rates. "Let's go get your bags and hit the road."

"Fine, but we're also supposed to pick up Amy. She's coming in from Toronto. Her flight—"

"Amy? As in our new stepsister Amy-the-Legend? We're picking her up?" This was another surprise.

"That's what the message said." Holly clearly hated this business of having to operate just on messages her secretary transmitted. "I never got to actually talk to Mom and Hal about it."

"I thought she never went to this place. When did she decide to come?"

"I don't know. Apparently she was in the middle of taping a TV special when she hurt herself and had to take a break from skating. I know nothing about it."

Holly was starting to sound very tense. "I'm not blaming you," he assured her. "But, Holly, think about it, you, me, Nicky, and now Miss Amy, that's four people. Excuse me for sounding excessively detail-oriented"—he was probably the least detail-oriented person on the continent—"but I have a truck, a pickup. It only holds three people."

"Oh." Obviously she hadn't considered that. "You don't have one of those little bench things in back? I thought you did."

That had been five years ago. "Different truck, different time. You were just in this one last month, remember?"

"Now I do." She sounded rueful.

"I'll take the bus up," Nicky called out. "I've already checked it out. There's bus service to a town about twenty miles away. I can hitch the rest of the way."

91

He was still over at the newspaper machines. He wasn't supposed to have been able to hear them. Jack had thought headphones had destroyed the hearing of all kids his age. "No, you are not taking the bus up." Jack could imagine what his mother would say to that plan. And what kind of kid had already checked the bus schedule? He had probably been planning his escape route. Jack almost admired that. "We'll figure something out."

"But we all have to have our own seat belts." Nicky ambled closer. "Remember, I was brought up on *Sesame Street*. My generation wears seat belts. We use drugs and we commit suicide, but we wear our seat belts."

"How commendable of you. But we'll figure something out. Maybe Amy's so badly injured that she's on a stretcher, and we can load her into the back of the truck." He took her flight information from Holly and went over to the monitors. Amy's plane was coming in at Gate 67.

"The two of you go on down to her gate," Holly called to him. "I've got a couple calls to make. I'll meet you there."

"And I'll meet you at the baggage claim," Nicky said.

"No." Jack was firm. "We're all staying together."

He knew his sister. She would call work and then never get off the phone. He didn't know Nick—he didn't want to know Nick—but he suspected if he let the kid out of his sight, he would end up furthering the acquaintance in the company of a bail bondsman. He took his sister by the arm, glared at Nick, and began marching off down the concourse. He got them down the Gold Concourse across the airport to the Green Concourse, then out to Gate 67. He almost had them corralled into chairs when Holly spied a bank of phones and broke free. Nick slumped down into a chair and shut his eyes. A moment later he started tapping his feet and drumming out a beat on the leg of his black jeans.

The flight's arrival time neared. Other people were gathering. Right on schedule the stately silver plane rolled up to the gate. Jack caught Holly's eye and gestured her to get off the phone. He planted himself in the center of the people waiting to meet the disembarking passengers.

Okay. It was time to admit to a certain amount of male vanity here. In the best of all possible worlds, it would be nice to make a good first impression on Amy-the-Legend. He didn't need her to be instantly smitten with his multifold masculine charms, but it would be nice if she didn't leap back and make the sign of the cross.

But he had been driving for two days, he had spent the morning at the Ax Man, he was towing one juvenile-delinquent and one chained-to-her-fax lawyer. A good impression wasn't likely. Probably not even possible. Oh, well, that was life in the regular-guy world. And Jack considered himself to be a regular guy to end all regular guys. He jammed his hands into his pockets.

He looked over his shoulder. Holly was still on the phone.

The ticket Agent opened the gate. Two businessmen came out, and right after them was Amy Legend.

There was no question about it. This was Amy Legend, the sunny blonde hair, the clear features, the blue-green eyes. Her smile didn't quite have the full-wattage incandescence of her pictures, but that was hardly to be expected. She was getting off a plane; what was there to smile about? Jack stepped forward.

"Amy, I'm Jack Wells." She was shorter than he had

expected.

She put out her hand and greeted him quickly. Her handshake was firm; her voice was pleasant but rushed. "I did check my baggage, I hope that's not a problem."

"No, no." But before Jack could say any more, she started off down the concourse. She didn't pause, she didn't turn her head to see if he was with her, she didn't leap back and make the sign of the cross, she just took off. So much for the good first impression. She had hardly looked at him.

But he had a bigger problem. One of his charges was still on the phone, another was plugged in and tuned out, and the third—the injured one—was speeding down the concourse.

Holly could take care of herself, and she was too much their mother's daughter to let anything happen to St. Nick. So Jack set out after Amy.

It took him a few paces to catch up with her. Then she stopped so quickly that he almost crashed into her. She gestured at the door of the ladies' room. "If a lady in a fuchsia blouse comes by, don't let her in. The blouse has tucks and a notched collar and a stain right here."

She pointed at her collarbone and disappeared inside the rest room. The door swung shut behind her. Jack stared at it. This was really great. What was he supposed to say if the lady in fuchsia had to go pee? "I'm sorry, madam, this facility is under surveillance." He wasn't even sure what color fuchsia was. And tucks and a notched collar? What did that mean?

Jack looked down the concourse. Indeed, there was an overweight woman in a bright pink blouse, puffing along as fast as she could. She had three kids with her, and they were all as fat as she was. "She must have come this way," the mother said. "We can't have missed her."

Jack now understood. America's sweetheart was hiding from her public.

"Maybe we'll see her at the baggage claim," one of the kids said, and the whole family lumbered off.

"Where's Amy?" It was Holly. Nick was a couple of steps behind her. "In the bathroom?"

Jack nodded, and a moment later the ladies' room door eased open and he could see the top of a honey-blonde head.

"You can come out," he called. "The wicked witch is dead. The house has landed on her."

Amy Legend came out of the bathroom. "I am sorry. That wasn't very dignified, was it?" Her smile was apologetic, but her gaze was very level and direct. "Thank you for helping. I don't like not being able to manage on my own, but sometimes I can't."

"I didn't do a thing," he pointed out.

"I was desperate," she continued. "They have not left me alone for one minute. They kept trying to make up excuses to come up to the front of the plane. It was hard on everyone, not just me."

"They're hoping to meet you at the baggage claim."

She made a face, then flicked a hand. "Oh, well, I didn't need any of that stuff."

"Do things like this happen to you often?" Holly asked.

Amy shook her head. "Most of the time I'm traveling with someone. And if you are clearly in a conversation, people usually don't interrupt."

She was, Jack noticed, standing a little closer to them than the casualness of this conversation warranted. About ten feet away two teenage girls were standing and staring at her. He made a shooing motion with his

95

hands, and they moved on.

Holly spoke. "I hope Jack introduced himself. I'm his sister Holly, and this is our cousin, Nick Curtis."

Amy and Holly shook hands. Before she could put out her hand to Nick, he stuck up his thumb again, and she returned his gesture. She had very pretty hands, fluid and graceful. "The message I got from my father was unclear," she said. "Are we all driving up to the lake together?"

"That's the plan," Jack answered. "Whether or not said plan is going to be carried out pretty much depends on everyone's hip size." If he had been speaking to a normal person, he would have said "butt," not hip. "We've got to squeeze four people into three seat belts. But we've got to get the luggage first."

They set off down the concourse. Amy stopped three times to speak to people or sign autographs. Each time they paused for that, Holly eyed the phones and Nick drifted toward one of the shops. Jack wished he had brought a rope in from the truck. He could have lassoed the three of them together and tied them to his belt.

Two suitcases and a box were the last remaining bags on the carousel assigned to the New York flight. Jack recognized one suitcase as Holly's. Nick picked up the other.

"The box is ours too," Holly said.

That surprised Jack. Traveling with a roped cardboard box was not his sister's style.

He lifted it off the carousel. It wasn't heavy. But the knots were well tied, a bowline in one end, a slipknot in another. That was one thing about being a navy kid. You learned your knots. Holly probably tied the best knots of anyone in her law firm. "What's in here?"

"A three-dimensional Scrabble game, a Twister

game, six bags of those loops you make pot holders from, and an American flag." Holly didn't sound happy about this. "And you want to know something? They do not sell pot holder loops on Wall Street."

"Mom had you buy all that? What for?"

"I have no idea. This all came in a message. Maybe she knows you're worried about getting bored and wants some nice craft projects for you." She stopped, having obviously realized how she was sounding. "I'm sorry, Amy. Please don't think this is Mother complaining. It's me. She's really been having a wonderful summer. She says that the lake is everything your father said it would be."

"Oh, don't worry about offending me." Amy waved one of her pretty hands. "You need to be careful around my sister and brother, but me, I hate the place."

"What?" Jack hadn't expected to hear that. "I thought this was Mecca, Nirvana, every person's dream."

"Oh, the rest of my family loves it. And I'm sure you will. Really. Don't let me put you off. It's just me." She was apologizing, even more than Holly had.

"Then it's good of you to come," Holly said, and they all started to walk again. Jack couldn't help noticing Amy's stride; it was long and graceful. And her posture was great. His sister stood reasonably straight, probably better than every other lawyer on the planet, but a lot worse than your average admiral. Amy-the-Legend had even the admirals beat; her posture seemed easy and effortless.

"I thought you were injured," he said.

"Who, me?" She was surprised. "No, it wasn't me. I'm never injured. It was Mark Widemann, the Canadian skater. I was about to start working on his television special, but he was having so many ankle

97

problems that they had to postpone the whole thing. So I suddenly had some free time and here I am."

"How long are you staying for?" he asked.

"I don't know. It depends on a lot of things."

She sounded deliberately vague, so Jack shut up. They were approaching the carousel where the bags from her flight had been unloaded. He hid her behind a pillar while he scouted the area. Her fans had given up on her. She had a pair of nice-looking leather bags. Jack balanced Holly's box on his shoulder and took one of Amy's suitcases from her. The workmanship on it was impressive, although there was something strange about the handle. It was small.

She must have had it made to fit her own hand.

Jack generally tried to get his clothes to fit him, although it wasn't certainly anything he obsessed about. It had never occurred to him to try to get luggage handles to fit him.

Out in the parking lot, he stowed the luggage in the back of his truck. Then he reached for Holly's attaché case. She tried to pull it away. "I'll just keep it with me," she said.

"For God's sake, Holly, do you honestly think you're going to be able to work on the drive up? There are going to be four of us, crammed into a space for three. You'll put someone's eye out just trying to get the damn thing open."

Reluctantly Holly gave it up.

Jack slammed the tailgate shut. "All right, folks, let's see if we fit."

His plan was to put Amy next to the window, then Holly next to her with Nick squeezed in between Holly and himself. Surely the pleasure of being crammed up to Nick for five hours belonged to his blood relatives.

98

But Amy had already gotten in, and Holly was sliding in next to her. Holly pulled out the middle seat belt and passed it over to Amy. Fortunately it was a long one without a shoulder harness. The two of them snuggled their hips together, and the seat belt clicked in.

"It's a good thing our butts aren't any bigger, isn't it?" Amy laughed.

She was being a good sport. Jack liked that. He could forgive just about anything in people as long as they didn't whine or think themselves too good for the rest of the world. And so far Amy Legend had been a very good sport. She looked interestedly at the dashboard of the truck. "This can't be the kind of transportation you're used to," he said.

"That's why it seems so exciting. It feels like we're all going to summer camp." She sounded as if she thought that would be fun.

"I think that's what Holly's worried about." Jack put the key in the ignition. "Now, who knows where we're going?"

"I have the instructions in my attaché case," Holly said and pointedly looked toward the back of the truck.

"Too late," Jack told her. "You know how to get there, don't you?" he asked Amy.

She shook her head. Her hair brushed against his arm. He could smell her perfume. It was light and woodsy. "Actually, no. We take a left turn somewhere, that's all I know. I don't pay any attention to where I am going unless I am driving, and not always then."

"That sounds safe." Jack put the truck in gear. "Let's just go until we get bored, and then we'll take a left turn."

"Jack!" Holly protested. "If you can wait two seconds, I'll get the directions."

"Oh, no, it will be more fun this way."

He was teasing her. He had checked a map while waiting for her plane, and he was reasonably sure he could get them within five or six miles of where they were supposed to be. Then they could start the left turns and see what happened.

By the time he was out of the airport traffic, Holly and Amy were already well launched into a conversation about clothes that was far too technical for him. If you had the arm holes in your jackets cut very high, he learned, it was more flattering to your waist. "You can't move," Amy reported, "but you look great."

Nick had pulled his earphones back on. Jack didn't blame him.

They were soon on Interstate 35 heading north. Holly and Amy were talking about shoes. Amy propped her foot up on the dashboard to demonstrate something about an "instep strap." Her knee bumped against the steering wheel.

"Sorry," she said to him and went back to talking to Holly. "It is hard to find a daytime shoe with a strap that doesn't make you look like a schoolgirl or a tart, but some years diagonal straps are out there in leather. If you can find a closed shoe with straps and a court heel, you can climb Everest even on three-inch heels."

Jack glanced at his sister. She was nodding. She had understood every word. "What are you doing about shoulder pads these days?" she asked.

That opened the gates for another vocabulary—"hair-canvas base" and "feathering at the neckline edge." Both of them were gesturing toward their shoulders, drawing curving lines over their clavicles. Each time one of them moved, Amy was crowded closer to him. He put his arm along the back of the seat to give her more room. When, a few minutes later, she leaned forward to struggle out of her jacket—he now knew it to be reversible, washable silk—so that she and Holly could figure out how the inner jacket had been "turned"—whatever the hell that meant—her elbow poked into his chest.

Finally Holly changed the subject. "So tell us more about this lake. Your family has three cabins?"

They did, Amy answered, but all three were quite small. The one that the family had had from the beginning had only one bedroom. It was log-sided, and they called it the "main cabin." "Even though it's probably the smallest, it's where we always eat and such."

The "new" cabin actually had been purchased next. It was called the "new" cabin because it had been built only a few years before the family bought it. "It's the most comfortable. It has two bedrooms and lots of windows, so it's light and it has a much more open floor plan. The kitchen's separated from the living room only by a counter, things like that."

"Then why don't you eat there?" Holly asked.

"Because we don't. The important thing about the lake is to go up and do exactly what you did the year before."

The third cabin was called the "log" cabin because, it was made of logs, not just sided with them. "It's pretty dark. So my brother's and sister's families alternate years—one year Phoebe and Giles stay in the new cabin, the next in the log. Everyone likes it when it's their year in the new cabin."

"So your parents stayed in the main cabin, your brother and sister traded off between the other two," Holly said. "Where did that leave you?"

"Usually in Amsterdam or somewhere like that. I don't come very often anymore. But there's a bunkhouse. I suppose that's where we'll all be staying."

"A bunkhouse?" Holly didn't sound happy.

"It's okay, but the mattresses are kind of crummy, and there're no lights or mirrors or anywhere to put your clothes."

Jack imagined that she was used to lights, mirrors, and places to put her clothes. "So why do they put you there?" He hadn't said anything in a while.

She looked up at him. "I'm never there for as long as the others, so it doesn't make sense for me to take one of the better beds."

"But doesn't sleeping on a lumpy mattress tend to make your stay even shorter?" Holly asked. "It would mine."

Amy smiled and wrinkled her nose, her answer obvious.

"There's no reason for us to whine about this." Jack had no patience for martyrs. "If the mattresses are lumpy, we'll go into town and buy new ones. And how far is it from the propane tank? Why not trench a gas line out to the place and put up a light? How long could it take?"

"Two years if you're lucky," Amy laughed. "More likely five. You have to understand the culture up there. They don't make changes."

Well, they were going to have to. Jack knew that his mother expected her two children to be good sports. She expected them to be accommodating, to respect the fact that the Legend family had been coming to this place for years and years. She would put up with endless inconvenience herself and expect them to as well. But she would draw the line somewhere. And Holly having

102

a decent place to sleep would probably be it. He didn't know how that would sit with the travel-soccer, Cub-Scout-Blue-and-Gold-banquet parents, but they would have been at this precious lake for twenty-four hours by now. They were at last going to have to admit that changes were taking place.

# CHAPTER 5

PHOEBE GOT IN THE BACKSEAT WITH THE KIDS. SHE didn't want to sit in the front with her brother. If she did, he would start to fuss and complain, and she didn't think she could stand that.

The drive outside the cabin was narrow, a pine-needle-covered lane threading between the birches and pines. Ian had to concentrate, steering the car as tightly as he could so that the boat trailer didn't crash into the trees. But once he was out on the road, an open, sandy trail that circled the lake, he could drive with more ease.

He hooked his arm over the back of the seat. "Weren't you surprised that the power boat wasn't put in? Mom and Dad always launched the boat first thing."

*It's not Mom and Dad anymore, Ian. It's Dad and Gwen now.* "I don't see that it's any big deal."

"I didn't say that it was. I was just surprised, that's all."

He was lying. But then so was she. It did seem important. Last year had been horrible. Coming up here without Mother had been so awful that they had all left after a week and a half, but this year, with Gwen and the changes . . . it almost seemed like this year was going to be worse.

It had started with the milk. On their way up to the

lake yesterday, she and Giles stopped to buy milk. Of course they had. That's what they always did.

All three of the cabins had refrigerators, but they were old and small, very small. They couldn't be replaced because they ran on propane, and no one in the United States manufactured refrigerators like that anymore. When these finally died, they would have to send to Sweden for new ones.

As a result, there was never enough cold storage when the whole family was there. So on the way to the lake people stopped and bought milk. That's the way things were done.

But yesterday after all the flurry of greetings, as Giles lifted the cooler out of the back of the station wagon, it was clear that Gwen hadn't expected them to buy milk. She had plenty of milk. She had been to town the day before. Every inch of every refrigerator was full. There was nowhere to store three gallons of milk.

"We'll put it in the lake and hope for the best," Gwen had said.

The little kids, Alex and Claire, had loved the idea, putting milk in the lake. They had danced down to the water, happy as could be, to rig up some infinitely elaborate system of storing milk under the dock.

"Putting it in the lake, that's a good idea," Giles said as he closed the cooler. "I wonder if it will work."

"It won't." Phoebe was not feeling very gracious. "You're supposed to store milk at forty degrees, and the lake's nowhere near that cold. It will spoil before we have a chance to drink it."

"It's only a couple gallons of milk," he said mildly. "We'll survive the loss."

She knew that. But she had made a mistake. She didn't like that.

There was a system to everything here. There had to be. The kitchens were so small, the arrangements so primitive, town so far away, that you needed good systems. Phoebe's mother had established them. And Phoebe knew them. She knew how to store the boats, she knew how to light the refrigerators, she knew how to prime the pumps. She knew where the tea towels were kept, how the latrine was cleaned. She understood life at the lake.

But it had all changed. Someone else was buying the groceries; someone else was putting the tea towels away.

At least it was her family's turn to have the cheerful, airy new cabin. As great as all summers up here were, the best years were when she, Giles, and their kids had the new cabin. Earlier in the spring Ian had tried to suggest that his family should have the new cabin again this year. "I know last summer was our turn, but we were there such a short time that it shouldn't really count."

"Forget it," she had said. That's why they had such a careful system of taking turns so that they didn't have to negotiate everything every year.

But yesterday as she was unlocking the top carrier, Dad had spoken. He told them about Amy coming. "So with her and Holly and Jack, we need to rearrange how we sleep."

Phoebe handed Giles the first duffel bag. "Aren't they going to be in the bunkhouse?" That's where Amy had slept the last time she had come.

"No. That's not fair to them. We want Holly and Jack to feel welcome and comfortable. They're a part of the family now."

He outlined the plan. All of the school-age children

were to sleep in the bunkhouse. Ian and Joyce, Phoebe and Giles, were to each have one of the bedrooms in the new cabin. Thomas, Phoebe and Giles's toddler, the one born after her mother's death, would be in with his parents, and the other three adults—Amy, Holly, and Jack—were to be in the log cabin.

"We've discussed every other arrangement," Hal said. His voice was firm, this decision was made. "This is the best."

"The kids will like all sleeping together," Giles said. He reached up for another duffel bag.

Something in Phoebe shrieked.

She hated to admit it even to herself—and she would have never said a word to her mother or father—but Giles, her dear, wonderful husband, was not crazy about the lake. He never complained, he came year after year because she loved it so, but he would have been happier at a resort where a tanned college girl in track shorts and a tank top served frozen margaritas on the beach.

Giles was disabled, having been born with a withered leg. With his special built-up shoe, he could walk adequately, but there was enough of a lurch to his step that hiking was no pleasure. He certainly couldn't water ski or bike.

Two things made the lake tolerable for him—fishing in the old wooden rowboat that he had restored himself and having his own family all in one cabin. They spent the day with everyone, but mornings and nights were theirs, just the five of them—now the six of them. At night the kids would pile into bed, and Giles would read and read to them. Then once the kids were sleeping in the other bedroom, she and Giles would make love under heavy quilts as quietly as they could, listening to rain fall on the roof. In the mornings she would often go

106

over and help her mother get breakfast started, but Giles would stay in the cabin with the kids, chatting, playing games, doing all the things that you did when there was no newspaper to read, no TV to watch. He never cared whether they were in the log cabin or the new cabin, as long as he and she were in it alone with their children.

Phoebe watched him swing the duffel bag onto the pile with the others. He was a realist; his disability had made him so. It made him great at his job; he was one of the most able general counsels that the University of Iowa had ever had. He accepted setbacks, he moved on, he didn't look back, he didn't regret.

But he was disappointed with these new arrangements. Phoebe could tell. And she minded for him, she minded terribly.

They had to unload quickly because the car was needed. Mother and Dad had stopped driving a big family car a couple of years ago, and so Phoebe and Giles's station wagon was used to pick Ian's family up at the little airport an hour away in Hibbing.

It was a sensible arrangement, the wisest thing to do, but there were problems. Ian didn't really like it that her family was already settled and organized before his. On the other hand, it meant that she and Giles had to make their plans around Ian's, and sometimes it did seem that he chose a flight precisely so that it would be inconvenient to them.

The top carrier was empty. Phoebe hopped down and nodded to her father. The car was ready.

"Are you coming, Gwen?" He spoke to his new wife.

She turned to Phoebe. "Do you need some help with the children? I'll be happy to watch them while you unpack."

In the past Giles had watched the kids while she and

her mother unpacked. Phoebe had always liked that hour or two, that private time with Mother. Then her mother would leave her alone, and she would have the cabin to herself. She could arrange it just as they liked it, shifting a few little odds and ends that Joyce and Ian had rearranged the year before. "No, we'll be fine. If you want to go into town, go on."

"I am eager to meet Ian and his family."

Phoebe picked up Thomas so he wouldn't stagger behind the car, and holding his sturdy little body, she leaned against Giles. Together they watched the station wagon ease out of the narrow drive. The kids' bags had been set in front of the bunkhouse, and down the woods-lined path that ran parallel to the road, she could see her and Giles's suitcases set in front of the new cabin.

She felt Giles's arm close around her shoulders. "Let's not unpack. Let's just swipe the best room, make a big mess, and go swimming."

It was a wonderful idea. They called out to fourteen-year-old Ellie, telling her to get the little blue bag, that all the kids' suits were in there.

Giles changed quickly hurried back to the bunkhouse to help Ellie get Alex and Claire ready. This was one problem with the kids being in the bunkhouse. Ellie was going to end up working harder, doing more for the younger ones. If she would be helping with only Alex and Claire, Phoebe would not have minded. But Ian's kids were also going to be in the bunkhouse, fifteen-year-old Maggie and little Scott and Emily, who were the same ages as Alex and Claire. And Maggie was not helpful. It was going to be a struggle all month long to be sure that Ellie didn't end up responsible not just for her own little brother and sister, but for Maggie's too.

Phoebe changed slowly. She could hear voices down at the lake, the first splashes and shouts. She found her book, gathered up Thomas, and crossed back toward the main cabin. On this side of the lake the bank was steep, and a set of logs embedded in the sand served as steps leading down to the water. A short dock ran about fifteen feet into the lake, and anchored out in the deeper water was a wooden raft.

It was a beautiful afternoon. The lake was a rough oval, about three-quarters of a mile in length, perhaps a half mile across. The bottom was sand, trees ringed the shoreline, and the water was tinged a rust red. They had always thought that the redness of the water was from the rich veins of iron ore that lay under this part of Minnesota, but recently some people had suggested that the color might come from the needles of the tamarack trees. Phoebe didn't know which was right, and it didn't seem to matter.

They had a wonderful time. They swam, they swamped the canoe, and they sat on the raft in the sun. Phoebe had brought down cards, and they played Hearts and King's Corner on a towel spread over the planking of the raft. It seemed all so normal, to be at the lake again, with the sun shining on the water and the kids splashing. Thomas fell asleep inside an inflated ring. Phoebe covered him with a towel. It was so good to be back. She couldn't imagine life without the lake.

"Mom, we're starving." Ellie splashed over to the raft. "Can I go get us something to eat?"

"Sure. Do you want me to go?"

"No, no, I'll be glad to."

"Then go see what Gran has."

Phoebe watched her older daughter scramble up out of the water and hurry up the bank. It was like watching

109

herself. She remembered doing that, offering to help, liking to help, feeling important because she was the one helping. She knew what it would be like for Ellie to walk into the cabin alone, feeling so pleased to be responsible, to be the one whom your mother trusted. That's how Phoebe had always felt when she had helped her mother. They were in a line, the three of them, Eleanor, Phoebe, and Ellie, each one the oldest daughter. It meant something.

"Mom?"

Phoebe looked up. Ellie was back down on the bank, empty-handed. "Mom, would you come up here?"

"Sure, sweetheart."

She checked to be sure that Giles knew she was going and then splashed back to the dock. "What is it?"

"I don't know. I wasn't quite sure what to get."

Phoebe followed her daughter up the steps and across the narrow lakeside porch of the main cabin. Ellie held back. Phoebe opened the screen herself.

The table was set for dinner. That was the first thing she saw. Then she realized that she hadn't been in the main cabin yet this year.

All the furniture was in the same place. The little braided rugs, the candlesticks and hurricane lamps, were all in the same places. The mugs were stowed on cup hooks, the books were on the right shelves.

But it was all different. It was so *clean*. The windows sparkled. Every single tiny little pane had been washed inside and out. The floors had been oiled. A faint lemony, woodsy smell rose from the narrow pine planks. The globes of the gas lights shone. Even the dark build-up around the edges of the door latch was gone.

Gwen must have cleaned for days and days, Washing

110

all those tiny window panes would have taken forever.

Why had she done it? The cabin had always been good enough, clean enough.

Mother had looked down on people who were fanatic about cleanliness. It seemed petty to her, small-minded.

A bouquet of wildflowers was set in the center of the table. They were tansies, a vivid yellow flower with buttonlike blossoms. They were arranged in a blue pitcher that had been in the back corner of one of the upper cupboards. Phoebe didn't think that her mother had ever used the pitcher. It was always the wrong size, too big for a creamer, too small for anything else.

Why had Gwen set the table so far in advance of dinner? Of course, it made sense. They would all be getting back from the airport just at dinnertime, but still Mother wouldn't have done it, and there would have been a mad scramble to get everything ready. But Mother had been no more afraid of a mad scramble than of a little dirt. These careful preparations felt too fussy to Phoebe. It seemed bourgeois to worry about details like that.

This was not getting the children their snack. Carefully Phoebe went into the kitchen, her mother's kitchen, the kitchen she had been working in for more than thirty summers at her mother's side. She felt like a stranger. It too was immaculate. Every window pane, the edge of every shelf, every canister, gleamed.

Such a clean kitchen seemed so unforgiving, as if not a drop or a smudge would be excused.

"I didn't know what to do," Ellie said. "It all felt different."

"It is different," Phoebe said. "We're going to have to get used to it." She hoped she sounded like Giles, accepting, strong.

Even the pump, the old iron long-handled pump at the side of the sink, had been painted. It was a pump, for God's sake. Why would anyone paint a pump?

Ellie spoke again. "Down at the lake you called her 'Gran.' Is that what we should call her?"

Tears stung, sharp, hot tears. "Honestly, honey, I wasn't thinking. It just came out, and I was talking about Gran as if she would be here." Phoebe couldn't imagine her children ever calling anyone else "Gran." "We'll ask her what she would like to be called. Now let's see about a snack."

Phoebe stepped out onto the enclosed roadside porch where the pantry shelves were. The table in there was pulled out from the wall, and it too was set. Six places at each table. Clearly Gwen was planning an adults' table and a children's table. Mother had never done that. She had always opened the big table all the way and put everyone together.

Phoebe opened a couple of cupboards, looked into the refrigerator. "You were right," she said to Ellie. "It's hard to know what she"—they couldn't go on calling Gwen "she" and "her"—"what Gwen has planned."

There were several boxes of crackers, both the kinds that were always there and some kinds that Mother never bought. The wire hanging basket was full of fruit, oranges, apples, and bananas. Mother would have intended them for snacks, but maybe Gwen was planning a fruit salad. Phoebe didn't know.

And she wasn't used to that, not knowing.

"Look, Mom," Ellie called out. "This might help."

Posted on the wall beside the refrigerator was a list of menus. Phoebe quickly scanned them. Nothing seemed to require unusual amounts of fruit or any of the crackers. Gratefully Phoebe gathered up some apples

112

and told Ellie to pick a box of crackers.

And she tried not to notice how ordinary the apples were. Mother had always bought interesting apples, Prairie Spies, Harrelsons, Honey Golds. These were Red Delicious.

The afternoon had lost its glow. There was no pretending that things were the same, and it wasn't much longer before she heard the horn honk and car doors slam. Ian had arrived.

Alex and Claire dashed up the bank, eager to see their cousins. Phoebe followed more slowly, carrying Thomas, matching her pace with Giles. By the time they rounded the cabin, everyone was out of the car. The two little girls, Emily and Claire, were shrieking and hugging. The boys, Scott and Alex, were jumping off the stoop in front of the bunkhouse. They were all happy. But among the adults Phoebe could sense the tension. Her father was tight-lipped, disappointed. Ian looked harassed, Joyce defensive. Gwen seemed calm, but she wasn't smiling.

Phoebe greeted her brother and sister-in-law, then turned to Gwen. "I gave the kids apples and crackers," she said. "I hope that was okay."

"That's what they're there for," Gwen answered pleasantly. "And there are tons of cookies."

Phoebe hadn't thought to look for cookies. Mother hadn't liked sweets. "Where are Maggie and Ellie?"

"I think they went to the biffy," Gwen answered. That's what they all called the outhouse, a "biffy." Phoebe had no idea why, but that's the word they had always used.

And a moment later Maggie and Ellie did come down the path that led to the biffy. Ellie was pale, her features pinched. Maggie was clearly sullen and angry.

So this was it. Maggie wasn't happy about something, and she was making sure everyone else knew it.

The four little kids were now running in and out of the bunkhouse, slamming the two doors, thrilled at the notion of sleeping there. Hal and Ian were unloading the top carrier. A bright pink duffel bag was clearly Emily's. A Mighty Ducks soccer bag was Scott's. Simpler cases came, and when Ian directed Hal to put one in front of the bunkhouse, Maggie whirled toward Joyce and burst out, "Mom! You said—"

"We said we would talk about it," Ian said.

He finished unloading the top carrier and then came over to Phoebe. "Maggie's really upset about having to sleep in the bunkhouse with the little kids," he said quietly, "so we figured if it was all the same with you, she could sleep on the sofa in the new cabin. She can keep her stuff in our room. She won't be in the way."

Maggie not in the way? Maggie was a slob, her stuff would be everywhere.

Although Ian had adopted her, Maggie was Joyce's daughter, born during a brief first marriage. While she was a very bright girl—Ian and Joyce certainly never let you forget that, how smart Maggie was—she was also, Phoebe thought, selfish and indulged. Joyce gave her all the privileges of being an oldest child and none of the responsibilities.

"I'm not going to have Ellie in the bunkhouse all by herself with four little ones." Phoebe was firm on this. "It's not fair, it's too much responsibility. I don't mind having her have occasional responsibilities for Alex and Claire." Phoebe had done the same in her time. "But not all four of them. If Maggie sleeps in the new cabin, then either you or Joyce need to sleep in the bunkhouse with your two."

114

Joyce heard half of this. "You know I don't think it is fair to expect Maggie to do a lot of baby-sitting. The younger children are not her responsibility."

"They aren't Ellie's responsibility either. Either all"—Phoebe stopped and counted up—"all eleven of us sleep in the new cabin, or we stick to Dad and Gwen's plan."

"I don't see why we can't do what we've always done." Joyce's voice was close to a whine. "Why can't Gwen's kids sleep there?"

At home Joyce wore long, loose skirts in earth-tone tribal patterns topped by either roughly embroidered peasant blouses or cotton poet's shirts under handwoven vests. The clothes suited her. The gauzy layers softened the sharp angles of her face and hid her extreme thinness. But at the lake everyone wore jeans, and without the flowing fullness of her normal wardrobe, Joyce looked gaunt, and the poorness of her posture was exposed.

"Gwen's kids aren't kids, they are adults like us," Phoebe returned. There was nothing like opposition from Joyce to turn her into Gwen's ally. "I don't want to sleep there. You don't want to sleep there. Why should we make them sleep there?"

She pivoted, marching off before they could answer.

Ian and Joyce had insisted, had absolutely required, that everyone come to their house for Christmas last year. It had been awful, and in one of their rare moments alone, she had fussed about it to Giles.

"Remember," he had said, "if we lived in a patriarchal culture, Joyce would be holding all the cards."

She had stared at him. "What are you talking about?"

"In a real patriarchy, what happens when the queen

115

dies? Who runs things at the castle? Who plans the menus? Who gets the good jewelry? The oldest son's wife, not the daughters."

"We don't live in a patriarchy." And Mother's will had had a clause about her jewelry; it was to be divided between Phoebe and Amy. That had mortified Joyce. She had expected a third of it. She had adored Eleanor, even been in awe of her, and so had insisted, at every turn, that she be thought as much of a daughter as Phoebe or Amy—or as much as Phoebe and a whole lot more than Amy.

Of course, this wasn't about jewelry—although since Amy had said she didn't want any of it, Phoebe had it all—it was about who had power in the family, who made the decisions, and Joyce clearly wanted that too. "Given Joyce's politics, it's awfully strange of her to be counting on patriarchal property laws." Joyce professed herself to be a socialist.

"I know," Giles had agreed. "That's why this has all been so interesting."

But since that conversation the King had found a new Queen. As strange as it might be to have Gwen in Mother's place, that was probably a whole lot better than having Joyce there.

Phoebe walked over to the main cabin. Gwen was in the kitchen. "What can I do to help?"

"Nothing this evening," Gwen answered. "I was thinking tomorrow that we might post a duty roster. We can't have you, me, Holly, Joyce, and Amy all trying to help at the same time, to say nothing of Ellie and Maggie."

You certainly didn't need to worry about Maggie helping. The girl wouldn't. Nor would Amy either, for that matter.

"But you can stay here and talk to me," Gwen said pleasantly. "I've already told this to Ian and Joyce. We picked up the mail on the way in, and apparently my nephew—actually, he is my grand-nephew—is coming out with Holly and Jack. He's sixteen. He can sleep in the boys' half of the bunkhouse, and help Ellie and Maggie out with the children."

*My Ellie doesn't mind helping. It's not Ellie who's objecting to sleeping out there.* But Phoebe kept her mouth shut. Gwen was a smart woman; it wouldn't take her long to appreciate the difference between the two teenage girls.

As Mother had always done when they were all together, Gwen had set up a buffet line on the narrow pine server, but when everyone was coming in, Gwen asked Phoebe to help her move the server away from the wall. "That way we can have two lines at once."

"This is how I met her," Hal laughed. "She was having the caterers move the buffet table away from the wall."

Gwen smiled at him. "At least there are no extension cords for me to stand on."

It was obviously a private joke, but Joyce insisted that they explain it. Of course, once explained, the incident didn't seem very interesting, but things like that never were. Phoebe didn't blame her father or Gwen for how mundane their story was; Joyce shouldn't have asked.

It was amazingly easy to get dinner served. For thirty seconds Phoebe tried to pretend it was because the kids were all older than they had been last year, better able to manage for themselves. But it wasn't just that. Everything was better organized this year. Nothing had been forgotten on the buffet or left off the tables. There were two serving spoons for each dish. The bread and butter, the salt and pepper, the drinks and the napkins, were on the tables, not on the buffet. Gwen had done a good job.

Phoebe filled her plate, sat down next to the high chair, and started cutting up food for Thomas. She felt Giles nudge her under the table, and she looked across at him. His smile was questioning—*Are you okay*? She nodded. *Yes, for the moment.*

There were more flowers on the mantel above the fireplace. They were goldenrods; vibrant, heavy-headed blossoms arched over a tall stone jar. The oak mantel glowed a soft honey-yellow. Last year the mantel had been almost brown. The aging varnish had grown sticky, and it had trapped a haze of dust, dulling the wood's sheen. Gwen must have stripped the varnish and refinished the oak. The actual work probably hadn't taken all that long, but there were so many different stages involved in refinishing wood, and it was such a mess . . . Phoebe wasn't sure that she herself would have ever bothered to do it, but it did look wonderful.

She glanced over her shoulder. Her father and Gwen were getting their food. Gwen was going last, as if she were the hostess, which of course she was.

Gwen laid her plate down at the end of the server and put the covers back on the pots to keep things warm. She picked up her plate again and turned to sit down. There were no more places at the adult table.

Maggie had taken a place at the adult table.

Before dinner Gwen had said that the kids were to eat on the back porch. She had been absolutely clear. Maggie had to have heard her. But Maggie had gone and sat at the adult table anyway.

Phoebe was furious.

Ian instantly scooted his chair over. "Here, Gwen, there's plenty of room. We can get another chair."

But Giles was already on his feet, lifting his plate. "No, I'll go out and help Ellie. She's stuck out there with the little ones. Here, Gwen, please sit down."

This wasn't Giles on vacation, this was Giles, general counsel of the University of Iowa, thinking quickly, acting quickly, being so decisive that no one had a chance to argue. He had already taken Gwen's plate from her, was already guiding her to the chair. "I haven't touched a thing. Everything—glass, napkin, fork, they're all clean."

But being general counsel was exactly what Giles did not want to do on vacation.

Ian was flushed, mortified. He knew he should have made Maggie move. Phoebe could see Joyce start to bristle. Joyce would have defended Maggie. *Maggie enjoys adult conversations so. She is simply too intelligent for some other teenagers.*

And just whom was Maggie too intelligent for? Ellie was the only other teenager here. Phoebe's own sweet, helpful, responsible Ellie.

Phoebe turned back to the high chair and started mashing up Thomas's lasagne again. Now it was too fine, and he was having trouble eating it.

None of this would have happened if Mother was still alive.

## CHAPTER 6

THERE WERE FOUR OF THEM IN A SPACE DESIGNED FOR three. Amy could tell that Jack didn't like having to crowd his passengers like that, but she wasn't uncomfortable. Neither he nor Holly seemed to mind being bumped and poked—being touched drove Henry

119

nuts—so Amy wasn't having to hold herself forward and stiffly upright as she would have if crowded between Henry and Tommy.

She was having a good time. She really liked these people. Of course, the boy Nick, fair-skinned, dark-haired, seemed a typical sullen teenager, but compared to the teenagers Amy knew, the determined little near-anorexics who viewed Amy as the once-idolized enemy, the person they wanted to dethrone . . . compared to them, Nick was just fine.

Holly was great, the ideal person for Amy to share a long car trip with. She had a cooler, more detached nature than Amy herself did, but like Amy, her clothes and shoes had the place in her life that other women reserved for husband and children. She was also dreading the inconveniences of the lake even more than Amy. "I don't know how I'm going to survive without a hair dryer."

"You have to tell your stylist," Amy had laughed, "that you are going to Europe and don't have room to pack an outlet adapter. That's the only way to make them understand that you really won't have a hair dryer."

Physically Holly and her brother were attractive people. They both had rich, warm coloring—their eyes were a hazely topaz, they had freckles across their noses, and their hair was chestnut with coppery highlights . . . although Holly freely admitted that while Jack's highlights were natural, streaked into his hair by the strong Kentucky sun, hers was a product of her hair salon. "I made him go in with me," she said, "so that they could see exactly what I wanted."

"Every woman should have a brother," he remarked. "We're so useful."

120

He was driving easily, his left hand cocked at the top of the steering wheel, his right arm stretched along the back of the seat to give Amy and Holly more room. Holly played up her coloring; she was wearing a shirt of tobacco brown that looked marvelous on her. Jack's waffle-knit, Henley-collared shirt was navy, and the best thing that Amy could think of to say about his choice of color was that it proved that he wasn't vain. His hair was shaggy—Holly had already asked why he hadn't had it cut—but Amy liked how soft and rumpled it looked.

He seemed like a familiar type to her. He was a guy, one of life's practical types. She knew a number of such men. In her world they were road managers, sound engineers, and lighting technicians.

They were great. Outgoing, easy-tempered, and strong, they could always put a smile on your face; they could always get things done. They could open car doors when the keys were locked inside; they could get electricity back to an arena when the main circuit kept blowing; they could get the ice to refreeze when the rink was covered with huge puddles only hours before a show. They never gave up; they believed they could fix anything. They were wonderful people to have around.

But they were impossible to get to know. They hid behind all that practicality. They never asked themselves any of the hard questions; they were too busy trying to get the streets clear. They lived entirely in the moment; the past was over, the future had not yet happened. So as fun as they were to be around, they weren't very interesting.

But they got things done. If anyone could persuade Dad and Ian to get light into the bunkhouse, it would be someone like that.

Amy had last seen her family at Christmas. It hadn't been easy to arrange. The holidays were always busy for her. She was either riding a float in a parade, skating in a big holiday ice show, or both. The Christmas one month after her mother's death had been no different. She was fulfilling commitments made long, long before her mother had gotten sick.

But the following year, this year, she had been determined to join her family for at least part of the holiday. Christmas Day would be out of the question, of course, but she carefully arranged her schedule on the twenty-sixth so that she could make the best possible connections from New York to Iowa.

Then the day after Thanksgiving Phoebe left a message to say that the family would be gathering at Ian's house in California this year.

Amy called her right back. "California? Why?" They had always celebrated everything at home.

"We were all pretty miserable last year," Phoebe answered. "So Ian suggested we do something dramatically different this year. Break the pattern. And Dad agreed."

"When did we decide?"

"I don't know. I guess we started talking about it in the summer, but we really didn't decide for sure until yesterday."

In the *summer?* Amy couldn't believe it. Why hadn't they told her? If she had known this in the summer, she could have scheduled her holiday appearances for LA and been with them the whole time.

Tommy had had his family in LA a couple of Christmases ago, and they had all had a great time. He had gotten tickets for the Rose Bowl parade and had set up a "back-door" tour of Disneyland so that his nieces and nephews could get on the best rides without ever waiting in line. The local promoter had provided suites for everyone, and the kids had used room service and had gone swimming in the hotel pools, and the women had had facials and massages. It had been a Christmas they would remember forever.

Phoebe had said the Legend family needed something dramatically different. How about Christmas in a luxury hotel, arranged by Amy? That would have been different.

But it was too late now. She was committed to being in New York.

So she had to reroute herself, and then she almost missed the plane. Pestered by a talkative seat mate— someone traveling on a frequent-flyer upgrade who was thrilled, so *thrilled,* to be sitting next to *Amy Legend*— that Amy could not sleep during the flight. She was exhausted by the time she got to Ian's.

As was the rest of the family. Ian and Joyce's house wasn't big enough, and everyone felt the lack of privacy. Joyce had planned extraordinarily elaborate meals, and every other plan had to be subordinate to their preparation. Ian and Joyce were very environmentally conscious—and Amy knew that was right—but feeding thirteen people three meals a day and never using a single paper plate or cup? Amy felt as if she and Phoebe and Joyce were chained to the kitchen, and she hated kitchen work.

*Let's go to a restaurant*, Amy wanted to shriek. *Call for pizza, Chinese, anything. I'll pay for it.*

But this was clearly Joyce's show. Her sister-in-law was determined to be as in charge of this holiday as Mother had been of all holidays past.. So Amy said nothing about pizza, nothing about Disneyland. She just loaded and unloaded the dishwasher over and over.

And at the lake there wouldn't even be a dishwasher.

Suddenly Amy wanted to warn Holly and Jack— these two nice people she was squeezed between— about her family. She wanted to caution them about what the lake meant to Ian and Phoebe, how odd her brother and sister were about so many things. *Please be careful. Let them have their own way.*

But why should Holly and Jack have to accommodate Ian and Phoebe? Why couldn't Ian and Phoebe be generous, why couldn't they compromise?

Because they couldn't.

Nick was listening to his CD player so loudly that Amy could hear a tuneless rasp coming from the headphones. Holly and Jack were now talking to each other about the financing of a business deal he had just done. They had carefully explained it to her so that she would not be excluded from the conversation, but once she started thinking about Phoebe and Ian, it was hard to concentrate on anything else.

For the early part of the drive they had been on the interstate; the terrain had been open, the Minnesota prairie falling away from either side of the graded highway. For the first half hour there had been billboards for an outlet mall, then ones for casinos on Indian reservations. After they passed the reservations, they left the interstate, and then there was nothing to advertise. The fields were dry, and slender-trunked trees lined the streambeds.

The afternoon shadows lengthened, and they entered mining country. The road curved around huge mounds of earth excavated from open-pit iron mines. This was the Mesabi Iron Range. Ore from under this earth had been mined and made into the steel that had won two world wars.

"I'm going to stop at Nashwaulk," Jack said. "My sense is that that is the last place to get gas."

"That sounds right," Amy said.

Nashwaulk was a very little town, perched close to the edge of a mine. It was T-shaped; the county road ran along the edge of the mine, and Main Street ran perpendicular to it, meeting the county road and dead-ending at the mine. The town had an odd air to it. As small as it was, the houses were built close to the street on cramped lots. Even the churches crowded toward the curbs. No one wanted to waste on building lots land that might have ore beneath it.

The filling station was at the intersection of the county road and Main Street. Jack pulled up to the pumps, and Holly and Amy got out to go to the bathroom. This wasn't only the last gas station; it was the last flush toilet, the last running hot water.

When they came out, Jack was going inside to pay for the gas. "Do either of you want a soda?" he called over his shoulder.

They shook their heads. "Is Nick in the bathroom?" Holly asked.

"I don't think so."

Holly made a face. "Where can he have gone?"

There was a bar across from the filling station. In fact, there were several bars along Main Street, almost more bars than stores. Holly sighed. "I think we're about to have to turn ourselves into Carrie Nation."

"There's an observation platform over there," Amy said, "where you can look at the mine. Maybe he's there."

At the end of Main Street was a small wooden tower

outside the high fence that surrounded the mine. There was someone up on the platform. It was Nick. Amy and Holly went over to it. "This is sort of cool," he said as they were climbing the steps. "What is it?"

It was the first time he had initiated conversation. "It's an iron ore mine." Amy reached the top of the platform. "Well, no, I guess it's now a lake."

The last time she had climbed this tower had been in her childhood. The mine had been closed for only a year or so then, and you could see down into the pit, into the glowing orange-red earth. It had been a man-made canyon, with roads gradually spiraling down the walls to the floor of the mine.

But over the years it had filled with water, dark, still water that looked icy and deep. All you could see of the mine was a steep rust-colored bank topped by a cyclone fence designed to keep people out. The water was not used for boating, swimming, or fishing. It was just there.

Holly started asking questions about mining, most of which Amy couldn't answer. "My dad will know."

Jack joined them on the platform, and the platform suddenly seemed smaller. He took one look at the water and shuddered. "This gives me the creeps."

"It does?" Amy was surprised. "Why? It's so peaceful."

"I guess that's it. It sort of looks like a thousand people drowned there, and that's why it's kept so peaceful, because it's a graveyard."

"It's not," she said. "At least not that I know of. It filled gradually. Long after the mine closed."

"I know." He shrugged. "I guess I just don't like deep water."

Amy looked at him. Was she wrong about him,

126

thinking he was like the sound engineers and the lighting technicians? Those men would have never admitted even to themselves that they didn't like deep water.

The business deal that Jack and Holly had been talking about, the one that had kept him from getting his hair cut, had been his. The kind of men she had been thinking of also didn't start their own businesses. They became head supervisor in someone else's.

"Why don't you like deep water?" she asked. "You can swim, can't you?"

"Yes, but how is swimming going to help you if you're stuck in a submarine?"

Amy didn't understand. Puzzled, questioning, she glanced at Holly.

"Our father was a submariner," Holly explained. "He was under water deeper than this for long periods of time. Jack doesn't think it would be his cup of tea."

"Jack doesn't *think* anything," Jack answered. "Jack *knows*."

"You've never been down in a submarine," Holly said.

"I have too," he protested. "When I was thirteen. The male-dependents cruise." He turned to Amy and Nick, explaining. "We were in South Carolina and Dad had his own boat, so he set up a three-day male-dependent cruise—the guys on the boat could take their sons or nephews out. Some of the younger ones took their own fathers. And Dad took me."

"I had forgotten about that," Holly said, obviously now remembering.

"That's because you didn't have to go," Jack told her. "If you'd gone you would have remembered."

"I remember how mad I was," she answered. "I

couldn't believe that you got to go and I didn't. I was the older; I felt that I should have gone."

"They should have let you. You probably would have liked it fine, and right now you'd be in dress whites with a couple of stars on your shoulder."

"I could never be in the navy," Holly said. "I look horrible in blue. I'd have to be in the army. I can wear olive."

Those sounded like good reasons to Amy. After all, she had chosen her career because it was one of the very few that allow a person to wear marabou. "I take it that you didn't like the submarine," she said to Jack. Her body was still facing the water, her elbows propped up on the top rail of the tower's protective fence, but she had turned her head so she could look at him.

"I *hated* it." He raked his fingers through his shaggy hair. "It was torture, the longest three days of my life. And it wasn't just routine adolescent hate-everything-associated-with-your-dad, although I certainly had enough of that. I honestly felt like I couldn't breathe down there. I was just starting to grow, and I was having trouble managing my body up here on God's green earth, and then they put me in a narrow little metal tube on top of a nuclear reactor. When it was finally over, I don't think I went inside for a week. I was so glad to see the sunlight and the stars again."

"Dad must have been disappointed," Holly said.

"It did not exactly improve our relationship," Jack acknowledged.

He had disappointed his father. Amy looked down at her hands. She knew all about that. Her parents had hardly known what to do with a child who didn't like to read, who couldn't organize her thoughts into tidy paragraphs, who refused to learn about primitive

128

cultures because the clothes weren't pretty enough.

"You probably weren't delighted with yourself either," Amy said.

"I sure wasn't," he agreed. "It probably seemed like I was determined to piss him off at every possible moment, but I wasn't. It just worked out that way." He pushed himself away from the railing. "All these folks who write about male-initiation rites—they never seem to talk about the kids who fail. What happens to us? Where do you go when you have failed not only your male parent but your entire culture?"

He was exaggerating, making this into a joke. But it wasn't a joke. Amy knew that. It still bothered him.

And she knew something else. Although Nick had crammed himself into the far corner of the platform, although he had his back turned and had not said a word, he was listening, listening hard.

They were heading back to the truck when Amy remembered milk. "Should we get some milk? I wonder if we should get some milk."

"Beats me," Jack said. "I didn't hear anything about it."

"Me neither," Holly added.

"It's just that there isn't much refrigerator space at the lake," Amy explained, "so people always stop and buy milk on the way up."

"I don't mind if we get some, but if Mother expected us to, she would have told me," Holly said. She sounded very confident.

"I don't know . . . my sister always buys milk on the way."

"We can do whatever you want," Jack said. "But I can't imagine Mom leaving anything to chance. This has all been planned to the last carton of milk. And if

129

she did expect us to bring some, we'll turn around and come back. I don't mind. In fact, I'm assuming I'll have to drive into town every time my sister needs to go to the bathroom."

"That's the way to think," Holly said approvingly.

But Amy shifted uneasily as they slid back into the truck.

*You are twenty-six years old,* she reminded herself. *You have an Olympic gold medal. It doesn't matter whether or not you buy milk. This is not a female-initiation ritual, not like going down in someone's submarine.*

But it did matter. Mother's lips would tighten. "Oh, Amy, you should have known—"

But Mother wasn't going to be there.

Oh, well, Phoebe's lips could tighten with the best of them. Actually, Phoebe probably cared more about details than Mother had. Mother would have seen Amy's failure to buy milk as an inconvenience. Phoebe would see it as yet another sign that Amy was an idiot.

They drove on. Nick leaned his head against the car window and closed his eyes, but Amy didn't think he was asleep. She wondered about him, who he was, why he was here.

Just as the prairies had given way to the mines, so now the mines gave way to the forest. The trees grew taller and closer together. The maples and box elders were gone now; this far north the winters were too cold. Except for the birches and the popples—which was the term people around here used for aspens—the trees were evergreen: spruces, balsams, jack pines, white pines, and Norways. The light was filtered, and the only wildflowers were in the ditches at the side of the road. The power line swooped into one final house and then

130

stopped. Beyond that house there was no electricity, no phones. The road became a thin ribbon slicing through a wall of trees.

A State Forestry Service sign, brown with incised yellow letters, directed travelers to a public campground. Jack turned off the blacktop, and gravel spat out from underneath his tires. After another mile and another sign they turned again.

This was the trail that led to the lake. It was a narrow, sandy lane, winding and only wide enough for one car. The original growth had been logged, but it had been so long ago that the popples, jack pines, and birches were nearly full-grown. Moss, wintergreen, and silvery blueberry plants grew in the sandy soil along the edge of the trail.

"This is really nice back in here," Jack said.

"It is," Amy agreed. She always forgot that about the lake—how beautiful it was.

It was familiar, even after all this time. The open spot where above the wild grasses she could see the lake for the first time. The little rise in the trail. The names on the signs in the front of each cabin. Familiar names: Henson, Pinianski, Nutting, some locals, some summer people.

Amy had hated coming up here. She really had. They had come for the whole summer in those days, and she had to go for two and a half months without skating. None of the other girls she trained with could believe that her family made her do this. The lake had come to symbolize that—having a family who didn't understand.

But none of those girls, girls whose families had understood skating, whose families had treasured their daughters' efforts and had nearly bankrupted themselves . . . none of those girls were still skating competitively.

131

And she was.

During her break last summer she had volunteered to participate in a medical study of female athletes. In so many of the athletes, their rigorous training schedule had delayed the onset of menstruation for years and years, often resulting in bone-density levels of post-menopausal women.

But Amy's menstrual cycle and her bone density were those of a normal twenty-six-year-old. And she had never had a serious injury. Yes, she was careful about warm-ups, but there was a resiliency about her bones, muscles, and ligaments that not all skaters had.

The examiners were fascinated. When had she started skating? How much had she trained as a child? What had her schedule been? Her diet? They asked about her family history, her mother's bone-density levels, her sister's.

She answered their questions as well as she could and then added, "Until I was in senior competition, my parents didn't let me skate in the summer. I took two to three months off every year."

There was a sudden quiet in the room. This was important.

The trail flattened as it came to the longer side of the oval lake, and there now was her family's sign—THE LEGENDS, HAL AND ELEANOR, PHOEBE AND IAN AND AMY.

The sign had been made before she had been born, so the "and Amy" was squeezed into the corner, ruining the symmetry of the spacing.

Twenty-six years, and no one had made a new sign.

Surely a new sign would be made now, one that included Gwen, Holly, and Jack.

The strip of land between the trail and lake was

132

densely wooded, and none of the cabins could be seen from the road. The only breaks in the wall of trees were the narrow driveways. Of course, they weren't driveways in the suburban sense, graded and paved. These were sand-covered lanes twisting between the trees.

Jack swung wide and turned into Amy's family's drive. A big Norway was rooted right in the middle. He eased the truck around it, and then they could see the cabin.

"It's lovely." Holly was astonished. "I had no idea. It's like something out of a children's book."

This was the "main" cabin. Sided with logs of honey-colored pine, it was small with a sharply sloping roof of green and brown shingles. More birches, their white bark peeling in papery layers, filled the spaces between the road and the lake while tall pines shaded the cabin itself. The cabin sat to the right of the drive while to the left was the bunkhouse and the path leading to the other two cabins.

Amy peered through the windshield. The screen door of the cabin opened, and out came her father, followed a moment later by a fair-haired woman. The woman was carrying Phoebe's son Thomas on her hip.

Jack reached across Amy, touched his sister's arm, and pointed at their mother and the little boy. "We can go home now. She's happy."

Holly and Amy had to wait while Nick got himself organized. Jack got out of the truck and crossed the pine needle-covered sand. An instant later he was at his mother's side, his hand on her shoulder, and he was speaking to her softly and quickly. She was nodding, as if to say, yes, yes, she already knew.

She came toward the truck with a smile. "Nick," Amy

133

heard her say, "what fun that you're joining us."

Nick didn't resist her one-armed hug—she was still holding Thomas—although he did not return it. "They didn't give you a chance to say no, did they?"

"They didn't need to. They knew that I wouldn't."

By now Amy was out of the truck, and her father's arms were closing around her. "How wonderful of you to come, sweetheart."

He felt good. He had been thin and pale at Christmas, and for the first time Amy had thought about him growing old, but he had regained the lost weight and there was strength in his arms again. "How's your ankle? Are you going to be okay? You've never been injured before, have you?"

How the messages had gotten garbled. "It wasn't me. I'm fine. It was someone else."

"That's good. How long can you stay?"

"I'm not quite sure. It depends on a lot of things."

"Fine." Then he turned her around and introduced her to Gwen.

Her father's new wife was very pretty—that was the only word for it; even at her age, she was pretty. Her hair was light. She had her children's high cheekbones, but not their warm coloring or their strong jaws. She was wearing khaki slacks and a white turtleneck. She looked crisp and trim. Mother had insisted on everyone wearing dark colors at the lake so that they didn't have to go into town and do laundry so often. But Gwen obviously didn't mind doing laundry.

Gwen said that she had been dying to meet Amy, and Amy said the same about her . . . and then, although she wanted to kick herself for saying it, she couldn't help it, she had to say it—"We didn't bring milk. I hope that was all right."

134

"Goodness, yes. It would have been a disaster if you had. There's not an inch of refrigerator space. We're absolutely set for at least the next twenty minutes."

"So where is everyone?" Holly asked. "I thought there were going to be whole hordes of people."

"Mom has murdered them all," Jack said, "so she can keep the baby."

Gwen swatted him on the arm. "Maggie and Joyce are out in the canoe, and Giles is asleep. The others went to launch the boat. We're baby-sitting this little man here." She poked Thomas in his tummy. He giggled at her.

"So where do we put our stuff?" Jack asked. "Amy said something about a bunkhouse. Is that it?" He pointed at the aging building.

"That's the bunkhouse, and Nick will be sleeping there with the other kids, but the three of you are in the log cabin."

"We're in the log cabin?" Amy was surprised. "Then where is everyone else sleeping?"

"All four adults are in the new cabin," Gwen said firmly and went around to the back of the truck. "Now, I know these are Holly's bags"—clearly there was to be no further discussion about who was sleeping where— "so either Jack's taste has improved a lot or these beautiful leather ones are yours, Amy."

"They are." Amy wondered how her brother and sister were reacting to this decisiveness. Badly, she assumed.

*This has to be so much harder on them than it is on me. I'm not going to mind changes. They will.*

The log cabin, the one where Amy, Jack, and Holly would be sleeping, was the oldest building on the lake, the only one built pioneer-style from notched and

135

stacked logs. It was designed for harsh Minnesota winters; the walls were thick, the window openings small. As a result, the cabin, while a snug fantasy after nightfall, was dark, even gloomy, during, the day.

Amy followed Holly and Gwen inside. Each paused for a moment, waiting for her eyes to adjust to the dim light. The first room was a small, square kitchen furnished with an enamel-topped table, a gas stove, and a squat little refrigerator. There was an old-fashioned pump mounted next to the sink, and two big teakettles set on the gas stove.

Beyond the kitchen was the main room, which was warmed by a wood-burning stove fashioned from an old oil barrel. Two more teakettles sat on the barrel stove. That's how you got hot water up here; you pumped it and then heated it. A small bedroom with a pair of twin beds was nestled next to the kitchen, and along the lake side of the cabin was a narrow enclosed porch with a set of bunk beds.

Holly and Amy were to take the bedroom, Gwen said, leaving Jack to sleep on the porch. He went back to the main cabin to get the rest of the luggage, and Gwen showed Holly and Amy where the coffee and tea were and explained how to light the stove. She told them what to do if they thought the pilot light on the refrigerator was out. She showed them how to prime the pump in case the prime gave out.

Holly was paying close attention. "I think I've got it," she said, then looked at Amy. "But you understand it, don't you?"

Amy winced. "No, I'm afraid I don't." And she had not been paying attention. She was the little sister up here. She didn't have to understand how things were done. Everyone else understood, and if they needed her to do anything, they told her.

Tommy said that she acted this way out of choice, that she didn't have to be the little sister for ever and all time. Everything would change, he said, if she started exerting herself more, and he was probably right, but it didn't seem worth the effort, not when she was around so little, and not when Phoebe and Ian were Phoebe and Ian. "I just know to sleep with some windows open so a propane leak won't kill us."

"We can do that," Holly said.

Jack brought the rest of the luggage in, carrying hers and Holly's into the bedroom. Holly lifted her suitcase onto one bed; her mother was standing ready to help unpack. Jack was at the door of the little room. "So how's it going, Mom?" he asked.

"Wonderful," Gwen answered. "As you can see, it is a beautiful place."

That was no answer. Amy suddenly realized that she was the outsider here, that Gwen couldn't speak honestly in front of her, that the most helpful thing she could do, the only thing she could do, was get out and give the three of them a chance to be alone.

"If you all will excuse me," she said, "I want to go see the lake."

"Do you need some company?" Jack drew back, out of the doorway, letting her pass.

He was being polite. He wanted to stay and talk to his mother. "No, no. I think the lady in the fuchsia blouse has given up on me by now."

"Good thing. Since you probably wouldn't want to hide out in the bathroom here."

"That's for sure." She smiled and went outside. A little set of steps led down to the lake in front of this cabin, but the only dock was at the main cabin. She went in that direction. As she grew closer, she could hear children's high-pitched voices, and a moment later the four little kids, Alex and Claire, Scott and Emily, came scrambling up the bank. They greeted her exuberantly, carelessly, and dashed off.

A moment later her sister came into view. Phoebe was carrying what looked like nearly a dozen life jackets, the old orange kapok Mae West type. She had thrust her arms through the neck openings and so at times had to turn sideways to maneuver between the trees.

Amy hurried to meet her. "Let me help you. What can I do?"

"Actually I'm okay. They aren't heavy, and I've got them all balanced."

"Where are you taking them?" Amy stepped out of her way.

"We've been keeping these under the bow of the boat for ages," Phoebe said over her shoulder. "I can't imagine we'll ever use them again. So I thought we should store them in the garage."

*If no one was going to use them, why store them at all? Why not throw them out?*

But Amy didn't say anything. She was not going to interfere.

"Dad and Gwen were delighted you could come," Phoebe said. "How long are you staying?"

"I don't really know. It depends on a lot of things." Amy quickened her step so she could open the side door to the garage.

This big, free-standing garage was between the road and the new cabin. In the male-dominated culture of the Iron Range, garages were occasionally bigger than a family's house, and this was certainly true here. The garage, built by a man who had been an electrician in the mines, was bigger and perhaps even better built than the new cabin itself.

To get through the garage door, Phoebe had to turn sideward again. The late afternoon light fell full on her face. She looked pale, and her eyes were tired and tense.

That wasn't right. Phoebe wasn't supposed to look like this at the lake. Phoebe was supposed to be happy at the lake.

Phoebe's life in Iowa City was busy and fragmented. Whenever Amy spoke to her, it seemed as if a million things were happening at once; she was always planning Girl Scout trips, baking cupcakes, planning class parties as well as working, worrying about the law students, the legal aid cases. She worked hard at the lake, of course she did, she was Phoebe, but up here she only did one thing at a time. She was soothed, made peaceful again.

Not this year.

*Let me take those life jackets . . . let me massage your shoulders.* Amy longed to do something for her sister. *I brought a cashmere robe, please take it, it's so soft, it will warm you, comfort you . . .*

Phoebe never did anything nice for herself. She never bought herself scented bath oil or thick feather-edged writing paper. She never took time for herself. When did she make herself a cup of tea and sit in the sun on a spring afternoon? When did she ever buy flowers just for herself?

Amy followed her to the garage. There was a loft across one end of the building. Phoebe dropped the life jackets there.

Then it was Phoebe who got the ladder—Amy didn't know where it was—and it was Phoebe who climbed up the ladder, balancing precariously while Amy handed the life jackets to her.

"I'm glad that's over," Phoebe said, brushing off her hands after she had put the ladder away. "I'm not crazy about heights."

*Then why not have me do it?* Amy wanted to ask. *Heights don't bother me at all. Why not me?*

And for a horrible, overpowering, swamping moment Amy wondered why she was here. What was the use? What was the point?


Whoop-di-do. Two whole laundry baskets shoved underneath the lower bunk for his stuff. Was this ever first-class treatment. The two little dudes he was bunking with—Nick couldn't imagine ever being able to keep their names straight—got only one basket apiece. But Aunt Gwen had given him two.

*Thanks, Brian. Thanks a heap. Look where you got me.*

Nick was lying on his bunk, staring up at the underside of the mattress above him. Aunt Gwen had said that cocktails would start at five-thirty. *Oh, does that mean there will be a cocktail for Cousin Nick?* He hadn't even bothered to ask.

It was five forty-five. He could hear voices outside the bunkhouse. This place was some kind of trip, all right. The full-scale isolation might be cool if there weren't so goddamn many people all living on top of each other. He levered himself upright, swung his feet around, and stood up. There was no point in putting this off any longer.

The driveway ended in a little clearing in front of the cabin. A couple of rough-hewn boards had been laid across some sawhorses, and Gramps—Aunt Gwen's new husband—was tending bar. Aunt Gwen herself was passing around crackers and cheese. The kids were playing some kind of game, the two teenage girls were sitting together on a picnic bench, and the other adults were all standing around being too polite. That always signaled the start of something weird—when grown-ups were being too polite.

He looked over at the two girls. They were not exactly read-each-other's-diaries-forever friends. He had picked up on that right away. The tall, dark one—Maggie was her name—did not want to have one thing to do with the other one, the mousy one, Ellie.

Maggie was a looker. She wasn't pretty-pretty like the icky-sweet cheerleaders at school. She was super pale with big soft lips and dark eyes. Her eyebrows grew low and close to her eyes. She was wearing a man's black shirt. She was tall, but the shirt was big on her, drooping down over her shoulders. Nick wondered if she was self-conscious about her boobs, which—based on his insufficient eyeing of them—looked quite majestic.

He had less of an impression of Ellie. She seemed pretty boring, even a little pathetic, but Nick supposed that was what happened to you when your folks gave you a name that worked best on a cow.

He watched the two of them from the corner of his eye. Ellie was turned toward Maggie, trying to talk to her. Maggie was looking straight ahead, obviously ignoring her.

"So what will it be, Nick?" Gramps asked. "We're making the little kids drink powdered lemonade. Otherwise we'd be surrounded by half-drunk cans of pop. But you and Maggie and Ellie can certainly have pop."

Pop. That's what people, around here called soda.

141

God, it was a stupid word. Pop, pop. No wonder people thought Midwesterners were stupid; they ran around saying "pop" all the time. It didn't exactly scream sophistication.

Unlike the words "bourbon, gin, and vodka." Those items were also on the table. Gramps could have shown himself quite the sophisticate by uttering those words in Nick's direction, but clearly that was not meant to be. He was a member of the pop brigade. He took a Sprite and sauntered over to where the two girls were sitting. Maggie instantly moved over, crowding Ellie, making room for him. Clearly he was to sit by her.

Not cool. A mistake, a misstep, too obvious by half. Sorry, sweetheart, but Cousin Nicky wasn't here to make things easy.

He sat down next to Ellie.

Joyce couldn't believe the junk that Gwen had set out for the kids—potato chips and cheese curls. The cheese was Brie, soft, full of fat—there was more fat in that wedge of cheese than her family ate in a week. Gwen had cut apple slices, but they were accompanied by one of those pre-prepared caramel-chocolate dips. The little girls, Emily and Claire, were using the apple slices as spoons. They would scoop up a wad of the dip, lick it off the apple slice, then stick the apple back into the dip dish. Joyce's own kids, Emily and Scott, would be wild before the evening's end. But it wouldn't be her fault. They weren't used to that much sugar.

At least that boy Nick was here so Maggie wouldn't get stuck with Ellie all the time.

"Ellie's such a dork," Maggie had said on the airplane. She and Joyce were sharing an aisle and a window seat while Ian was in the row behind them with

Scott and Emily. "I just can't stand her."

Joyce agreed . . . and she would have said so except that there was a chance Ian would overhear. "You know that Phoebe and Giles wish that the two of you were better friends."

"Oh, come on. She's a baby. She's dumb."

"You're exaggerating, Mags. She's not stupid."

*But she's not like you.*

It was a source of nearly immeasurable satisfaction to Joyce that her child was so very, very smart. Maggie might not have any Legend blood in her, but she had the kind of abilities that the Legends so valued.

From the earliest days of her marriage to Ian, Joyce had known that she was in competition with Phoebe. Who was the first Legend grandchild? Ellie, the first child born to any of their children? Or Maggie, older than Ellie, brought in the family before Ellie's birth but not officially adopted by Ian until well after?

Phoebe had named her daughter Eleanor after her mother. Why had she done that? Joyce knew. Phoebe had been drawing a line in the sand; she had been trying to make sure that everyone knew that her daughter was the one who counted.

But then Maggie started to read at three and a half. She was labeled gifted and talented during her first semester in kindergarten. And Ellie? All anyone could say about Ellie was how sweet she was, how nice, how helpful. Ellie was clearly one of life's Miss Congenialities, someone people sort of liked, but never respected or feared.

Joyce looked across the clearing at her daughter. All three teenagers were sitting together. Ellie was in the middle, but both Nick and Maggie were leaning forward, talking to each other, ignoring her.

143

And in addition to being smart, Maggie had her father's striking looks.

How many people had said "I told you so" when Matt—Maggie's father—had let his heroin problems get the best of him? Joyce would like to be able to gather all those people up in a room now and make them look at Maggie, listen to Maggie. That would show them.

# CHAPTER 7

JACK HAD BEEN ASSIGNED QUARTERS IN THE NARROW enclosed porch of the log cabin. It had a set of bunk beds, and rather reluctantly he flipped back the covers on the lower one. He had never particularly liked bunk beds; that's where men slept on a submarine. But this one wasn't too bad, he decided a couple of minutes later. The bunks had been wedged along the narrow wall at the end of the room. There were windows along one side of the bed, and at the foot were more windows that faced the lake. The dark plaid curtains were drawn, but behind them the windows were open. The fresh air was cool, and the pile of quilts was heavy on his body.

Everyone had survived the evening without any hissing or snarling. Jack attributed it to his mother. People tended to behave themselves around her.

But the hissing and snarling were bound to come. There was too much tension for it not to.

Phoebe's husband Giles, the one with the bum leg, seemed okay. In fact, he seemed like a pretty good egg. Phoebe herself Jack was less sure about; she seemed like she was swimming through a fog, forcing herself to eat and speak. But he had heard enough about her life, how busy and active she was, to know that she couldn't

144

always be this way.

Ian was tedious; he had spent most of the evening talking to Hal, which is what Jack would have liked to have been doing, but of course Ian was the Real Son, so Jack could hardly complain. Ian's wife Joyce—the only good thing Jack could think about her was that she hadn't been sleepwalking like Phoebe. But the world probably would have been a better place if she had been. Her energy was nervous and jangling, and she seemed to have her antennae pitched only to notice people's mistakes, especially those she could interpret as criticism of herself.

His mom and Hal must have noticed all this—except maybe Ian's tediousness, Hal didn't seem to see that—but they were letting it happen.

His own father wouldn't have. No, sir. Dad would have taken charge. He wouldn't have let snippy Miss Maggie get away with her rudeness. Such rudeness would have been considered insubordination in the ranks and treated as such.

But apparently Hal Legend didn't view himself as commanding a submarine. He was an adult, playing host to other adults.

Jack woke to the muted sound of the screen door being eased shut. He hitched himself up on his elbows, listening for a moment. Morning light edged the curtains, but he heard nothing else. It was probably only Amy or Holly going to the outhouse. He punched his pillow and crooked his arm across his eyes.

A moment later he heard a rustling outside his window, followed by two whispering voices.

"I haven't done this in ages," he heard Amy say.

"I don't think I've ever done it." That was Holly. "Do

you think anyone will see us?"

"So what if they do?"

"That's easy for you to say. You probably have a gorgeous body."

"No, I don't," Amy returned. "I have no waist, no hips."

Jack sat up. Two splashes were followed by a muffled shriek.

Holly and Amy had gone skinny-dipping.

He heard more little yelps. The water must be cold.

This could *not* have been Holly's idea, but it sounded like she was having fun.

Jack swung out of bed and pulled on his jeans. Embers were still glowing in the barrel stove, and so the water in the kettle was warm. He poured some into a saucepan and put it on the gas stove to get it hot enough for coffee. He built up the wood fire and draped a pair of blankets in front of it.

He was pouring the water through the coffee grounds when he heard the two of them returning. He glanced out the kitchen window. They were coming around the corner of the cabin. Both had towels wrapped around them, and they were mincing barefoot through the pine needles, their nightgowns in hand. He pulled open the screen door. "Hello, ladies."

Startled, Holly shrieked, stopping so suddenly that Amy crashed into her.

"You scared the daylights out of me, Jack," Holly reproved.

He smiled and held the door. They crowded past him into the little kitchen. Their hair was wet, their shoulders damp and bare.

Amy did have a narrow torso and almost boyish hips. Her arms and legs were long for someone her height.

"I am freezing," Holly shivered. "Why did we do that? Why did I think I minded being dirty?"

Amy giggled. That was the only word for it. She didn't laugh, she didn't chuckle, she giggled. "I had fun."

"But you must be used to freezing your tuckus off," Holly returned. "I'm not."

Amy made a face.

She had been quiet at dinner last night, hardly saying anything, but he had heard Holly and her talking softly in their bedroom late into the night.

"Do you 'girls' want some coffee?" he asked. Holly loathed being called a "girl."

She didn't even notice. "Coffee? Oh, Jack, you're wonderful."

She had already started to pour it, so he stepped into the living room and grabbed the blankets, folding them back in on themselves to hold in the warmth. He draped one over Holly, rubbing her shoulders briskly. She purred at the warmth. Even admirals like being taken care of once in a while.

He turned to give the other blanket to Amy. She looked up at him and smiled.

The early morning light from the open door shone against the smooth skin of her shoulders. The curve of her arms was lean and muscular. Everything about her was so . . . he didn't have a good word for it . . so compact. She was slender, even petite, and yet every ounce of her was muscle. He stepped forward with the blanket, ready to swirl it around her.

But then at the last moment, just as he was about to shake the blanket open, he stopped. He handed the blanket to her politely and moved to get her a cup of coffee.

He was interested in her. No, not interested. That was too polite a world, too cerebral. This was about bodies. He was drawn to hers, attracted to hers.

Which did not seem like good news.

It made no sense. His instincts were as good about women as they were about business and safety. If a woman was trouble, it didn't matter what she looked like, he wasn't attracted to her. Ever. He would walk into a room and be immediately drawn to the one woman who was funny, good-hearted, and wise long before he could have a clue that she was funny, good-hearted, and wise. His body was more astute than his mind.

Lurking at the ends of his consciousness had been wispy impressions of Amy—her posture, her gait, her perfume—and now suddenly *Whammo!* here it was—full-scale, industrial-strength attraction.

*She's in a towel. Who wouldn't be attracted to a beautiful woman in a towel? And not only beautiful, but famous and incredibly fit as well. Who wouldn't want her?*

He wouldn't, that's who. Since when did he ever care about beauty and fame . . . although fitness, well, that could have its merits.

What could possibly be right about this? He was here for his mother and his sister; he needed to make sure Mom was okay and to try to get Holly to relax a little.

He wanted his mother to be happy. That's what he cared about. No question about it. Two of Hal's kids were having a lot of trouble with the idea of their dad having a new wife. Surely Jack's attempting to seduce child number three wasn't going to make the family-blending process any easier.

So his instincts were wrong.

148

But his instincts were never wrong.

With a deft move Amy swirled the blanket around her and then pulled her wet towel off from underneath. She bent her head forward and wrapped the towel turban-like around her hair. She straightened. Her neck was graceful, swan-like.

He wasn't supposed to be noticing stuff like that.

What was it about her that attracted him? Was she funny, good-hearted, and wise? He had kept hearing hushed laughter in the dark last night; she and Holly had amused each other. And everything he had ever read about her talked about all the charity work she did and about her ability to comfort, to make people feel that someone cared. She must have a good heart.

But was she wise? She seemed a little childlike, a bit passive. *Should we get some milk?* she had asked. *I wonder if we should get some milk.*

When had he ever been attracted to a woman who couldn't decide whether or not to buy a gallon of milk?

"Would you like a dry towel?" he asked.

"No." She shook her now turban-covered head. "The rule is one towel a person. If you forget to hang yours up, you are out of luck. It's too hard to do laundry."

That might have been *her* mother's rule, but it wasn't his mother's. When he had carried the suitcases into the little bedroom last night, he had seen a nice pile of towels on top of the dresser. Hadn't she noticed them?

Holly had gone to sit in one of the rocking chairs. She rested her toes on the stove. She sipped her coffee. "You know, this isn't so bad."

Jack tried to focus on his sister. "You two sure were whispering late last night," he said.

"I know." Amy laughed again. "It was fun. It was like being at camp."

149

"No, it wasn't," Holly said. "At least not any camp I was ever at. My counselors were all tyrants. They never let you talk after lights out."

"I don't want to hear that." Amy made a face again. Jack was still watching her; he couldn't help it. "Can't you humor me? I never went to camp. It always sounded like such fun. Go and make friends you could pour your heart out to and have a wild summer romance—"

"A wild summer romance?" Holly interrupted her. "Where did you get your ideas about camp from? I never had a wild summer romance at camp. Did you, Jack?"

He had to clear his throat before answering. "Fortunately not. I went to Boy Scout camp."

Amy protested. "But I thought there was always a girls' camp down the road or across the lake and there would be dances and raids on each other's tents, and so there would be someone to have a wild summer romance with."

"Not at the camps our parents sent us to," he said, and then spoke more briskly. "I hope the two of you sit here buck naked spinning tales about summer camp until high noon, but Mom gave me a list . . . and"—again he couldn't help himself, he wanted to talk to her; he pointed a finger at Amy—"it includes trenching a line to the bunkhouse, something that you predicted would take five years."

She smiled. "I still bet it takes you two."

She did have some kind of smile. He had to get out of there.

He jerked open the screen door and stepped out in the sunlight. He looked over his mother's list. He'd like to find one where he'd have half a chance of being alone

150

for a while. He settled on number four, get the old sauna to work.

Just outside the log cabin was a little shack with a chimney. Jack pulled open the door. He stepped into a small room that had clothes hooks screwed into two of the walls. It must be a changing room. Beyond it was the sauna itself, another small room heated by an old, airtight wood-burning stove surrounded by rocks. Next to the stove was another old-fashioned hand pump like the one in the kitchens. It fed a thirty-gallon cistern. A pipe carried water from the cistern through the stove and back, and there was a drain in the floor. Clearly the place had been designed as much as a bathhouse as a sauna.

His mother's letters had said it had been cold when they first arrived. Bathing in the lake couldn't have been any fun. If he got this going, she and Holly—and Amy—would have thirty gallons of hot water and a warm place to wash their hair. Surely that would make a big difference to everyone's comfort. Not as much as a generator would, of course, but still it would be nice.

So why hadn't the Legends ever tried to use it? Of the three cabins, they had purchased this one the most recently, but they had bought it at least ten years ago. Oh, well, the past wasn't any of his business. He started to take the stove pipe apart.

He was up on the roof, knocking the soot off the galvanized wired cage on top of the chimney, when he heard a voice on the ground. It was Ian, Hal's son, Amy's brother.

Ian was tall and lean like Hal, and he wore his light hair cropped close to his head, although Jack had seen in the main cabin some family photos no more than five years old that showed Ian wearing a ponytail. Jack

151

wonered what made him cut it off. He was also thinner than he had been in the photos. Actually, Jack thought he looked gaunt. And maybe he was. His wife Joyce had gone on and on about low-fat cooking last night. Maybe the man simply wasn't getting enough to eat. That would make Jack plenty foul-tempered.

"Dad says you're taking a look at the sauna," Ian said.

"I think we'll be able to fire it up this afternoon." There had been a few problems, but they had been minor.

"You really think it's safe?"

*No. I think it is a major fire hazard. That's why I am doing this. I want to roast my mother and my sister and burn down the entire forest if I can.*

Jack generally liked people. That's the way he was. But this guy . . . you could make all the starvation excuses in the world, but Jack still didn't like him.

Ian was a linguistics professor who learned and recorded Native American Indian languages. Apparently there were a bunch of these languages that were down to their last couple of surviving speakers. When they died, the language would. Ian found such people and had them talk into a tape recorder for a year or so.

*Why?* That had been Jack's first thought. He hoped that he wasn't anti-intellctual or anything, but he couldn't see any practical value in Ian's work. There weren't any books or documents written in these languages. They were dying for a reason—no one wanted or needed to speak them anymore.

He supposed he could understand it as a matter of curiosity, and admittedly he had on occasions felt some regret when he closed up a ceiling. With an unfinished ceiling you knew exactly what was there, where all the

152

wires and pipes were, but once the ceiling was up, everything was by guess and by golly. Of course, with a ceiling if you really had to know, you could rip it down, but on this language thing he supposed there was no going back once the old guys were dead.

Looking at it that way, Jack felt a little more sympathy. Maybe it wasn't so bad, maybe it even was something worthwhile and important to be doing, but Ian didn't have to talk about it as if it were second only to spiritual salvation.

And the Indian part didn't make sense. Jack couldn't say that he was an informed cultural anthropologist, but wasn't Indian culture closely bound to nature without a lot of artificial laws—now that he thought about it, he probably would have done okay himself if a tribe had kidnapped him from the wagon train when he was six. Indian culture was earthy, moist, mysterious, and dark, whereas this guy, this Ian fellow, was cool and dry. He'd freeze-dry anything he looked at.

Jack swung back down the ladder. "It looks in pretty good shape. Whoever built it was a little nutty, but I don't see any reason why it shouldn't be fine."

They were in the sauna now. Ian was looking around like he knew what he was talking about—and maybe he did. "The stove seems too close to the wall."

"It's probably not up to code." Jack didn't think they had to worry about the building inspectors descending on them . . . unless Ian called them. "But that's why there's all this brick work here." *And for how many years were you a professional firefighter, Mr. Dr. Professor of Dead Indian Languages?*

"What about the window?" Ian continued. "Shouldn't the window open freely?"

There was a little casement window on the sauna's

outer wall, and in the best of all worlds, Jack supposed yes, it would open. That would be a quick way to cool the place down if it got too hot. But it had been painted shut years ago.

"If people feel in peril, they can break the window." Jack had found an old ballpeen hammer and had suspended it near the window. The window was too small for an adult to climb out, but it would let in enough fresh air to keep a person from cooking.

"Breaking glass is dangerous business," Ian said. "I wonder if any of the children know how to do it safely."

He sounded like he worked for OSHA. "If no one's taught them, then they probably don't."

"What about this door? It should open outward."

The door opened inward, and that had given Jack pause. You were going to have people throwing water on the rocks. Humidity would cause the door to swell. That might make it hard to open, and you couldn't put your shoulder to a door that opened inward.

"I suppose that theoretically that might be a problem," Jack admitted. "But the thing fits so badly in the first place. As it is, you're going to have to fold towels along the bottom to block the drafts."

"I don't think we can trust the children's safety to that. The door needs to be rehung." Ian spoke flatly as if this were his decision and his alone.

"Okay." There was no point in fighting this battle. Ian was peeing on the fire hydrant. Hal was his dad, he was the Real Son, and this was his turf. "I'll get a screwdriver." Jack knew that his mother would want him to let Ian pee wherever Ian wanted to pee.

"No, no. I'm the one who thinks it needs to be done. I'll do it."

"Do you need any help?"

"Rehanging a door?" Ian was faintly sarcastic. "I shouldn't think so."

"Fine." Jack nodded and turned, going through the small dressing room and then outside into the light.

Jesus, what an asshole.

Jack spent the rest of the morning working on the gas line, bringing it to the bunkhouse in order to install some lights. It should not have been a big deal. Hal had the lights and all the necessary fittings, and the ground was sand, the easiest thing to dig through. But within five minutes of starting he had a horrible feeling that Amy did have at least some degree of wisdom. She might be right about this taking two years.

The four young kids wanted to help.

Jack looked down at their cheery little faces. What was more important to his mother, getting propane to the bunkhouse or having him spend a wonderful morning bonding with these children? He tried hard, but there was no way he could convince himself that she would have voted for the propane. So he marked the line with some spray paint and turned over his shovel. In a minute Hal came out.

"Are you all right?" Hal asked him. "I don't want you to feel abandoned in a sea of children."

"We're doing great." It was a lie, but it was, he knew, the lie that his mother would want him to tell.

What a shame. She really had worried about him during his adolescence, worried that he would flunk out of school, wrap his car around a tree, or both, that he would get a girl pregnant, that he would murder his father or that his father would murder him. If she could have peered into the future and seen how docile and obedient he was being this morning, she could have had

155

an extra decade's worth of a decent night's sleep.

Hal brought out two more shovels, but that only made everything worse. Now there were three shovels and four kids, and one of the shovels was more desirable than the others, so Jack had to spend the entire morning keeping track of whose turn it was to have the good shovel and whose turn it was to have none at all. Then Thomas, the one still in diapers, appeared and wanted a piece of the action too. Fortunately he brought his own tool—a bright red plastic spade—but he was always getting in everyone's way, and that was something else for Jack to monitor.

Eventually Amy and Holly appeared. They were coming over to the main cabin to help fix lunch. "What wonderful progress you're making," Amy remarked.

They were making horrible progress, and Amy knew it. Her eyes were dancing, and Jack would have loved to have—

To continue happily supervising his very non-union crew of child laborers. Oh, yes, that was precisely what he wanted to be doing in this moment. Nothing else could have made his world so complete.

Fortunately after lunch it was warm enough to go swimming, and Jack lost all his helpers. He worked quickly, wanting to get this over with before anyone else could get involved. When he was sure that everyone else was down at the lake, he sneaked into the tool compartment of his truck, got out his battery-operated drill, and had the lights up in no time. He was done by two o'clock. As he carried his tools back to their hiding place in his truck, he realized that if he started the fire in the sauna now, the water would be hot when people came up from the lake to get ready for dinner. So he went back to the log cabin and, gathering up an armload of wood, he hooked the handle of the screen door with his little finger and used his hip to bounce the door open. He went inside the changing room.

And dropped the wood with a crash. The sauna door wasn't up. He marched over to the opening. The hinges, were off, but Ian hadn't even gotten around to chiseling the niches to reposition them. He had been working in here most of the morning. What had he been doing?

The door itself was lying on a pair of sawhorses. On top of it was a card with the most absurd measurements. The measurements alone would have taken a person over an hour to do. To a sixteenth of an inch, Ian had calibrated the uneven slope of the concrete threshold. Why? Sure, there were things you could do about an uneven threshold, but a folded towel would work almost as well as any of them.

It was clear to Jack that Ian planned to let this task take a couple of days. Everyone else was going to have to wait to use the sauna while Ian did exactly what Ian wanted.

That was bullshit. Jack checked the battery in his drill and picked up the chisel.

His mother was furious. "You should not have done that, Jack. Ian had started the project."

"Come on, Mom. It would have taken him forever, and Holly wanted to wash her hair."

"Holly can wash her hair in cold water. She did it this morning."

Everyone had again gathered for cocktails in front of the cabin. All the women obviously felt clean and happy, having relished the abundant—and until now unprecedented—supply of hot water. His mother had felt that way too until she had heard Ian's very stiff questions about Jack's hanging of the door.

"Don't you understand?" she went on. "It was important to him. He wanted to be the one who got the sauna going."

"But, Mom, he had ten years to do it."

"Jack, you need to stop and think. Try to respect their position."

*Stop and think.* This was like being a kid again. Everyone telling him to stop and think. Especially his dad. His cautious, precise father. His dad would have measured the floor. A folded towel would not have been good enough for his dad.

You couldn't go around wadding up old towels to plug leaks on a nuclear submarine. Jack was willing to grant that. But why did everything have to be done according to submarine standards? Why not just make do once in a while? Duct tape was one of God's finest gifts to mankind. Jack's whole life was held together with it.

But his father had used duct tape only on ductwork.

# CHAPTER 8

GWEN WAS MAD AT HER SON. AMY FOUND THAT interesting. Obviously Ian had planned on doing something in the sauna, but he had been taking forever, and so Jack had finished it for him.

Amy could see why Gwen didn't like that . . . on the other hand, she herself did. At Christmas last year, Ian had been always making everyone wait for him. He wasn't a congenitally tardy person. If he was doing something alone or with one or two others, he was prompt and efficient, but if the whole clan was trying to get out the door at one time, Ian was always busy completing something important and everyone had to wait. It seemed like some kind of power move. She had been mildly irritated by it; Phoebe had probably been incensed.

So she was glad that someone had called Ian's bluff.

It had been a nice day, probably the best time she had had at the lake since she had started skating. At family gatherings she usually drifted, uncertain of what she was supposed to be doing, how she was supposed to be helping. She never knew what she would be doing in the next twenty minutes.

She hated it. She was used to a day rigidly organized around ice time, flight time, curtain time, warm-up time, and every other kind of time. A structureless, scheduleless day probably should have been a relaxing change—she couldn't help thinking that a sane, normal person would have found it so—but she couldn't cope with it.

When she and Holly had come over to the main cabin for breakfast that morning, however, there was a big sheet of paper posted on the cabin wall. It listed the day's schedule. Chores had been divided up; activities had been given a time. It was all very structured.

"Mother spent her whole adult life as a navy wife," Holly explained. "She believes in order."

"Don't apologize to me." Amy loved knowing what she was supposed to do. "There can't be any group of people who are more addicted to routine than skaters. We can't stand having any choices." She was looking for her name on the duty roster. Sweeping the porches, clearing the lunch dishes, setting the table at dinner—these were all things she could do. She wasn't going to have to ask a million questions.

She and Holly stuck together all day like two first-time summer campers. They swam, played cards with the kids, rode bikes out to one of the logging roads to see if the raspberries were ripe. Holly was her friend, her bunk mate, someone even more of an outsider than she, someone even more ignorant of the routines.

After lunch Giles launched his wooden fishing boat, the one he had restored so beautifully, and he took the kids for rides. Amy started to swim alongside the boat, and as her muscles warmed and eased, as she could feel the strength in her legs and across her back, she started to feel like herself again. The water was wonderfully soft. She could open her eyes and see the spray of diamond water drops flung out by her rising arm. She could hear the rhythmic splash and pull of Giles's oars.

She didn't get enough exercise when she was with her family. She was always too busy standing around waiting to unload the dishwasher.

She stuck her head out of the water. "Could you row across the lake?" she asked Giles. "I'd like to see if I can swim it."

"Of course," he answered. Giles was always happy to be in his boat.

The lake was about a half mile across, and she made the round trip easily. Then Jack came down to the dock and quietly beckoned to Gwen, Holly, Phoebe, and herself.

"The sauna's ready. You four go first, before the kids get to the hot water."

Amy had hardly known what he was talking about, but it turned out that the little building next to the log cabin which her family had always used as a woodshed had once been a sauna. Gwen had cleared it out; Jack had got it working.

It was deliciously warm, and the tank was full of hot water. The four of them lay on the benches until their skin was rosy and moist. Then they poured bucket after bucket of hot water on themselves. There was usually never hot water at the lake for anything but washing dishes, and the warmth, the cleanliness, was a luxury. Amy washed everyone's hair, loving the way that she could feel each one of them relax under her fingers. Even her sister had eased.

"I didn't think anything could make the lake better," Phoebe sighed. "But this really does. I can't believe that it's been sitting here this whole time, and we've never used it."

"I knew that Jack would run mad if he didn't have some projects," Gwen said. She was speaking mildly, but she was clearly pleased. "Although we may have to put our heads together to think up some more. It's only been one day and he's making too much progress."

The clouds thickened and lowered as they ate dinner. Amy lingered at the table with her dad and Gwen, Gwen being eager to ask all the questions everyone always asked Amy, how she had gotten started, what her life was like, what her daily routine was, what was she going to do when she wasn't able to skate, and the final, completely unanswerable one—what it was like to be famous. She usually answered those questions the same way each time, but now she found herself concentrating on her father's role in her career, how he had steered her onto the right path early in her career, how much of her music he was still finding. He even passed some along to Tommy and Henry. It was an enormous help. All three of them did their own choreography now. They didn't like being dependent on other people's creativity—many skaters just waited for their choreographers and coaches to have good ideas—but finding new music was extraordinarily time-consuming, and Hal's help was invaluable. He had grown to understand what a skater needed in a piece of music as well as any of the professional choreographers.

He waved a hand, dismissing his role. "I've learned a lot. But tell us, how long are you going to be able to stay? That was never clear in any of the messages."

"I don't know," Amy answered. Yesterday she couldn't have imagined being here for more than forty-eight hours, but clearly she was going to be able to make it for longer than that. "I've still got the four days left over from the television special." That committed her. Now she had to stay for at least four days. "At some point we need to start thinking about our fall programs and what we're going to do this spring."

"Who's 'we'?" Gwen asked.

"Henry Carroll, Tommy Sargent, and our coach Oliver Young. We're planning a tour next spring, primarily the three of us. We're really going to try to keep the ticket prices down." That was particularly important to Tommy. The ticket prices for the big spring tours always seemed way too high. The venues usually sold out, but some of the people who cared the most couldn't go. "But keeping the ticket prices down is our only idea so far."

"It's a good one," her father said.

"Yes, but it's hard to skate too."

He laughed. "I can't disagree with that."

She liked seeing him laugh. He hadn't laughed last Christmas. "So I don't know. Mostly it's ideas I need, and I don't have to be in Denver to come up with ideas."

"Stay as long as you like," Gwen said, "but in the meantime would you help me bring all the towels in? It looks like it's going to rain tonight."

Taking towels off the line—this too was something Amy could do, and she happily followed Gwen outside.

The towels were still damp. "When it was just your father and I," Gwen said, "I hung them up in front of the fire for the night, but there's too many now. What did your mother do?"

"I don't know," Amy admitted. "But whatever it was, it wasn't very effective." In fact, whenever Amy smelled mildew, it reminded her of towels at the lake. She thought for a moment. Laundry was her hobby, her sole domestic skill. She couldn't cook, she couldn't tell one cleaning product from the next, but every time she moved it was to get better laundry facilities. She owned five different shapes of tailors' hams, and her ironing board was German with a vacuum-producing motor that pulled the steam through the garment. She should be able to figure out what to do with damp towels even if there were almost twenty of them. "What about if we hung them in the sauna? Wouldn't they dry in there?"

"That's a good idea. We can add another log on the fire, and they'll be perfect in the morning."

As they were carrying the baskets over to the sauna, they met Phoebe coming toward the main cabin.

"We thought we would hang these in the sauna," Gwen explained. "So they can dry overnight."

"That should work," Phoebe said. "It's a good idea."

A good idea? Phoebe had just said that she had had a good idea.

*This is laundry,* Amy reminded herself. *Just laundry. Surely you are not such an idiot as to be pleased that your sister likes your idea about laundry.*

163

Of course, Phoebe didn't know that it was Amy's idea. She probably thought it was Gwen's.

The three of them draped the towels over the benches, and while Phoebe built up the fire, Amy carried the empty baskets back to the main cabin. She set them in their place—she had watched Gwen pick them up—and then went back outside, letting the screen door shut behind her.

She started back down the path. Then she heard a noise from the far side of the bunkhouse. She went around and looked.

It was Jack. He was halfway up on a small ladder, caulking a window. He was working quickly, his grip on the caulking gun sure and strong. He jumped down from the ladder and bent over, tilting his head to do the underside of the window.

Amy watched him work. He was so busy with all his tasks. It almost seemed as if he were a handyman paid to work while the rest of them vacationed.

He finished the underside of the window. He ran his fingers lightly over the seam and then began rubbing his thumb over his fingertips. He must have gotten some of the caulk on his hands and was trying to bead it up.

He saw her. "This stuff is supposed to be quick-dry," he said, "but I'd feel better if the rain held off until after midnight."

"The towels are in," she said lightly. "So we laundresses are prepared."

"Good for you. Now tell me, have you taken a look at that limb?" He was speaking again, now pointing at a tree overhead. "Don't you think it ought to come down?"

Amy looked up. She saw a mass of green leaves. She supposed that the leaves were attached to a branch, and if they had been silk leaves, she probably could have figured out how to iron them if that proved to be necessary, but since they were real, she didn't have one thing to say about them. "If you think it needs to come down, then take it down."

"I shouldn't do it without talking to your dad."

"Then talk to him. He was inside a couple of minutes ago."

Jack shook his head. "Not anymore. He's doing something with your brother. And they'll probably want to do it themselves; they must have their own way of working."

"That they do," she agreed.

He closed up his ladder and picked it up. "So what are you up to?"

"Nothing." She stopped herself. She was not going to be that way. She was going to make her own plans. Even if they were little and pointless, they would at least be her own. "I'm going to go on a walk. If anyone asks where I am, will you tell them I've gone down to the Rim?" She had been meaning to do this ever since she had arrived yesterday.

"The Rim? Where's that?"

"At the other end of the lake. Would you like to come?"

He paused for a second. "Sure. Why not? Let me put this ladder away. It will only take a second. Shall we try to find Holly?"

"That's a good idea." Amy watched as he picked up the ladder, levered it across one shoulder, and started carrying it to the garage. Then she changed her mind about finding Holly. "Actually, I'm not so sure that it is a good idea. While we're looking for her, we'll run into everyone else, and they'll want to come, and people will need to get sweaters and the kids will have to use the biffy and someone else will think of one other quick little thing that they have to do first, and someone else will think of another, and it will be dark before everyone gets ready, and then we won't be able to go."

He came out of the garage, brushing his hands. "I like my sister, but not that much."

He scooped up a wool shirt that had been lying on the steps to the bunkhouse, and they started down the driveway. He threw a last glance at the tree hanging over the bunkhouse.

His shirt was plaid, browns and camels with a touch of gold.

They started walking up the drive. "That's a nice shirt. It must look good on you," she said.

He had hooked the shirt on his finger and slung it over his shoulder. At her words he twisted his head to look at the shirt as if he remembered nothing about it.

"The colors," Amy continued. "They must look good on you."

He shook his head. She could have been speaking Greek for all he understood. "If you say so. Holly gave it to me."

At the end of the driveway they turned right, heading away from the campground and the turn-off from the main road. He was walking easily, his shoulders back, the kind of effortless posture that came from good abs and traps.

Amy was used to male figure skaters. They were leanly built, often quite short men. And her father and brother, although tall, also had trim, sleek builds. But Jack was crafted on generous, solid lines with broad shoulders, big hands, and a strong chest.

Holly had told her all about him last night, about his

166

different business ventures, his different romances. In terms of romance, Holly had called him a "rescuer." His relationships were with women who were making important transitions in their lives, returning to school or starting a business. Jack gave them a lot of practical support, from cleaning their gutters to advising them when a client wasn't worth the effort. Once the woman emerged from her transition, Holly said, she and Jack amicably lost interest in one another.

Amy felt that "rescuer" was too strong a word. She was involved in enough mental health organizations to know that the true rescuers fell in love with people who were transitioning from manageable drug addictions to ones that were completely out of control. It didn't sound as if Jack were rescuing these women; he was giving them a helping hand. There was a big difference. Maybe the mental health professionals would say that he was avoiding intimacy, but what woman starting her own business had the time for a lot of emotional intensity?

Of course, Amy had to pretend that she didn't know about any of this. "Holly said you just sold a business. Do you know what you're doing next?"

"I think it would be fun to learn to fly helicopters."

"Helicopters?" Amy herself found helicopters noisy and uncomfortable, but the men flying them always seemed to love them. "Do you have a reason? Or does it just sound like fun?"

"It just sounds like fun. But if my past history is any guide, I will figure out some way to turn it into a business, and I'll have it for about five years and then I will get restless and sell it to someone."

Apparently he had done that twice already. Amy was used to her father, who had only had one profession, and to figure skaters, most of whom would need a second profession but could rarely find one. "Does that seem okay to you?"

"It seems like what will happen, so it had better be okay."

That was probably a good attitude. "You don't have any control over it?" she asked.

"Apparently not."

They walked on for a minute or so. Then he spoke. "Why did your brother cut his hair?"

"Ian?" Amy blinked. That seemed like an odd question. Ian had always worn his hair long, puffed back into a ponytail, but sometime between Mother's funeral and when she had seen him the following Christmas, he had cut it. "I have no idea. Maybe he did it out of sympathy for me. Maybe he knows how much I want to have long hair, and so he cut his to share in my misery."

This was, of course, unlikely in the extreme. Ian could not have given her hair one moment's thought in his entire life. If you asked him to shut his eyes, he probably couldn't have said what color it was.

"Why can't you have your hair long?" Jack asked. "Because of your skating?"

"No. I could pin it back or spray it. It's that I would look really horrible in long hair."

"You would?" He looked down at her, squinting a bit, as if trying to picture her with long hair. "I find that hard to believe . . . but I don't know one thing about it."

Amy had to agree with him there; anyone who had his coloring and wore navy did not know one thing about it. She hoped that all the ladies in transition understood that.

The trail did not make a complete circle around the lake. The far third of the shoreline was marshy and reedy, with no solid ground for building a road. So before they reached the trail's dead end, Amy turned away from the lake onto an old logging road. Heavy flatbed trucks had worn two sandy ruts through the forest, but now that the trucks were gone, wild grasses grew between the ruts. The road ran at an angle away from the shoreline, and after a bit they turned down an even more overgrown trail.

The last time Amy had come on this walk, it had been simple. One old logging road ran away from the lake; then another road cut back toward the lake. But the logging roads were now crossed by snowmobile trails and all-terrain vehicle routes. She stopped for a moment.

Jack noticed. "Are we lost?"

"I don't know. I thought I knew this road, but that was because there was only one."

"We came out from the trail at about a thirty-degree angle, then we took a pretty sharp turn—maybe eighty degrees or so—and now we're heading back toward the lake again. My guess is it's about a hundred yards away—but I don't know that for sure."

She was impressed. "You have a good sense of direction."

He nodded. "But I don't have my dad's sense of distance. He would be right about the yardage."

"Well, I don't care about the distance so long as we're going the right way." Then she saw a No Trespassing sign. "Oh, good, we are in the right place."

"Because we're trespassing?" he asked as she went past the sign. "That's how we know we're in the right place? I thought I was the only one who said things like that."

Amy rolled her eyes, but didn't answer . . . because

169

she wasn't trespassing.

A moment later they rounded a bend and came to a chained gate with another No Trespassing sign. But the gate was not attached to a fence. It was designed to keep cars out, not people. In fact, there was a distinct footpath leading around the gate.

A short lane opened onto a clearing at the edge of the lake, the one stretch of firm ground between a little swamp at the end of the trail and the marshy land around the inlet stream that brought water into the lake. The clearing was almost meadow-like, flat and open and sunny, full of wildflowers—lavender-blue asters, lemon-scented evening primroses, the fuzzy pink dome-shaped clusters of the Joe Pye weed. Their blossoms were little dots of color in the pale green grasses. Raspberry bushes spilled from the edges of the woods, growing over a pile of brush.

The site was low, and there was a sandy beach at the lake's edge, the only beach on the lake beside the one at the campground.

Amy and Jack crossed through the meadow and flowers. The property was at the longer end of the oval lake, so the length of the lake stretched out before them. Normally at this time of day the sun would be nearing the treeline and long streaks of light would glitter off the water, but of course this evening was cloudy.

Jack was looking around. Amy sat down on the lone big boulder that rose out of the sand.

"What is this place?" he asked. "It's a great spot. Why hasn't anyone built on it? The access stinks, but that could be fixed. Who owns it?"

She started to shrug, but then she spoke, her words coming out in a rush. "Can you keep a secret?" She was standing now. She didn't remember getting up off the

170

boulder. "I do. I own it. It's mine."

He had been looking out across at the lake, but at her words his head jerked toward her. "You what? *You* own it?"

"Yes." These grasses and flowers, the raspberries, the soft beach, they were hers. "The last time I was here, it was three years ago, the property was on the market, and apparently some resort developers were looking at it to be some sort of fly-in hunting and fishing retreat. So there would have been little planes landing on the lake all the time. They would have brought in electricity, and that would have changed so much. My family would have hated it. So I was in town one day, and I just picked up the phone and told the people who take care of my money to buy it."

Pam and David—her financial advisers—had said it wasn't a good investment, but she hadn't cared. The summer people had been dreading the resort, and the locals hadn't wanted it either because the potential purchasers were terrible employers, and here all by herself she, little Amy the Afterthought, had fixed everything with a single phone call.

Jack was shaking his head. "I guess I've opened businesses with about that much thought . . . but how big is it? Those No Trespassing signs were a good ways back."

"It's a hundred acres."

"A hun—" He whistled. "That's a lot of land. But why the secret? Why aren't you telling people?"

"I had to keep my name out of it during negotiations. Otherwise the price would have gone through the roof And then . . . I don't know. I guess I wasn't sure how my family would react. My mother always talked about how far the place was from the other cabins, how

171

inconvenient it would be to have a cabin there."

"Inconvenient? You have no plumbing up here, no electricity, you've got to drive twenty miles to make a phone call, and another half mile seems *inconvenient?*"

"Well, when you put it that way, I guess it does seem a little odd, but my mother's opinions were always so settled that it was hard to even think about disagreeing with her. And I supposed I was also a little embarrassed about doing it. I didn't want it to look like I was flashing my money around."

"Okay." It didn't sound like he completely understood. "I take it you don't have any plans for the place?"

"No. None."

But as she spoke she realized that she probably had had, if not plans, at least a hope that someday, somehow, she would feel enough a part of her family to want a cabin up here. There'd be the main cabin, the new cabin, the log cabin, and Amy's cabin. Amy's cabin—she liked the sound of that. A place where Amy would decide what they all would eat, a place where Amy would decide where they all would sit.

Of course, a good rainfall would wash out the road to Amy's place. So much far that fantasy.

Jack had moved over to the edge of the clearing and then stepped into the woods. She could hear twigs cracking and leaves rustling as he moved around.

He called out. "Is the swamp at the end of the trail yours?"

"I think so."

He reappeared. "If you built a little footbridge across the swamp—laying down a few dock sections would work fine; it would be at most two hours' work—then people could get from the trail to the beach in two

172

seconds."

Amy had never thought of that. "The kids would love being able to walk down here."

"But you'd have to tell everyone that the place is yours."

There was a leaf caught in his thick hair. He must have tangled with a branch while crashing through the swamp. Amy wanted to reach up and brush it out.

"I'll think about it," she said.

But she knew she wouldn't.


Gwen sat down on the steps to the main cabin. It was the first moment she had been alone all day. The sky was dark and low. At home she would have turned on the Weather Channel to find out when the storm would be coming, but there was no Weather Channel up here, no TV.

She could hear voices. The younger kids were playing in the road with Giles and Phoebe. Maggie and Ellie were in the new cabin playing cards with Joyce. Nick was by himself in the bunkhouse. Holly had gone to the log cabin to do some work. Hal and Ian were looking at the bank, checking for erosion. Everyone was accounted for. Except Jack, but she wasn't worried about him. He could take care of himself.

She sometimes thought that he should have been born a hundred and fifty years ago. He could have gone west, and once he had learned the road, he could have become a wagon master, paid to guide the covered wagons full of settlers across the Rockies to Oregon. He would have never settled himself, never found a little plot of land and tried to raise cows or grow corn, but he would lead others to their new homes.

An instinct, a mother's instinct, turned her eyes

173

toward the road, and there he was, her wagon-master son, at the end of the driveway, talking to Amy. Oh, yes, Amy. She had forgotten to keep track of Amy. She must have been out in the road with Giles, Phoebe, and the younger children.

Jack was wearing the wool shirt Holly had given him, the one he looked so good in.

He was still talking to Amy.

He had his hands in his pockets. Amy's were linked at the back of her neck, her forearms together. They were still talking.

"Amy! Aunt Amy!" It was one of the little kids, calling her. Amy dropped her arms and gestured to the kids that she was coming. She turned back to Jack, no doubt smiling a little farewell.

He, still keeping his hands in his pockets, moved his elbow and lightly nudged her arm with his.

It was the lightest of touches, but Gwen felt her shoulders drawing together, her neck starting to stiffen.

Why hadn't this occurred to her? Jack and Amy. Both unattached, neither with enough to do. She watched her son come down the driveway. He was built like her own father, tall, broad-shouldered, but he had John's warm coloring. Both the children did. She raised her voice. "What have you been up to?"

"Caulked that window and then went on a walk with Amy."

So there had been more than a chat at the end of the driveway.

Gwen moved over on the stoop, making room for him. He sat back, bracing himself on elbows. She leaned back a bit so that she was touching him, her back against his arm. They were quiet for a moment; then he spoke:

174

"Mom, how bad would Amy look in long hair?"

Gwen forced herself not to react, not to sit up, pulling herself away from his arm. She tried to answer. "I don't know . . . it's hard to imagine her looking anything but wonderful, but her features are very delicate. I suppose she could be overwhelmed by a lot of hair. And her jaw and throat are so perfect, you wouldn't notice them as much if she had longer hair." What on earth was happening that Jack was thinking about how Amy wore her hair? "Why do you ask?"

He shrugged. "We were just talking. I was wondering why Ian had cut his hair, and then she said something about wishing her hair was long, but that she wouldn't look right in long hair. I don't get it. If she wants her hair long, she should let it grow. Surely she's earned the right to have what she wants."

Gwen had to agree with him on that. "Well, it was nice of you to go on a walk with her. It doesn't seem that she's as comfortable up here as the rest of her family."

"She's not," he agreed.

"But I think she's really enjoying having you and Holly here. She's closer in age to the two of you. It's as if she finally has a brother and sister who can play with her."

Jack was still leaning back on his elbows. "She and Holly certainly have gotten chummy."

"And that's nice for both of them."

Gwen knew that he was getting her message. *Amy needs a brother too. And you're a good brother, Jack. You're wonderful to Holly. You're the only person who can get her to stop working. Her life is so much better because you are her brother.*

*That's what Amy needs too. Don't fall in love with*

175

*her. Be her brother.*

Was she asking her son to set aside his own happiness? She hoped not, she desperately hoped not. But everything was so complicated this summer, so difficult. Phoebe, Ian, and Joyce were having such trouble adjusting to Gwen's being here. Phoebe was a mass of unresolved grief; Ian seemed unreachable, unknowable; Joyce swaddled herself in critical bitterness. The cord that was holding Hal's family together was thin and fraying.

And if by summer's end the cord broke, Gwen knew that everyone would blame not the worn sections of the cord itself, but the new knot at its end, the knot that had tied her family to theirs.

*So not now, Jack. The necklace can't take any more weight.*

*I'm trying, Mom. I suggested that we take Holly on the walk with us. I knew we needed to take Holly with us. And I didn't ask her to tell me that secret. I would have stopped her if she had given me a chance.*

*I'm not going to give in to this. I'm not.*

# CHAPTER 9

YEARS OF STAYING IN HOTELS, A DIFFERENT BED NIGHT after night, had given Amy a routine for falling asleep. She lay on her side and let her body relax until she felt as if she were floating, until she could almost feel the inch-deep cushion of air between herself and the mattress.

Then her mind grew still. and she waited, and during this peace, this waiting, her body sent messages to her.

She would notice a slight stiffness in her hip and know that she needed to stretch more; a swelling in her fingers told her she had eaten too much salt; soreness in her breasts said that her period was coming. Sometimes she would simply notice a part of her body, there would be no specific message, just a noticing, and she believed that was a warning of injury and so for the next few days she would be careful.

Then after she had heard from her body, she went to sleep.

But tonight she was lying on her back, and she was thinking of Jack.

Jack was also lying on his back, also alone in a single bed, but he was not thinking of Amy. He was deliberately, determinedly not thinking of Amy. He thought about the roof over the woodshed; it looked like it needed some new shingles. And the steps down to the dock, they could use some work. And that limb over the bunkhouse. He was thinking hard about that. He should have taken it down. Bad weather was coming. There might be some strong winds.

See, this wasn't going to be so hard. He didn't have to think about her. This was not going to get the better of him. It wasn't.

The rain came at midnight. Wind gusted across the lake, hurling rain against the three little cabins, against the big garage and the sauna. It pounded against the peaked roof of the bunkhouse, a hard drumbeat against the roofs and windows. Nick couldn't sleep. Last night—his first night up here—had been okay; he had dozed on and off, but the sound of the wind and the dark rain was keeping him awake tonight. Weather never sounded like this at home. The rain was blowing in at a fierce slant. He could hear it hammering at the high little windows at the end of the bunkhouse. It was a sort of spooky sound. He wasn't scared, but it did make him think about Brian. Thunder boomed.

He turned over and tugged his sleeping bag over his shoulder. Once he started thinking about Brian, it was really hard to do anything, much less sleep. At home thunderstorms like this came in the late afternoon and were gone by nightfall. But this turbulence had come in from the Rockies. He didn't know anything about that kind of weather.

The rain went on, pounding away, each little drop hurtling itself against the windowpanes, like an army of Japanese warriors sacrificing themselves in a hopeless onslaught.

A sharp crack ripped overhead. Something rumbled, then thudded.

Nick sat up. Oh, shit. A tree limb had landed on the roof. He waited for more, for cracking beams, smashing wood, whatever, but all he heard was the wind and the rain. He fumbled for his flashlight.

"Nick?" It was Ellie, the boring one. Her voice came over the partition that separated the bunkhouse into the boys' half and the girls'. The partition came up only eight feet. So there was a big space between the top of the wall and the peak of the roof. She would have seen his light. "Are you awake?"

Was he awake? What did she think? That he had turned his flashlight on in his sleep? He might have his problems, but if there was one thing on earth he respected it was batteries. He didn't waste batteries. "Yes."

"Do you hear something?"

Why did she think he had turned on the light? "Yes."

He twisted his head and shoulders out from the lower bunk and shone his light on the ceiling. He moved the white circle of light along the boards. They were pale and yellowish. He didn't know what kind of wood it was. He never knew stuff like that. His light moved on, and he wondered why he was doing this, what he was looking for.

Then the light caught and glistened. Something was moving and cool, a rivulet of water. Oh, great, they were taking in water. That's how it always started in the movies, with this little tiny stream of innocent-looking water that you knew was loaded with radioactive poisons.

The water ran down a board until it hit a nail head, and then it started to drip. Nick couldn't hear the drip over the sound of the rain. But it was right over a top bunk. One of the little dudes was sleeping up there. He had forgotten about them.

"Do you think everything's okay?" It was Ellie again.

"Sure." There were two sets of bunk beds on this side of the partition. Nick was in a lower bunk while the two kids were both sleeping on a top bunk. He got out of bed and went over to other bunk, the one underneath the drip. His light shone against the navy blue nylon of the little dude's sleeping bag. Right in the middle of it was a dark circle, shining and wet.

"Are the boys okay?" It was Ellie again.

Nick wished she would shut up. "They're fine." At least the one who wasn't under a hypothermia watch was.

It was weird how little space the kid took up. More than half of his sleeping bag was just flat. "Is Maggie awake?" Nick didn't know why he said that.

179

"She's not here," Ellie answered. "She went in the new cabin to read, and I guess she fell asleep there."

The wet circle was growing larger. Nick didn't like the looks of that. He needed to do something.

Someone was passing out the wrong script. He wasn't supposed to do things. He was Nick, negative Nick, do-nothing Nick. When you live with two hysterics as he did, that was the smartest thing to do, nothing.

But here he was, with the wind howling around like some horror movie, and instead of getting to be the vampire who goes around chewing on people's necks, he got cast as the what-were-they-called? The governess. Yes, Negative Nick was the governess responsible for the wee ones.

"I think one of the kids is in a draft." A draft? Where had he come up with that? It must be nineteenth-century governess lingo. "Will he wake up if I move him?"

"He'll go back to sleep. Pick up the whole sleeping bag if you can," she advised. "But are you sure you need to move him? A little draft shouldn't be a problem."

This wasn't fair. Why did he have to sound simpering and prissy, and she got to sound like a normal human being?

"Do you want me to come over and help?" she asked.

He would love it. Let someone else deal with it. In any given situation that was by far the safest thing to do. But there was no door in the partition. To come over here, she would have to go outside and get all soaked herself "No," he said. "It's nothing."

Nick set his flashlight down and put one foot on the slat at the edge of the lower bunk and hoisted himself up. It wasn't going to be an easy feat, scooping the kid and his sleeping bag up and then stepping backward and down. Nick supposed he couldn't have done it last summer, but he had been on the wrestling team this year, and that had taught him a thing or two about moving other people's weight around. The kid murmured as Nick lifted him, and for a moment it looked like he was going to wake up, but he went limp and still again. Nick stepped back and down, then leaned forward to lay the boy on the lower bunk. The sleeping bag bunched up underneath him. Nick tugged it. The boy straightened out and rolled over, but didn't wake up. Nick picked up his flashlight and shone it on the sleeping bag. Now the wet spot was right on the boy, but at least it wouldn't get any bigger. If they were lucky, the lad was a champion bed-wetter, used to sleeping in puddles.

Nick got back into his own sleeping bag. At least he wasn't thinking about Brian anymore. That was something. Brian would appreciate the humor of that.

Oh, shit. The roof was still leaking. Should he do something about the mattress? Probably. But what?

There were a couple of forty-gallon trash bags under the bed. The sleeping bags had been stored in them.

He got up again, found his flashlight, fished the trash bags out from under the bed, and again perched himself on the edge of the lower bunk. He needed one of those helmets that coal miners wore, the kind that had a headlight. Spreading garbage bags was a two-handed operation.

*Okay, Val, Barb,* he said to his mother and grandmother, this is it, *resourcefulness, responsibility. That's what you wanted. Can I leave this joint now?*

Of course, the minute he had the garbage bags spread out all nice and neat, he remembered that Jack had put in a gas light that afternoon. He could have lit it. How was that for stupid?

Oh, well. He moved back to his bunk.

Cra-ack. A rumble like an oncoming train. The bunkhouse shook.

Double shit. It was another tree. What was this?

"I think a tree's fallen." It was Ellie again. She sounded worried.

"Yeah, I suppose." Nick tried to sound cool. "But sh . . . stuff like that must happen all the time around here, doesn't it?"

"No." She didn't make any bones about it. "We've never had a tree fall on any of the buildings."

That was because they had never had Cousin Nicky up here before. Nick shows up and the trees start falling.

Okay, time to think. Were they safer inside the cabin or out? He didn't have a clue. Wasn't someone supposed to teach you junk like that?

They probably had, but if so, old Nick hadn't been listening.

"I'm going to go tell my folks," Ellie said. Nick could hear her moving around, getting out of bed, finding her shoes. "No, wait, someone's coming."

Nick looked up. Through the narrow windows he could see the sweep of a flashlight. He supposed it was one of the dads riding to the rescue. God, he hoped it was Giles, Ellie's dad, not that asshole Ian. But Giles was lame. It probably wasn't so cool for him to be stumbling around in the dark.

He heard his name, then the door opened. It wasn't either one of the dads. It was Jack. He was wearing a dark poncho. Rain was streaming off him.

Oh, great. Nick would have preferred Ian the asshole. Jack might have tried to hide his reaction to Nick at the airport, but it had been clear. Sweet little Nicky was not what Cousin Jack had hoped the tooth fairy would bring. And now Jack had had to come out in the rain to rescue him.

"There's a tree on the roof," Jack said. "We need to get you guys out of here."

"The roof is leaking." Nick shone his flashlight up to the spot of the roof.

Jack moved over to that bunk. He had a halogen flashlight. The beam was bright and focused. "I *knew* this would happen." He sounded irritated. "I don't know *why* I don't listen to myself." He was clearly pissed off. "Did you put the plastic down?"

Nick nodded.

"Then you're thinking better than I am. And you were right not to light the lamp. We'll need to check the gas line in the morning. Now, how do we go about moving these kids?"

Why was he asking him? Nick pointed at the other side of the bunkhouse. "Ellie seems to be our resident expert on that."

They could hear her moving around in the other room, speaking in a low voice to the little girls. Apparently she was already getting them up.

"Stand them up," she called out softly. "They'll walk, but you kind of have to steer them because they won't be completely awake and they'll run into things."

Jack had brought over a pile of ponchos. He tossed a couple over the partition to Ellie. Nick went to one of the lower bunks and got the little dude out of his sleeping bag. He sat down on the bed, propped the kid up against his knees, and tugged the poncho down over him. Jack was doing the same for the other one. Nick slipped on his own poncho and started propelling the little boy toward the door. The ponchos were adult-size,

183

and the kid kept getting tangled up. Nick picked up the hem of the poncho. If he ever got asked to be a bridesmaid, he'd have practice.

Outside, the rain was really slicing down. It was only a step or two to the door to the girls' side, but the kids' faces got wet and that woke them up.

Ellie had single-handedly gotten both the two little girls into their ponchos. They were slumped back over on one of the bunks, asleep again.

"Shoes," Jack said. "Dammit, we forgot the shoes."

His flashlight was pointed down, shining on the edge of one of the girls' ponchos. Peeking out from underneath the plastic was a little foot wearing a scuffed-up pink sneaker. Nick shone his own flashlight down. Beneath their ponchos the boys' feet were shiny and damp, with a few pine needles and bits of leaves already clinging to them.

"They can go barefoot," Ellie said confidently. "They do it all the time."

"We can carry them," Jack said. "You look like a strong guy, Nick. Turn around."

Nick was a strong guy. It had been a fairly recent development in his life, but he liked it. It was a good way to scare people.

So he didn't need to turn around. He squatted and took one of the boys' arms. A second later the kid was on his back. He was awake enough to clamp his legs to Nick's waist and link his arms around his neck.

"Nice work," Jack said as he did the same thing. Ellie had already picked up one of the little girls. Jack took her in his arms, cradling her like a baby. Ellie turned to get the other one. She was obviously planning on carrying her, but Nick moved quickly and held out his arms. If Jack was carrying two kids, he was carrying

184

two kids.

Ellie opened the door. The rain cut in on Nick's face. The kid tightened his arms around his neck, making it hard to breathe.

The main cabin, where Hal and Aunt Gwen were sleeping, was dark, as was the one where Ellie's and Maggie's folks were staying, but the one beyond that, the one made of logs, was all lit up. Ellie was walking first, she had two flashlights, and apparently she had paid attention to the class about how to walk with a flashlight. She held one ahead of her so she could see where she was going, and she pointed the other one behind her so Nick and Jack could. She held both of them high so they illuminated as much of the little path as possible. At the tricky places she stopped and turned, shining both onto the path. The raindrops glinted in the light.

Holly and the ice skater had the door open, and the cabin was all light and warm. The skater took the girl out of Nick's arms right away. Then he squatted down by the sofa and let the little dude climb off by himself He rubbed a hand over his windpipe. He supposed it would uncrush itself sooner or later.

"Where are we going to put everyone?" Holly asked. "Can some of the kids share a bed?"

"They don't need to be in a bed," Ellie said. "They can sleep on the floor, just so long as they don't get cold."

She suggested spreading one sleeping bag out in front of the fire, lining all four kids up, and dumping a bunch of blankets on them. And wonder of wonders, for what had to be the first time in recorded history, three adults listened to a teenager and did exactly as she said. She was real confident, not one bit mousy. Nick was impressed. Knowing how to put a bunch of little kids to bed might be pretty dorky, but it was better than not knowing anything at all. And it was quite awhile before any of the three grown-ups remembered to ask where Maggie was.

Nick slept fine the rest of the night. It was weird to wake up to the morning light and to feel that he was halfway rested.

He lay still for a moment. The cabin was quiet. He had slept out on the enclosed porch in the upper bunk of Jack's bed. The porch was low and the ceiling was just a few feet over him. It was all flat and close, and the bed had a railing on the side, and suddenly it all felt too much like a coffin.

He rolled over and swung himself to the floor.

Jack's bed was empty, all neatly made. Jack didn't seem like the make-your-bed-every-morning-kind of guy, but he was. He never left crap lying around either. Nick supposed it came from having a father who was in the military. Apparently the military turned a person into a neat freak. Nick jerked the blankets off his bunk, but he couldn't get them to lie smooth. He flung the blankets back and started with the sheet. Even then it was tough because of not being able to get to the other side of the bed. What a display of talent—he couldn't even make a stupid bed.

He went into the main room of the cabin. The blankets that the little kids had been sleeping on were all folded up and piled on the sofa. Holly's room was empty too, and both those beds were neatly made with bedspreads that were made up from little squares of fabrics—patchwork quilts, he guessed they were called. He crossed through the little kitchen and pulled open the screen door.

He had to squint. The sun was bright, the sky clear. The only signs of the storm were a few little puddles on the ground and the twigs that had snapped off the trees. Their leaves were still fresh and green.

He could hear a thin grinding sound coming from the road, starting and stopping. He guessed it was a chain saw. A tree must have fallen across the road. He had never used a chain saw. He supposed it might be pretty cool if you knew what you were doing because those things could really rip, but of course he didn't know what he was doing, so he was bound to cut his leg off.

The psychologists and the sociologists never talked about that, did they? How the disintegration of the nuclear family unit was leaving a whole generation of America's youth unable to use chain saws.

By now he was almost at Aunt Gwen's cabin. He heard a whistle, then someone calling his name. He looked up. Jack was on the roof of the bunkhouse. "A couple of shingles worked loose last night. Why don't you come up and help me?"

There was a ladder propped up against the bunkhouse. Nick climbed it and stepped onto the roof. The tree had already been cleared away—Jack would certainly know how to use a chain saw—and a square of roof about four feet by three feet was exposed. Jack had a bunch of tools in his tool belt, and a couple of flat packets of new shingles were stacked at his elbow. He already had one line of new shingles installed; they were brighter than the old ones.

"We were lucky. None of the beams were broken, and Hal had some new shingles," Jack said. "So this won't take any time at all."

"I hope you aren't counting on me for well-informed

187

aid," Nick told him. "I'm clueless about all this handyman stuff."

"That's okay. I'm hoping to drag this out as long as possible. I'm hiding out from the logging crew. Some trees fell across the road, and the others are out clearing them away. Do you hear how the saws are always starting and stopping? I'll bet you anything that they are discussing where to make every single cut. It's going to take them forever. They're probably following parliamentary procedure."

Nick didn't see what was so bad about that. There was nothing else to do up here. Why shouldn't people chew the fat endlessly if they wanted? So long as they didn't involve him, that is.

But clearly it bugged the hell out of Jack. Nick watched him work for a while, his hands flashing quickly between staple gun and hammer. "Are you sure there isn't something you need me to be doing?"

"With this? It's nothing," Jack said as if that were obvious, as if Nick could look at this activity and see that it was easy. "But as long as you're up here, why don't you fill me in on this shoplifting stuff?"

"Shoplifting?" What was he talking about? "Who's been shoplifting?" How could you shoplift here? There were no shops.

"I thought that you had; that was why your mother and grandmother had sent you here. Some sort of shoplifting charges."

"Jesus, is that what they told you?" Nick raked both hands through his hair, squeezing his scalp. "*Shoplifting*?" Two guys that he sort of knew had gotten picked up last week for that, but he hadn't had anything to do with it.

Jack nodded. "At least that's what your mother told

188

Holly."

Nick tilted his head back. Wasn't that just like the two of them? To dump all their problems on someone else and then not even tell them?

Jack had stopped working. "So that's not it. You didn't steal."

"No . . . I mean, yes, of course I have. But I've never been caught." Everyone stole. That was part of being a teenager. "And I probably won't be."

"So?"

Nick's first impulse was not to tell him. But to equate Brian with shoplifting . . . it was such an insult. And he didn't want Jack thinking he was the sort of idiot who got caught shoplifting. He shrugged and spoke. "One of my friends offed himself a couple of days ago."

"What?" Jack stopped working. "You . . . you don't mean suicide, do you?"

"The funeral would have been yesterday. Those bitches wouldn't even let me go."

"Suicide? A friend of yours committed suicide?" Jack was now looking all major-issue worried.

Nick waved his hand. "Look, it's not a problem. I'm not going to toast myself. Brian was sick, man. He knew it, there were a couple of us, we all knew it. It was like he had cancer or something. He used to joke about shaving his head so he would look like he was in chemo."

God, it had made him so mad. That Val and Barb thought that this was like a cold, something he could catch. It wasn't. None of them had a clue what it was to be Brian, to have that black weight pressing down all the time. This wasn't something Brian had done on impulse; it wasn't a stupid teenage prank. He didn't do it because of a fight with a girl or bad SATs. Maybe that

189

was why some kids commit suicide, but this had been in the works for years.

He'd been cool; he had done it while he had been in the hospital. That was one thing he had said. "Be sure that I do it so my mom doesn't have to find the body." You weren't supposed to be able to kill yourself in a psychiatric ward, but Brian always said he had ways. Nick didn't know what he had done. If Val knew, she wasn't telling him . . . like it would give him ideas or something.

Jack was still looking at him with all this grown-up concern. "I'm okay," Nick assured him. "I did not come up here to kill myself. Val and Barb just flipped out. They couldn't handle it, so they sent me up here. Look, I know you wish I were on Mars. But trust me, I'm not going to kill myself."

Jack was shaking his head. "I can't believe they weren't straight with us."

"Oh, believe it."

"Then I really think you should tell my mother and Hal."

"Why? Don't they have enough on their minds wanting everyone to get along?"

"Secrets aren't going to help."

Nick supposed he had a point. Val and Barb loved secrets. They were constantly keeping things from him or each other. That in and of itself suggested how bad the secrets were.

So reluctantly he agreed. He would tell Aunt Gwen and Hal. He would do it at lunch.

He thought it might be hard, getting the two of them alone, but everyone decided to eat outside, and Gwen and Hal took their food to a pair of lawn chairs that had been put off to the side.

"Jack tells me that Mom and Gran"—the only time he ever called Val and Barb "Mom and Gran" anymore was when he was talking to Aunt Gwen—"have concocted this story about shoplifting to explain why they sent me here."

"We don't care why you're here," Aunt Gwen said. "We're just glad you are."

From anyone else that would have sounded like total bullshit. But Aunt Gwen could say an incredibly dopey thing like that, and it would almost seem true.

"What is the real reason?" Hal asked.

Nick had not been able to figure Hal out. He was like this crystal mountain—there were no cracks, no fissures or ledges for you to grab hold of, no way to start figuring him out. That wasn't good. Grown-ups had too much power. A kid's only chance was to figure out where the weak spots were.

Or maybe it was just that Hal was a dad, and dads were one thing Cousin Nicky didn't know too much about.

So he couldn't figure out what to do except launch into his little tale of woe and destruction. Halfway through the first sentence Aunt Gwen gasped and started to say something, but Hal put his hand on her arm. They stayed quiet, and so Nick ended up telling them a whole lot more than he had planned. Finally he saw what Hal was doing—being quiet so he would ramble on—and he shut up.

"It seems like such a terrible waste," Aunt Gwen sighed, "a young person killing himself."

"This wasn't something he was going to outgrow. It didn't have anything to do with how old he was."

She ducked her head almost as if she were apologizing.

Hal cleared his throat. "We're going to have to trust you on this one, Nick. We have no way of knowing if you really are okay."

"I'm fine."

"I hope you would tell us if you weren't." Hal didn't sound like he expected Nick to do that . . . which was shrewd of him. "And I do think your mother and grandmother were wrong not to let you go to the funeral."

Nick jammed his hands in his pockets, knotted his fists.

Everyone—the counselors at school, his various therapists, everyone—was always saying that he had to accept responsibility for his own life, saying that he couldn't blame others. When he would try to give them the picture—not because he was excusing himself, but because he thought they had to understand how mind-bogglingly silly Barb and Val could be, how pointlessly frittering they were, all caught up in their little head games of guilt and reproach—the reaction was always the same: *I'm sure they meant well . . . we're here to talk about you, not them.*

It was so frustrating because he could never get anyone to agree with him. That's all he wanted was—for someone else to acknowledge what he was living with. But no one would admit that they were jerks. Even Aunt Gwen, who had to know, who had to *see,* would never breathe one word of criticism about Barb and Val. Everyone was always pretending that Barb and Val were models of responsibility and maturity.

But here this Hal fellow, who couldn't know the half of it, had said it flat-out, no quibbling. *They were wrong.*

That was cool.

# CHAPTER 10

SUICIDE. PHOEBE COULDN'T BELIEVE IT. HER FATHER had drawn her aside to tell her about Nick's friend.

"It's hard to assess how Nick really feels," Hal said, "but he's not ready to listen to any criticism of his friend. Right now he doesn't want to hear anyone questioning his friend's decision."

Suicide. Another death.

Gwen joined them. Phoebe could hear herself saying all the right things, about depression sometimes being a fatal illness, about the rapid advances being made in treating it, about the shame, the waste—but that wasn't what she was thinking. Inside her a horrible, selfish monster was shrieking.

*How dare anyone bring these problems to the lake?*

It was an awful thought. She hated herself for it.

*This will ruin everything. We're supposed to be happy up here.*

Giles not getting to share a cabin with the kids, and now this. It wasn't right. It wasn't fair.

*There's a child who is dead. And his mother. . . her pain . . .* And she could only think about the lake. What was wrong with her?

"Nick knows that we're telling the adults," Gwen was saying, "but he says that he'd rather Maggie and Ellie didn'know."

"That's fine," Phoebe murmured. "Kids don't need to know everything."

"I've already told Amy, Jack, and Holly." Gwen spoke softly. "I'll tell Joyce or Ian as soon as I have a chance."

It didn't sound as if Gwen was looking forward to

that. "Shall I do it?" Phoebe offered . . . not that she wanted to. If *she* had reacted badly, God only knew how Joyce and Ian would be.

"No, I don't mind."

The two of them were standing in the road at the end of the driveway, waiting for everyone else to assemble for an afternoon hike. The day was cool after last night's rain, and no one was very interested in swimming, so Gwen had suggested a hike instead.

Gwen planned activities. Yesterday they had taken a boat trip across the lake to have a tea party at the campground; last night there had been family charades. The kids had had a Jello-eating contest at lunch today. Now they were going on a hike, and this evening there would be a campfire. Gwen wrote up a schedule every morning.

She had said over and over that everything was voluntary, that each person should do whatever he or she wanted. And Phoebe believed her; Gwen was not going to force anyone to have a good time.

Except her own children. Gwen clearly expected Holly and Jack to participate in everything. They were to stick to the schedule; they were to be good sports.

And Phoebe was not about to indulge herself at their expense. If they had to be good sports, she would be one too. Even when she was aching to stay home and read, even when the craving for a book was a throbbing behind her eyeballs and an itching in her palms, she went along. She knew that if she excused herself even once, Joyce and Ian would never do another activity for the rest of the vacation.

Each activity was fun, Phoebe was willing to admit that, and the kids were having a marvelous time, but at moments in the midst of all this organized summer-camp activity, she missed her mother so much that she wasn't sure she could stand it.

The hike today was a color chip hike. Once everyone had assembled, the two little girls passed out paint-chip cards that Gwen had picked up at the hardware store last time she was in town. She had chosen natural colors, earthy browns and pale leaf yellows, every shade of green. They were each given a card and told to find something along the trail in that color.

"Is it a race?" Ian asked politely as he took his card. "Or a contest—who has the closest match?"

"Oh, no." Gwen laughed. "You just do it."

"We did it all the time as kids," Holly said. "Mother always kept paint chips in the glove compartment of the car."

Gwen laughed again. "Of course I did. They were free."

Phoebe knew about Gwen's first husband and his long tours at sea. "Keeping everyone's spirits up, that must have been hard," she said to her. "Especially without a lot of extra money."

"You're right about the money," Gwen acknowledged.

Mother had had money; there'd always been money for lessons, outings, restaurant meals. They had never had to think twice about using an extra tank of gas. Perhaps that was why Mother hadn't been as inventive as Gwen about games and such; she hadn't needed to be. Surely she would have been if she had had to be.

"Do we have a goal here?" Ian asked as he took his color chip. He was not being critical. He simply didn't get it.

Gwen shook her head. "No. Unless you count having fun as a goal."

They all set off down the road. Surprisingly it was Amy who had the best eye for color. "Don't you see that the paint has a little more blue in it than the leaf?" she would say. She would step out into the sun to see the colors better, and the bright light would shine against the fine grain of her skin.

The rest of them would laugh. No, they didn't see it.

"Keep looking at it," she would say . . . and yes, when you really stared at it, really paid attention, you could see that she was right.

She was walking between Holly and Jack, obviously having a good time. It was strange seeing her talking and laughing. She was usually so quiet.

"Have you had a lot of art training?" Holly asked her.

"Goodness, no," Amy answered. "But I have spent my life trying to match sequins to chiffon."

Phoebe looked at her. She was so graceful. Once you started looking at her, sometimes it was hard to stop. Even in her smallest gestures her arms curved and, her fingers arched.

Her fingernails were shorter than they had been last Christmas; they were filed to a square tip and polished with a clear finish. It probably made sense to do your nails like that up here. The clear polish wouldn't show chips, and the flat tips would be stronger. Phoebe always broke a couple of nails each summer . . . probably because the only thing she ever did to take care of them was file them while sitting at stoplights, and she never sat at stoplights at the lake.

She glanced at Holly's nails. They were done just like Amy's, clear polish, blunt tips. That couldn't be a coincidence. Amy had probably suggested she do it; Amy had probably lent her the polish. Amy might have actually even done the work. It would have been like a preteen slumber party, all the giggling girls gathering around to do each other's hair and nails.

*Doesn't it bother you that Mother's not here? Isn't it ripping your heart out to see each change? It's fine to like Holly and Jack—they're nice people, and Gwen too. But remember why they are here . . . because Mother is not.*

Ian came up to her, broke into these thoughts.

He must be missing Mother. Surely he was missing their mother.

"Don't worry about the boats tonight, Phoebe," he said. "I'll do them."

The boats? It was two in the afternoon. Why talk about the boats now?

Tying up the boats at night had always been her dad's responsibility. Giles had, of course, taken care of his fishing boat, but Dad had gone down every night to be sure that the motorboat was anchored well away from the shore, that the canoes were pulled up on the bank and flipped over. It was important to do it properly so that a sudden wind wouldn't crash the boat into the dock or the shore. And, of course, Phoebe could do it properly.

Dad hadn't minded when she offered to do it the first evening. "That's good of you," he had said.

But goodness had nothing to do with it. She had to have something that she was in control of, in charge of.

The kitchen had slipped away. They had had chili for dinner last night, and when Gwen had carried Mother's heavy stock pot in from the kitchen and realized that there was no trivet to set it on, who had she looked to for help? To Phoebe—the one who had always been the right hand, the one who knew where the trivets were? No. Gwen had looked at Holly.

197

"Holly, quick," she had said. "I need something to put this on."

*But that's my job,* Phoebe had wanted to cry out. *Getting trivets. I am the responsible one, the helpful one. I help Mother, and Ellie helps me. That's how it works.*

But that was also how it worked for Gwen and Holly. Holly was Gwen's first daughter, her right hand. Gwen didn't need two first daughters. So where did that leave Phoebe?

Ian too needed something to have control over. If she felt that Holly was easing into her place, then Ian must feel that Jack was dynamiting his way into his. Projects that Ian and Dad had talked about for years—the gas line to the bunkhouse, checking out the sauna—Jack had done on his first day here. Dad was openly exhilarated about all the work that was getting done. He loved having Jack to hurry things along.

Ian had told her yesterday not to worry about the boats.

"It's no bother," she had said, and after dinner she had gone down to take care of it.

He had tried to stop her. "I said I would do it," he had called after her. "I'll be there in a minute."

But Ian wasn't doing anything quickly this summer; his "minute" would stretch out and out. She was done long before he could get himself down to the dock.

Phoebe could see this going on night after night. The two of them would be in a stupid little competition, who could get down there and tie up the boats, and of course she would always win. It was pathetic.

So after dinner that evening, she forced herself to sit still. The cabin was too warm, and it was noisy, with the kids clearing the table and Holly and Joyce struggling to get the dishes organized. Phoebe couldn't even help them because it wasn't her turn. To help them would be saying to Gwen that she didn't approve of her system of dividing chores, and that wouldn't be right.

It would be cool down by the lake, cool and quiet. The loons would be out, and there might be an evening fisherman trolling along the edge of the lily pads. The water lilies had glossy green heart-shaped leaves that floated on the surface of the lake; the yellow blossoms were tight and cup-like. Soon the green and yellow would disappear as the trees on the west shore cast deep shadows across the water, bordering the lake with dark fringe. It would be peaceful down by the lake, beautiful.

But Phoebe stayed inside. She let Ian tie up the boats.

Amy looked at her sister. It wasn't like Phoebe to be sitting, not knowing what to do with herself.

That was Amy's part.

It was as if they had reversed roles up here. Finally, miraculously, Amy was having a good time at the lake. She felt as if she belonged, as if she had a place. She knew what she was supposed to be doing, who she was to be with. And Phoebe was feeling the opposite.

*Let me be the one who feels that way. I've felt that over and over, I don't mind so much; I'm used to it, you're not.*

It was nice to be having a good time, of course it was . . . but not at Phoebe's expense, not when the lake mattered so much to Phoebe.

Except what could Amy do? Pretend that she didn't like Holly and Jack? Pretend that she didn't think the world of Gwen? How would that help Phoebe?

Phoebe noticed her regard and stood up instantly. "I guess I should go see if Jack needs help with the

199

campfire."

Jack? Need help building a campfire? Amy didn't think that very likely. "Why don't you go read for ten or fifteen minutes?" That was how Phoebe coped; reading was the one thing, the only thing, she ever did for herself. It was the only way she knew how to say no to other people; it was the only way she could manage to be alone, by putting a book between herself and the rest of the world.

"And we need to be getting the kids into jackets." It was as if Phoebe had not heard her.

Maybe she wasn't ready to start coping.

Silently Amy followed her out of the cabin. The kids were playing in the drive. A pile of jackets was lying on the bunkhouse steps. Ellie must have already gotten them. She hadn't needed to be reminded. Here she was, fourteen, and she knew what to do. Phoebe would have been like that when she was fourteen.

*Is Claire going to grow up like me? In the shadow of this perfect older sister, the one who always knows what to do?*

Amy watched as Phoebe touched Ellie on the arm, silently thanking her for getting the jackets. Then Phoebe moved up behind Claire, scooped her up, turning her upside down. Claire shrieked and laughed, her small arms closing around Phoebe's thighs, hugging her.

Amy did not remember her mother ever doing that to her. *Ellie may be as helpful as Phoebe used to be, but Claire will always know that she is loved.*

Amy went down the path toward the log cabin. That's where the fire circle was. Her family had never used it very much. They had always read in the evenings. If anyone wanted to sit by a fire, they had done it indoors.

Gwen had had the kids rake the leaves and twigs out of the circle. Jack and Nick had dragged away the rotten logs and split new ones, arranging them for seating. The older kids would pop popcorn over the fire; the little ones would roast marshmallows.

Jack was squatting in the middle of the cleared space, already at work building the fire. He looked up at her. "Hi."

"Do you need me to pick up more sticks or something?" she asked. "I don't know the difference between tinder and kindling, but at least I remember the words."

He smiled. "I'm doing fine."

"I thought you probably would be."

Amy sat down on one of the logs. She wrapped her arms around her knees and watched him work. Little wisps of bluish flames were licking up the twigs, and he was gradually adding more small pieces of wood.

Finally he sat back and watched the fire. The first twigs had already burned through, their orange-red embers collapsing onto the dark ashes of older fires.

"Holly told me that you used to be a firefighter."

He nodded. "Right after high school."

"Why did you quit?"

"It was a government bureaucracy. I'd rather be in a burning building than a government bureaucracy."

"Have you ever done any disaster-relief work?" she heard herself ask.

"Disaster-relief work?" He looked up. The light was too dim for her to read his expression. She could see only the square lines of his cheekbones and the almost parallel set of his jaw. "What are you talking about?"

"I do some work for the American Red Cross. When there's a flood or a hurricane or an earthquake,

201

sometimes they ask me to go in and get on the air, letting people know what kind of services are available and where funds are needed and—"

"You know about that stuff?"

"Someone hands me a piece of paper." She didn't want to talk about herself. "Anyway, at disaster sites there are always these people who are there to get things working again. People who can figure out how to get electricity from that side of the causeway to this one or who can lay a clean water line across the San Andreas fault. It's very short-term work, very 'let's just get this done before nightfall,' no worrying about permits or environmental impact statements."

"You don't have to worry about permits? That sounds like heaven to me."

Amy had thought it would appeal to him. "I think the people who do it love it. They'd never admit it because of the disasters being so awful, but they always seem so alive when they're trying to get things working again."

"And you're suggesting that I might like it too?"

"I don't know about that." That was nearly a lie; she thought he would love it. "But when you were talking about laying dock sections across the swamp, it occurred to me that you would be good at it." And if what his sister had said about his love life was even half true, he was at his best when helping other people.

"I probably would be reasonably adequate," he acknowledged, "especially if they let me use duct tape."

"They don't care what you use. They only care about results."

Jack was still squatting like a baseball catcher, his elbows on his knees. "That's what people ought to care about, but the older I get, the more it seems like results are the one thing a lot of people *don't* care about. They think they do, but they don't. Either they want to control your process, or they want to know that you're feeling the right thing. You can completely screw up, but as long as you were feeling the right thing while you were screwing up, all is forgiven."

"We're a sentimental people," Amy said. You had to understand that all the way down to your toes if you ever wanted to be successful in American popular culture.

"I suppose," he agreed. "But me . . . I don't want to be judged on what I say or how I feel, but on what I do. Talk's cheap; it's actions that count."

Amy agreed with him on talk. "But feelings . . . they aren't cheap, they do count."

"But they shouldn't be excuses."

"No," she agreed again.

"In fact, they—" He broke off. "Am I ever yammering on about myself. Let's talk about you."

This time Amy did not agree with him. She wanted to go on talking about him. "I'm a professional figure skater."

He looked up at her. "Guess what? I already knew that. And you live in Denver, and you train with two guys that I have actually heard of, and you are on TV a lot."

"So what else do you want to know?"

He put the first log on the fire. Amy thought it looked too big, that its weight would smother the fire, but flames began curling up its sides. "You could start by telling me why you told me about that property of yours."

Amy straightened. That was out of the blue. "Was I wrong to?" she asked carefully.

"I don't like secrets. I don't think families should

203

have a lot of secrets from one another."

*But secrets are fun.* The figure-skating world was full of secrets—what music you were working on, what contracts you were about to sign. Most of the secrets were common knowledge, but still officially they were secrets and were the currency of friendship, how you let someone know you were pals.

He continued. "I worry when people start telling me secrets. They usually want something from me."

"That's probably often true," she said.

"So what do you want from me?"

What did she want from him? She let out a breath. She hadn't thought of herself as wanting anything from him. Yes, she wanted to have a good time at the lake. She wanted to feel that she had a friend up here, an ally.

But his sister was providing that. So why hadn't she told Holly about the property? Why had she told him? She didn't know.

He spoke again. "I don't want to be the boy at the camp down the road. If you want a wild summer romance, you need to look elsewhere."

Amy felt her eyes widen. She quickly disciplined her expression . . . not that it mattered. It was too dark for him to see.

A wild summer romance? Was that what she wanted? She hadn't thought about it.

But the idea did have some merits. Physically Jack was attractive, there was no question about that. Even when he was wearing blue, he had a natural, earthy magnetism. He was interesting, he was generous, he was trustworthy. For a wild summer romance he probably was an ideal candidate . . . although if that had been her reason for telling him about the property, she certainly hadn't been conscious of it.

"First of all," he continued, "I'm not a kid, and second, this isn't summer camp."

"Okay." What else could she say?

"Stop me if I am making a complete idiot of myself here. I'm not saying that I wouldn't be flattered or that if things were different, I wouldn't—oh, hell." He broke off. "Would you please say something? I'm talking way too much."

It was too late. He had already exposed himself, not in what he had said, but in what he hadn't said. *First of all*—this is what he could have said, should have said— *I don't think of you in that way*. But he hadn't said that. Clearly the issue was not *her* wanting a wild summer romance, but him doing so.

Amy was not often surprised by people. Her intuitive powers were strong enough that she usually at least half expected whatever happened. But all this was surprising. Jack, her father's new wife's son, her new friend's brother, was attracted to her.

"What would you like me to say?" she asked.

"You could be making violent gagging noises because me being even as close as the camp down the road makes you sick."

"If I put my mind to it, I'm sure I'd decide that you on the other side of the fire circle was too far."

He cursed. "Don't say things like that. It's stupid to say things like that. Try the violent, gagging noises."

"You're really worried about this, aren't you?" Amy imagined that he was like herself, all instinct and intuition, trusting first impressions far more than orderly thought. But he had obviously been thinking about this for some time. He was attracted to her, but he was determined to resist the feeling.

"I wasn't worried about it at all because I was

205

counting on you to be repelled at that idea."

She was not. She quite liked the idea . . . in fact, the clarity of her feelings suggested that her subconscious had been addressing the matter for some time.

She didn't understand his reluctance. There was no privacy up here, she would admit that, but they could at least get to know each other better.

"I think I should go away for a couple of days," he said.

"Go away?" Was this really such a problem that he had to run away? "Why? I don't want to be chasing you off. That's not fair to your mother."

"You're not chasing me off . . . well, maybe you are, but I figure I can kill two birds with one stone. Mom told you about Nick's friend, didn't she? I don't see how he can think straight with so many people around. So I'm thinking I should take him away for a while. That will be fine with Mom. She'll want me to do what's right for Nick."

Amy imagined that he was right. "But where would you go?"

"I don't know . . . there's not a lot of choices, but there is a whole bunch of federal land up by the Canadian border, National Parks and such, and the only way to get into it is by canoe. Maybe we could do that."

"Do you like canoeing?" Amy had not seen him out in any of the boats. He tended to avoid the water.

"I haven't been in one since Boy Scout camp, but I can probably manage for a couple of days. He and I can go out in the wilderness, paint our faces blue, and march around the campfire howling until he feels a little better."

Amy had to smile. He was joking about the face painting and the howling, of course, but the rest of it was so like him. All the other men up here would want Nick to talk—actually, Ian might just want Nick to listen—but Jack would want to act, to move. They might go the whole time without saying one word about Nick's friend, but Nick probably would come home feeling better.

"When would you go? How long would you be gone?"

"I don't know. I just had the idea about five seconds ago."

That too was like him. "So I guess you haven't told Nick about it yet."

He shook his head. "Haven't had a chance."

The screen doors were banging, and voices were growing closer. In a moment the others joined them, the kids carrying bags of marshmallows and a jug of lemonade. Gwen followed with a metal dishpan full of the popcorn supplies. Phoebe was carrying a Coleman lantern. Jack took the dishpan from his mother, gave it to Holly, then drew Hal and Gwen aside. He said a few words. Gwen glanced at Hal, Hal nodded, and Gwen reached up, patted him on the cheek.

He didn't spend much longer with Nick. The boy started in surprise and then looked down, kicking a little trench in the sand with the side of his shoe. He shrugged and nodded, still looking at the ground. Amy suspected that he liked the idea better than he was admitting.

Jack looked back at his mother. She nodded again. The whole thing was settled. How quickly they made decisions. It was amazing. Her family would have had to talk about it for a week. At the very minimum.

Of course, her father had been part of the decision. He had been able to decide as quickly as Gwen. He was changing. How odd to think of your parent as changing.

207

Gwen waited until Phoebe was done shaking the long-handled popcorn popper and the kids had roasted their first marshmallows. Then she spoke. "Nick and Jack are going on a canoe trip for a couple of days."

The group exploded. "A canoe trip? Oh, Nick," Ellie sighed, "you're so lucky."

"Can I go?" seven-year-old Scott chirped.

"Me too," piped up Alex. "I want to go too."

"When did you make these plans?" Ian asked.

"Jack doesn't make plans," Holly answered. "He just does things."

"You'll need to plan this," Ian said. "You need to get permits."

"Permits?" Jack's head shot up. He did not like the sound of that. "From the government?"

"I think that's right," Amy's father said. "I'm not sure that you can hop in a canoe and go anymore. They restrict access. You'll need to go into town and make arrangements for a permit."

"The wilderness areas have gotten too crowded," Ian explained. "It's a major issue in the management of our national park system. So they have had to limit access. Only so many people can launch a day."

"Oh, well, a *day*." Jack was clearly prepared to launch at night rather than go through permit application.

Amy saw her father start to laugh, but Ian missed Jack's point. "And I believe the permits get snapped up pretty fast. You probably can't get one for this year."

"That may be true for weekend access," Giles said. "Mid-week might be a different story."

That made sense to Amy.

"But still," Ian went on, "I think you'd be better advised to wait until next year."

208

Amy looked at him. Didn't he ever listen to himself? Didn't he ever hear how pompous he sounded? *Don't you care what Gwen and Holly and Jack must think of us?*

Maybe he hadn't cut his hair. Maybe his ponytail had just fallen off, unwilling to be a part of such pomposity.

"Obviously we don't have enough information." Amy's father was speaking, sounding more like himself again. He loved to collect information. "I'll go into town tomorrow and make some calls."

"Why don't I go?" Ian volunteered.

Amy could think of a thousand reasons why Ian shouldn't be the one to make the calls. He would make sure that the trip didn't happen this year.

"Oh, let's have Holly do it," Gwen said lightly. "She's very good at finding things out on the phone."

"Me?" Holly was startled. "I'm not going on a canoe trip."

"I didn't ask you to," Gwen answered. "I just want you to make the arrangements."

"Arrangements I can make. I will do anything as long as you don't expect me to sleep in a tent."

"But you were planning on including the rest of us, weren't you?" Joyce asked. "We've never split up like that before."

"This was something Nick and Jack had planned to do together," Gwen said quietly.

"Is there a reason why others can't go with them?" Joyce persisted. "It doesn't seem fair."

What did fairness have to do with it? Surely Joyce realized—

Amy stopped. She looked across the fire circle toward Gwen. She was standing at the picnic table, salting the popcorn, and the light from the Coleman lantern shone

209

on her face. Her expression was tight.

She had not yet told Joyce and Ian about Nick's friend. Surely even they would have been cooperative if they had understood.

It was wrong of Gwen not to have told them right away, of course it was . . . but Amy couldn't blame her. Joyce and Ian could be difficult. Amy would have put off talking to them too.

"If there's a reason, tell me what it is." Joyce was not going to give up.

The other adults exchanged glances. They couldn't tell Joyce and Ian about Nick's friend right now. Nick had not wanted Maggie and Ellie to know.

Joyce saw the glances. She knew that something was being communicated. She felt left out. And she couldn't stand being left out. It had been going on since the day she had married Ian. She had wanted to be as important to Eleanor as Phoebe was. She was constantly on guard, ready to be offended.

"And we *really* want to go," added little Emily.

Nick suddenly spoke. "Maybe they should go."

The little kids all dashed to him. Here was someone on their side. "Can we go? Can we go?" they clamored.

"It's fine with me," Nick said. "The more, the merrier."

Amy saw Jack tug the ends of his hair. Being merry was the exact opposite of what he had planned.

Ian's kids whooped with joy. They went dancing around the fire, thrilled at the idea of going.

"Can we go, Mom?" Alex was now leaning on Phoebe's knees, pushing his face into hers. "Please please please please *please*."

"We'll see," Phoebe said.

"No, Mom, don't say that, please don't say that. Just

say yes. You can say yes."

"Not until Dad and I talk about it."

This seemed typical. Ian and Joyce's kids were taking it for granted that they would be able to go. Phoebe's knew that they needed permission.

"But if Scott gets to go, then I—"

"Alex." Giles's voice was firm. And Alex shut up.

"All right." Gwen spoke decisively. "Everyone who plans on going must tell Holly by eight a.m. tomorrow morning." Ian's kids immediately started to squeal again. Gwen held up her hand. "But I don't think any of the younger kids can go unless one of their parents goes."

"Oh," Joyce said. She hadn't wanted to be excluded, but it wasn't clear that she really had wanted to be included either. "Is that really necessary?"

"Yes," Gwen said.

Amy waited for someone to protest Gwen making so many of the decisions, but no one did. Wasn't this what they were all used to? Her mother had always had the final say. This might be the first time people were completely comfortable with Gwen . . . because she was finally doing something Eleanor's way.

An hour later it was bedtime. Giles was burning the sugary gunk off the end of the marshmallow sticks; Holly and Phoebe were picking up the paper cups, gathering up the popcorn supplies. Amy tossed her cup into the embers of the fire. The wax sizzled; the remaining drops of lemonade popped.

"If I'm going on this thing with a hundred people, then you're going too."

It was Jack. He was at her elbow, speaking softly.

"But I thought—"

211

"I know what you thought," he interrupted, "and that's what I thought at first too, but Mom's not going, and Holly isn't either, so you have to come and protect me."

"Protect you from what?" Amy had to smile. "I thought *I* was the big danger in your life."

"Maybe you were awhile ago, but don't flatter yourself. You aren't half as threatening as all these plans and this organization. That's what I need protection from."

Amy laughed. If he had been anyone else, she would have touched him, put her hand on his shoulder. "I think you'll need someone a lot bigger and stronger than me to protect you from that."

Gwen looked across the campfire. Just apart from everyone, underneath the shadows of the trees, Amy and Jack were talking. Her head was tilted back, and he was looking down at her. It was too dark to see their faces, but she could tell that they were laughing.

Last night, as she and Hal had lain in bed waiting for the rain, they had made love for the first time since the others had arrived. And afterward, perhaps because their children were here, reminding them of their late spouses, they had talked about the private parts of their first marriages.

Her story was simple. She had had only theoretical information when she married John, and he had known little more, but over the years they had both learned, and they achieved pleasure simply, straightforwardly, even efficiently—sometimes too efficiently perhaps, but that was one of the realities of marriage.

Hal's marriage had been different. When he had met Eleanor, she had been, in sexual terms, casual and experienced. "I was a Midwestern farm kid," he said. "I was dazzled."

Sex was great fun to Eleanor. But that was all. It wasn't sacred or romantic; it was fun. Her mores were aristocratic. "It never occurred to her that once the children were born, we would continue to be faithful to each other."

"And so she wasn't?" Gwen tried to keep the shock out of her voice.

"No, she was, but only because she realized how important it was to me. Still, I think it always puzzled her."

Then Amy had been born. "She wasn't planned, she was a mistake," Hal continued, "and after that Eleanor started to feel that the game wasn't worth the candle. It was as if she had fallen once too often while fox hunting. Once upon a time this was fun, but it's not worth the risk anymore."

They had continued to have relations, but their encounters were occasional and flat. "Sometimes I look at Amy—she's so very lovely—and even though I know that this is foolish, it seems as if her beauty is the result of, the compensation for—I don't know what—the end of her parents' sex life."

It wasn't like Hal to be so hesitant in his expression, but he probably had never spoken of this before, not even to Eleanor.

"And yet," he continued, "her performances are fairly sexless. I don't think I'm saying this because I'm her father. She can be warm, funny, sad, elegant, but she's never sexy."

Gwen agreed with him. When she was getting to know him last winter, she had scrounged the corners of her local video store and found tapes of various figure-skating performances. She had managed to see a number of Amy's important numbers, and at least on video there was no sexual fire in her performance.

The other night she had asked Amy about her life, and Amy had unconsciously revealed the extent to which she was surrounded by gay men. That was no great surprise considering her profession, and artistically, financially, these men served her well, giving her excellent advice and solid support.

But surely their role in her life was more solid if she remained unattached. Was she a Sleeping Beauty and they the palace guard, slaughtering all intruders who might come armed with different sexual weapons?

Gwen looked again at her son and this exquisite young woman. They were obviously about to say good night. Jack had his hands in his pockets, just as he'd had when he had been talking to her at the end of the driveway the other day. He almost never stood with his hands in his pockets. Perhaps it was the only way he could keep from touching Amy. And her body was leaning toward his; her hands were clasped under her chin, as if she were keeping them from reaching out to him; her shoulders were arched forward, as if drawn to him.

Amy didn't have Rapunzel's long hair. She needed Jack to crash through the thick brambles that had grown up around the palace walls; she needed him to draw his sword before the armed guards; she needed to be rescued, awakened.

And Jack needed to be needed. In so many ways the two of them were so well suited to each other . . . but not like this, not here, not now.

# CHAPTER 11

ELLIE OFFERED TO PUT ALEX AND CLAIRE TO BED. "I know that you and Dad need to talk about the canoe trip."

Phoebe thanked her. "But it's just Alex and Claire we have to talk about. If you want to go, you certainly can."

"I was hoping you would say that." Ellie scooped up her brother and sister and danced off to the bunkhouse.

Giles waited until the kids were out of earshot. "Ellie's getting a crush on Nick, isn't she?"

Phoebe nodded. At home thirteen-year-old Ellie and her friends socialized with boys only in groups. If she had particular feelings for any one boy, Phoebe suspected, they were directed toward the son of one of the physics professors, an intellectually gifted kid who was shy enough that he might never date until college. Nick's confident independence had clearly driven every other thought from Ellie's mind. Flushed and breathless, she watched him whenever he wasn't looking at her and nervously shifted her gaze away whenever he was.

Giles grimaced. "Actually, he's not a bad kid, but he's probably very unhappy. And she's going to have a lot of competition from Maggie."

"That's for sure." For Maggie's fifteenth birthday, Joyce had taken her to the gynecologist for birth-control pills. "I want her to be able to make an informed decision about physical pleasures," Joyce had said.

Phoebe thought that was crazy. Joyce wasn't helping Maggie make an informed decision; she was encouraging her to make an impulsive one.

Phoebe rose from her place at the campfire and went around the circle to get Thomas from Gwen. Already half asleep, he was heavy and limp. Giles opened the door to the new cabin, and they went into their bedroom. Joyce and Ian were still outside. They could talk.

"So what about Alex and Claire?" Phoebe asked. She laid Thomas on the bed and began taking off his overalls. They were dirty; the knees were out-and-out filthy. "They're dying to go too."

"And we'd be monsters if we didn't let them. The only question is which one of us goes with them and which one of us stays home with this little munchkin." Giles tickled Thomas's chin. He usually liked that, but tonight he was too sleepy. He lifted his chubby little fist as if to bat his father's hand away, but even that was too much effort.

Phoebe looked up at Giles. Why was that a question? Yes, half of each day would be spent sitting in a canoe, but there would be portages across uneven, rocky paths; the campsites were often up steep banks. That sort of thing was difficult for him.

He went on. "I know you must have assumed that I would stay home—and of course I will if you want to go."

"But you want to go too." This did surprise her.

"Whatever Jack and Nick might have been planning originally, they're going to have to take an easy trip now that the kids are going. And yes, I do want to go."

Giles rarely spoke up like this. He certainly could have strong opinions, and sometimes he did impose them on everyone else, but he only ever thought about what was right for a whole group: he never worried about what he wanted for himself Phoebe knew that because there had been so much he couldn't do as a kid, he had learned not to have a lot of preferences so that he

216

wouldn't be disappointed.

"I know it isn't fair of me," he went on, "because the minute I say I want to go, it's a done deal in your mind, you would never dream of going yourself, but that just shows you how much I do want to."

He was right. If he wanted to go, there was no question whatsoever that he would go and she would stay home with Thomas.

She put Thomas in his crib. "Do you want to get away from the lake?" she asked.

They never talked about this, about the fact that Giles didn't love the lake as much as she did.

"That's part of it," he admitted. "We haven't had an easy time of it this year, but I also just want to go." His voice lightened. "I think I have finally figured out what I want to be when I grow up."

"Oh?" Phoebe looked over her shoulder with a smile. He was already the most grown-up person on the face of the earth.

"Yes, I want to be Jack."

"What?" Phoebe stared at him. Thomas's clothes fell to the floor. "You want to be what?"

"You heard me. And it's a who, not a what . . . at least I think it is. I want to be Jack. He's so good at all this guy stuff—the tools, the outdoors. I want to be like that."

"Giles!" Phoebe had to laugh. "You want to be *Jack*?" She liked Jack, she did, and yes, he did have both large motor and fine-motor skills, and his problem-solving skills were superb, but . . .

"Yes. I want to be him, but in my own life. I want to keep my family and my house and my job, but just be him."

Phoebe started to undress. "I don't suppose I need to

217

point out that Jack doesn't have a family, a house, or seemingly even a job, and that's probably no accident. Can you imagine him doing your job?"

"Absolutely. He would keep a chain saw behind his desk, and the minute anyone started being a pain in the butt, he'd fire the thing up and start slicing the furniture. People would learn to behave."

"If Jack had your job, he would probably use the chain saw on himself."

"I have been known to lock up all sharp objects."

Phoebe did love this man. She knew how their marriage must look to outsiders—oldest daughter marries crippled man so she can go on having someone to take care of. But Giles was, in so many ways, the least needy person she had ever met. She came around to his side of the bed, sat next to him, slipped her arm through his, and rested her cheek against his shoulder. "I'm really glad you want to go."

The first summer he had come up here had been difficult. There had been so little for him to do. Then the next summer he had asked if he could restore the old wood boat that had belonged to the previous owners of the log cabin. Restoring it had taken him years, and ever since the boat was his; it was the one thing up here he really cared about.

And now he wanted to go on the canoe trip. She was glad.

Staying here wouldn't be so bad. Gwen, Dad, and Holly had already said that they weren't going, and Amy probably wouldn't either. So she wouldn't be alone. It might be odd to be here with so few people, it wouldn't seem like the lake, but she wouldn't think about it.

Jack stayed to put out the fire while the rest of the

family settled down for the night. The screen doors banged, people called to one another, and through the trees he could see the flashlights bobbing down the paths to biffies. In the moonlight he could see Amy in the large cleared patch through which the clothesline ran. The kids always flung their towels over the line in wrinkled wads that would never dry. So each night Amy checked the line, folding the dry towels and rehanging the ones that were still damp. Apparently she liked doing laundry. That seemed strange to him, but he liked watching her, a shadowy figure moving through the moonlight.

He had certainly made a mess of that conversation with her. Why had he tried to be subtle? He was the least subtle person on the planet. He should have just come out and said what he had to say. That was the only thing that worked for him.

*If you were any other person and I had met you at any other time, I would have come calling at your door, but you're Hal's daughter and I'm Gwen's son, so I'm not going to.*

He sprinkled another juice can of water on the fire. He was putting it out correctly, using perfect Boy Scout procedure. Normally he just threw a couple of buckets of water on a fire and let the big logs soak, but tonight he didn't have anything else to do, so he was doing it right, drizzling the water a little at a time. If you used too much water, it was hard to build a fire on the site the next morning.

Some footsteps rustled in the pine needles behind him. He looked up. It was Holly. She had an armful of neatly folded towels; Amy must have given them to her.

"You doing okay?" he asked. He hadn't seen a lot of her.

"I am . . . although I would have died without the sauna. I don't think I could have stood skinny-dipping in the lake every morning."

"Is the lack of privacy getting to you?" he asked. She was used to being alone in the mornings and evenings, and she had grown to like it.

"Surprisingly not. The times when I would have been alone at home, I'm with Amy, and I love being with her."

"She's good company," Jack said and dipped the juice can back into the water bucket. He was glad that the lake was working out for his sister.

"I saw you talking to Amy after the campfire."

The juice can suddenly sank to the bottom of the bucket. He must have let go of it. That was stupid. Now he would have to roll up his sleeve and fish it out.

He unbuttoned his cuff. "I wanted to be sure that she felt welcome on this canoe trip." The water in the bucket was cold. "Sometimes it seems like her family doesn't think about including her in things."

"You like her, don't you?"

"Sure. I just said she was good company, didn't I?"

He shouldn't have sounded so defensive. He had probably given himself away completely. Oh, God, what would she say?

When they were kids, Holly sometimes turned herself into Junior Mom and lectured him with a persistence that their mother never had. He supposed that she would launch into something like that now. *The fragility of a blended family, Jack . . . Phoebe and Ian aren't happy with so many changes, Jack . . . so much other stress, Jack . . .*

He was not in the mood to hear any of it. Not at all. He stood, picked up the bucket with a jerk, and dumped

220

the water on the coals. The embers hissed, and grimy puddles formed among the gray ashes, exactly the kind of puddles the Boy Scouts didn't like.

Well, forget the Boy Scouts. They might have taught him to use a compass and lash a table, but none of those merit badges were doing a thing to help him through this.

Holly spoke. "As much as I like it here, I'm starting to get concerned about things at work. I think I probably ought to go home to New York when you get back from this canoe trip."

Jack blinked. Where had that come from? Not that it was a complete surprise; she had made it clear from the beginning that if she really hated the place, she would leave. But she didn't seem to hate it. "Mom would be really disappointed."

"She would understand."

He picked up a stick and turned one of the logs over. He really shouldn't have thrown so much water. "Is there anything I can do to make you stay?"

"Short of running phone lines, probably not . . . but I haven't made up my mind. I'll see how things are at the office when I go into town tomorrow."

This was not about the office. Jack knew that. She hadn't spoken to anyone there in a couple of days. And it probably wasn't about having to pump dish water or not being able to blow-dry her hair.

Was it about him and Amy?

Holly wasn't an idiot, and she was sleeping in the same cabin with Amy and him. If anyone had a sense of how he felt about Amy, it would be her. Her notions probably wouldn't be far enough advanced for her to lecture him in the way he had imagined her doing. She probably just felt a vague unease, one she might not fully understand.

But it was enough to make her think about leaving the lake.

Amy was her pal, her summer camp buddy, the person she spent most of her time with. They got up together, went on walks together, planned their day together. What if he suddenly started romancing Amy? Holly would want to give them privacy; she would linger outside the cabin every evening, get up early every morning. She would hold back, never wanting to make plans with Amy until she was sure that Amy had had a chance to make plans with him. She would feel as awkward, as out of place, as the third party in any courtship . . . and she would leave the lake.

This really stank. He had been all worried about Phoebe and Ian, thinking that they couldn't handle any more family complications, but it turned out that Holly, his side of the family, couldn't either.

If there had been any doubt in his mind about keeping Amy at arm's length, now there was none. He didn't want Holly to leave the lake. He wanted her to like it here. He wanted her to want to come back. He wanted this to be where Mom, she, and he saw each other.

Because he was starting to love the place.

At breakfast everyone was full of talk about the canoe trip. Quickly, firmly, Phoebe announced that she wasn't going.

"Gwen and I discussed that last night," her father said. "She suggested that Thomas stay here with the two of us. We will take care of him so that both you and Giles can go."

Thomas stay here? That had never occurred to Phoebe, the little one staying home with the

222

grandparents. A lot of families did make arrangements like that.

But hers hadn't.

It wasn't that Mother hadn't loved the children, that she wasn't a wonderful grandmother, but she wasn't a playful person by nature. And any lapses in her grandparenting weren't her fault. They were Joyce's.

Maggie had been less than a year old when Ian married Joyce after the briefest of courtships. They had come back to Iowa when Phoebe herself was pregnant with Ellie.

Maggie had been a difficult, colicky baby, and even after she had grown out of the colic, she was sensitive and irritable. "She doesn't like being so helpless," Joyce had said—which had seemed absurd to Phoebe. How would a baby know whether she was helpless or not?

Joyce had allowed no one to do anything for Maggie. Phoebe supposed that such protectiveness and jealousy was natural of a single parent, but her message—*I don't want your help, I can do this*—had set a pattern for Hal and Eleanor. They had not wanted to interfere; they had not wanted to offend by doing too much.

At least that's what Phoebe had always told herself.

But this summer had been different. Thomas had become Gwen's special pet. The two of them had developed their own little routines. They had a plastic bucket which they—to no purpose whatsoever—filled with pine cones every morning. They had a special stick with which they made elaborate designs in the sandy road. They dusted the cabin together. They sorted the clean silverware together. He was her little shadow.

And it had made life easier for Phoebe.

"I don't know," Phoebe said now, "about leaving him here. I'm just not sure." She really wasn't. "He'd

223

probably do all right, but he's never been away from us before, and there would be no way of reaching us if there's a problem." She heard herself sigh. It would have been fun to go with Giles and the older kids. "I don't see how we can make it work."

Her dad suddenly smiled. "Gwen is way ahead of you on this, sweetheart."

"What do you mean?" Giles asked.

"I thought we might do a little trial run first," Gwen answered, "and see how he does here without you. The two of you could go into town and spend the night there. It will just be for one night, and if Thomas is really miserable, at least Ellie and the other kids will be here for him. He won't feel completely abandoned."

*Go into town . . . spend the night. . .* what an odd idea.

"It is true," Giles was speaking, "that Ellie being here would make all the difference to him."

"And even if we find out that the canoe trip isn't a good idea," Gwen continued, "the two of you will at least have a night in town."

"A night in town?" What were they talking about? Town was a place to be avoided. Whenever you went to town, you rushed through your errands, trying to get back to the lake as soon as possible.

"I don't suppose it would be the most thrilling trip you've ever taken," Gwen answered. "But you'll have some time to yourselves."

"Actually, it will be the most thrilling trip the two of us have had together in the last thirteen years," Giles said. "It's very generous of you, and we accept."

Phoebe stared at him. They were accepting? Just like that? She had barely finished her first cup of coffee.

He went on. "My folks took Ellie a couple of times when she was a baby, but my dad's health isn't what it

224

should be. So this is great."

"Then why not go today?" Gwen suggested. "If you left in an hour or so, you could have lunch in town."

"Leave right now?" Phoebe stared at her. "Today?"

"I know I'm going to sound like Jack"—Gwen smiled at the thought—"but what's the point of waiting? It's not like you can plan anything or make any reservations from here."

Phoebe could feel the objections welling up in her. "But we don't need groceries. Shouldn't we wait until we need to go again?"

"No, no, no." Gwen took Phoebe by the arm and turned her around to face the path toward the new cabin. "Go get ready. You are not going to do one single errand. No groceries, no laundry, nothing at the hardware store. You are not to do a single practical thing."

"Shouldn't we at least call about the permits so Holly doesn't have to go into town?"

"She would never forgive you." Gwen was shooing them down the path. "She's having telephone withdrawal and is dying to get on the phone and start throwing her weight around."

Phoebe shook her head. This had happened so fast. As soon as she and Giles were back at the new cabin, she said, "I wonder what made her offer to do this."

"Jack and Holly will say that she wants to have Thomas all to herself and that she's wired a bomb to the ignition of the station wagon to be sure that we don't return, but I think the truth is that she likes you and she wants to help you."

Phoebe stopped. "Me? Help me?"

"She remembers what raising kids is like, and she wants to do something to make it easier for you. But

225

you aren't the easiest person to help, my love."

"Is that why you accepted so quickly, because you thought I'd say no?"

"Let's just say that I knew right away that I really wanted to do it."

"And what precisely do you think we're going to do in Hibbing?" Hibbing was a town of fifteen thousand people, smaller than even Iowa City.

"What are we going to do?" Giles asked. "We're going to have sex."

And that was precisely what they did. Yes, they went out to dinner, and yes, they went out to see the big mine and they visited the high school with the crystal chandeliers and marble staircases paid for by the mining company. But mostly they had sex.

There was nothing they were supposed to be doing. No meals to prepare, no phone trees to distribute. And not once did Phoebe worry about Thomas.

And as they got in the car to drive back to the lake, she scooted over and buckled herself into the middle seat belt so that she could sit right next to Giles. She couldn't remember when she had last done that. Certainly not in the lifetime of this particular car.

"I haven't been much fun for the past year or so, have I?" she said.

Giles checked the rearview mirror and then lifted his right arm to put it around her shoulders. "Phoebe, my love, having fun has never been your strong suit."

"But it's been worse since Mother died, hasn't it?"

"Yes," he said simply. Giles never lied to her. "You've been grieving."

Her Jewish friends told her that their religion gave them one year to mourn a death. After that a person was

226

obliged to resume living to the fullest, to find life's joys again. Phoebe had always thought that sensible and healthy.

But Mother had been dead for more than a year and a half. "I'm stuck," she said, "I want to stop thinking about Mother so much, but I can't."

Giles nodded. He knew.

"Have you been worried about me?" she asked. She didn't like people worrying about her.

"Yes," he said again, "And I've been a little hurt," he added honestly. "It sometimes has seemed that being your mother's daughter was more important to you than being my wife or the children's mother."

Phoebe felt a prickling heat at the back of her neck. It spread to her face, down her arms to her hands. She was mortified. "Oh, Giles . . ."

His arm tightened around her shoulders. "Don't be so hard on yourself. We just had a wonderful twenty-four hours. Let's view this as a new start."

They were close to the cabin now, past the spot on the trail where you could first see the lake over the wild grasses. Giles was driving slowly, obviously in no hurry to get back. As they crested a little hill, they saw a small group walking toward them. It was Ellie, the two little girls, and Amy. Claire and Emily started jumping up and down when they saw the car, shrieking for Giles to stop so they could ride home on the tailgate.

The lake was the only place where the kids were allowed to sit on the tailgate of the station wagon and dangle their feet. Giles stopped the car, got out, and lowered it for them. They dashed to the side of the road to get sticks so that they could make designs in the sand while the car was moving. Amy said she would ride in back with them; Ellie squeezed into the front seat next to Phoebe. Phoebe put her arm around her.

"Thomas did great," she reported. "Gwen had Nick and Maggie and me eat over at the new cabin so he wouldn't see me so much," Ellie reported.

"I hope that was fun," Phoebe said.

Ellie ducked her head, but Phoebe could see that she was blushing. "It really was."

So Nick must not have openly favored one girl over the other.

Phoebe was grateful to him.

Giles was driving even more slowly now because of the open tailgate, but they were soon at the cabins. Holly and Gwen came out to greet them.

"Thomas just fell asleep," Gwen reported.

"Then let's not wake him," Phoebe said. She'd love seeing him, but she wasn't in any great hurry.

"What do we know about the canoe trip?" she asked Holly. "Did you get the permits?"

She had. For such a large group they needed two permits, but by leaving mid-week they were able to get them. "So you're leaving on Wednesday," Holly said.

Today was Sunday. "I guess we should start thinking about menus," Phoebe said. There was a lot to be done, planning, shopping, packing. "We'll probably need to go into town on—"

"You don't have to worry about any of that," Holly interrupted. "The outfitter is packing all the food and the equipment for you. You just have to show up."

"The outfitter?" Phoebe knew that outfitters provided such services, but it would have never occurred to her to use them. "Isn't that expensive?"

"Hideously so," Holly answered cheerfully. "But we put it all on Amy's credit card."

Amy's card? Why Amy's card?

Because Amy had more money than everyone else. Phoebe kept forgetting that.

"So what am I supposed to do with myself," Phoebe asked, and she was only half joking, "if I don't get to spend the next day and a half packing Tang and dried skim milk into Ziplock bags?"

"You could have fun," Gwen suggested.

Phoebe let herself make a face. "My husband just told me I'm no good at that."

"Then you need to start practicing."


Nick believed that when you fucked up, you ought to admit it to yourself. Lie to the rest of the world, but be straight with yourself—it was a point of honor with him. Stare in the bathroom mirror and admit that you had screwed up.

There weren't any bathroom mirrors up here—there being no bathrooms—but he could admit it anyway. He had loused up this canoe trip something fierce, so much so that he was almost considering apologizing—and that certainly was not a part of his code.

He had not wanted to go out in the wilderness alone with Jack. Right away he understood that this was a mission of mercy. Let poor fatherless Nick grieve. That bugged him. He could handle his shit himself. And a canoe trip? What a mismatch that would be—Jack could start fires, Jack could split wood, Jack could have probably melted down the canoe and built a B-52 bomber out of it. And what could good old Nick do? Nothing, zippo.

So like the jackass idiot that he was, he had suggested that everyone should come . . . just to protect himself from feeling like an ignoramus. Now the trip had become this huge, expensive production, and of course he was still feeling like an ignoramus.

They were renting four canoes—three seventeen-foot canoes and one fifteen-footer. There had been a lot of discussion about who should be in which canoes. There would, he was sure, be a lot of discussion about everything; these people didn't do anything without a lot of discussion. This subject simply happened to be the first.

Maggie wanted to be in a canoe with him. It took him two seconds to figure that one out. She was being smart about it, never saying that she wanted to be with him; she simply objected to every other arrangement. But the idea was stupid. Neither he nor she knew a thing about canoes. They had to be split up.

Ultimately Nick ended up with Jack, but they were going to have the two little boys riding in the middle of their canoe. Ellie's parents had the two little girls and a knapsack full of Barbie dolls in the middle of theirs. Maggie would be in the last of the larger canoes with her parents, while Ellie and the ice skater had the smaller one to themselves.

Canoes—Nick learned—had a front and a back, a bow and a stern. And there was a real power ladder about who sat where. The person in the stern was the boss. He—or she—got to steer the boat. Nick would be hard pressed to say that any canoe stroke was interesting, but the person in the front had only two strokes, forward and reverse—"straightaway" and "backwater" was the lingo—while the person in the back led a life of fun-filled drama with an arsenal of at least four or five strokes.

So it was cool to sit in back. It was less cool to sit in front. It was totally uncool to sit in the middle, because you didn't have a real seat and just had to squirm your way around the big trail packs. So the dads—Giles, Ian, and Jack—were all in back.

Ellie had automatically gone to sit in the front of her canoe. After all, she was a kid riding with an adult, and adults always kept the cool jobs for themselves.

"What on earth are you doing?" the skater called out instantly. She went over to the smaller canoe . . . and Nick had to admit that it was something to watch her move. It was like that with coaches who had once been really good wrestlers. You could tell just from the way they walked, and her walk was even better than theirs. Her torso hardly moved. From her collarbone through her rib cage down to her pelvis, her body remained in a clean, straight line. "You aren't expecting *me* to steer this thing, are you?"

Ellie turned and looked at her. "Don't you want to? It's more fun to be in the stern."

"Not for me it wouldn't be. I've never sterned in my life. Actually, I ought to be with Claire and Emily playing Barbies. I'm probably very good at Barbies."

Nick had never paid a minute's attention to ice skating, but he did know that Amy had a gold medal from the Olympics. Maybe that's why she could stand there and admit that she couldn't stern a canoe without looking like a doofus because she knew she was really great at something else.

He'd have to remember that.

"And," she continued, waving Ellie out of the canoe, "to be in the stern you have to be power-mad, and I am terrified of power and responsibility."

"I'm not power-mad," Ellie protested, laughing.

"I know it doesn't seem like it," Amy returned, "but you're an oldest sister. You have to be power-mad. Now get into the back of this stupid boat or we'll both

231

drown."

This arrangement left Ellie in the stern, and Maggie not even in the bow like Nick, but in the middle, between her parents. Maggie was clearly not thrilled with the arrangement.

So they set off. The first lake was long and narrow. They launched at its tip, and there was a small cluster of cabins near the launch site, but after fifteen minutes of paddling there was nothing on the banks except trees. No power lines, no road, just water and trees—that was all there was between here and Canada.

At the end of the first lake, they had to portage—unload everything and carry the canoes and packs on a trail around some rocks and swirling currents. Jack asked him if he thought he could carry one of the canoes. "Giles is strong," Jack said, "but his footing isn't sure enough. So will you try?"

"You'll have to show me how," Nick answered.

It was fairly straightforward. The canoes had padded shoulder pads attached to the center crosspiece—"thwart" Jack called it—so you carried the canoe overhead like a gigantic hat, its weight resting on your shoulders. It wasn't horribly heavy, maybe sixty pounds or so, but it was mostly awkward. If you looked down, you could see your feet, but if you looked straight ahead, all you saw was the inside of the canoe.

Then they loaded up again, and Nick wasn't surprised to see that this time Maggie was in the bow of her canoe, and her mom was sitting on the packs in the middle.

They ate lunch at the next portage, paddled a couple more hours, then started looking for a place to camp. It was still pretty early, just the middle of the afternoon, but the kids were clearly getting restless.

He hadn't known what to expect. The maps noted "established campsites," but these sites made the bunkhouse at the lake look like the Ritz. The one they chose was on an island. It had a couple of nearly flat tent sites and a fire circle, but no tables or shelters of any sort.

"Where do we pee?" the skater asked cheerfully. "In the woods?"

"There should be some sort of latrine away from the water." Ellie's mom gestured toward the center of the island. "It's probably down that path."

The kids all dashed down the path and then returned to report that there was a box with a hole in it, and you were supposed to sit on the hole, but if instead you looked down the hole, there was—

Ellie's mom stopped them. "We get the idea."

Apparently that's all there was to the latrine, just a box over a pit. There wasn't even a little house around it. The woods were starting to sound pretty good to Nick.

"It's times like this"—Jack was suddenly at his elbow, speaking softly—"that you're glad to be a man."

That was for sure.

Nick had finally, *finally* figured out something about Jack—he had the hots for the skater. Nick wasn't entirely sure how he knew; it wasn't like Jack was flirting with her, putting the moves on her, or even looking at her too much, but Nick knew anyway. He spent too much of his life observing grown-ups, trying to predict their behavior so he could keep one step ahead of them, to be wrong about something like this.

And while it should have been cool to finally have some information on Jack, Nick found that it wasn't giving him any power . . . because Jack wasn't doing anything. Nick supposed that that was admirable. Weird perhaps, but admirable.

Clearly not something his own father had done.

Nope, his dear old dad, his pops, hadn't resisted a thing. Nick wasn't accusing the guy of rape; Val would have been a willing participant. She might talk a good game, but in the end she did whatever she wanted to do.

He knew nothing about his father. "He was just a boy," that's all Val and Barb would ever say. "He was just a boy." She wouldn't even give him a name. It really pissed him off. How the hell were you supposed to grow into a man when your father had been "just a boy"?

The guy might be a rat, Nick was well aware of that possibility. But he might be a decent enough sort who'd never been told that Val had changed her mind about giving the baby up for adoption. Maybe he'd be somebody like Giles or Hal or—

Nick stopped himself. He wasn't going to turn this into an Afterschool Special, a made-for-TV movie with ninety minutes of heartwarming complications followed by a bittersweet happy ending. Dads were not the solution to much these days. As far as he could tell, his friends were getting next to nothing from their dads or stepfathers. The men did three things—they drove to work, they worked, and they got mad. They would come to soccer games or wrestling matches and yell. They would yell at their sons, they would yell at the coaches, they would yell at the refs. He and Brian had always said they were better off not having dads at all.

*Brian . . . what's it like? What's being dead like?*

Suddenly he wanted to be alone. He went over to Giles. He didn't mind asking permission from Giles. "Is it okay if I take off for a bit? We're on an island. I can't

234

get lost."

"Go ahead. Just keep your eye out for firewood."

The island was a rock-studded mound poking up from the lake, and Nick started to climb toward the center. The only path was the one to the latrine, but it was easy enough to move without one. Some of the tree limbs were low; he ducked under them. The sheets of rock were covered with silvery, gray-green lichen, and where there was as no rock, tree roots arched out of the sandy soil. Pine cones crunched under his feet.

He could tell when he reached the high point of the island, but he couldn't see anything, just the thick, furrowed bark of the trees. He didn't know their t, not dense and packed like Christmas trees. One of the branches was low, and testing it with his hands, he swung himself up and started to climb.

It had been ages since he had climbed a tree. In fact, he didn't know if he ever had. They'd never had a good one at any of the places they had lived.

He eased himself up to the last of the thick limbs. It didn't make any sense to go higher; the branches wouldn't support him. His view was framed and filtered by other trees. Some of their needles were blue-green and soft-looking while others were paler and twisted. He could see the lake, and from here it almost looked black, but the water was so pure that they were just dipping their cups straight into the lake to drink. It was unbelievable that anything was that clean anymore. It must be amazing up here in the autumn with the birches firing up golden and the flocks of birds and geese flying in V's overhead.

And suddenly it seemed so wrong, overwhelmingly wrong, that he was here and Brian was dead.

Brian used to wonder if he should wait. There were

such advances being made; maybe someday they'd find the drug that would work for him, the drug that would keep each day from being a torment.

It was impossible to imagine that kind of suffering, and one thing that Brian had liked about Nick was that Nick never pretended that he understood. "You never say that you know how I feel," Brian used to say. "That means a lot."

So how could Nick say what was right, what was wrong? How could he know what thoughts Brian had had? How could he judge? But it was really something up here. Brian should have seen it.

A heavy rustling broke into his thoughts. Someone else was climbing the island. He heard twigs snap, pebbles scatter.

"Nick? Nick?"

He peered down through the pine boughs. It was Maggie. She was keeping her voice down. "Nick?"

"I'm up here."

She tilted her head back. "In the tree?"

"Yes."

"Oh . . ." She was a little disconcerted. "Could you come down?"

He didn't answer. Instead of climbing down, he inched along the limb, and just as it started to bend, he dropped, landing neatly like a gymnast. He was, standing closer to her than he expected.

"I've been looking for you," she said.

"You found me."

"I hear a friend of yours committed suicide." There was a little thrill in her voice.

Oh, great. He hadn't wanted Ellie and her to know. He had asked Aunt Gwen not to tell them.

And Aunt Gwen wouldn't have. "How did you find

that out? Eavesdrop city?"

"My mother told me. She doesn't believe in keeping things from me. How did he do it?"

How did he do it? Nick kicked a pine cone. What kind of question was that? Did she really want an answer? Little globlets of brain tissue on the living room couch?

"Believe it or not, I don't know." He sat down on a flat plate of rock. "He was in a psychiatric hospital, and they aren't releasing any details. I suppose I'll find out sooner or later."

"Why did he do it?"

Maggie sat down next to him. Her thigh was right up against his leg. He could feel its warmth. He expected her to move away, but she didn't. And in a moment the contact lengthened as she moved her leg even closer.

He knew what it meant.

*Did you figure on that, Brian? That your frying yourself would make me sexy?* Brian would like that. He would laugh.

Nick had first done a girl at fourteen. He had read all these old books—Phillip Roth, *Catcher in the Rye,* all about the terminal sexual frustration of the young male. Well, it wasn't like that anymore, ladies and gentlemen of middle America. Girls were aggressive. They started things, and they intended you to finish.

Admittedly he didn't hang out with the most well adjusted of young ladies, and usually a whole lot else was going on besides a girl's passion for his pasty white body. There was a bigger scheme; she was trying to get back at her mom, her stepdad, or sometimes even her regular boyfriend.

There was nothing, not anything, that Nick hated more than being a pawn in someone else's scheme. That wasn't for him. It was better just to jerk off.

But of course he had his reputation to think about. He couldn't have people thinking he was saving himself for marriage. So he had developed another way. He scared the daylights out of the girl. That way everyone saved face. She got to be the one to say no, and he got to pretend to be frustrated.

So Nick let Maggie move closer still, and he answered her questions, about how Brian had been depressed, seriously, chronically, clinically depressed, that some of the drugs would help a little for a while, but then he would be worse.

"When did you talk to him last?" She was fascinated; it didn't occur to her to offer sympathy. "Did his parents feel like it was all their fault?"

Nick could see where her thoughts were going—standard teen stuff, kill yourself so everyone will feel bad afterward. But it hadn't been like that. Brian had hated what this would do to his mother. The thought had probably kept him alive for another year.

Maggie was sitting really close to him now, and rather than answer he put his hand on her leg. She leaned forward and kissed him. She knew what she was doing, and all of a sudden that was seeming like a fine idea. She wanted it, and he certainly did too, and it would be easy enough to—

But you couldn't survive in the jungle giving in to temptation. You had to hold fierce to your resolve. Nick made up his own rules, and the only difference between him and the other kids who were also out in the jungle alone was that he stuck to his.

So it was fear-time, scare the girl. He pulled Maggie against him tight and hard. She was a good-sized girl, but he was strong. He rolled over with her and used his knee to open her legs. The rock must have been cold and hard against her back. He thrust his tongue into her mouth and ground against her, letting her have it for a minute or two, kind of mean and angry-like. Only he wasn't just angry-like. He was angry. Brian was no sideshow. He hadn't suffered for this girl's amusement.

It should have been over by now. She should be protesting, she should be scared. *No, Nick, no, please stop.* And he would instantly turn himself into a poster child for the date-rape laws. "You said you wanted to stop," he would say when the girl started looking hurt and rejected.

But Maggie wasn't reading the right script. Nick could feel her flattening her back, pulling her legs up, giving him a better angle at her crotch. She was squirming. She liked this. It turned her on.

That made him sick. He sat up, straddling her, one leg on either side of her thighs. "So is this a turn-on for you, guys whose friends commit suicide? Is that who you do?"

She looked stunned, horrified. She drew a breath, about to speak, but he didn't want to hear. He scrambled up and plunged down the hill. He was running, and pine needles were snapping against his face. He almost lost his footing as the pine cones rolled across the rocks. At the bottom of the hill he stopped and wiped a hand across his face.

Shit. That had not gone according to plan. He had really pissed her off.

What a major mess lay ahead. When you had a fight with a girl at school, maybe she and her friends would be cold and prickly for a while, but who cared? Up here all the adults were going to get involved, and it was going to be hell on Aunt Gwen.

Even Val and Barb couldn't have caused this kind of trouble.

He was down by the water now, and there was nothing to do but circle the island shoreline until he reached the campsite. He climbed over an outcropping of rocks and almost landed on Ellie, who was stowing two life jackets in a canoe. She was wearing a bright yellow Iowa Hawkeyes sweatshirt, khaki shorts, and heavy hiking boots with thick socks rising out of the top. A navy fanny pack bunched the sweatshirt in stiff folds at her waist. As fashion looks went, it was imperfect, but if he had owned hiking boots or a fanny pack, he would probably be wearing them too.

She looked up. "Oh, hi. We don't have much wood here. I was about to paddle over to the shore. There are a couple of brush heaps."

Giles had asked him to keep his eye out for firewood. He hadn't. "Who's going with you?" He pointed at the second life jacket.

"My mom. She'll be here in a second."

But it was her dad who appeared at the top of the rocks. He had heard her. "No, sweetheart, you're getting dear old dad instead. At least you will when he gets down these rocks."

Going up and down the rocks was hard for Giles. "I can go with her," Nick heard himself say.

"That would be great by me," Giles said. "You don't mind, do you, Ellie?"

Ellie was suddenly busy, checking stuff in her fanny pack, not looking up. "It's fine," she mumbled.

She headed toward the bow of the canoe. "No way," Nick called out. "I'm still a major league amateur. You have to do the hard stuff."

She brushed her hair off her face. "Okay . . . if you're

sure."

"I'm sure."

It wasn't far to the mainland. Ellie didn't say anything, and that was fine with him. She steered them in parallel to the shore, and at the first brush heap they were able to break off dry wood while still in the canoe.

But the second wasn't so conveniently located. "I'll get out," she said.

She was closer to the more solid ground. It made sense for her to get out, but all of a sudden Nick shivered. There was something wrong with this brush heap.

He never had thoughts like that—instincts, he guessed they were called—but he couldn't get rid of this one. There was something wrong. He couldn't let her go.

"No, Ellie, I'll do it."

He tried not to move too quickly, he tried to be careful, but he didn't want to dawdle. Otherwise she'd argue with him, and he didn't know what he could say without sounding like some sort of macho jerk.

He hadn't paid any attention when the canoes were first being loaded, but once they were out on the water, he could see that his and Jack's canoe rode lowest in the water; Jack had taken the heaviest packs himself. That's what guys like Jack did, take the heaviest packs, climb the risky paths first.

Nick's first step, the one that took him out of the canoe, was fine. And his second one was okay too. So he tested his third step. The tangle of branches and brush seemed solid, but just as he was lifting his back foot, he heard the wood crack, and it wasn't just a single crack but a whole series of little firecrackers. Everything was still cracking and popping as the wood

241

gave way. He slipped and then there was a pain, a slicing pain, followed by warmth, warmth and liquid and pain.

"Nick, Nick . . . what happened?"

"I don't know." He was feeling strange. Weak. Woozy.

Ellie was fumbling with her fanny pack. She pulled out something shiny and raised it to her mouth. Three shrill blasts spat out across the water. It must have been a whistle.

She was blurring. He felt like she was getting farther away, although he knew she was coming closer. The pain in his leg was fierce. *Was this what it was like, Brian? Is this what it felt like?*

## CHAPTER 12

THE BLAST WAS SHRILL. IT WAS INSTANTLY FOLLOWED by two more. Then a pause. Then another three blasts. The pause made it unmistakable. This wasn't a kid playing. This was the international distress signal, coming from somewhere across the lake. A moment later Jack was in a canoe, sweeping it through the water. He knew how to paddle a canoe alone. You sit in the bow, facing the stern. His dad had told him that when he had been canoeing in Boy Scouts.

The blasts sounded again. He could hear shouts from the campsite, but he was already off, following the sound. It was coming from behind a pile of brush on the shore. He grew closer, saw the canoe. He called out. "Hello?"

"Dad?" It was Ellie.

"No, it's Jack."

He rounded the brush heap. Nick was at the shoreline, tangled in the brush, slumped over, and Ellie was in water to her knees. "The pile gave way. He's caught on something."

Jack pulled the canoe next to her and splashed into the water. He felt along Nick's leg. It was clear what had happened. Some idiot had dropped an open knife. It had wedged in the brush and Nick had fallen onto it. His leg was clammy with blood.

Jack pulled off his shirt. "Okay, when I lift him, you get this underneath. Get it on top on his cut and hold it there. Really keep the pressure on." Ellie was nodding. She understood. "You won't pass out or anything?"

She shook her head. He got his arms under Nick's knee and around his shoulders. He lifted, and Ellie slipped her hand underneath. "I've got it."

Another canoe was coming; Jack could hear the splash of their paddles. "What happened?" It was Phoebe; Amy was with her. "What can we do?"

"Get that canoe out of the way." He nodded toward Ellie's canoe; it was full of firewood. "Then can you get into this one and hold it steady?" Jack had already turned with Nick in his arms. Ellie was bent low, still holding her hand in place.

Phoebe swung herself in the empty canoe. The thwarts kept Jack from laying Nick in flat, so he let Phoebe cradle him in a crouch. She reached out to place her hand over Ellie's; the pressure on the wound never let up. As Ellie pulled her hand away, Phoebe gasped sharply.

"We need to get him to a hospital, don't we?" Jack asked.

Phoebe nodded.

Before they left, Ian had spent what had seemed like

243

hours discussing with the outfitter what to do in an emergency. Jack had taken it as a typical Ian make-everyone-else-wait power move. But to give Ian credit, it was good to know that there were ranger stations equipped with radios that they could call in little airplanes whose pontoons could land on water.

Ellie was now in the bow in the canoe. The legs of her jeans were dark and wet; a watery red trail ran down her arm. Phoebe was keeping pressure on the wound.

"What can I do?" Amy asked. She was still in the smaller canoe.

"Go back," Phoebe said. "Tell Giles to start cutting butterfly bandages about an inch and a half long."

"And tell the others to take down the pup tent and put together a trail pack," Jack added as he got into Nick's canoe. "We're going to have to go to the ranger station."

Amy nodded and quickly pivoted in her seat so that she too was in the bow facing the stern. Jack gave her a helpful shove.

He leaned over Phoebe's shoulder to look at Nick. The boy was ashen, and if Phoebe took the pressure off, the bleeding would start up again. Jack told Ellie to start paddling.

"Do you know how far we are from a ranger station?" Phoebe asked. "Is it closer than where we launched?"

"By about an hour, and remember, there may not be anyone at the launch. We could still have to drive for another twenty minutes and then figure out who to call."

"Are there portages?"

"Yes."

"Then Giles shouldn't go. You and Ian will have to."

Jack grunted. He supposed it made sense, but he certainly would rather go with Giles. They would need to go fast, and Ian would want to check the maps, think,

244

deliberate. He would want to be in charge. He would want to tell Jack what to do.

Everything was ready for them at the campsite. A poncho was spread out, and all the first-aid supplies were lined up. The butterfly bandages were cut and ready. Joyce and Maggie were over at the kitchen packs, apparently making sandwiches, preparing a trail pack. Ian was taking down the little pup tent. Amy had made good time across the water

Of course she had. Pound for pound, who was the single strongest person here? It wasn't any of the men; it was Amy, beautiful, delicate-looking Amy. Even if you dropped the pound-for-pound requirement, she had more brute strength than anyone but Jack himself. And her endurance was probably better than even his. Why was he for one second even considering going with Ian?

Giles was doing the actual bandaging while Phoebe was holding the skin together. They were wearing rubber gloves from the first-aid kit, and the smell of alcohol rose from their hands. They had sterilized them even before putting on the gloves. Joyce and Maggie were still working, and the kids were sitting quietly, out of the way. Whatever else Jack might think of this family, they knew what to do in an emergency.

"I'm going to take Amy," Jack said to Phoebe. "She and I are going to the ranger station."

"Amy?" Phoebe glanced up, startled. "Why? What good will she be?"

"Muscle. She's stronger than Ian. Her endurance is probably better than mine. We've already paddled for six hours today, and the ranger station is another five. She's the only one with that kind of conditioning."

"You're right about that." Phoebe looked back over her shoulder. "Ellie, I think Amy is in Jack's tent,

245

finding dry socks for him. Go ask her if she's willing to go to the ranger station with him."

Ian overheard. "Wait, wait." He set the rolled pup tent on the ground. "Let me get this straight. You can't be thinking of sending *Amy*?"

Jack wanted to hit him.

It was Phoebe who answered. "No, Ian, we aren't going to wait, not while you get this straight, not for anything. Face it, Amy's stronger and in better shape than any of the rest of us."

"But Amy? She has no outdoor skills."

"Jack has enough for the both of them. We need muscle. That she has. We always think of her as having sequins on her brain, but she is a professional athlete."

*Argue with that,* Jack dared him.

He couldn't; he wasn't stupid. He couldn't say that he was in better shape than Amy; he wasn't. He tightened his lips, not liking anything about this. Then he spoke. "Your boots are wet, Jack. I've got an extra pair of really good wool socks if you'd like to take them."

Jack wasn't sure he had heard right. Ian was being decent about this. Jack supposed he needed to be gracious in return. "That would be nice."

*I don't want your stupid socks even if they are wool.*

But wool socks were great. Jack didn't own any because he could never bring himself to spend that kind of money on comfort.

Ian went off to get the socks, and Jack knelt by Nick. Nick was biting his lip, struggling not to cry out. Jack touched his arm. "Hold on, kid. You'll be fine."

Jack did believe that. If the butterfly bandages didn't hold, Phoebe and Giles would keep pressure on the wound all night if they had to. They were that sort of people. Nick wouldn't bleed to death, but he did need to have the wound stitched and a doctor check his tendon.

Ian handed Jack the socks, and they were thick and light and soft, exactly what you wanted when your boots were wet. "Thanks," Jack said.

"My younger sister's usually the one in the family with all the right clothes. She and I seem to bc changing places."

When the stakes were high enough, apparently even Ian could be a good sport. It was the nickel-and-dime stuff that made him impossible.

Amy was already down by the canoes. They were taking the smaller one. They had two packs, a bulky, light one with their sweatshirts and sleeping bags, a smaller, heavier one with the tent, the food, and a few pieces of equipment. Jack changed his socks while Amy went to get an extra paddle.

It was five-thirty; their light would hold until nine. Jack glanced at the map. They could camp about an hour from the ranger station and then reach it just after dawn the next morning. It would be a long haul, but he was sure they could make it.

"Ready?" he asked Amy.

"Ready," she answered.

The person in bow sets pace, and Amy set a swift one. If it had been anyone else, Jack would have said something about the need to pace themselves, but Amy had to know her strength. She must know more about her body than anyone he had met. So he kept quiet. They shot through the water, their paddles digging deep, then lifting and circling through the air in perfect unison. Drops of water danced off the end of the paddles, arcs of ripples splaying out on either side of the canoe. They didn't speak as their muscles warmed and loosened.

Amy pulled off her sweatshirt. She was wearing her black bathing suit, the one that was cut surprisingly high in front, almost to her collarbone, but then swooped low in the back.

Jack had never seen anything like Amy's back. He had noticed it the first time he had seen her in a bathing suit. Her muscles were lightly, even delicately defined, curving across her back in graceful arcs, but they were so well developed that it was almost as if she didn't have shoulder blades.

They sped through the portages. Amy could carry both packs at once, the bulky one on her back, the smaller one on her chest while Jack carried the canoe. At the end of each portage, he stepped to the water's edge, hoisted the canoe off his shoulders, and flipped it into the water. It landed with a splash and a little aluminum echo. Amy unloaded her packs directly into the canoe, took up her paddle, and was ready to go.

They traveled on, making excellent time. The rhythm of Amy's strokes was nearly perfect, never wavering, never intensifying. He felt completely in tune with her, with his body, with hers. The hours passed. Their shadows on the water lengthened as the sun fell. They approached the spot where he had planned to camp; they paddled beyond it.

It was as if time had disappeared. There was no past, no future, just the moment and the tightening and lengthening of muscle, the movement of arms and back. The task, the moment, was all that mattered, not the goal, not the reason, just the doing, the now. This was what Jack lived for, moments like this. The tool in your hand, whether a hammer, a drill, or a canoe and paddle, became a part of you, an extension of yourself, and every motion sang with the harmony of you and your task and your tools.

And to be out here, away from phones, beepers, and clients, answerable to no one but himself and his partner, it was—

Was it how his dad had felt? He had commanded a fast-attack submarine, and most of his missions had been covert. Jack used to bug him for details, and his father would give him only vague answers. Jack now supposed that the missions involved things like slipping into a Soviet port to photograph its fleet, the kind of thing that you couldn't have your kid bragging about on the playground.

When the boat was on these missions, it would be alone, out of even radio contact for days. Its C.O. would be answerable to no one for anything except the safety of his men and the result of his mission.

Maybe that's what his father had liked about his career, not the deskwork or the ranks and saluting, but being out on a submarine, deep underwater, the one place you didn't have the admirals breathing down your neck every instant. And all that caution, that insistence on doing everything right, on never using duct tape for anything, maybe that was one of the ways you kept the admirals off your back.

*Did you hate authority as much as I do, Dad?*

Jack suddenly and with complete certainty knew the answer. Yes, his father had hated authority, had hated it maybe even more than Jack did.

Mom occasionally mentioned how his dad had been one of the few enlisted men at the Naval Academy, a tough coal miner's kid with a few years' service under his belt. The other midshipmen would have been suburban college boys.

That couldn't have been easy.

But you don't get ahead in the military by rebelling. All his career John T. Wells, Sr., had played the game and followed the rules.

Then what had happened? They went and made him an admiral, stuck him behind a desk so that he was breathing down the necks of the guys who were having all the fun.

*I couldn't have choked it back that long.* Jack knew that about himself.

But he wasn't a tough coal miner's kid. He was an admiral's son. It was probably a whole lot easier to take risks and make changes when you had a little privilege in your background.

Jack shifted uneasily in the cold aluminum canoe seat. He didn't like to think of himself as being privileged, but he had been. And it wasn't fair to his dad to pretend otherwise, not when the guy had struggled for so long.

The sky had darkened, and they were traveling by the moon, its pale golden light marking a highway across the black water. They were only fifteen minutes from the ranger station, but there was another portage, rocky and steep.

"I hate to stop when we're so close," Jack said, "but it's too hard to carry a canoe in the dark."

"We have a flashlight." Amy looked back over her shoulder as she spoke. Before he could shake his head, she went on. "My sense of balance is good, and I'm very used to falling. I know how. Let me carry the canoe."

Jack paused. Let her carry the canoe? He always took the hardest jobs, he always carried the heaviest load even among other men, and Amy was a woman.

*Okay, Dad, what would you have done? You didn't*

*have girls on your boats.*

His father would have done what was best for his crew and the boat. Amy's sense of balance had to be better than Jack's, and she was plenty strong. Her sex was irrelevant. She should carry the canoe.

They went slowly. Leaving the packs behind, Jack walked sideward, pointing the flashlight at her feet, his other arm up to steady the canoe if she stumbled. But she never wavered.

At the end of the portage, he helped her lower the back tip of the canoe to the ground. He lifted the front end so that she could slip out from underneath. He flipped it into the water, and they went back to get the other packs.

"You're very strong," he said.

"Of course I am," she answered. "I don't know why that always surprises people."

"I suppose it's because you're pretty."

How irrelevant that seemed right now—what she looked like. She was so like him, all instinct and motion. That's what mattered, not her beauty.

He had made a hash of his conversation with her before the campfire last week, but it was probably better to have things out in the open. He would take honesty over dignity any day.

When they were on the water again, they could see a light halfway up the lake. It was the ranger station.

"We made good time," she said.

"We made very good time," he answered.

The ranger station was simply a little cabin with a big antenna. It was set up on a rise so that people could see it from anywhere on the lake. Jack turned the canoe toward the shore. There was a narrow strip of sand at the water's edge. Amy hopped out of the canoe, and

251

with his weight keeping the stern low in the water, she easily pulled the canoe onto the shore by the painter rope attached to the bow.

"I need to pee," she announced as he got out of the canoe. "You go distract the ranger while I sneak into his biffy."

Jack started off toward the cabin, and Amy went to the little outhouse at the edge of the woods. He saw a small campsite set back from the water. He whistled, caught her attention, and pointed it out to her.

The ranger was straightforward and affable, radioing for a plane immediately. "It's great that you came in now," he said. "They can get themselves organized tonight and then take off the minute it is even half-light. They should get to your people just as the sun is rising."

Jack thanked him, took the lantern and pot of hot water the man offered, and went back to the little campsite by the water. Amy had unrolled the tent and had the first flickerings of a fire going. The tinder was flaming brightly, and the bigger pieces of kindling were ignited.

Jack hung the lantern on a tree. "And your brother said you had no outdoors skills."

"I don't. But I've got a visual memory. I conjured up a picture of what fires looked like before the match was lit and did my best to duplicate that."

The technique had clearly worked. Jack started to assemble the tent poles. Amy began to unpack the food. He watched her. She had put on her sweater, and its chunky knit hid the clean, hard muscles of her arms and back.

Her fire was doing well. It was an A-frame with a little tepee built on the crosspiece. Her brother laid a tepee fire; her sister built a classic A-frame; he himself

252

combined the two in the way Amy had done. Any one of them worked fine, but when she had "conjured up" an image of a fire, it had been his.

"You knew that you, not your brother, ought to come, didn't you?" He didn't wait for an answer. "If no one else had thought of it, would you have said anything, or would you have just let Ian go?"

Her answer was immediate. "Oh, I would have let Ian go."

"Why? If you were sure you were right . . . why not stand up for yourself?"

"To Phoebe and Ian? You have to be kidding."

"Why not? If you know you were right."

"Well, it wasn't like they were completely wrong." She poured some of the ranger's hot water into their smaller pot, set it on the grate to reheat, and emptied packets of dried soup into their cups. "Ian would have done all right."

He started to unpack the sandwiches and dried fruit that was the rest of their meal. "Are you like this about everything?"

There was a chance that she wouldn't even understand his question. She might be so passive about everything, letting agents, managers, whatever, make so many of her decisions that she didn't even know that it was happening.

"You don't stay where I am by being someone's puppet."

So she did understand. "Go on."

The water was hot. Pulling the cuff of her sweater down over her hand for a pot holder, she poured water into the cups and handed him one. She took hers and sat down, leaning against a big rock. She told him about how she and these two other skaters had gradually

253

accepted a lot of responsibility for their own careers, doing their own choreography so they weren't dependent on other people's ideas, now even planning their own tour. "You don't have to be creative to do well as an amateur, you just have to be expressive. But to last for any length of time, you do need to be imaginative. And fortunately the three of us are."

The broth was thin and salty, but the powdered stuff always was. "Go on."

She sat down again. "Everyone says that figure skating is the one sport in which things get easier when you turn professional. Athletically that's true. The Olympic-division skaters do routines that are technically harder than what we do. But there's so much more to this than just the skating. If you're going to keep selling tickets, you have to be a celebrity. The public has to love you."

People didn't understand fame, she said. When it first happened, you were too busy to know about it. In the weeks leading up to the Olympics, she hadn't realized that her face was everywhere. It would have thrilled her, there was no question about that; it was one of her dreams to walk into a store and see her face repeated again and again on magazine after magazine. But she hadn't gone anywhere during those weeks; she had either been practicing or been holed up in a little conference room giving the interviews that were behind those cover stories. Even after the Olympics, walking through the airport to fly home, she had been surrounded by other people and too distracted to notice the newsstands. Of course, she had seen individual copies of the magazines later, but that wasn't the same as seeing people buying them, reading them.

Then publicity became something to worry about—

were you getting the right coverage? were the good photos used? how misleading were the quotes? Publicity brought no joy. The best possible feeling was relief.

"What's the good part about being famous?" Jack wanted to know.

"You can get things done," she said. When you were famous, you got your phone calls returned. "Amy Legend is on the line." People noticed that. They opened their checkbooks, their hearts. An ill child got air transport to a bigger hospital, and a hotel chain donated a room to his family. A desperate blood bank suddenly had a hundred donors snaking a line down their hallway. A water-soaked school library received boxes and boxes of children's books and plenty of volunteers to clean, catalogue, and shelf. "Henry still cares about winning the professional competitions. Tommy and I can't make ourselves care about that anymore, but we're more satisfied, we're more content than Henry because we do more good."

"Is that why you thought I ought to go work for the Red Cross?"

She shrugged. "Maybe. Doing good works for me."

Jack finished his sandwich. Amy shook open the little bag of dried apricots, took a few for herself, and handed him the rest. The little fire danced and flickered. The wind rustled in the pines. Jack sat forward, his elbows on his knees, his hands clasped loosely. Suddenly he felt a cool splash against the back of his hand. It was a raindrop.

Amy looked up at the sky. She must have felt the rain too. "Is it raining?" The moonlight was still bright. "It can't be raining. The sky's been clear all day. How can it rain?"

She did not want it to rain, she wanted to go on sitting

by the fire, but what she wanted didn't make any difference to Nature. It was definitely raining. Jack stuffed the last of the apricots into his mouth and stood up. He started kicking the fire apart; it would be easier to put out that way. "You can keep asking how all night, but you'll be talking to yourself because I'm going to be somewhere dry."

Amy hopped up. She started moving quickly, scooping up the trash, gathering the dirty dishes. "It's okay just to give these cups a good rinse and call them clean, isn't it?"

Of course it was. "Go in the tent. I'll do this. There's no sense in both of us getting wet."

"Don't be silly. I can do my share."

The rain was increasing. A gusty wind blew clouds across the moon; the light grew dimmer. Amy dunked the cups into the remains of the hot water. Jack scrambled the rest of their equipment into the Duluth pack. He carried the pack back to the water's edge, stowing it under the overturned canoe, quickly arranging their tin pot, cups, and plates on top of the canoe.

Amy helped. "Why are we doing this?" she asked, balancing a plate on the curving canoe bottom. "If we want the dishes to air-dry, this may not be the best spot."

The raindrops were hitting the aluminum canoe with light metallic pings. Little puddles were already gathering near the rims of the plates.

"It's in case of bears." Bears weren't too big a problem around here, not like in Yellowstone, where the bears had gotten so used to humans that they could open dumpsters and pop car trunks. "If a bear tries to get at the pack, the plates will rattle and scare him away. It's good that your family still uses metal plates and cups. Plastic doesn't make enough of a racket."

"Two tin plates and a three-cup pot are going to scare a *bear*?"

She had a point. "At least it will wake us up and scare us."

"I can't wait," she said.

Jack could feel the rain starting to bead up in his hair, but everything seemed to be packed. He prodded Amy, urging her to get under cover. He detoured back to the fire site to grab the lantern.

When he got to the tent, she was already inside. He lifted the flap and carefully passed the lantern in, not releasing it until he felt her grip it firmly. Then he crawled in.

He had to sit cross-legged. The tent was an old-fashioned pup tent with triangular ends and steeply sloping walls. It was no more than seven feet long and four and a half feet wide. Its center ridgepole was only a bit more than four feet from the ground.

Amy was holding the lantern at arm's length. Its green metal shade was beaded with raindrops, and the whole thing was hissing. "Why is it making this awful sound?"

Jack had no idea. "Because it is. But don't worry. It's not about to blow up." He looked around the tent for something to do with it. A shiny metal hook on a ribbed tape was sewn into the center seam. He took the lantern and hung it up, letting go of it gently, hoping that its weight wouldn't pull the tent down.

"You're going to bump your head," Amy pointed out.

The lantern was right in the middle of everything, and its base swung about three feet above the tent floor. "You're just as likely to bump your head as me," he

257

said.

"No, I'm not."

She started unrolling the sleeping bags, spreading them out. She knew that he was watching her, waiting for her to bump into the lantern. So she started to make a show of it, flinging her arm, thrusting her shoulder, tossing her head, always coming within a half inch of the lantern but never touching it. And she did all this without ever looking at it. She simply knew where it was. What a sense of space she had.

"How do you do that?"

"I don't know. I just do it . . . although this is easy, because there's also a sound and a temperature change."

That wouldn't have helped him in the least. "But you could have done it without the sound or temperature change."

"Probably."

Which meant "of course." Jack shook his head. He had thought that he had decent reflexes, but compared to her he had the reaction time of a large hibernating animal.

She waved him over to sit on the unrolled sleeping bag so that she could do the other one. To unroll the bag in such a small space, she had to flip it out in front of her, scoot over onto that part, and then turn and smooth out the rest. The lamp's sharp light shone against the fine grain of her skin, and a faint woolly smell rose from her sweater.

It was time for a little conversation. Surely they were both on the same page here, both committed to their roles as noble rescuers, as fleet-footed messengers, but it probably did behoove him to make dear the purity of his intentions. *You're one hot number, babe, but I ain't gonna put the moves on ya.*

258

Also, she was hardly a "hot number." She seemed remarkably unaware of her sexuality.

He took a breath. This wasn't easy, but he had to do it. "Last time I tried to talk to you about anything"—he was referring to the disaster of a conversation they'd had before the campfire back at the lake—"I made a total hash of it."

She smiled. "You did reveal more than you intended."

That was no big surprise. "When I was a kid, I had this book about King Arthur and all those guys, and whenever a knight rescued a lady and they had to travel together, he'd always talk about sleeping with his sword between them. I didn't get it then, but of course I do now and while I don't exactly have a sword with me, I suppose we could use a canoe paddle, except that the paddles are even wetter than we are, and—"

He stopped. He was getting nowhere. "You know what I mean."

Now, that made sense. *You know what I mean.* That was all he needed to say. She knew what he meant.

"I know what you *think* you mean," she countered. "But I assume you did enjoy this afternoon."

What did that have to do with anything? "I loved every second of it. You know that. I don't think I've ever felt that close to a—no, not just to a woman, to anyone." Oh, Lord, he was starting to do it again, starting to talk too much. He never talked about himself So why did he keep blathering on? "But that's probably only because I didn't have a dog as a kid. I might have higher standards for companionship if I had had a dog."

"And when the bear comes, I'm sure it would be better if I were a dog, but in the meantime, don't you think there are some advantages associated with the fact

259

that I'm a woman?"

"No," he said bluntly. That was good. *No.* You couldn't get any simpler, any clearer, than that. "It's an incredible inconvenience, because all I can think of is that folded up over there is your nice dry sweat suit, and not only are you probably going to want to put it on, but you're also going to insist on taking off your wet clothes first, aren't you?"

"Of course, and it's worse than you think." Amy lifted her sweater to her ribs. Her midriff was covered in black. "I have my bathing suit on underneath this. I have to take *everything* off."

"Oh, Lord . . . that is bad news." Jack shook his head. "But I'm strong. You do your thing, I'll do mine, and we won't pay any attention to each other." He crossed his arms in front of him, yanked his sweater off over his head, and promptly crashed into the lantern, sending it swaying.

Amy started to laugh. "Don't laugh," he protested. "That hurt."

"Poor thing." She reached over and started rubbing the spot where he had bumped his head. The knit of her sweater was brushing against his face. She was still laughing. "Are you rejecting me?"

"No," he protested. "No, of course not."

"Then what are you doing?" She mimicked his voice. " 'We won't pay any attention to each other.' If that's not rejection, what is?"

She was still sounding happy and light. He was confused. "Why are you acting like this?"

"I guess because I'm propositioning you since you don't seem to be propositioning me. Or is it a seduction? What's the difference between proposition and seduction?"

260

Jack had no idea. "Amy, are you out of your mind?"

She had both hands on his face, tracing her fingers down his throat. "All I know is that I had a wonderful day, a glorious day, and tonight is an opportunity that doesn't come along very often."

"But what about the family? What about everything we were talking about at the campfire?"

"I don't recall that *I* was saying any of it," she replied. "Jack, my family never knows where I am or what I'm doing. Why should they know about this?"

That made sense. Or did it? Jack didn't know . . .

"No one has to find out. We don't have to go back to the lake and shriek it from the treetops. We can keep it to ourselves when we're around everyone else, and then at the end of the summer, we can do whatever we want."

Well, if no one found out . . .

"You said I don't stand up for myself." Her fingers were at the round neck of his T-shirt. "I'm doing it now. I don't meet many people I can trust, Jack. And I can trust you."

That was true. She could trust him. He liked her so much. Yes, she was beautiful and strong, but he also just liked her.

So if they trusted each other . . . if no one found out . . .

He put his arms around her and bent his head, kissing her. Everything about her was soft and fragrant. Well, almost everything. Her sweater was damp. It was one of those Icelandic things, in which the sheep's rich lanolin caused water to bead up and stay on the sweater's surface. She might be staying dry, but he was getting wet.

"Your sweater's like hugging a barnyard. Take it off

261

and then turn around."

"Turn around? Why?" She pulled off her sweater and swiveled away from him, but craned her head over her shoulder so she could still see him. "Why did you want me to turn around? Are you being modest?"

"No. I want to look at your back."

The delicate lines of her muscles ribboned down her back, framed by the deep U of her black swimming suit. The delts, the lats, the . . . she had muscles he didn't know the names of. He couldn't stand the way female bodybuilders looked, so bulky and bunchy, but her back was feminine, almost fragile-looking.

He blew on his hands to warm them, and then he touched her, stroking up and down, following the lines of her muscles. He leaned forward, resting his check against her.

He moved his hands down to her waist. She had said to his sister that she had no hips or waist, and indeed her body fell cleanly below her rib cage without the inward curves of most women.

She was leaning back against him now, her head resting back on his shoulder. His hands slid upward. Compressed under the Lycra of her suit were her breasts, their softness reined in by the tightly knit fabric. Her nipples were hard, but they wouldn't be visible; her suit was keeping them flat. He pulled the shoulder straps down off her arms, and then against his palms he could feel the soft weight of her breasts, the tight bud of her nipples. She leaned back against him, her head in the curve of his neck.

She liked this. So did he.

But now what?

Jack considered himself a reasonably competent lover, no Don Juan by any means, but certainly someone who could maneuver his way through a romantic episode without a woman having to worry about logistics, about what happened next and what went where.

But at the moment the logistics were a problem. He was sitting sideways across a narrow tent, his back hunched to follow the slope of the walls, his legs pulled up because there was no space for him to stretch them out. Amy was sitting between his legs, facing away from him.

Normally a graceful pivot would solve everything, but there was no room for a pivot of any sort, and there was that goddamn lantern still swinging from the last time he had banged his head.

How long did he have before she got cold? You always had to figure that in, at what point a half-naked woman was going to get cold . . . although she was an ice skater; ice skaters were probably used to being cold.

Thank God for something.

Amy twisted her head again, trying to see his face. "What's so funny? Why are you laughing?"

"Haven't you noticed that we are stuck in this position?"

"No," she answered and leaned back against him again, shutting her eyes. "Keep going. I'll tell you when I notice."

He looped his forefingers into the belt loop of her jeans, hoisted her out of his lap, and deposited her in a corner of the tent. Then he clambered to his knees and tugged on her feet, stretching her out, hitting his head only twice.

Her black bathing suit was bunched up at the waist of her jeans. He unzipped her jeans and gave them a good pull. A moment later she was naked.

263

Her body was sleek and compact, her hips narrower than her rib cage. Her pubic hair was dark gold, and she had surprisingly little of it, just a narrow triangle. He had never seen anyone with so little pubic hair.

"Do you do something to yourself down there?" he asked.

"Of course. Skating costumes don't provide much coverage."

"Do you shave?"

She shook her head. "Wax." He must have looked puzzled for she continued. "They paint hot wax on your skin, and then when it cools, they rip it off and the hair comes with it."

Ouch. Hot wax on your pubic hair? This was *not* something Jack wanted to think about. He was as realistic as the next guy, but really . . . did he have to know about this?

Amy was running her hands over the V-shaped crease at the top of her legs. "I haven't had it done in a while. I'm getting a little stubbly. You want to feel?" Obligingly she flattened her back into the sleeping bag, raising her pelvis up. "Really short pubic hairs are like daggers; they can poke through a pair of tights."

If there was anything on earth that would make Jack not want to touch her pelvis, it was this . . . and she knew it. "My sister said you were amazingly unself-conscious about your body." She was chattering away stark naked while he was fully clothed. That would have given most women pause.

"I suppose I am. My body is what I skate with. I don't usually think of it sexually."

He wasn't surprised. "Doesn't that cause some problems?"

"Not in the least. Given that I have no sex life, it's

264

probably an advantage."

"But you have had one at some point, haven't you?"

"Occasionally, but it never seems to work out. You know how it is—sleep with someone and he thinks that gives him the right to control your publicity or produce your shows."

"I think I can promise that won't happen to me."

"I know. That's one of your charms."

They had been talking a long time. Jack didn't mind. He liked shooting the breeze with her. It seemed like a waste of time with most people, but not with her.

But he had to wonder if they were avoiding something by all this talk. "Tell me about yourself when you do have a sex life. What do you like?"

"Actually, I'm very efficient. A little bit here"—she gestured to her breasts—"a little there"—she waved her hand near her pubic region—"and I'm done."

That did surprise him. He would have expected things to be more difficult for her. That was true of many women.

"Why are you surprised?" she asked . . . even though he hadn't said anything. "I can focus, I can be in the moment, my muscle memory is great. It's really just a physical thing, isn't it? And I'm good at physical things."

*Just a physical thing.* That seemed like a pretty stark way to describe sex. But maybe her encounters had been on the stark side—female orgasm, penetration, male orgasm, and then on to the good stuff, producing her shows. No wonder they were chatting away here; it was her way of prolonging what she assumed would be very brief.

"If you're so efficient," he asked, "does intercourse sometimes feel like an afterthought?"

265

She lifted her head, startled. "An afterthought?"

"Or something like that." He tried to explain. "Sometimes when you make love, everything seems like it's in very separate, defined stages, and—"

She interrupted. "I know what you mean. It's just the word, afterthought. That's how I used to think of myself, as an afterthought. Amy the Afterthought."

He suspected that she was probably Amy the Mistake. "Well, do you? Think of intercourse as an after-thought?"

She sighed. "I suppose I do."

He suddenly felt very . . . well, he wasn't sure. She was like Sleeping Beauty or Rapunzel, one of those fairy-tale ladies who was trapped inside a castle. Her profession made her very matter-of-fact about her body and left her surrounded by men who were uninterested in her sexually.

That didn't seem right. Sex shouldn't be efficient. It should be an extension, a continuation, a part of the way you lived. Its roots should thrust all the way down to the moist, urgent earthiness that connects your body to your soul. Despite all the frilliness in her life, the fancy clothes, the sequins and TV cameras, in her core she was like him, a physical person, someone who lived through her body, someone who expressed herself through her body, someone who loved the here and the now of sensation and exertion.

She shouldn't be efficient in bed.

Tenderness . . . that was what he was feeling. Desire and tenderness—he hadn't known that they could go together, but clearly they could. He wanted to help her escape from that castle . . . not because it was some big, macho challenge—the whole high-walls, pretty-girl thing—but because she shouldn't be stuck in there, not

266

when her body was so alive in every other way.

He wished that this could be perfect for her. But there was no way. There was no music, no soft lights, not even any cushioning under any of the sleeping bags. The tent was so cramped that in the end he was going to have put her underneath him in the most old-fashioned of ways, and since neither of them had come prepared, everything was going to have to be more incomplete than he liked.

It couldn't be perfect. But maybe it would be a little better than what she had had.

# CHAPTER 13

AMY ROLLED TO HER SIDE AND TUCKED HER HAND under her cheek. She could hear the wind in the trees. The heavy pine boughs were rustling thick and soft; the slender branches of birches flicked against one another with light clicks. The morning light filtered through the gray-green tent walls.

Last night had been wonderful. It had been so . . . so simple, so natural, unstudied, and honest. She didn't like it when a man tried to create an atmosphere with soft music and low lights. That always made her feel uncomfortable; music and lighting were things you worried about when you were performing. But with Jack she hadn't felt that she was performing. It had been more like the canoeing, something the two of them had done together, using their bodies because that's the kind of people they were. Maybe that wasn't the most romantic comparison, making love and paddling a canoe, but she had had a really good time paddling that canoe.

Jack started to stir. She leaned forward to kiss him.

He lurched back, turning his head, holding up his hand. "My breath will be awful."

She laughed. What a perfect thing for him to say. People had morning mouth—not a pretty thought but the truth. And Jack viewed it that way, as a simple physical fact. More romantic types tried to pretend it away . . . which didn't work.

"I don't care," she said.

"Oh, yes, you do." He sat up, rummaged among his clothes, and triumphantly pulled out a toothbrush.

They began to dress. Jack found it difficult to maneuver in the tight space, and she made sure to get in his way so that he was always bumping against her with his elbow or hip. "You have to be doing this on purpose," he said at last. "I'm no model of grace, but I'm not this clumsy."

They scrambled out of the tent, Jack going up to the ranger cabin to return the lantern and see if the ranger could spare some hot water again while Amy went to the water's edge to get the food pack. The plates and cups were still on the top of the canoe. They were slick with rainwater, and Amy had to brush the pine needles off them with the side of her hand.

Jack returned from the ranger cabin with coffee. Their menu was the same as it had been last night, tuna fish sandwiches and dried fruit. The ranger had offered to give them a hot breakfast. "But he's a talker," Jack said. "We would be there forever."

"This is fine." Amy sat down on a rock to eat her breakfast. It would have been more fine, she decided an instant later, if the rock had been dry, but it hadn't.

Jack squatted down, resting one knee against one of the logs. The knee of his jeans would be damp and dirty,

268

but better to have a damp knee than the wet tush that she had.

He picked up his sandwich. "Do you really think we can keep this from everyone? I think it's important that we do."

"I don't see why it would be a problem."

"Everything would be different if there wasn't this family stuff. I'm not a one-night-stand kind of guy."

"I know that."

She had answered instantly, and he looked up, a little suspiciously. "You do? How?"

"My great insight into people, and the fact that I'm sharing a room with your sister. Don't you think I know everything there is to know about your love life?"

He groaned. "So I suppose you've heard this whole Jack-as-rescuer thing?"

She smiled. Of course she had. Holly said that Jack had never been in a true partnership. The women had needed him; he had probably not needed them.

"Well, it's not like Holly says." He was determined to defend himself. "It's just that I'm not so great in the expressing-my-true-feelings department, so I do better with women I can do stuff for. You put a new radiator in someone's car, and she gets the message that you like her. You don't have to rattle on quite as much."

"I think you express yourself very well."

"Then you're the only one." He drained the last of his coffee. "So this will all work the best if you give me a list of chores. Like your gutters . . . do you need your gutters cleaned? I like cleaning gutters."

He wasn't talking like someone who was planning on a secret relationship. "I don't have gutters. I live in a highrise, and the building has a maintenance staff."

He grimaced. "A maintenance staff? No woman who

already has a relationship with a maintenance staff would have any reason to have a relationship with me."

"I think I can find something to do with you." Amy folded the Saran Wrap her sandwich had been in and stood up. "But we've got plenty of time to sort this out, because we can't really do anything until the summer's over."

"I guess that's true," he agreed.

They packed up quickly, and as Jack was pushing the canoe out into the water, she turned in her seat. "Let's see how fast we can go."

It was an absurd idea. There was no need for speed, and yesterday had been grueling.

"Sounds good to me," he said.

As quickly as they had traveled yesterday, they had at least been prudent. They hadn't known what difficulties lay ahead; they'd had to stop and check maps. But this morning they knew the route, and there was nothing stopping them.

The wind was at their back, and they flew through the water, carried on by the air currents and their own strength. They made a game of it, plotting where to beach on each portage to save themselves a few steps, a few seconds. Even though the sun was still low in the sky, their shirts were damp with sweat. It was utterly pointless; it was completely exhilarating.

"Wouldn't it be fun"—Amy spoke over her shoulder—"to come up here sometimes and really push ourselves to see how far we could go?"

"With your strength and my lack of sense, we'd probably be at the Arctic Circle in a week's time."

That was what she needed, not a repairman but a playmate, a buddy. She would love to try new things physically. She'd always wanted to roller-blade, mountain bike, cross-country ski, horseback ride, but she never had. She wanted to go to a state fair, ride the roller coaster, and have someone win her a big stuffed animal. She wanted to have fun.

They could have their own camp, the two of them, Camp-Amy-and-Jack. It would be a traveling camp. They would meet for weekends in Montana, New York City, Maine, wherever there was something to do, and they would have fun.

It didn't have to be hard. As soon as the summer was over and the family was all scattered around again, they could pick some dates. Amy's assistant Gretchen would make the travel arrangements. It would hideously expensive, but very easy.

She knew that this would work. She always felt doubts first as a tightening in her throat. It has harder to swallow, harder to exhale when she felt a doubt. When she doubted herself on the ice, it seemed that she never quite got all the air out of her lungs. The old air would settle in her stomach and her legs, weighing her down.

Confidence she felt in her arms, a prickling, flashing, bubbling certainty, making her arms curving and graceful. Beauty flowed from that confidence, and she would know that however she moved her arms, however she held her fingers, the line would be beautiful.

Time and again she would find a piece of music and no one else thought it would work, and she wouldn't know how it would work, and for days, weeks, everyone would keep questioning her, joking with her, urging her to give up, and then suddenly it would work, and everyone else would be grimacing, apologizing, acknowledging that she had been right. "It was my arms," she would say. "I knew it in my arms."

Most people dreaded summer's end. Amy could

271

hardly wait.

Other canoes, other parties, were entering the water. The ones going upstream were struggling against the wind. Across the surface of the larger lakes, waves broke and foamed against the silvery canoes. The shore curved away from the lakes in arching shells, the deep green of the trees reflecting a fringe on the blue-brown water.

One more portage and they would be in sight of the island campsite. It was not even nine o'clock. They had been gone for only eighteen hours.

The four little kids crowded down the rocks to meet them, shrieking and jabbering. It wasn't until Ellie reached the shore that Amy and Jack could piece together the story. The plane had come at five this morning. It had found the campsite easily. They hadn't even had to paddle out to the center of the lake and flap orange ponchos to identify their location. The kids had been looking forward to that.

"Nick got off okay?" Jack asked.

Ellie nodded.

By now the adults had joined them. "I'm wildly impressed," Giles said immediately. "You just left twenty minutes ago, didn't you?"

"You got to the ranger station last night?" Phoebe marveled. "We couldn't believe it when the pilot said that was when the message came in."

"But you didn't really get all the way there on your own, did you?" Joyce asked. "That's what I said. You must have found someone with a motor or a cell phone." Motors were not allowed in canoe country, and cell phones didn't work. Joyce knew that. Amy couldn't imagine what she was thinking.

"No, we made it there ourselves," she said quietly.

Ellie and the kids were unloading the canoe, obviously planning on carrying up the packs. The two boys were already fighting over who was to carry what. Amy and Jack followed Phoebe and Giles to the longer but less steep path up the rocks.

Phoebe and Giles confirmed that everything had gone well. The butterfly bandages had held, although the wound had oozed throughout the night. They'd had to send Nick off alone; otherwise there would not have been enough adults to bring all four canoes back.

"He'll be all right," Jack said.

Everyone agreed. Nick was a survivor.

"If he went alone," Amy put in, "then where's Maggie?" She had not seen the other girl.

Phoebe and Giles exchanged glances. Then Phoebe spoke carefully. "She's in her tent. She is in a bit of a snit."

When wasn't Maggie in a bit of a snit? "What happened?" Amy asked.

"We haven't pieced it all together"—Phoebe was speaking softly—"but Ellie says that she thinks something happened between Maggie and Nick. He went off for a walk yesterday afternoon, and the little kids said that Maggie followed him."

"And?" Jack asked.

"That we're not sure of, but they are a pair of teenagers. Then a half hour later he was out collecting wood with Ellie—"

"Which he clearly volunteered to do," Giles put in. "I was planning on going with her."

"So no doubt," Phoebe continued, "Maggie viewed that as a kind of rejection."

"Do you think they had sex?" Amy asked. Both Maggie and Nick did have an alert animal presence to

273

them, an awareness of their bodies, their sexuality.

Phoebe shrugged. "Who knows? She was probably willing."

Jack was shaking his head. "If there is one person on earth Nick has any respect for, it is my mother. He might have had a sense of how disruptive this could be, how tough it would make things for her."

"And that's why he didn't have sex with a willing girl . . . out of respect for his aunt?" Giles didn't sound convinced.

Jack grimaced. "It does sound a little lame, doesn't it?"

They were now at the worst part of the climb, and Giles waved for Amy and Jack to go on. A moment later Amy spoke to Jack softly. "When you were talking about things being disruptive for your mother, it wasn't Nick you were talking about, was it?"

"I was supposed to be this great role model for him, and so far all I've seemed to manage to teach him was how to seduce family members."

Amy would have slipped her arm through his if she could have, but Giles and Phoebe were behind them on the path. "First of all, if you check the timing, whatever did or didn't happen, Nick and Maggie went first, and second, it's not clear that Nick was doing the seducing . . . or you either, for that matter."

Jack rolled his eyes. He was not convinced.

Amy longed for something to say that would persuade him of what she knew, that Camp-Amy-and-Jack wasn't going to hurt anyone, that it was a perfect way for them to be together.

With Amy and Jack back safely, the others decided to leave the tents pitched and take a day trip to a little waterfall. Phoebe urged Amy and Jack to stay at the campsite and rest. "You've paddled so hard. Take it easy for the rest of the day."

That sounded wonderful. Amy hadn't expected to be alone with him until after the summer's end.

But of course, the minute Maggie heard that the two of them were staying behind, she announced that she wasn't going either That left too many people for two canoes, but not enough for three, so Joyce said she would stay back too.

And rather than spend the day with the two of them, Amy and Jack quickly chose to go on the day trip.

The obvious arrangement for the return trip home the next day would have been to move Maggie out of the middle of her parents' canoe and have her take Nick's place in Jack's. But the obvious thing was never done when Maggie was involved. Complicated negotiations started, and Amy was not going to get involved. This was not regression, this was not a return of Amy the Afterthought, this was just smart. She went and sat on a rock. A minute later Ellie came to sit by her.

"You're keeping out of this too?" Amy asked.

Ellie nodded.

Ellie didn't have Maggie's sexual presence; she simply did not.

Amy reached over and ruffled the girl's hair. "Does it drive you nuts that Maggie gets her way all the time?"

Ellie looked up, startled. She hadn't expected to hear that from Amy. "Yeah, I guess. It just doesn't seem fair that she should be so smart and so great-looking."

"Maggie has a very dramatic look, and that's in fashion right now. In the fifties people would have thought that she was ugly."

"They would have?" Ellie looked hopeful for a moment, but only a moment. "That doesn't change anything now."

"That's true," Amy had to agree. "But her being gorgeous and smart does not change the fact that Nick could have bled to death if you hadn't acted so quickly."

"I just blew the whistle."

"You had a whistle; you knew the distress signal." Amy herself had not known what the three blasts meant. Phoebe had explained it to her when they were in the canoe searching for the source of the sound.

Ellie shrugged. "That's Girl Scouts; they're always teaching us stuff like that."

"But you applied it."

*This is me. I am being myself.*

When new girls joined the big spring tour, some of them were painfully young, fifteen, sixteen, and while they could skate exquisitely, they had no idea how to be a professional, how to get along with the others, how to remain focused. Increasingly each year Amy found herself reaching out to any who would listen to her, dropping a hint here, a suggestion there, reassuring some, questioning others.

She went on. "I'm sure I'm scheduled to visit a hospital or a health-care facility sometime this fall." She had no idea if that was true, but as soon as she got back to Denver, she would make it so. "Would you like to come?"

"Me?" Ellie asked. "Why me?"

"If it's a group of other adolescents, you could talk about how something as little as carrying a whistle and not panicking can save someone's life." *Or you could just come and see what I do.*

"I'd love to," Ellie said. "If Mom and Dad will let me

miss school."

"I'm sure they will." Giles, at least, would say yes.

Suddenly a whoop broke from the cluster of decision makers, and the two little boys were tearing down to the waterfront, shrieking.

"I get to go first," one shouted.

"No, me, me, me, *me*," the other one shrieked.

"What do you think that's all about?" Amy asked Ellie.

"It sounds like someone told them they could take turns in the bow," Ellie answered, "but it makes no sense. They're too small, they aren't strong enough. I can't imagine whose idea it was."

Amy could. The two little boys had been in the middle of Jack's canoe. "I'm willing to bet that Jack got fed up with all the discussion and just said he'd go with Alex and Scott."

"Would he really do something that stupid?" Ellie asked.

"Yes."

Jack broke free from the others and came over to the two of them. His expression was rueful, and he was shaking his head as if he knew that he had made a mistake. "I figure that two eight-year-olds makes one sixteen-year-old, and we won't miss Nick and his wrestling muscles one bit."

Ellie giggled. "But they're only seven."

"Seven, eight . . . what's the difference?" Jack waved his hand. "We're all men."

"Why don't you take the smaller canoe?" Ellie offered. "Aunt Amy and I will do fine in the bigger one."

"Oh, no. We need no concessions made for us. We are men. We will do great."

They didn't. Jack's stroke was so much stronger than the boys' that it was nearly impossible for him to steer the canoe. They trailed way behind the others.

At the first portage the rest of the group had to wait nearly ten minutes for the "all-men" canoe. Ian was, Amy noticed, very subdued. He must have known that this would not be happening if Joyce or Maggie had been more accommodating.

When they at last arrived, Jack came straight up to Ellie.

"You're clearly the only person around here with any sense. Thank you, and yes, we accept your offer of the smaller canoe, and I don't care if you and Aunt Amy are miserable because this is all your dad's fault."

"Dad's fault?" Ellie was giggling again. "How do you figure that?"

"Yes," Giles put in, "how *do* you figure that?"

"Because you just stood there"—Jack glanced over his shoulder to be sure that neither Ian's family nor the two boys could hear—"and let me make an idiot of myself and you didn't say one word to save me."

"I guess it is my fault," Giles agreed. "For that I will take one of your packs."

"Deal."

Amy and Ellie took a couple more packs, and with the smaller canoe and only one pack, Jack and his crew managed to keep up.

They reached Ely in the middle of the afternoon. Nick had left messages both with the outfitter and the hospital. They were not to call his mother and grandmother. He had gotten a judge to approve his treatment. He was all stitched up and had spent the night at the home of one of the nurses. Apparently Giles had given him a credit card if he needed to get a motel room, but Nick had managed to get himself a free billet.

"Don't thank me," the nurse said. "He was a godsend. He played cards all afternoon with my kids. I took a nap. I haven't taken a nap since my husband walked out."

"That does it," Giles sighed. "Nick, you are now a danger to the entire human race. You have learned what grown women truly want—some sleep. This is knowledge so powerful that a lad of your years ought not to have it. Use it wisely, my boy."

"Yes, sir." Nick grinned.

The nurse gave them all the necessary information about changing the dressings, when to have the stitches removed, and such. Nick was a very lucky young man, she reported. No tendons had been cut, no muscle damaged. He was sore but able to walk.

Maggie had not gotten out of the car.


Although Thomas had been quite happy during his parents' absence, the instant he saw their station wagon turn into the drive, he burst into tears and punished his mother by refusing to look at her for a full five minutes.

"You little pill," Phoebe said to him. "I love you anyway."

Amy hugged her father, Gwen, and Holly.

"How on earth can you be out in the wilderness for three days," Holly demanded, "and still look so good?"

"Just wait—" *Just wait until we're alone and then I'll tell you everything*—that's what Amy intended to say.

She wanted to tell Holly what had happened with Jack. They had talked late into the night about their equally empty love lives, and Amy would love it this fall if she got a giddy, gushing phone call from Holly reporting that Holly had Found Someone. Amy would want to know everything about him, how Holly had met him, what he was like. She and Holly were friends; they were sisters.

But how could she tell Holly about Jack? It was supposed to be a secret from the family, and Holly was family.

Maybe this was going to be more complicated than she had thought it would be.

"I guess"—she revised her answer to Holly's question about her looks—"it was all the exercise."

The little kids were all talking at once, telling Gwen, Hal, and Holly about the plane that had come to get Nick. Phoebe, Giles, and Ellie were clustered around the wailing Thomas. Maggie was leaning against the garage sulking.

At dinner Maggie took her plate and ate by herself on the front porch. Gwen pretended not to notice, but Amy knew that she did.

After dinner Maggie was scheduled to help with the dishes. She didn't.

When the kitchen was almost clean, Ian came to apologize for her. "She must have forgotten to look at the kaper chart. I'm sorry." He was obviously sincere. "Is there anything I can do to help?"

Gwen shook her head. "We're almost done." Then she laid down her dish towel. "I hope you remember that Hal and I want to take care of your kids so you and Joyce can have a night in town as Phoebe and Giles did. Why don't you go tomorrow?"

"Tomorrow?" Ian sounded surprised.

"Why not? Everyone must have had their share of togetherness on the canoe trip. Scott and Emily will be fine here without you."

"I know they will." Ian paused. "That actually sounds

like a pretty good idea. I'll go talk to Joyce."

He left. When they heard the door bang shut, Holly spoke. "Do you think they will go?"

"I hope," Gwen answered, "although the rest of us may be in for a rocky time. It will be interesting to see how Maggie handles herself when her mother isn't around to make things perfect for her."

But Gwen's curiosity was not to be satisfied. The next morning they all discovered that Maggie was insisting on going into town with Ian and Joyce.

"But I thought the point was for each couple to have some time to themselves," Jack said.

"Indeed." It was clear that Gwen did not approve. "They let that child make all the decisions. That's why Scott and Emily are so demanding. They know they are second."

It was easy to lump all four of the younger kids into one squirming little mass, occasionally dividing them by their sex, the two boys, the two girls, but there was, Amy knew, another division—Phoebe and Giles's two did behave better than Ian and Joyce's. All four always wanted to go first all the time, but it was usually Scott or Emily who shrieked a claim ahead of the others. Their voices were more urgent, their need to have things their way more desperate.

And Amy could see that they knew they weren't as important as Maggie.

"Why does Maggie want to go?" Giles asked. "What does she think there is to do there?"

"You and Phoebe had a great time," Jack pointed out.

"Yes, but it was not entirely family entertainment."

"Oh"—Jack grinned—"I see."

"At least," Giles continued, "I hope it doesn't result

281

in any more family."

Ian sensed everyone's disapproval, and when he came over to the main cabin to get the keys to Hal's car so that he could drive into town, his face was tight and tense. He wanted everyone to think that he was doing the right thing, and he knew that no one did. It wasn't clear that *he* felt he was doing the right thing, but obviously he felt trapped. Maggie was too insistent, Joyce too determined.

Amy had never thought much about her brother's life, but as she watched the car ease around the big Norway in the center of the driveway, she longed to be reassured that he was well, that there were joys and satisfactions in his life.

At the campfire that night, she sat down next to her father. "Dad, this is embarrassing because I should already know this, but how is Ian doing professionally?" Here she had pitied herself, because her family seemed to pay so little attention to her career, but did she pay any attention to theirs? "I know what he does—learns dying Indian languages—but is he doing well?"

Gwen and Holly both stopped their conversations. They were interested. Amy supposed that they too wanted to be reassured that something was going well for him.

"He's doing great," Hal said easily. "He's terrific at what he does. He can learn a language, figure out its grammar faster than anyone. The whole linguistics community has known that since his first year in graduate school."

"So it was easy for him to get tenure?" Holly obviously knew something about academic careers.

"Not at all." Hal shook his head. "Everything's always been a struggle for him. He's a practical linguist, and when he was in school, no one was doing practical linguistics. They were all theoreticians. His department was completely unsupportive of his dissertation. It didn't seem to matter that he would have been, at best, a B-plus theoretician while he is really gifted at what he does. They wanted him to change, but he stuck to his guns."

"So why is he doing so well now?" Holly asked.

"Funding. He's the only linguist who can get any kind of funding. The government is not interested in the theoretical stuff, but he has a couple of California congressmen who are really behind him, and his money is solid. He supports three or four graduate students year in, year out, on his grants, and in this day and age that's incredible."

Amy had only the haziest notion of the difference between practical and theoretic linguistics, but she heard the larger theme. Everyone had told Ian to change, to stop doing what he was good at, to start doing what everyone else was doing. "So it is like my not being able to jump," she said. "It would have been easier if he had done the theory stuff, but he ended up better off because he did it his way."

Her father turned to her, obviously not having made this connection before. "Yes, I guess it is the same."

It was so odd to think this, that her career and Ian's had something in common.

Hal put his arm around her. "I suppose that's your mother in you; she always made her own rules. She wouldn't have had children who follow the crowd."

# CHAPTER 14

IAN, JOYCE, AND MAGGIE WERE BACK AT THE LAKE hours before any one expected them. From the way that Maggie slammed the car door it was clear to Phoebe what had happened. Joyce would have let the whole trip be about pleasing Maggie. Where did Maggie want to eat? What movie did Maggie want to see? And you didn't treat sullen teenagers like that. They just got more sullen, trying to see how much more they could get.

"Teenagers are difficult," was all Gwen said.

"I wasn't," Holly said.

"No." Gwen patted her arm. "You weren't."

And Phoebe hadn't been either.

"What's the history here?" Holly asked. "Why does Joyce let Maggie get away with this?"

There were only four of them on the lakeside porch of the main cabin, Dad, Gwen, Holly, and Phoebe herself. She had no idea where Jack and Amy were.

Dad answered. "Joyce's mother remarried when she was a girl. Her stepfather already had a couple of kids, and then he and her mother had some more. Joyce felt that no one paid any attention to her, that she was never heard. Ian understood that. That's why he has stepped back and let Maggie have more of a voice than most kids. But clearly he has let things get too far."

Phoebe was surprised. She had never heard her father criticize anyone in the family behind their back.

He continued. "Ian has probably spent his entire married life trying to prove that he loves Maggie. He does, but I suspect that Joyce doesn't believe it. There's probably nothing he can do to convince her that he does."

That made sense. Phoebe had never thought of it that way.

This was strange. She knew her father was a quiet, observant man, but she had never had any idea how much he truly did observe. He understood Ian and Joyce so well. She felt suddenly uneasy. What had her father observed about her?

"Are you going to say anything to him?" Gwen asked.

"I have never interfered in the kids' adult lives, and this doesn't seem like the time to start."

If anyone was going to say anything to Ian—Phoebe certainly was not—he needed to be told not to overact. He was furious with Maggie, and after all these years of indulgence, he was suddenly getting tough.

At the evening campfire he was after her constantly, wanting her to help as much as Ellie was. He was quiet about it, he was trying to not humiliate her publicly, but it was also very clear that he wasn't taking no for an answer. She had to help the little kids put their marshmallows on sticks. She had to shake the popcorn popper. He was trying to turn her into Ellie.

It was too much, too fast. *You can't make an Ellie overnight,* Phoebe wanted to caution him. Teenagers were so fragile, so explosive. Maggie wasn't going to accept these changes meekly. She would thrash against the new leash, she would struggle, she would fail, not caring what or whom she damaged.

Phoebe could only hope that the damage didn't happen at the lake.

The sky was dark, the usual pelter of stars hidden behind thick clouds. The wind came up, and they put out the campfire early. Giles's leg was hurting him; he

285

had done too much on the canoe trip. He was restless all night, and Phoebe kept waking, hearing the sharp gusts outside their window and fierce crackling of lightning overhead.

But there was no rain, and the strong winds took the clouds with them. When Phoebe woke the next morning, the light pouring through the little four-paned bedroom window was bright. She could hear Giles up in the kitchen making coffee, talking to Thomas. She shoved her feet into her slippers and was coming back from the biffy when she heard the kids rushing along the path.

"Dad, Dad . . . your boat." Their voices were frantic, urgent.

"Uncle Giles, the boat, the boat."

Giles heard and came out of the cabin, his face tense, puzzled, his brow lowered. "Go on," he nodded to her. He didn't have his built-up shoe on yet. "Go see."

She grabbed Thomas, ran down the path, slipping down the log steps, the kids milling around her.

There was already a crowd on the dock. Dad and Gwen, Ian and Joyce, Amy. Jack was calf deep in the water, standing by Giles's boat.

It was ruined. Giles's beautiful wood boat was ruined. The heavy winds had first smashed it against the shore and then swung it back into the dock's steel uprights, splintering its sides. Heavily filled with water, it was listing, the starboard stem resting on the sand at the bottom of the lake.

"The rope must have come untied," Scott shouted. "The rope at the dock must have come untied."

"Be quiet," Ian ordered.

Giles always tied the boat at an angle from the shoreline, knotting one end to the dock and the other to

286

a tree on the bank. He left enough play in the ropes to give them strength, but kept them taut enough so that the boat would hit neither the dock nor the shore. Now the boat was tied only at the shore.

Phoebe saw her father step toward the end of the dock. She looked up. Giles was coming down the steps.

These steps were always hard for him. They were awkwardly spaced for his gait and there was no rail.

*Why didn't we ever put up a rail? All these years . . . Giles has been coming here for all these years, and we never put up a rail.*

Giles was coming down slowly, not looking at his feet. He was staring at the boat. Everyone was watching him.

This boat had been his. The one thing that had belonged to him here.

"I don't know much about boats." It was Jack, speaking from the water. "But this looks bad."

Thomas was squirming, pushing Phoebe's chest with his little fists. She was holding him too tightly. The other kids were, for once, silent, aware of the adults' distress, frightened by it.

"Did the rope break?" Giles asked. It was the first thing he had said.

They all glanced at the upright. No. There was no line dangling from it. The knot had come undone.

This made no sense. Giles's knots were good. The rope might break, but Giles's knots wouldn't come untied. Giles tied good, clean, strong knots.

Giles didn't answer.

"It was me."

Nick's voice came from the steps. He looked rumpled, still in the sweats he had slept in. Maggie was a few steps behind him. Obviously the noise had woken both of them up. "Giles asked me to tie it up last night."

"My leg hurt," Giles said.

"Did you forget to come down, Nick?" Gwen spoke carefully.

"No. No, I did. I tied it up. I thought it was pretty cool that he had asked me." Nick was mumbling a bit, looking at his feet, seeming young. Then he lifted his head, looking straight at Giles. He came down the steps, moving easily despite the sutures in his leg. "I know what the boat means to you. I thought it was cool that you trusted me. But I must have screwed up. It was my fault."

Everything Phoebe had ever heard about Nick's home life suggested constant evasion of responsibility, continual blaming of others. But Nick was stepping right up and accepting the blame here.

It was good for him . . . but oh, what he had done to Giles. He could never know.

"He didn't screw up." Jack was out of the water now. He had kicked off his shoes before going in to check the boat, but he hadn't rolled up his jeans. The lower part of the legs was dark and wet. "I'm sorry, Nick, I know this is insulting, but I heard Giles ask you, and I came down afterward and checked your knots. Giles may have trusted you, but I guess I didn't. I should have. I always hated it when my dad checked everything I did. But they were good knots. I tugged hard on them. There was no way they could have loosened. The ropes would have snapped before those knots came undone."

Nick ducked his head. Phoebe supposed that he didn't want anyone to see his relief.

"Then how did it happen?" Ellie asked. "What about when you came down, Maggie? Were the knots—"

"I didn't come down last night," Maggie snapped.

288

"Yes, you did. During the campfire you left. I thought you were just going to the biffy, but then we broke up a minute later, you were coming up—" Ellie stopped.

She turned toward Phoebe, her eyes desperate. Phoebe knew her daughter. Ellie didn't know what to do. She was confused, anguished. Ellie never accused anyone of anything.

"I don't know . . ." Ellie's voice trailed off. "Maybe I'm wrong."

Before Phoebe could speak, before she could urge her responsible, observant daughter to have confidence in what she had seen, Ian spoke. "No. You wouldn't have been wrong about that." His voice grew stern. "Maggie, did you come down to the dock last night? Did you untie the boat?"

Maggie glared at him. "You all think this place is so all-fired wonderful. Everything about it is so la-de-da precious—"

"Maggie, did you untie Giles's boat?"

"No. I mean, I was leaning against the post a bit, and maybe I may have loosened the knot a little, I don't know. Why should I care?"

Maggie had untied Giles's boat. It had been deliberate; she had meant to do it. At the campfire they had all been talking about how the winds were coming up. She knew what might happen.

"It's just a boat," she protested. "So what if—"

"Shut up," Ian snapped.

"Well, all right, I will." Maggie whirled and marched up the steps.

"She wouldn't have done it"—Joyce would, Phoebe knew, defend Maggie in any situation, she would excuse any behavior—"if she wasn't so unhappy here. It's not her fault. You can't blame her." And she went racing up

289

the hill after her daughter.

Ian watched her go. "Maggie's fifteen years old. You can too blame her," he said. Slowly he turned to Giles. "I know this isn't something money can fix, but—"

Giles held up his hand. "Not yet."

Giles usually didn't admit that things hurt. He had suffered so much as a kid, and then in his job, he couldn't take anything, not anything, personally so he had learned not to mind.

But this hurt.

He spoke slowly. "Jack, I don't want to see it again. Would you take care of it? Sink it, burn it, I don't care."

Jack nodded. "Sure thing."

Giles turned and began to clump up the bank. Phoebe moved to follow him. Gwen stepped forward, her arms out for Thomas. *Thanks.* Phoebe mouthed.

Ellie caught up with her at the top of the steps. "Mom, Mom. Is Dad okay?"

"He will be. But for the time being he's pretty upset."

"I hate Maggie." Ellie was pale. Her freckles stood out. "She's awful."

"She does seem that way right now."

Nick appeared at Ellie's shoulder. "Do you want us to get the little kids out of the way? We could take them to the sand pit or something."

"That would be a big help," Phoebe, said. "I don't think they've had breakfast. Take a box of cereal and the paper bowls." Joyce had made such a fuss about the disposable bowls Gwen had bought that no one had used them, but right now Phoebe didn't care what Joyce thought. "Make it into a picnic. Gwen has Thomas. I'm sure that's okay with her, but ask her anyway to be sure."

Nick was nodding. "And, Phoebe. . . will you tell

Giles, I'm really sorry about his boat."

Phoebe touched his cheek. "We know you are."

She hugged Ellie and followed the path to the new cabin, but through the open screen she heard Joyce and Maggie. Giles couldn't have gone in there, not with the two of them. Nor would he have gone to the log cabin, not when they weren't staying in it. She peeked in the garage, where he had worked on the boat, but of course he wasn't there. The garage would be full of too many memories of the boat.

Here he was, suffering, and he didn't even have a place of his own to go to.

She rounded the three-sided woodshed. There he was sitting on a stump, his hands linked between his knees. The stump was used as a chopping block. It was surrounded by a thick layer of wood chips; they were pale and fragrant. Phoebe went over, put her hands on his shoulders.

How grateful she was that Gwen had been there to take Thomas, that she didn't have a child on her hip, that at this moment she was here as Giles's wife, not as someone else's mother, not as a dead woman's daughter.

"Oh, Giles, I'm so sorry, and I know it won't be the same, but let's just go buy another boat. Let's go into town today."

How she had minded all the changes Jack and Gwen were making. Talking, planning, taking years to do something . . . that was part of being at the lake. Giles had been quick to understand that code. That's why he had refinished the boat in the first place rather than buying a new one; that's why he had spent two years fishing from a canoe while he had worked on it, because he had been willing to do things the Legend way.

But things had changed. It was time to accept that.

Giles shook his head. "I know everyone else would feel better if we did. But I don't want it to look fixed when it's not."

She ran a hand through her hair. As always, he was exactly right. She was too willing to accept solutions that looked fixed.

"You know you're paying for Ian's mistake. He was coming down on her so hard last night. She wanted to lash out at some dad figure, but she was scared to hurt him, so she hurt you."

"I don't really care."

Phoebe heard the motorboat starting. Who would be water skiing now? Then she remembered. It would be Jack getting ready to tow Giles's boat somewhere.

Giles heard too. He stood up. There were deep V-shaped cuts in the stump. Nick had been learning to split wood; sometimes he used too much force, and his maul drove the wedge all the way into the stump. "The boat was one thing I loved here. So, from my point of view, there's no reason to come back. Other lakes have better fish. God knows there's more comfort and privacy anywhere else."

"What are you saying?" Phoebe sank back against a tree.

He put his hands in his pockets. He didn't do that often. He didn't feel balanced. "For sixteen years I've been coming here for you and the kids. I know it's great for them, this time with their cousins, and I know it means the world to you, but it's my turn now, Phoebe. I'm a grown man. I have a tough job and I make a decent living. But on vacations I come play son-in-law. At first I did it for you. Now I do it for the kids because they do get so much out of this. But what's in it for me?

292

The boat. And now it's gone."

Phoebe knew that all of this was true. She knew it. But she couldn't bear hearing what was going to come next.

"It's time for us to get a place of our own."

"Somewhere else?" She could hardly breathe.

"Yes. I don't care where. It can still be in Minnesota if you want. The place is full of lakes. Let's find a new one and build our own cabin, one that's exactly right for the six of us and not worry about anyone else."

"And not come back here?"

"Not like this, not for a month. Maybe a week. That's what most people do, Phoebe. They don't spend a whole month with their families."

"But the kids—"

"The kids will be fine. Cousins and grandparents are important, but they need to understand that their mom and dad and brothers and sisters are first."

*Are first* . . . Phoebe felt sick. She agreed with Giles. But had she lived by it? Or had her mother always been too important to her? Not just since her death, but always? Had that kept her and Giles from starting their own family traditions?

She couldn't protest, not now. Not ever. There was nothing to do. This was going to happen. She could only sit here, her back against a birch tree, her palms pressing into the moss. She wanted to shriek apologies. I've *been wrong, all wrong.* Tears were smarting in her eyes. Guilt was biting at her, and fear too. This was going to happen.

She was going to lose the lake.

She loved Giles. She loved him with all her heart. She respected him more than anyone else on earth. And she was going to have to give up the lake for him.

The whole time on the dock Hal had not said a word. Gwen tried to imagine what would have happened if John, her first husband, had been here. He would have taken over. He would have barked at Maggie, sent her to her room. He would have dismissed Joyce, refused to listen to her excuses. The two of them would have forgotten their guilt, letting it sink beneath their anger of him, and everyone else would have felt useless, unable to act.

Gwen further suspected that if Eleanor, Hal's first wife, had been here, she too would have taken over, meting out justice as she saw fit.

Sometimes it was better to let things play out.

She took Thomas up to the main cabin and settled him down for his morning nap. She finished up the breakfast dishes, and when Hal came up, he said he would stay with the sleeping boy. She went to the new cabin. She knocked lightly and went in.

She hadn't been in this cabin since everyone arrived. She had forgotten how light it was, how bright the view from the plate-glass windows. The bank in front of this cabin was rocky; there were fewer trees, and so you could see the lake from inside the cabin. The main cabin, where she and Hal stayed, had a more wooded site and little windows; all you could see through them was branches and pine needles.

The living arrangements here made no sense. This should be the cabin where everyone ate and cooked.

Ian, Maggie, and Joyce were all here, and they were all reading. Ian was at the table looking through a catalogue. Maggie and Joyce each had a murder mystery. It was as if they were all alcoholics, desperately fumbling for a drink in the face of stress.

What would this family be like if you took away their

books? It might make them face things. It would force them to spend time together. Gwen now understood why it was so important to them to come to a place where there were no phones, no televisions or newspapers. They didn't believe they could be a family when there were outside distractions. They didn't trust themselves to pay attention to each other when there was a morning paper to read or phone calls to return.

Ian looked up at her, and Gwen thought she saw a plea in his eyes. *We're stuck. We don't know what to say to each other. We don't know what to do first. Help us.*

She spoke. "Maggie, you need to make two apologies, and I expect you to do them before lunch."

Maggie started to protest. Gwen ignored her. "You must first apologize to Giles. At this point in your life you can't possibly understand what you have done to him, but you must still apologize. Second, you must apologize to everyone, from Claire and Emily on up to your grandfather, for being so disruptive and spoiling everyone's morning."

"Isn't anyone going to apologize to *me?*"

Gwen supposed she shouldn't be surprised by that. How unfair it was to allow a child to be this self-centered. "No," she said firmly, "no one is going to apologize to you."

"This isn't any of your business, Gwen," Joyce said.

"How you choose to raise your children is not my business. But the peace of the family table is my concern, and we aren't going to pretend that this didn't happen."

"I'm not going to apologize." Maggie slammed her book to the floor. "I don't give a fuck about your stupid family table. If anyone cared about this stupid shit about

295

the fucking family—"

"Maggie—" Ian's voice was stern, shocked.

"Oh, for God's sake, Dad. Don't you be such a hypocrite. You and Mom have done nothing but complain about Gwen. Every time her back is turned you whine and complain. Now all of a sudden you—"

"Maggie! Now you must apologize to Gwen."

What a family. Maggie had destroyed Giles's boat, and everyone was up here reading. Say what Gwen knew to be the truth, and they were at last ordering the girl to apologize.

"What's all this crap about apologies?" Maggie stormed. "It's not going to change anything. What was so goddamn important about Giles's boat anyway? Let him buy another. You guys have always said that they aren't using any of Gran's money like we are. Let them start."

Gwen had no idea what she would do if a child of hers spoke like that. Was it too late for Maggie? She honestly didn't know.

But she had done what she could. She had set down her rule. The rest was up to Giles and Joyce.

"I meant what I said," Gwen spoke softly, firmly. "You will not sit down to eat with the rest of the family until you have apologized."

"Like I'm supposed to care about that. So I don't get to eat with the ankle biters and Miss Goody-Goody. My heart is broken."

Gwen turned, walked out. She let the screen fall shut behind her. She went back to the main cabin, put together a snack, and bicycled it down to the kids at the sand pit. Nick and three of the kids were playing "Mother, May I?" The cereal box, milk carton, and used bowls were neatly piled at the side of the road.

296

"Where's Ellie and Emily?" Gwen asked.

"They're in the ladies' room, I believe." Nick made a bit of a face.

Apparently this wasn't a simple pee in the woods. "Do you have toilet paper?"

"Ellie has her fanny pack, and if I know her, she has an itty-bitty but fully usable chemical toilet in it."

It was odd, wonderful, to hear Nick speak so positively about someone. "She's a good kid, isn't she?"

"She does step up and do her share." He looked down at his feet, then looked back up at her. "How come Val and Barb never do their share? Why do they dump everything on you all the time?"

"Because I let them," Gwen answered. "I probably shouldn't. But habits are hard to break. Barbara's my little sister; Valerie is her child. But don't feel guilty because you are one of the things that have gotten dumped. You've been a joy this summer."

Nick ducked his head. "I don't know about that." Then he looked off into the woods. "That really was shitty, what Maggie did, wasn't it?"

Gwen nodded. "Yes, it was."

"I sort of feel like maybe it was my fault."

Phoebe had told her what had apparently happened on the canoe trip. Gwen shook her head. "No, Nick, whatever you did, you can't possibly think of it as your fault. Maggie's spent her whole life getting her way. That's not your doing. And"—Gwen wasn't quite sure how to put this—"word on the street is that you didn't do anything." That was Jack's position; he was maintaining that Nick hadn't had sex with Maggie, although he didn't seem to have any reason for thinking that.

Nick grinned, and for a moment Gwen thought of

297

Jack, how naughty and gorgeous he had always looked at this age. "That's the bitch of it. I can't help thinking that all of this wouldn't have happened if I had."

Gwen was not about to endorse that position. "I doubt that, but let's not look backward."

Ellie and Emily reappeared. Emily was having "tummy problems," Ellie reported, and would like to go back to the cabins. "Is that okay?" she asked Gwen.

"Of course." Five-year-old Emily with her routine stomach complaint had just as much right to her parents' attention as did Maggie. But she wasn't going to get it.

Gwen took the bike back to the cabins and asked Hal to go pick Emily up in the car. Thomas was awake. She picked him up and went along the path to the other cabins. Ian came out to meet her. "Maggie and Joyce are packing," he said. "They're going home."

"Oh, Ian," she sighed. "Is that really necessary?"

"Joyce seems to think so. All morning Maggie's been insisting how much she hates it here. She really doesn't, she's just horrified by what happened. She's painted herself in a corner, and I think we ought to help her get out of the corner, even if it means walking over wet paint and having to do the work all over again, but Joyce doesn't. I think you were right to tell her to apologize, that would have been a good first step, but Joyce can't see that."

"Are you all going or only the two of them?"

"Joyce thinks we all should leave, but I'm not going to give Maggie the power to drag Scott and Emily around. So I'm hoping it's all right if the three of us stay."

"Of course it is. You know that." Then Gwen remembered why she had come. "Emily's not feeling well. I think it's a very routine little case of diarrhea, but this isn't the most comfortable place in the world to have the runs. Maybe Joyce will want to stay at least until she feels better."

"I'll tell her," Ian said. "But I don't know that it will make any difference."

It didn't. Although she was only five, Emily knew her job, she knew her place in the family. "I'm okay, Mommy. If you and Maggie need to go somewhere, that's fine. It's okay. Ellie's here."

Her soft little voice broke Gwen's heart. Children shouldn't have to be that good.

## CHAPTER 15

AMY OFFERED TO HELP JACK WITH GILES'S BOAT, AND together they towed it over to the Rim, pulling it up on the beach. It could dry out there, and then they could burn it. Jack took a sledgehammer with him and, raising it high over his head, smashed the boat into smaller pieces so it would dry faster. He didn't want to use the chain saw. Noise traveled across the water, he said, and Giles would be able to hear.

Amy lined the broken pieces along the beach, separating them so they would dry more quickly. Even smashed and splintered, you could tell that the pieces had once been a boat. Many of the pieces still curved with the boat's graceful arch, and the varnish on the finished surfaces shone in the sunlight.

Of all people, Giles did not deserve this. Amy longed to do something, but what? There was no wealthy philanthropist she could call, no friendly reporter, no generous rink manager. Being famous wasn't any help.

299

Giles didn't ask what they had done with the boat, but Hal did. "The Rim?" He hadn't expected that answer. "You do know that is private property, don't you?"

Jack glanced at Amy. She understood. He was asking if they should tell her father. *The Rim is mine, Dad. I bought it a couple of years ago to keep those developers from building a resort.*

But before she could speak, before she could decide whether or not to speak, her father waved his hand. "Oh, I can't imagine it matters in the least. Whoever owns it never comes up. So let's just pretend to ourselves that they would understand."

"And we'll have it out of there in a couple of days," Jack added.

The rest of the day was quiet. When Ian returned from the airport, he said that he was going to move out to the bunkhouse to be with Scott and Emily. "So why don't you have your kids move back into the new cabin with you?" he suggested to Phoebe and Giles.

"We would appreciate that," Giles said quietly.

But it was too little, too late. In the late afternoon Amy sat on the porch of the main cabin with Hal and Gwen. Phoebe came outside, and standing with her back to the wooden-framed screen door, she told them that she and Giles would be looking for a cabin site of their own.

"At another lake?" Amy couldn't help herself. Phoebe at another lake?

Her sister nodded.

Phoebe was leaving the lake. Phoebe was not coming back here. Amy heard her father take a sharp breath.

"Oh, Phoebe—" Amy stepped forward, but Phoebe held up her hand, stopping her. She didn't want sympathy. She didn't want to cry.

But Phoebe loved the lake; she needed the lake. How could she be thinking about going someplace else?

"We'll still come visit." Phoebe was trying to keep her voice cheerful. "It's not like you're rid of us."

Visit. That's what Amy had done all these years, visit. Stop in for a couple of days, get what bed was left over, not have any say in the plans, the improvements. That's what you do when you visit.

And that had been all right for Amy. She was used to it. She didn't expect to have a voice. But Phoebe . . . Phoebe wouldn't be able to stand it. She was used to being heard. She had earned that, she deserved it. She worked so hard, she was so responsible, that she was entitled to be consulted.

Now she was going to visit.

*You should cry. This is sad. Maybe you are doing the right thing, but it is still hard. You should cry.*

*Why did I let you stop me? Why didn't I go ahead and put my arms around you? You are my sister You need comforting. Why didn't I do it?*

Standing, Hal came across the porch and put his arms around Phoebe. She drew back, she stayed stiff, but she couldn't push Hal away. He was her father.

Hal smoothed a hand over her hair as if she were a child. In a moment Phoebe leaned against him. Her neck bent, her shoulders hunched forward. "I never thought I'd"—her voice was muffled against his shoulder—"be the first one to stop coming, that I'd be the one to end our summers together."

*The first one to stop coming.* How like Phoebe that was, to be judging herself, to be worrying how her actions would affect everyone else.

Amy felt a touch on her arm. It was Gwen, motioning for her to come down off the porch, to leave Phoebe and

301

Hal alone.

"This is really sad," Amy said as soon as they were on the other side of the cabin. "I can't imagine Phoebe without the lake. And then her feeling like she's breaking up the family somehow. . ." Amy shook her head.

"She'd probably rather blame herself for causing changes than put the blame where it truly belongs."

Amy didn't understand. Gwen couldn't be talking about Joyce or Maggie. Phoebe wouldn't have minded blaming them.

"She doesn't want to blame your mother," Gwen explained. "It seems harsh to blame the dead since so few of them choose to die, but if your mother hadn't died, your family would not have changed."

That was probably true. Her mother had made the decisions; there had been no room for the others to act. If Mother were alive, Joyce and Maggie wouldn't have left. If Mother were alive, Giles and Phoebe wouldn't be getting a place of their own. If Mother were alive, Amy would have never met Jack.

She felt a shiver of guilt.

Gwen was still speaking. "And Phoebe doesn't want to be mad at your mother."

"No, I'm sure she doesn't."

Gwen tilted her head back and looked up the trees. "When John—my husband—died, I faced his death in stages. First, I admitted that he was dead on a normal weekday, and I could accept that because I was secretly counting on the fact that he'd be back for Thanksgiving and Christmas. It took me awhile to accept the completeness of it all, that he was really gone. I suspect that the lake was the one last place Phoebe has still been trying to keep your mother alive. Now she's having to

302

face that she truly is dead, that she won't ever come back."

So Phoebe was losing the lake and Mother.

Amy had prepared herself for losing the Olympics. She had known precisely what to do when she started to lose . . . that's why she had won. But how could Phoebe have prepared herself for this?

"Getting a new cabin may be the only way for Phoebe to move on. As long as she keeps coming here, she'll feel like your mother's daughter," Gwen continued. "But it does seem like a shame that they'll have to go so far. It's too bad there's no sites left on the lake."

So much of the other side of the lake was marshy that every possible cabin site was built on. Very few cabins ever came up for sale. When the original owners got too old, someone in the family or a friend or a neighbor usually wanted the place.

Of course, there was still one site.

Amy spoke carefully. "I thought Giles wanted the six of them to start all over."

"Yes, but if they were on the other side of the lake, they would still have the privacy that he's looking for. They couldn't be running over here every two seconds to eat breakfast with everyone, but Phoebe wouldn't feel that she was the one to break up the family summers." Gwen shook her head. "It really is too bad there's not some place on this lake."

But there was. And it was the loveliest site on the entire lake. With a beach so Giles would not have to climb down the steps. With a hundred acres so they could build whatever they wanted to build.

Yes, the road cut back into the forest to avoid the marsh, making the distance three times as long as it really was, but that would give Giles the sense that this

303

was their own place, their own cabin. And if Jack was right, they could lay dock sections across the marsh so that the kids could run back and forth.

It was perfect. The Rim would be perfect for Phoebe and Giles, and it was Amy's. It was hers to give to them. A flood of joy gushed though her.

She wanted to dash back out to the porch. *Phoebe, Phoebe, I've got it. I solved your problem. Me, Amy the Afterthought. I'm going to fix everything.*

Phoebe and Giles's children were moving their things out of the bunkhouse, dashing along the path carrying clothes, stuffed animals, and sleeping bags. They were shouting, laughing, this morning's anguish forgotten. They did love the lake.

And Amy would make sure that they didn't lose it. This wasn't like hanging up the towels in the sauna; this was important. She had to tell someone. But not Phoebe, not yet. She was still on the porch with their father, perhaps still crying, still mourning the loss, not just of the lake but of their mother.

*I can't bring Mother back. But I can let you keep the lake.*

She would tell Jack. That's what she would do. Until she could tell Phoebe, she would tell Jack.

He was more than someone to have fun with. He was someone she could share her thoughts with. This was new, this was wonderful. She didn't have to be alone in her family ever again, not with him a part of it.

She found him in the big garage. A long pole was propped up along three sawhorses, and he was sanding it, the sandpaper curved in his hand. He had the broad double door raised to make the most of the evening light.

He looked up. "Did you talk to your sister?"

304

So he already knew. "Yes." She held up her hand, stopping him from saying something sympathetic or sorrowful. There was no need for sympathy or sorrow. Amy was going to fix everything. "I have the most wonderful idea. What about if Phoebe and Giles built a place on the Rim?"

Jack was good at new ideas. He didn't need time to think. He would drop his sandpaper and stretch and smile. He would agree with her. He would think that this was perfect.

"Wouldn't it be exactly right?" she continued. "It's so beautiful there. They would have their own beach, so Giles wouldn't have to climb steps. They could be off by themselves, but still close enough to see the rest of us. Don't you think it's great? Isn't it perfect?"

Jack spoke slowly. "You'd give them the Rim?"

"Give, sell . . . I don't care. Wouldn't it solve everything?"

"But I thought you bought it, hoping that someday you'd have a place of your own on it."

Amy waved her hand. "That was just the smallest part of it." She had him. Why did she need her own cabin as long as she had him? "I really bought it to keep those developers out. And Phoebe needs it much more than I ever would."

"That's probably true," Jack conceded. "But how are you going to approach this with them? They don't even know that you own it."

What was wrong with him? Why wasn't he excited about this? Couldn't he see that this was perfect? "You don't think this is such a good idea, do you?"

He nodded. "There is something that doesn't sit right with me."

"What? What on earth could be wrong? I just don't

305

see the problem."

"I think I would have trouble accepting such a generous gift from my sister."

"But this is different. This is the lake."

He shrugged. "Would you give the whole tract or just the part on the lake?"

"I don't know." She didn't care. "I could talk to Pam and David—they're the people who handle the money—if that would make you feel better."

"My feelings aren't the issue here, but I do think you ought to slow down and think a bit before you do anything." He was looking serious; then suddenly his expression cleared, and, just as she knew he would, he dropped his sandpaper and smiled. "Do you hear me? Telling someone else to slow down and think? That's what people are always saying to me."

"And do you ever listen to them?"

"Rarely," he admitted.

"Then I'll show you that I'm better than you, because I will listen to you. I will go slow, I will talk to David and Pam," she promised. "But I'll still end up doing the same thing."

"It's a generous thing to do." He pulled off his leather work glove and lifted his hand to smooth a lock of her hair off her forehead. "It's crazy, but it is generous."

"It's no crazier than something you would do." How good it was to be standing this close to him.

"True," he admitted. "But remember, even though you're crazy and I'm crazier, Giles and Phoebe are not." His hand was on her shoulder now.

She slipped her arms around him. "Maybe they need to be a little crazy sometimes."

And he would have agreed, she knew he would have, except that he was kissing her, his mouth warm on hers,

306

his tongue—

Then it all happened so fast—footsteps, shadows in the broad door opening, all happening so fast that neither of them could move. Then came the gasps, Gwen's and Holly's voice calling out his name, and Phoebe's calling out hers.

# CHAPTER 16

THE GARAGE DOOR WAS BROAD, DESIGNED FOR TWO cars, and the three women, his mother, his sister, her sister, were silhouetted in the fading light.

There was no chance that they wouldn't understand. The way he had his arms, the angle of her head, there could be no question about what kind of kiss this was.

The light was at their backs. Amy couldn't see their expressions, but she had heard the gasps and now she felt the silence. She looked down. Jack's gloves, leather and worn, lay at her feet. A narrow rectangle of sawdust coated the floor beneath the pole he had been sanding.

Footsteps stumbled through the tamarack needles. It was Phoebe, whirling, leaving.

Amy's eyes shot to Jack's. *What shall I do?*

*I can't fix this for you.*

No, of course not. He had his own family to face.

Murmuring something to Gwen and Holly, she brushed past them, wanting to find her sister. They were dividing into two families, the Legends and the Wellses.

This was all wrong. She and Jack should be facing everyone together. It should be the two of them together facing a single family together.

Nothing was happening as she had planned.

She could see Phoebe going down toward the lake.

307

She called out, "Phoebe. Phoebe, wait."

Phoebe stopped on the steps, the split logs embedded in the sand. Her back was stiff. She turned slowly. She faced Amy, but she wasn't looking at her. *I don't want to talk to you.*

Phoebe was angry, bitterly angry. Amy knew that she had frustrated Phoebe, that she had irritated her, had made her impatient, but had she ever made her angry before?

*Say something, Amy* willed herself to speak. *You need to go first. You're the one who has to explain. You don't have to apologize. You've done nothing wrong. But you need to explain.*

Explain what? Explain it how? Camp-Amy-and-Jack? How on earth was she going to explain that? *I needed someone to have fun with. We wanted to go roller-blading together.* That would sound ridiculous. "Phoebe, I—" Amy could feel herself starting to apologize.

Phoebe interrupted. "You're having a relationship with him, aren't you?"

It wasn't supposed to be like this. Amy hadn't imagined how it would be when her family found out, but it wasn't to be like this.

"When you went to the ranger station, that was when it happened, wasn't it?" Phoebe's voice was insistent.

What could Amy say?

Phoebe's lips tightened, and she tilted her head back, looking up to the sky. "And I agreed with Jack, I thought it was a good idea for you to go." She leveled her chin, looked at Amy. "What were you thinking of? Don't you care about anyone else?"

"Of course I do." Amy struggled to keep her voice calm. *Phoebe's upset about everything else; she thinks she is losing the lake. It's not really me that she's mad at.* "But my relationship with Jack doesn't have to affect everyone else."

"It doesn't? Here we all are, struggling to get along, struggling to make some kind of a family, and you are sneaking off to have a little fling?"

"It's not a little fling," Amy protested.

"Then what is it? For God's sake, Amy"—Phoebe was lecturing her as if she were a little kid—"aren't things hard enough already? I know you're full of resentment. I know you think Mother and Dad didn't understand you, that they didn't treat you well, that spending tens of thousands of dollars on your skating every year wasn't enough, but does that justify the way you treat the family?"

"The way *I* treat the family?" Amy had no idea what Phoebe was talking about.

"Yes, the way you treat the family, the way you waltz in late, for every single holiday . . . why come at all? If it's not important to you to spend the actual day with us, why come at all?"

"I'm *working.* Holidays, that's when I work. Don't you understand that?"

"I don't know what I understand. I just know that by now you must have a choice. Maybe you're making the right choice—you probably are, clearly being in some stupid parade somewhere is more important to you than anything else, but don't pretend it's not a choice."

A stupid parade . . . was that all Phoebe knew about her work, knew about all the good she did? The libraries, the blood banks, the Special Olympics? Now Amy was mad too. "Nobody else at my level has to dash home after every single holiday. Sure they do sometimes, but sometimes their families come to them."

"So?" Phoebe clearly didn't see what this had to do with anything.

"You'd never come to me, would you?"

"You've never asked us."

That couldn't be true. "Would you have come?"

"How do I know? It's never come up."

Phoebe seemed very sure that Amy had not invited them. But it didn't matter. Invited, not invited, what difference did it make? They wouldn't have come. Amy knew that with all her heart.

"You come up here this summer and won't say how long you're staying for," Phoebe continued. "How is anyone supposed to plan around that? And what does it mean? If we're all nice to you and treat you like a princess, you will stay an extra day?"

"No, it doesn't mean that at all. I don't want to be treated like a princess. It has to do with creativity, with whether or not I have any new ideas while I'm here—"

Phoebe waved her hand, dismissing that argument.

Of course she dismissed it. Amy's career was all about sequins and makeup to Phoebe, and maybe even about athleticism and technique. But creativity, inspiration, no, no, you couldn't use those words to describe what Amy did. Amy was the pretty one. The pretty ones couldn't do anything important, anything hard . . . because the smart ones wouldn't let them. "You do not know what you are talking about."

Phoebe didn't like that. "What about when Mother died? You wouldn't even come when Mother was dying. Is it unfair to say that?"

Amy had had it. For a year and a half Phoebe had been holding this over her head. *You weren't at Mother's side when she was dying.* Phoebe hadn't said it, but Amy knew that she was thinking it. It had been a

310

test, Mother's deathbed, and hey, Phoebe had passed, and Amy had failed. Amy had failed big time . . . because Phoebe had designed the test. "They didn't tell me. You know that." Amy had said this over and over.

"And do 'they' still work for you? Did you fire them?"

No, no, she hadn't. They had made one bad decision, that was certainly true. But did Phoebe have any idea how hard it was to find people you could trust? Two, three pieces of bad advice, and your career as a public figure was over. Life in the public eye was that fragile.

And that's why Amy was not going to feel bad about her relationship with Jack. Phoebe was lucky. She had met Giles her first year in college. She probably thought it was easy, that men like Giles were everywhere. Well, they weren't. They were almost as rare as good advisers. Maybe more so.

But Amy had finally found one too. She wasn't about to give him up.

So it wasn't a matter for discussion.

She needed to make that clear. She wasn't going to be angry, Phoebe wasn't going to be angry, because there wasn't an issue. She and Jack were a fact. The family was going to have to accept that and move on.

She spoke quickly. "You know what you said earlier this evening about you and Giles looking for another place? Why not build on the Rim? That site is perfect; it's beautiful and there are no steps to the lake, and—"

"The Rim?" Phoebe stared at her. "What on earth are you talking about?"

"The property at the end of the lake, with the beach—"

Phoebe interrupted. "I know what the Rim is. It is beautiful. So what are you proposing, that we try to homestead it, that we simply build there and hope that the owners don't care?"

"No, of course not." Amy forced herself to be patient. This was what was going to help everyone move on. "I'm the owner. The Rim is mine."

"What?" Phoebe stared at her. "You own the Rim?"

Amy nodded. "Back when everyone was so worried about developers buying the place—"

"Developers? What are you talking about?"

"Three years ago. I was up here, and people were all talking about someone buying the place to build a fly-in hunting resort—"

"A resort? Why would anyone build a resort here? We're so far from everything. There's plenty of places like that already. Why would anyone build one where there was no utilities?"

"But don't you remember, that day we were at that picnic the weekend after the Fourth, at the campgrounds, and that's all people were talking about, how much they didn't want a resort on the lake."

Phoebe was shaking her head, puzzled. "A Fourth of July picnic?" Now she remembered. "Amy, everyone was drinking, especially that group from Chisholm. Don't tell me you bought a piece of property based on what a bunch of drunks said?"

Amy was speechless. What was Phoebe saying? A bunch of drunks?

She tried to remember the picnic. Maybe it had been that one group that kept bringing the matter up; maybe it had just been that one group forcing everyone else to talk about it. And no, of course, no one had wanted a resort on the lake, but that didn't mean that anyone except the drunks were actually worried about it.

Amy drank so little—and no one else in the figure

skating world drank very much either—that she didn't always have her antennae up about other people's drinking and what alcohol was making them say and do. So, yes, it was possible she had listened too much to people who had been drinking too much.

"Maybe it was an impulsive thing to do," she admitted. "But it's worked out for the best now because you and Giles—"

"You want to give Giles and me the Rim?" Phoebe drew back. "Oh, God, Amy, don't start now."

"Start what?"

"One thing I could say for you, you haven't thrown your money around, insisting on a lot of power because you have more money—"

Insist? Now Amy was mad again. She could own the Taj Mahal, the Mona Lisa, and all of Lipton College, and she would still have no power in this family.

"—Sure, your gifts to the kids are a little pricey, but that's understandable. We can live with that. But don't all of sudden start thinking you can fix everything with money. Don't start that, not when it's the only thing you're doing right."

Phoebe marched back up the stairs. She was done with this conversation.

Amy glared after her. *I am not a little kid anymore. I will not be dragged to every stupid Science Fair that you and Ian won blue ribbons at. I have a right to be happy. I've earned it.*

Of course, Phoebe might be right about the Rim. Amy forced herself to be objective about that. No one would have been more upset about a resort on the Rim than Phoebe. If she said it wasn't a threat, then it wasn't.

Amy remembered when she had told Pam and David to buy the Rim. It had been a hushed, hurried conversation outside the laundromat where her mother and Phoebe had been folding clothes. David had wanted to investigate; she had told him not to, that she wanted this done right away. If he had investigated, she realized now, he would have found out that the threat existed only in the minds of a group of drunks from Chisholm.

Why had she been so urgent? Why had she had to buy the property immediately? Because she had wanted to do something important. She had wanted to stop feeling like Amy the Afterthought.

Okay, she hadn't needed to buy it. It was a mistake, a bad investment, but she hadn't hurt anyone. She wasn't going to feel bad about it.

She heard footsteps behind her and knew without looking that it was Jack. She tilted her head back. "Did you talk to your mother and sister?"

He nodded. "They weren't all that surprised. They had both guessed how I was starting to feel about you. What about your sister?"

"She was completely surprised." How typical—that his family understood him well enough to have anticipated this while her family had had no idea what she was thinking and feeling.

"Are things okay between the two of you?"

Amy waved her hand. "It will blow over. But it turns out that I was completely wrong about needing to buy the Rim." She shook her head. "That whole idea of a resort coming up here, that was just alcohol talking."

"I wondered," he said. "There have to be hundreds of lakes in Minnesota where development would be easier. But why did this come up? I thought you weren't going to talk to her about the Rim."

Amy shrugged. "Things got a little out of hand."

"It sounds like it was more than that."

314

Amy didn't answer.

Jack persisted. "Is she angry with you?"

Amy didn't want to talk about it. "You could say that."

His lips tightened. "I don't want you to be fighting with your sister about this."

"She's got to stop judging me. She knows nothing about my life, about what it's like to be me."

"She can't help judging. That's who she is, but you have to admit that she's harder on herself than on anyone else."

He did have a point there.

"Amy, I think we need to go to everyone and say that we're sorry, say that we made a mistake. We can't pretend that it didn't happen, but we can—"

"A mistake?" She couldn't be hearing this. "You think the other night was a mistake?"

"I do." He was facing her squarely, looking straight at her. "You know it's not you. If we had met each other in any other way, if—"

"But it was so wonderful. How can it have been a mistake?"

"Because of what it's doing to you and your sister."

"But I don't care about my sister." That wasn't true. "I only care about you."

She was sounding like a child, a selfish child. *I'm the only one that matters.*

She wasn't like that. She was nice. That's what everyone said about Amy Legend, that she was nice. She wasn't a stuck-up star, she wasn't a prima donna, she was nice.

It was only when she was with her family that everything got so jumbled up.

She took a breath. The shadows were deepening

315

along the shore of the lake. The water almost looked black.

It was odd to see the dock without Giles's boat. The boat was always there, either tied up at the dock or out on the water, but now it was spread out on the sand of the Rim's narrow beach, smashed to pieces.

Jack thought they ought to break up. She couldn't accept that. She wouldn't. Did that make her selfish? Did that make her a child?

But she would acknowledge that this was a difficult moment in her brother's and sister's lives, that perhaps this wasn't the best time for her and Jack to be doing the happy-young-lovers thing. The original plan had been to keep this a secret for the rest of the summer, and then the two of them would get to know each other better in the fall.

As far as she was concerned, that was still the plan. She took another breath. "I agree that we need to keep things light until summer is over. But I want to see you again in the fall."

"Nothing will have changed by then. We will still be in the same family."

But in the fall he would see how different her family was from his, how none of them ever knew what she was doing. He would see that this could work.

He had his hands in his pockets. "I hope you know," he said slowly, "how much I hate this, how much I wish . . ."

She touched his check. "I know."

She was letting him misunderstand. She would let him think that she was agreeing with him. There was no point in arguing with him. He would never see how wrong he was until the summer was over.

"I'm going to go talk to my mother," he said. "But I

316

don't suppose you're ready to talk to your sister, are you?"

She wasn't. "I'll go to the log cabin for a while."

"Holly's probably in there."

"That's okay. It's my sister I'm mad at, not yours."

Through the screen door she could see Holly sitting at the round table. As soon as the door began to creak open, Holly jumped up and came into the kitchen. "Amy, I'm so happy for you. I think the two of you will have such fun together. But you have to promise me that whenever he drives you nuts, you'll call me. He's been driving me nuts since he starting teething."

Holly was trying, she was trying hard, but her voice was too bright. She had practiced this. She was not happy about Amy and Jack.

Amy had never thought about how Holly would react. She would have assumed that Holly would be happy for her, and clearly Holly felt that she was supposed to be happy, but she wasn't.

Why couldn't something go right? Why couldn't at least one person take this well?

"That's nice of you." Amy decided to pretend to believe Holly's words. "But unfortunately nothing's going to come of it. The family situation is just too complicated."

"Oh, Amy . . ." Now Holly's voice was sincere. She might not have been comfortable with Amy and Jack's relationship, but she did wish them well. "I'm so sorry. Are you terribly unhappy?"

"I'm not thrilled," Amy acknowledged. "But it's okay. It's not like we love each other or anything."

She hadn't planned on saying that. She didn't know why she had.

But it was true, wasn't it? They were both a long way

317

from talking about love. In fact, Jack thought they had broken up.

She went into the living room to sit at the table. Holly followed her. A legal-looking document was lying on the table, a pen on top of it. The document was densely typed and stapled across the top. Holly had been working.

"I really am sorry," Holly said again. "I do think you would have been wonderful for him."

"No, it's the other way around. He would have been wonderful for me."

*Going to be wonderful for me. Going to be. This might still happen.* She had to believe that.

Holly was speaking. "I sometimes think that Jack is lonely and doesn't know it."

"Jack? Lonely?" That was a new thought.

"Anywhere he goes everybody likes him. I know that, but I've started to wonder if either of us knows how to recognize loneliness. People complain that their parents didn't allow them to get angry or be sexual. I wonder if Mother ever allowed us to miss Dad. She always distracted us, made everything such fun, that we never faced up to missing him."

"I thought you liked it that you didn't mope around like some of the other families," Amy said. Holly and Jack had both told her about what fun they had had when their father was out at sea.

"Yes, of course. But we may have gone too far, leaving us as adults who don't know whether or not we're lonely."

"And you think this applies to you as well as him?"

"It has to, doesn't it?" Holly pushed her hair behind her ears. "Amy, I hate admitting this, but my first thought when I saw the two of you together was to feel

318

betrayed."

"Betrayed? How?" Amy was horrified. "Holly, I never—"

Holly held up her hand, stopping Amy. "I know you didn't mean to. It was all me. I guess I had been assuming that the two of us, you and me, that we would always have the same place in the family, the two career girls, the two maiden aunts." Holly glanced out the window, but there was nothing to see. The Norways grew close to the cabin on this side, and their soft needles filled the other side of the windowpanes. "I've always thought Jack would marry and it would be Mother and me and Jack's wife and kids, and that seemed fine. But after Mother married your dad and both your brother and sister were married with children, everything changed. The family was different. Everyone would have a partner and children . . . except me, and that would have been hard except that you were in the same situation too."

And then suddenly Amy hadn't been in the same situation. She had been with Jack. "I don't know what to say."

"Nothing. I know myself. I like living alone. I don't want to get married. I don't want to have children, but you can't let my choices influence yours. I was surprised, that's all. I'll get used to it."

"But there's nothing to get used to," Amy said softly. "It happened once. It won't happen again."

"Do you believe that I'm sorry?" Holly said. "That I am really not as selfish as I sound?"

"I do." She trusted the sincerity in Holly's voice. "You know I do."

It was her own voice she was worried about. *It happened once. It won't happen again.* That must have

319

sounded sincere too.

What was happening? Maybe Jack was right. Maybe the summer ending wouldn't make any difference.

Gwen was using paper plates for dinner. Eleanor had never done that. Paper plates were fine for lunch, but dinner was served on dishes. That had been Eleanor's rule.

Well, Eleanor wasn't here anymore, and this evening Gwen was using paper plates. She needed to talk to Hal, and that was more important than setting the table.

She found him still on the lakeside porch of the main cabin, standing, one foot on the railing, staring out through the trees, toward the lake. She went up and slipped her hand in his arm. He was still thinking about Ian's wife leaving, about Phoebe's husband wanting to find a place of his own. He didn't know about the latest problem, about Amy and Jack.

She wasn't sure how much to tell him. She had often concealed Jack's misdeeds from his father; John overreacted to everything Jack did. But Hal was so different. He observed, he watched, he waited, he thought.

Suddenly she felt as if she hardly knew him.

This summer was supposed to be their chance to learn each other's ways before they went back to Iowa and faced his world, his friends. But they had never had that chance. Since the moment Phoebe and Giles's station wagon turned into the drive, there had been nothing but everyone else's problems. She had, in effect, been standing on all the electric cords, keeping others from tripping. She had devoted all her patience, energy, and intuition to everyone except the one who mattered the most—Hal.

She loved Hal—she was sure of that, she did not for one instant question their marriage, question whether or not they had done the right thing—but she still didn't know him, not like she had known John, whom she had known better than he knew himself.

When would her generation ever get its turn?

"We were worried about the wrong couple, Hal." She decided to be direct. "It wasn't Nick and Maggie who had sex on the canoe trip. It was Amy and Jack."

Hal turned his head to look at her.

"When they went to that ranger station to get help, they shared a tent. He says that they both recognize that it was a mistake, that there's too much going on with the rest of the family. He feels awful about it. He really does. It's not like him to—"

Hal laid a hand over her lips. "You don't have to defend Jack to me. I'm not saying anything because I'm so surprised. That's all. I don't know what I think, but I'm not angry at Jack."

Gwen felt her shoulders ease. She had been more worried about that than she realized. "I was surprised too. I suspected that he was attracted to her, but I truly believed that he wouldn't let anything happen."

"Do they really think it was a mistake, or are they being noble, giving it up for the rest of us?"

"I don't know." That hadn't occurred to her although it was the sort of thing Jack would do. "That would be sad, wouldn't it?"

"Yes."

"So what do we do?"

"You know my answer to that. Nothing. We have to trust them to do the right thing."

"But what is the right thing?"

"How can we know that?"

Her first husband would have never said that. He would have believed that he did know what was right.

321

And his first wife probably would have too.

Thomas's little plastic pail of pine cones sat at the edge of the steps. It was still full from yesterday. When Gwen had first come to the lake, she had known nothing about pine cones. Now she knew that the light egg-shaped ones were from the Norways, the rosy brown ones were from the tamarack trees, the narrow, closed, curving ones from the jack pines. The beautiful white pine with its soft bluegreen needles dropped the ugliest of the cones, narrow yellow-brown cylinders.

Hal put his arm around her. "When I met you, I was so giddy, so happy, that I didn't think enough of how this would impact the kids."

"But they aren't kids anymore," she said.

"Sometimes they act like it."

She nodded slowly. They did. "Why do we always have to worry about them? Why can't they worry about us?" Even Holly, as considerate and attentive as she was, tended to think that Gwen could survive anything.

"Because we don't want them to. We still want to be Mom and Dad able to fix everything."

He was right. Holly thought Gwen could survive anything because that's what Gwen wanted her to think.

Why couldn't they all go back to being babies? Why couldn't they go back to having problems their parents could solve?

## CHAPTER 17

EVERYONE WAS SUBDUED FOR THE NEXT FEW DAYS. Ian's children, Emily and Scott, clung to him, and so Claire and Alex were quieter too, spending more time with their father in the new cabin. Gwen planned fewer activities, and Nick initiated more, taking the kids on walks, teaching them to throw horseshoes.

Phoebe apologized to Amy almost immediately. She was mortified, unable to forgive herself for speaking as she had.

*Are you always this hard on yourself?* Amy wondered as she listened. And she knew the answer instantly. Yes, Phoebe was. Phoebe had never learned to forgive herself.

Phoebe spent her life determined to make no mistakes. That's why she worked so hard, that's why she never relaxed or daydreamed; she might make a mistake. And because she never made mistakes, she had never learned to forgive herself for them.

Amy had won the Olympics because she had gone on after a mistake. Phoebe had never had to do this.

*How can I teach you this? How can I show you the one thing that I know?*

But Phoebe was locked into her own unhappiness, her grief at leaving the lake, her guilt at being the first one to do so. Amy couldn't help her. There was nothing she could say.

It was past time for her to go back to Denver. She had been here for weeks. Henry and Tommy were already at work, putting together new programs for the fall professional season and for their tour in the spring. They wouldn't be happy with her, but she didn't care. Holly wasn't leaving until the end of the week. Amy would stay as long as she did.

Jack offered to drive them to Minneapolis, but they refused. They would take the little commuter flight out of Hibbing. "Then I'll take you there," he said.

"I'll do it," Phoebe volunteered. "We'll have a mound of laundry to do."

"No," Jack said, "I'll take them."

His voice was low, quieter than usual. Phoebe understood. She nodded her head. Yes, Jack could take them to the airport. The laundry could wait for another day.

With Holly and Amy leaving there was to be yet another change in sleeping arrangements. Jack was moving into the bunkhouse with Nick; Ian and his children were moving to the log cabin. So while Amy was saying good-bye, there was another parade of children dashing along the path between the cabins, dropping T-shirts and shoes behind them.

Amy hugged her dad and Gwen, Phoebe, Giles, and Nick; she even hugged Nick.

"So when do I see you again?" she said to him. She really did like the boy. His pale skin had gotten more color in the weeks he had been here, and his close haircut had grown softer, making his narrow forehead, once bulldoggish, seem strong, not belligerent.

"Uncle Hal has been making noises about my coming to college at the place he teaches, so maybe in two years you'll be seeing me all the time."

Amy didn't want to tell him that she was almost never in Iowa. "I have a competition in Boston in November. Can I send you tickets? Will you have dinner with me afterward?"

"Is it on a school night? I'm not allowed out after bedtime on a school night."

"And that stops you?" she asked.

He grinned.

She hugged everyone again and got into Jack's truck. This time there were only the three of them, and she could sit without touching him.

The Hibbing airport was small, little more than one room. There was no gift shop or newsstand, just vending machines and an electric coffee maker. The coffee was paid for on the honor system, and a white foam cup served as the cash register. Amy and Holly checked their bags, got their boarding passes, and sat down to wait.

"I heard you making plans to see Nick," Jack said.

Amy nodded.

"It's good of you."

"I like him."

They looked at each other. She was going to see Nick; all her New York dates were already on Holly's calendar, but she and he were making no plans to see each other. Amy heard herself sigh.

But there was nothing to say.

The seats of the airport's molded plastic chairs had no armrests; the legs were pairs of chrome tubes that slanted down in long, narrow triangles. A chrome bar ran beneath the seats joining one chair to the next. They were the most ordinary sort of chairs, the kind you see everywhere.

How could she have nothing to say to him? She had never been able to be so straight with anyone before. They had been able to talk about fame, fears, bad breath, everything. She didn't think of herself as a witty person, but with him she had been funny.

Now there was nothing to say.

Holly stood up. "I think I'll go to the ladies' room."

Amy understood. Holly was trying to give Jack and her some time alone, a moment for a private farewell.

But what would be the point? "I'll go with you," Amy said.

The ladies' room had only two stalls, and the

women ahead of them had small children. They had to wait, and by the time they were finished, the plane was ready. People were already starting to pass through the security check in front of the airport's single gate.

Amy couldn't speak. There had to be air in her lungs; she could feel the rising swell in her chest, but she couldn't exhale, she couldn't breathe.

There was nothing to say.

She had wanted a relationship with him that didn't involve her family. Lots of women had that. They just took their husbands home for Thanksgiving and Christmas and stored them in the corner of the living room to watch football. The husband was polite to the family, and the family was polite back. That was all.

She didn't like herself when she was with her family. She didn't like how passive she was. That's why she wanted to keep her relationship with him separate from her family, so she could be her real self when she was with him.

But that wasn't possible. He didn't want to separate from his family, and his family was her family.

She and Holly moved to the security check. Holly put her purse on the conveyor belt. Jack hugged her. "I'll, call you whenever I can," he said.

Holly nodded. She knew that.

Amy laid her purse down for the X-ray inspection. Holly was walking through the metal detector. Amy looked at Jack. He had his hands in his pockets.

There was nothing to say.

# CHAPTER 18

THE NEXT MORNING SHE WAS AT THE RINK, LACING UP her skates.

The rink was light and airy, occupying a glass-covered courtyard space in the center of a large office complex. She and Henry and Tommy owned it. Throughout the year several other coaches rented ice time to give lessons, but in August and the first two weeks of September no one used it but them.

Henry and Tommy were already at work. Oliver, their coach, was standing on the ice, watching them, his arms folded. Amy pulled off her skate guards and stepped out onto the ice. The other three skated over.

"How was Minnesota?" Henry reached her first.

"Very nice."

How small he seemed. He was easily five inches shorter than Jack. Yet he was one of the largest of the male skaters.

"Gretchen said you'd be in today." Tommy was slightly out of breath. He'd already been working hard. "We've missed you."

Tommy was genuinely small, only two inches taller than Amy.

She wished that she could tell them. They were her closest friends. *Hey, I met someone, guys, and I slept with him. It was great, it was magic.* But things would be too hard to explain. *But be's also my dad's new wife's son, which makes him sort of my stepbrother except that he doesn't seem like a brother, although his sister, she does seem like a sister.*

Amy wasn't sure she herself understood.

Oliver eyed her arms and shoulders. He was always

worried about her upper-body strength. "How much conditioning do you think you lost?"

"Not much. I pumped water and paddled a canoe."

"Okay." That was all the greeting Amy was going to get from him. "You two"—he pointed at Henry and Ofiver—"more of the same. And, Amy, I suppose you know what to do."

"Warm up."

At their lunch break they talked about ideas for new programs. Or at least Oliver, Henry, and Tommy talked. Amy looked through her mail and listened. She had not had a single idea while on vacation. She noticed Henry looking at her suspiciously. Of all of them, Henry was the most ambitious, the most competitive.

*Oh, I could make you really suspicious,* Amy thought. *None of you liked it all the other times I got involved with someone. If you didn't like those men, what will you think of Jack?*

They would have liked him just fine. Jack would not have wanted to get tangled up in her career. He would not have wanted to produce her shows, arrange her publicity, or manage her money. He would have been perfect.

Would have been.

"Did your dad give you any music?" Tommy asked.

Amy shook her head. "He just got married. He's had other things on his mind. But I've probably got twenty, twenty-five tapes that we've never used. I can listen to them tonight."

She worked for another hour and then spent much of the afternoon at the beauty salon, getting a haircut, color, manicure, facial, and the long-overdue bikini wax. She returned to the rink for another workout—this was why they had their own rink, so they could have ice time whenever they wanted. At eight in the evening she returned home.

Her condominium building was across the street from the rink. She owned a three-bedroom unit on the top floor. It was full of ivory upholstery and burnished copper pillars. Professional designers had decorated it, of course. Everything in Amy's life was taken care of professionally. A maid service cleaned the apartment for her; the doorman and the front desk received packages and held her mail; the ground-floor deli fed her. Gretchen, in an office across the street at the rink, made travel arrangements, scheduled doctor's appointments, and took care of the bills.

She kept the tapes her father sent her in an antique Swedish pine pie safe. The tapes were nothing like a final piece of music. Occasionally Hal did the roughest of edits, but usually the music would come without introductions or closures. Sometimes he would simply play the melody on the piano. Other times he would talk over the music—"If you bring down the percussion here, Amy . . ."

Most of the tapes she was listening to now, she remembered having heard. She remembered why she had decided not to use each piece, and in general she still felt the same way. But every so often a tape would start and she wouldn't remember it. She wouldn't remember having heard it—although she had, her initials and a date were on the box—and she couldn't remember why she had rejected it. There were five or six such tapes, music that she couldn't remember hearing.

She listened to them all again. What did these pieces have in: common? Why hadn't she remembered them?

There was something about the tempo of all of them. Some were fast and some were slow, but there was a similarity, something she didn't have a word for. Amy closed her eyes, trying to see if she had an image instead of a word.

It wasn't an image, but a color—red. One piece was the deepest, smokiest burgundy. Another was fiery. A third was light and clear, a glassine filter. But all were red, the color of vitality, strength, aggression.

And sex. Red lights, scarlet women, flushed faces. That's what these were about—sex. Temptation. Longing. That's why she couldn't skate to this music. That's why she hadn't even remembered it. She hadn't understood what it was about. Despite her previous relationships, she did not know very much about sex.

She did now.

Could she skate to this music? Could she, sweet little Amy Legend, express herself sexually?

Why not? So what if it wasn't like anything she had ever done before? Jack wasn't like anything she'd ever done before. Maybe things weren't going to work out with him, and maybe things wouldn't work out with this music, but why not try? She didn't have to be little and sweet forever.

She was the first one at the rink in the morning. She had put all five pieces on a loop, and she cued them up for endless replay. She had no plan. She would simply listen to the music and skate.

This was why she had trudged through the biting wind one day so many years ago and skated into the middle of a hockey practice. This was why little girls everywhere begged their parents to get up before dawn and drive them miles to the rink. This was why people

330

gave up their friends, their Families, their childhood, even in some cases their health . . . because when you were on the ice, the speed and the grace, the beauty, it caught you and trapped you.

This too was magic.

Amy could tell that she was skating differently, using her arms in different ways, and she wasn't sure if the lines she was creating were beautiful, which was usually something she could feel immediately. But that was all right. This music would work. She knew it.

She rarely liked other people's sexy programs. They usually seemed thin and insincere. "The competitors are getting too young," the judges and skating officials would grouse, and so the coaches would try to make them seem older. Schoolgirls, compliant and obedient, were sewn into tight costumes and told to skate like temptresses, their hands stroking down their bodies. They did as they were told and understood none of it.

*If you're just doing what you're told, then sex isn't about sex. It's about power.*

Sex was another way of relating to a person, another way of getting to know him.

The music played over and over with a little pause as the tape rewound to its beginning. She deliberately avoided any of the conventional sexy moves—the eyes glancing back over the shoulder, the fingers tracing along the collarbone.

*Sex isn't about showing off your body. Sex is about sharing your body.*

The music was settling into her bones. Eventually, she knew, her body would take these pieces in, enfolding them into her auditory, her neurological systems, until it would seem that the music was not coming from a loudspeaker but from within herself, and

331

it would surprise her that if she stopped skating, the music would play on. In her best moments she could no longer distinguish between external and internal, between stimulus and response. It was all one.

She skated on, already putting together a few rough sequences. Suddenly she heard clapping. She turned toward the sound. Tommy, Henry, and Oliver were standing at the boards. They had been watching her.

"Okay," Oliver drawled, "who is he?"

She was getting her point across. "No one important," she answered.

She didn't mean that, but she didn't want to have to stop and explain. *He's not important to* you, that's what she meant. *He's not going to change anything for the three of us.*

But he had changed everything for her.

"If someone was making me skate like that," Tommy said, "I wouldn't call him 'no one important.' "

He was right. Even if she never saw Jack again, he would always be important. "Then I should have said 'no one you know.' "

Morning after morning Amy woke early. She would brush her teeth and come straight to the rink, unlocking the door, turning on the lights herself, working by herself The programs were starting to take shape. At least four were going to work out, maybe even all five. It was extraordinary; nothing like this had ever happened to her before, so much creativity, so many new ideas. It had never been so easy before. Henry, whose standards were absurdly high, was quietly approving. Tommy was openly, cheerfully, generously envious.

This was why she had always wanted long hair. She

had wanted to feel more sexual. Long hair was wild and romantic, uninhibited and exuberant. Short hair was practical, orderly, and professional. Of course, hair was only a symbol. Probably the best way to feel sexual was to have a sex life . . . which for one brief, shining moment Amy had had.

There was still a tremendous amount to do. She spent hours in front of the mirror in their ballet studio working on her arm movements; each turn of her wrist had to be studied from several angles. Every day she spoke to Jeffrey, the man who was developing the musical arrangements. That was hard, arranging the music, because there were so many choices, so many different things that could be done with a melodic line. You had to think about every note, every bar.

She often sent her father copies of arrangements they were working on, but there was no point in doing it while he was at the lake. It took a couple of days for anything to get to the lake—Federal Express did not deliver there—and then it took another three to get his response back. By then she and Jeffrey would have changed everything seven times.

She had to sketch ideas for her costumes and approve the final designs. She had to talk to the companies she had endorsement deals with to find out what they wanted her to do this fall. She had to pose for new publicity stills and sign stacks of photos. She had to lift weights. She had to try out new blades. She had to answer mail, return phone calls, get new clothes. There was always something to do.

Jack was running out of things to do. He stained the rails of the fence that ran along the road and replaced two rotting posts. He reroofed the main cabin biffy. He built better benches for the sauna. He dug a hole in the ground three feet wide and eight feet deep, and constructed a circular pull-up shelf to fit in it. At the end of the summer Hal could lower his cans of paint and tubes of glue down into the pit, and maybe they wouldn't freeze over the winter as they always had when left in the garage.

When it was too dark to work outside, he worked in the log cabin. He rehung the exterior doors so that the screen door wouldn't clip the back of whatever woman was standing at the sink. He niched little recesses into the interior wall between the bedroom and the living room, and installed shelves for a woman to store her toiletries. He repositioned the gas lamp that hung on the wall behind the beds.

Then because he couldn't think of anything else to do and because the real problem with the cabin, what Amy—and the others too—didn't like about it, was how dark it was, he got Hal's permission and cut four rectangular holes in the roof to install skylights.

"The skylights," Gwen gushed. She was in town to do laundry and had called Amy. "You wouldn't believe what a difference they make. The log cabin is so light now. You'll love it."

"But I thought Dad and Ian were worried about skylights leaking in the winter."

"Jack says that they are very well made now. A number of the other cabins on the lake have them, and they haven't reported any problems. Next year we're going to have him put some in our cabin too."

"Why are you waiting until next year? That doesn't sound like Jack, putting off something for a whole year."

Gwen laughed. "It doesn't, does it? That's my doing. Hal and I don't want to put up with the mess. And Jack is leaving on the thirteenth. We don't leave until the twentieth, but he's going early. He wants to give us some time alone."

Jack was leaving the lake August thirteenth? Amy fumbled in her skate bag for her Day Timer and flipped through the pages. She was supposed to be in San Antonio on August fifteenth for her costume fittings. She couldn't do that. What if Jack came?

She called JoElla in Texas, asking if she could come on the twelfth instead. The seamstress gulped and spoke slowly. "Okay . . . I guess I can have them ready by then."

Amy winced. JoElla was going to be sitting up late night after night to have Amy's costumes ready three days ahead of schedule. But she had to be in town on the fifteenth. Jack might come.

She was back from Texas on the morning of the thirteenth. He didn't come on the thirteenth. Of course not. Even he wouldn't have driven all this way in one day. And he didn't turn up on the fourteenth. Or the fifteenth either.

She asked the man who drove the Zamboni machine how long it would take to drive from Minneapolis to Denver.

"It's about nine hundred miles," he guessed. "And the route's not bad, 35 to 76 to 80, interstates all the way and nothing to speak of in the way of cities. So I'd guess sixteen, seventeen hours of driving time, not counting stops."

It took an additional four hours to get from the lake to Minneapolis. Jack should be here by now.

On the seventeenth she called Holly and asked her

335

straight out. "Where's Jack?"

"In Kentucky. He called a couple days ago."

"Kentucky?" *Why did he call you? Why didn't he call me?* "What's he doing there?"

"He lives there," Holly pointed out. "Although actually I don't know what he's doing there. He sold his business at the beginning of the summer, and he signed a two-year no-compete clause that really limits what he can do in Kentucky, Tennessee, or Virginia."

Denver wasn't in Kentucky or Tennessee or Virginia. He could do anything he wanted in Colorado. Why didn't he come?

"Is he going to learn to fly helicopters?" Amy asked. "He talked about that once."

"How would I know?" Holly answered.

Amy slid the antenna back into the phone. Jack wasn't coming.

On August nineteenth she had Gretchen send copies of the musical arrangements to Iowa by overnight mail. On the twentieth she had to shorten her morning workout to go to a meeting of a board for a charitable foundation. But she returned to the rink in the late afternoon. She was experimenting with a different way of squaring her hips in one sequence, and that meant all kinds of other things had to be changed as well. She was liking the effect the hips had, but she wasn't sure about everything else. There was nothing to do except repeat the sequence over and over, making tiny adjustments, working until things started to feel right. Every so often she would stop and skate one of the other programs completely simply to give herself a rest.

It was halfway through one of those programs when she became aware that someone was in the rink with her. She stopped skating. The overhead lights were on,

and she had to lift her hand, shading her eyes so that she could see into the bleachers. There was a person in the third row.

It was Jack.

She couldn't believe it. Jack. She called out his name and dug her toe pick deep into the ice to speed toward him. He rose and started climbing down the bleachers.

"You're here! I thought you were in Kentucky. I was so sure you weren't coming." The waist-high barrier was between them, but she reached out her hands and his closed around them, warm and strong.

He looked great. Even though he was wearing blue and the sleeves of his shirt were rumpled from having been rolled up and the upper thighs of his jeans were heavily creased from sitting behind the steering wheel and he hadn't shaven in two days, he really did look great.

"Let's go somewhere we can sit. My place is just across the street. I have to go out through the locker room because my stuff's there, so it's probably easiest if I meet you out front, but I'll just grab everything. I can shower at home. Do you know the way?"

She was chattering. Not saying anything, just chattering. She hadn't said this much in a week. It was so good to see him. The words were gushing out of her.

In the locker room, she tugged off her skates, crammed her feet into her street shoes, and pulled a big sweatshirt on over her skating dress. She was almost out of breath when she got to the lobby.

She hadn't cooled down. She hadn't stretched. That was stupid. That was how you ended up sore.

Oh, well. So what if she was sore for once? What difference did it make? Jack was here.

He was waiting for her, leaning against the wall near

the security desk, chatting with the guard. He straightened at the sight of her and held out his hand for her skate bag. He held open the door for her.

"Holly said that you went to Kentucky first. Wouldn't it have made more sense geography-wise to have come straight here?"

"Probably."

She wondered why he was here. Maybe it didn't matter. It was so wonderful to see him. She tucked her hand in his arm as they waited for the elevator in her building.

She got her keys out of the side pocket of her skate bag without taking it off his shoulder and opened the door to her condominium. Jack followed her inside.

"I have to take a shower," she said. "It won't take me long. Can I get you something first? Something to eat? A beer? Not that I have either one, but I can call the deli downstairs and they'll bring it up." She couldn't stop talking. She was so happy to see him.

"I'll go get it myself," he said. "I'd rather do that than wait around for a delivery. Do you want anything?"

Amy started to shake her head when the phone rang. Her cordless was on the side table next to the sofa. She answered.

"Amy?"

"Sweetheart, it's us."

It was her father and Gwen. That was odd. They were never in town in the evening.

But it was August twentieth, the day they were going back to Iowa. Amy, had forgotten. "Are you home? You must have just walked in the door."

On the other side of the room, Jack was shaking his head, crossing his hands in front of his face. He was not here.

Amy suddenly sobered. Jack had not told them that he was coming to Denver.

"We left the lake this morning," Gwen was saying. "We made it in just over ten hours. It was an easy trip."

"Jack had brought in the dock and closed up the other two cabins," Hal was saying. "It made leaving so easy."

"That's good." Amy didn't know what else to say.

"Gwen told you about the skylights, didn't she?" he continued. "You're really going to like them."

"That's what she said." This was awful. How could she not tell them he was here?

"Your tapes were here when we got home," her father continued. "I'm eager to listen to them. I'll try to get to them tomorrow."

He wouldn't *try* to listen to them tomorrow. He would do it. He would have guessed from the fact that she had sent them overnight, timing their arrival so carefully, that she was still working on the arrangements, that she would want a quick response.

How selfish she was. Just sending them like that, demanding his immediate attention, when he would have millions of things to do tomorrow, all the unpacking, the pounds and pounds of mail that would have piled up in his office.

Was this what Phoebe had been talking about?

"How is your skating going?" Gwen asked.

"Fine," Amy said. She was sounding too abrupt. But how could she talk about what she was doing, the new elements in her work, with Jack standing right there, pretending not to be there?

"What are you working on?" Gwen went on. "Are you coming up with new programs?"

Gwen wanted to chat. That was understandable. For the past two weeks she had seen only Hal and Jack. She was home now, but home was unfamiliar. It was still Eleanor's house. Of course she would want to settle in for a long talk with the one member of Hal's family she felt closest to.

And here Amy was acting all abrupt and distant, making it sound as if she didn't care about the family when she was working.

This too was what Phoebe had been talking about.

Gwen introduced another subject—how charming she found the house, how she was looking forward to settling in. But Amy only murmured the vaguest responses, and a minute later the conversation was over.

She hung up the phone.

"Well, that stank," she said.

Jack had his hands in his pockets; his shoulders were slightly hunched. "I hate having put you in that position."

"Why didn't you want them to know that you were here?" she asked. He had been the one who didn't think they should have secrets.

"I didn't want to have to explain my reasons to everyone."

"Are you going to explain them to me?"

He took his hands out of his pockets and then put them back in again. "That's pretty amazing stuff that you do on the ice."

"Were you surprised by the speed?"

He frowned. "Not particularly . . . should I have been?"

"No. But that's what people always say when they first see us live, how fast we skate. The speed doesn't come across on TV. But I guess the sequence I was working on was slower, wasn't it?"

"I have no idea. I was amazed by how sexy it was."

340

"Oh, that." She smiled. "Everyone is amazed by that, including me. It's completely new." *You changed me. You taught me things about myself and my body that I didn't know. I wouldn't be skating like this except for you.*

But this wasn't why he had come. Amy gestured for him to sit down. She sat across from him. She could see her blurred reflection in one of the copper pillars.

He put his hands on his knees. "I've said I'm no good at talking about my feelings."

Amy nodded.

"And you need to understand," he continued, "that I don't want anything from you, that I'm not thinking that what I'm about to say will change anything between us, because all the family stuff is still there."

He wasn't making any sense. "What are you trying to say?"

"That I love you."

Amy went still. Every nerve, every muscle, every vein froze.

He got up from the sofa and moved nervously to the windows, his movements chopped and jerky, not at all like him. "I've never said that to anyone before. I don't even think I've ever thought about it, ever spent time wondering whether or not I love someone, but after you left the lake, that's all I could think about. Did I love you? But why else was I putting skylights in the log cabin and new benches in the sauna? I wanted to make the place better for you. I wanted you to know that I loved you. And I thought maybe you'd come next time and you'd see the skylights and know that I loved you. But then that seemed pretty stupid since first of all, you may not go back there for another four years and second, you might see the skylights and think that they

341

were just about getting more light into somewhere dark. So even though this isn't my way of doing things, I figured I'd come out here and tell you."

"Oh, Jack . . ." She could feel her hand at her throat. She did not know what to say. *It's not like we love each other.* That's what she had said to his sister.

"Maybe it would have been better to keep my mouth shut since this doesn't change anything between the two of us, but I don't know . . . your career . . . the way the audience loves you. I thought maybe you would like to know that in addition to all of them, there's also one ordinary guy who loves you too. I don't know where I'll be, what I'll be doing, but there's one thing that you can count on—you are loved."

He loved her. Amy felt as if the floor had suddenly disappeared. She was plunging downward, head over heels, falling so fast that she could see nothing, hear nothing.

He loved her.

He stood up. "That's what I wanted you to know. So I'm going to go now."

"Go? You're leaving?"

"I can't stay here."

"You drove from Kentucky to Colorado"—Amy had no idea how long that took—"and now you're leaving? People don't do that."

"I do. And I told you that this doesn't change anything. This doesn't fix anything."

What was he talking about? This had to change things. "Wouldn't you please spend the night here?" she begged him. "It can't be safe to get back on the road."

"I won't drive long. I'll stop outside town."

"Then why not stay here?" Maybe in the morning she would know what to say. "You don't have to stay with me. There's a guest room."

He shook his head. "You know what would happen if I stayed, and I admit that once I saw you skate like that, I didn't give a damn about anything else. But that phone call from Mom made it dear. I can't stand having secrets from my family."

He was right. Amy knew that at this very moment Gwen was back in Iowa, making a grocery list or sorting laundry, feeling uneasy about how curt Amy had been on the phone.

"Amy, I've thought about this a lot. I have no role in your life, except to love you, and I can do that from anywhere."

"Where are you going? What are you going to do?"

He was at the door. "I'll go back to Kentucky, I suppose, although I don't have a clue what I'll do. Think about you probably."

"Oh, Jack . . ."

His hand was on the. knob. "Just remember—every time you put on your skates, every time you open a door and all sorts of cameras go off, just remember that you are loved."

Now her front door was open, and a moment later she was staring blankly at the elevator door sliding shut. She hurried back across her living room to the windows, and holding aside the sheer under drape with one hand, she waited for him to come out from beneath the awning that covered the stretch of sidewalk between the front door and the street. But she didn't see him. He must have used the side door.

All these weeks when she had been skating obsessively, he had been at the lake, struggling to decide whether or not he loved her.

He was right. His loving her did not solve anything. If

343

there was to be a solution, if there was ever going to be an Amy-and-Jack, the change had to come from her. She had to stop feeling like Amy the Afterthought; she had to stop being so passive when she was with her family. She needed to accept more responsibility. She needed to grow up.

And what had she been doing to achieve that? Nothing. She had been too busy skating.

When was she ever going to grow up? When was she ever going to stop always thinking of skating first?

Gwen smiled politely. "If you get started on it right away," one of the other music professors' wives was saying, "you'll be able to join us in September."

"It should work out fine," someone else added, two and a half weeks should be plenty of time to read *Anna Karenina*."

Gwen didn't agree. Two and a half weeks did not seem like enough time to read *Anna Karenina,* even if she had wanted to, which she did not.

She did not fit in. She had never felt that way before, but there was no question now. She was not like Hal's friends. They were all couples, People who had known each other for more than thirty years. They had been struggling young assistant professors together; their kids had grown up together. The women had been Eleanor's friends, and while they seemed like very nice people, Gwen could tell that she had little in common with them. She was the only woman in the room with polished fingenails; she was the only one wearing tinted stockings. Her skirt were linen, her shirt was silk; the other women were in easy-care knits.

They were more interested in politics than she was, and they had traveled more. They openly discussed their husbands' health, raising subjects which Gwen had always considered private. They spoke about the college administration in a way no navy wife would ever dream of talking about the commanding officers.

They were now inviting her to join the faculty wives' book club. Gwen had been in a book club in Washington, and she had enjoyed it. They read current fiction—some of it was rather difficult—and Gwen had liked reading the books that book clubs all over the country were reading. But this book club disdained contemporary fiction. They were reading *Anna Karenina* for the September meeting.

It had never been like this on a navy base.

The news from California was not good. Gwen ached for Hal every time he spoke to Ian on the phone,

Joyce had taken Maggie and moved out, withdrawing from Ian, Scott, and Emily's lives. "This is such a difficult time for Maggie," she had told Ian. "She needs me. Scott and Emily will be fine." Her identification with Maggie was complete. Maggie was all that mattered. it was as if the last fourteen years hadn't happened. Joyce was once again the abandoned mother of a helpless infant, unable to see beyond herself and her child. Even Scott and Emily had become a part of the outside world.

Ian and Joyce had chosen their house because of its proximity to her job, not his, and so if one of the kids had a dentist appointment, was in a school play, or became sick, Ian now had to drive for nearly an hour to reach them. The length of his commute added to time that they were in after-school-care programs.

His work was suffering. But how could he tell himself he could slow down? His subjects, these sole surviving speakers of Native American Indian languages, were dying, taking their linguistic knowledge with them. No one else had the funding to study them. On the other hand, his kids were desperate, floundering and bewildered, feeling deeply rejected that their mother had left, taking their sister but not them.

Finally he made a choice. He had to tend his own garden. He took a leave of absence for the rest of the semester.

But even that wasn't enough. He felt that he was doing nothing but going to the grocery store and trying to keep the clean clothes separate from the dirty ones. He and Joyce had been committed to public education for their children, but now that he went to the school activities, he could see how crowded and underfunded the school was.

The school was chaos; the house was in shambles; the kids were a mess; he was exhausted.

Reluctantly he picked up the phone. "Dad, Gwen, can I bring the kids home?"

Amy was outraged. "How can he do that to Gwen?" she fussed at Holly, who, had called to tell her that Ian was going home. "It's so unfair. Why should she have to pack lunches for his kids?" Ian had money, his share of their mother's trust fund. Her share had paid for her skating.

He could hire a housekeeper and put his children in private school.

"She doesn't mind," Holly answered. "She loves helping people."

But two hours later, Holly called back, her voice very different.

"What is it? What's wrong?" Amy asked instantly.

"I'm not sure. Jack asked me to call you. We spent twenty minutes bickering about why he couldn't just call you himself, but he seems to think that he can't."

Amy sighed. What a mess this was. He loved her, but he couldn't call her. "What did he want to say?"

"He's worried about Mother."

"Of course he is," Amy said. "Ian's about to descend on her."

"It's not that. She can handle that. She raised Jack, didn't she?"

That was unanswerable. Jack had probably been a naughty little boy, "So why did Jack want you to call me?"

Holly sighed. "Amy, I don't like doing this. I don't like putting this pressure on you, but he was so insistent. I feel like I'm having to choose between the two of you. It isn't right to ask you this, but he is my brother, and—"

Amy interrupted. "What is he asking?"

"For you to go back to Iowa for a week or so. I know it's impossible," Holly added immediately. "I know that this is the time you prepare for the entire year. I told him all that, but he kept saying that we needed to ask you."

Go back to Iowa? September? The professional season was getting longer and longer. Her first major competition was in early October. And her programs were promising to be so good. She wanted her skating to be worthy of them. She couldn't go back to Iowa. "I am keeping the whole week before Thanksgiving clear. I'll go back then, but I can t go now.

"I knew that. I'll call Jack and tell him."

"No, wait." Amy had no idea why she said that. "Don't call him, not just yet. Let me think. Why does he

347

think I should go? What good will I be? It's not like I'm going to be much help in the kitchen."

"I'm not sure he knows why. All he said was that you were on her side. He's having another one of these moments of his, complete certainty that he can't explain or justify."

That made Amy pause. "Isn't he usually right when he gets like that?"

"Well, yes."

Then perhaps she should go.

Last Christmas, shortly before her father had met Gwen, Amy had known that something was wrong with him. He had been thin and pale. She had been concerned.

But what had she done? Nothing. She hadn't given a minute's thought to doing something. It had never occurred to her that there was anything she could do.

But there had been. *Come on tour with us for a week.* She could have said that. He understood so much about the music; he might have enjoyed seeing everything else. *I've got five down days in Europe. Meet me in England. Show me Oxford. Show me where you met Mother.*

Had she done any of that? Had she made any gesture, assumed the slightest responsibility? No. If Dad needed taking care of, if something needed to be done, she had assumed that Phoebe would do it.

How could she help Gwen? She had never done anything for the family before. She had always stepped back and let Phoebe do everything.

But if Jack thought Phoebe could help, he would have called Phoebe. He had instead had Holly call her. Of course, he "knew" nothing, he understood nothing; these were only senses, impressions, intuitions. How could she disrupt her training schedule because of something so vague?

Because the senses, impressions, and intuitions were Jack's.

# CHAPTER 19

SHE COULD HARDLY TELL HER FATHER AND GWEN THE truth. *I'm coming because Jack thinks you need me.* Gwen would hate having anyone worry about her. Nor could she say that she was coming to help with Ian's kids. Who would believe that? So she had to make up a reason.

"I am having such good luck changing the content of my programs that I thought I might try shaking up my training routine a little."

How selfish that sounded. *I, Miss Amy Legend, am interrupting your lives on the slight chance this will be good for my training routine.*

But when she called before going to the rink the next morning, Gwen seemed so delighted that Amy was coming that she paid no attention to her reason, and Dad . . . well, he was probably used to Amy sounding selfish.

*I haven't meant to be. I didn't know I was.*

"That's wonderful," Gwen exclaimed. "When will you get here? How long will you stay?"

"I'll know more this afternoon," Amy promised. "I've got to work out the ice time first."

The others were already at the rink when she got there. At the first break, she told them. "My brother's marriage has broken up, and he's taking his two younger kids back to Iowa. I need to go too. I don't know how long I will be gone, but it will be more than a week. I'll train by myself."

Oliver's jaw sagged. Tommy's eyebrows went up. Henry stepped forward almost threateningly.

She held up her hand. "You can say whatever you like, but you aren't talking me out of it. I'm going. My family needs me."

"What are you?" Henry asked. "Cinderella?"

"Are you sure this is a good idea?" Oliver asked. "You've never trained alone."

"I know that, but this is necessary." She turned to Henry. "And I'm not going as Cinderella. My family may not understand me, but they aren't stupid. They know I'm hopeless in the kitchen."

"So why are you going?" Henry demanded. Then he stopped and waved a hand. He wasn't going to be able to talk her out of this. Why try to understand? "You're still with the program, aren't you?"

Amy knew what he was talking about, what the program was—the three of them skating together, touring together as long as their names would sell tickets and their bodies would hold together. Over time they would do more and more work for other skaters, producing, choreographing, designing. Skating would be their lives; they would never have to find other occupations.

She looked at Henry. He had always been the one most intent on their future—not only because he was the most intent about everything, but because the future would probably arrive first for him. His style of skating was more demanding physically than hers or Tommy's. She and Tommy would be skating in front of crowds at least a decade longer than he would be. Their routines wouldn't be is difficult as now, but they would find other ways to entertain.

350

Yes, she still wanted that, yes, she was still "with the program," but only if there was more in her life than that.

At lunch, she went into the office and settled down with Gretchen to make arrangements. She was serious about continuing her training, and she needed an Olympic-size rink with private ice time.

The college had a new rink, and even though Amy had contributed a fair amount of money toward the building of it and had skated at its opening, she could never get it for as long as she would need it. The college community needed it; that's why it had been built.

But a couple of years before the new college rink had been built, someone had built a private rink on the edge of town. Again Amy called her parents' familiar number, and it didn't seem odd in the least to have Gwen answer. "Is the rink out on Fifth Street still open?"

"I hardly know where Fifth Street *is*," Gwen answered, "much less anything about a rink. Do you want me to have your father call you? Although . . . wait, it's listed in the phone book."

Gretchen was on another line, rescheduling some things. So Amy called the rink herself. She could do that. She was a big girl.

During the school year, the manager said, the rink didn't open until one o'clock, and yes, of course, they'd consider leasing it to a private individual—Amy had not identified herself—oh, except on Tuesday and Thursdays at ten, there was a little kiddie class.

Five days a week, mornings only, except for an hour on Tuesday and Thursday morning for the preschool class—plenty of skaters would have delighted with that much private ice time. But Amy was used to much

351

more.

She hoped she was doing the right thing. This could be a disaster. She had never trained by herself before.

But Jack had asked her to do it. She took a breath, identified herself, and reserved the ice.

If she left tomorrow, she would arrive before Ian. That sounded like a good idea. She asked Gretchen to call the airline. "And a car," she said. "I will need a car." Whatever was wrong with Gwen wouldn't be improved by having to share a car with Amy.

At the beginning of the summer Tommy had suggested that Amy rent a car and drive herself to the lake, and she had dismissed it as far too adult. But here she was, two months later, renting a car.

She called Holly, catching her eating lunch at her desk. "I'm going to Iowa tomorrow."

Holly was shocked. "You aren't serious, are you? Isn't this when you practice so hard? How can you leave? Amy, Jack is crazy. Don't listen to him. Mother will be fine. If Jack's so worried, he should go himself. He's the one not doing anything."

Jack did want to go himself Amy was sure of that. He probably had had to slash his tires to keep himself from going. But he must know that he and Ian being together in one house would not solve a thing.

"If there's any chance that I can help your mother," Amy said to Holly, "then I'm going. I want all the best for her. I love her."

Holly was silent for a moment. "I can hardly argue with that."

That night as Amy was packing, Jack called. "I'm asking for more than I know, aren't I?"

How good it was to hear his voice. "Probably, but that's okay."

"So why are you going?"

"Because it was you who asked."

"Oh." Clearly he couldn't think of anything else to say. "Oh."

"Jack, what are you up to?" she asked suddenly. "What are you doing?"

"Nothing."

"What do you mean, nothing?" It was impossible to imagine him doing nothing. "How can you be doing nothing?"

"Because I have nothing to do. I thought maybe Pete—he's the guy I sold the business to—might need some help, but he doesn't."

"What about learning to fly a helicopter?" Amy sat on the bed next to her folded clothes. "I thought that's what you were going to do next."

"I'm not doing it."

"Then what are you doing? What's your day like?"

"Like anyone else's, except I'm not doing anything."

"Be more specific," she ordered . . . it was possible that Jack's definition of doing nothing included digging a new trench to reroute the Ohio River.

"I get up. I shower. Then I decide whether or not to go to 7-Eleven for coffee or make it at home. I read the newspaper. Actually, I read several newspapers, which is odd because I don't give two hoots for world affairs. Then I shoot pool or play pinball or go to the batting cage. That's what my day is like."

"And you're worried about *your mother*?" It sounded like he was the one with the problem.

"I do one other thing. I think about you. In fact, that's what I do most of the time. I think about you."

Even though she was renting a car, her father would

353

have liked to meet her at the airport. He wanted to help her claim her bags and get the rental car, but he had a class to teach.

"I'll be fine, Dad. I know how to get through an airport."

She did indeed manage fine. She got her luggage, signed the rental agreement, and drove the thirty minutes to Lipton, carefully parking at the curb in front of the big, square red-brick house. Gwen must have been listening for her car. She was waiting on the white-columned porch, and it seemed completely normal to see her, hug her warmly, and walk into the house with her. Together they carried Amy's luggage upstairs.

"Do you mind sleeping in Phoebe's room?" Gwen asked. "The one thing that made Emily agree to come was the promise that she could stay in your room."

Ian's daughter had just started first grade. "My room? Why would she want to stay in my room?" It was by far the smallest.

Gwen shrugged. "It seemed important to her, but that was before we knew you were coming."

"If it's important to her, then that's fine. I can stay in Phoebe's . . . even though I won't get a moment's sleep because I'll be so worried that someone will come in and holler at me for playing with her makeup."

Gwen smiled. "I think you can count on having to holler at Emily for coming in and playing with *your* makeup."

"I will not mind in the least."

"Yes, you will. She'll use your blusher brush in the eye shadow, and you'll find yourself with big brown streaks under your cheekbones."

"I guess I would mind that."

They were driving to Iowa City that evening to have

354

dinner with Phoebe and Giles. Amy had not been at her sister's house since before their mother had died. Like their parents' house, it was, brick, built at the turn of the century, with four square rooms on the first floor. The stairs were in a different location; the front porch was different; the kitchen had been redone, but it really was a lot like Mother and Dad's. Even the furniture was arranged in a similar way.

Amy hadn't noticed this before. *Didn't you trust yourself, Phoebe? Didn't you believe you could make a home for your family in a different* style *of house?*

"This is such a treat," Giles said, hugging Amy, his silky beard brushing her cheek. "How long are you here for?"

Amy hugged him back, hiding her grimace against his burly chest. Once again she didn't know how long she was staying. That was just the sort of behavior that Phoebe had complained about. It probably did make her seem very much the prima donna.

And she couldn't even give an honest answer. "That's so hard for me to answer because I don't know how training alone will go."

"You've never come home before," Phoebe said.

*You never came home when Mother was alive.* That was what Phoebe was saying.

Amy took a breath. *You're right. I probably wouldn't have come home if Mother was alive. Gwen feels more like my true mother than Mother ever did.*

Phoebe had, to know this, and it chewed at her, this sense of her younger sister's disloyalty. *By your standards I have been disloyal, but I cannot run my life by your standards.*

The next morning Amy drove herself to the rink and

adhered faithfully to the workout that Oliver had designed for her. During the hour that the preschoolers and their moms were using the rink, she drove to the college and used the weight room. Then she returned to the rink and continued with her practice. At twelve-fifty, the rink manager came to resurface the ice for the public session, and Amy went home.

Gwen was changing sheets, getting ready for Ian and his kids. "I'd hoped to get this done before you got back," she apologized. "I didn't want you to feel like you had to help."

"I don't mind." Amy moved around to the other side of the bed. "You'd expect Holly to help, wouldn't you? Think of me as Holly."

Ian was arriving on Saturday. Hal borrowed a station wagon, and Gwen and Amy drove to the airport with him. Scott and Emily were quiet, weary after the plane ride. Ian looked thin and tired just as Hal had last Christmas. He hugged Amy briefly. "Emily was thrilled that you were going to be here."

Amy glanced at the little girl. She had to admit that she had never paid much attention to this particular niece. At family gatherings Emily and Claire were together all the time, and everyone treated, them as a single being. The only time Amy had ever thought of her separately was when she noticed that Claire, Phoebe's daughter, was better behaved and less demanding.

And if she had thought about it, she would have assumed that Emily was paying no more attention to her. But here Emily was, slipping her hand into Amy's, asking if Amy would sit with her in the way back of the borrowed station wagon.

"I'd love to," Amy said. And suddenly brown eye

356

shadow on her blusher brush didn't sound so bad after all.

The flight had arrived in Iowa City, so they went directly to Phoebe's for lunch. Amy expected Emily to forget all about her as soon as she saw Claire, but Emily did not want to have one thing to do with Claire. She would not go see Claire's new bike, she would not play in Claire's room, she would not even sit with her at lunch. "What's going on?" Amy whispered to Phoebe and Gwen as they were clearing the dishes.

"Emily's mad at Claire," Phoebe said, "because Claire has a mother and Emily does not. Of course, it's really Joyce that Emily's mad at, but she won't admit that."

That was almost exactly what Gwen had said about Phoebe earlier in the summer, that Phoebe was mad at her mother but couldn't admit it.

"I hope you don't mind that she's turned to you," Gwen said to Amy.

"Not at all. I'm flattered."

Finally Ellie was able, to persuade all four kids to walk down the block to the park, and the adults were able to sit down and talk.

"Are things as bad as they seem?" Giles asked.

"Yes," Ian answered, but he wasn't whining and he didn't sound depressed. "All three of us are a mess, but we're going to get better."

"Do you have any expectation that you and Joyce will get back together?" Hal asked.

"Not in the immediate future. My focus right now is Scott and Emily and, to a lesser extent, myself I've been seeing a therapist," Ian said, "and I hope to find someone here. Yes, Joyce is needy and critical, but those are her issues. What I'm trying to figure out is

357

why I was drawn to someone like that, why I wanted to be coupled with a difficult person."

"Do you have any answers yet?" Amy asked.

"Not a one," he said almost cheerfully. "But I'll get there."

Like most skaters Amy needed a routine, and as a navy wife Gwen was used to one, so the newly expanded household immediately settled down. Scott and Emily remained quiet and fearful, but the predictability of Gwen's schedule was soothing.

"I don't think we are being much fun," Gwen whispered to Amy as they waited for the children to set the table one evening. "But this might be what they need."

The one thing Gwen had asked of Hal was that Ian not hang around the house all day. "Amy is fine," she had said. "She's a woman. But I'm not going to face having a man at home until you retire."

So Hal had found Ian office space at the college, and while the kids were at school, Ian went to the campus and worked on the tapes his students were sending to him. It was, Amy had to believe, as good for Ian as it was for Gwen.

Amy wasn't wild about training alone, but her skating was going well enough. For an hour every morning a student from the college came in and videotaped her practice. She watched it and then express-mailed it to Oliver, who would watch it and call her with comments.

She had been in Iowa nearly a week and felt that she had not seen anything that justified Jack's concern. Gwen really did seem fine.

Finally she called Holly from the rink. "Would you tell Jack I'm getting nowhere? Your mom seems fine."

"Of course she is. And why don't you call Jack yourself? You don't need me to be a go-between."

"Just call him, will you?"

"All right, but only because it means I can tell him he was wrong."

Two hours later, the college student who opened up the rink for Amy called her back to the phone.

It was Holly. "He wants to know if she is being herself or if she's just being the perfect wife and mother."

"What does he mean by that?"

"It can be really hard on a military wife of Mother's generation when her husband dies on active duty. She not only loses him, but she also loses her job. This sounds weird to us, but being a C.O.'s wife, then an admiral's wife, really was Mother's profession. But she did fine after he died. She got new routines for herself, she met all kinds of new people, went to museums, took classes."

Amy thought before she answered. "She's not doing anything like that now." Taking care of Hal, Ian, Scott, and Emily was her job now. And Amy. She was also taking care of Amy.

"But there are things to do, aren't there?" Holly asked. "With the college and all? And what about the house? At the beginning of September she was saying that there was tons to do. She said that the rooms needed painting, the kitchen needed updating, and every single window in the house had pinch pleats, but I haven't heard her talk about that in weeks."

"I haven't heard her talk about that at all."

Amy had almost completely cooled down by now, so she did a minimal stretch and went home. Gwen was out, and the house was quiet.

359

Before she even took a shower, she walked through every room. The walls did need painting, and every single window except those in the kitchen did indeed have pinch-pleat draperies, velvet on the first floor, chintzes on the second. Her mother hadn't been the least interested in interior design.

But Gwen had had wildflowers on the mantels and the side tables all summer long, emerald ferns arching out of earthenware vases, vivid masses of goldenrod, the soft, pale stems of the touch-me-nots. Gwen loved beauty in her home.

She heard Gwen's car in the drive and glanced out the kitchen window. The truck was open; Gwen was unloading groceries. Amy hurried out to help.

"I talked to Holly today," she said when they had the groceries inside.

"I'm glad. I love it that you and she get along so well." Gwen handed Amy a box of cold cereal to put away.

"She said that you'd been thinking about doing some redecorating."

Gwen started folding the grocery bags. "It was just a reflex. John and I always bought whenever we moved, and we never could afford what we wanted. So I would always spend the first year of a tour working pretty hard on the house to get it halfway tolerable."

"Did you enjoy it?"

"Yes. I got a little sick of doing the painting and sewing, but picking out everything was fun."

Amy had had nothing to do with the decoration of her Denver condo; she hadn't had time. But she could see that it might be fun. "Why don't we do some stuff, then? Why don't we do it together?"

Gwen shook her head. "I have painted with children

360

in the house, and trust me, it isn't anything you would want to do."

"We aren't going to paint ourselves," Amy said firmly. "We're going to pay people to do that, and we're going to pay them a huge amount to do it quickly. We'll just do the fun parts. Where do we start?"

"I always wallpaper my own bathroom first. It's cheap, it's fast, and you're in it every day."

"Then let's forget about making dinner"—Amy didn't like cooking any more than she ever had—"and let's wallpaper your bathroom."

Amy had never looked at a wallpaper book in her life. Her designer had always ordered reference samples and had taped them to the wall for her approval, but within ten minutes of arriving at the paint store, she was ready to wallpaper every room in her condominium. There were so many pretty patterns.

"We should bring Emily," Amy said. "I would have loved this as a kid. Maybe she will."

"If you don't mind, we could let her pick out a border to put up in your room. We wouldn't even have to repaint. Just slap something up. We can always take it down after she leaves."

That sounded like a great idea. Amy had never gotten to pick out anything for her room. "Did you let Holly pick out her paint colors and such?"

"Amy, I let *Jack* pick out what he wanted in his room."

Amy stuck a piece of scrap paper in one of the books, marking a pattern that she liked. "You really are a noble person."

Amy had no idea what the future held for her and Jack, but she knew one thing for sure. There was no way she was ever letting him pick out paint colors.

361

So Amy now spent her afternoons helping Gwen with the house. While Gwen was far more experienced, Amy's eye for color turned out to be better, and if it was Amy leaving the message, painters and contractors returned the call.

Gwen had long since met all of Hal and Eleanor's friends in the college community, but when she and Amy were in town, looking at fabrics and carpets, they occasionally ran into women whom Amy knew and Gwen did not. These women were the professional community, the wives of the doctors, lawyers, and bankers. Amy knew them because they ran the local charities, and they had appreciated the usefulness of her rising fame long before any of her parents' friends ever had. The first public speech of her life had been in front of the Lipton PEO, an organization her mother would have never joined.

They were orderly, elegant women who were accustomed to their order and elegance being essential to their husbands' careers.

When Amy and Gwen were comparing wallpaper selections with Mrs. Selfridge, a lawyer's wife, it occurred to Amy that Gwen would probably have more in common with these ladies than she did with Eleanor's friends. But she would never have a chance to get to know them. They would never think to invite a music professor's new wife to their homes. There was little socializing between the business community and the college. Gwen would never have met them through Hal. Her friends would hive to be Eleanor's friends.

Not if Amy could help it. She was going to introduce these ladies to Gwen. She would have a luncheon and invite them all. It would be strange, her guests would be very surprised at the invitation, but they would come.

Amy thought about the details. If she had it at home, Gwen would end up doing all the work. She could have it at Staunton's, the town's nicest restaurant, but she suspected the people she was inviting went there all the time.

It wasn't childish to call Gretchen for advice, she told herself. Having such poor problem-solving skills herself, she had hired Gretchen for hers. And Gretchen had the solution, the name of a company that air-shipped a complete New England clam and lobster dinner packed in its cooking pot. All Amy would have to do was set the table and add boiling water. This even Amy could do.

"My new stepmother is from the East," she said when she issued the invitations, "and misses the seafood. Could you join us?"

She invited Phoebe as well. She did it to be polite. She didn't really expect Phoebe to take off work to come eat clams with women she had little interest in. But Phoebe did. The two sisters did all the serving and clearing, leaving Gwen to entertain the guests.

By the end of the party Gwen volunteered to cut down and rehem the old bedroom drapes so that they could be used in the rec room of the local shelter. She appeared eager to hear a lecture on Oriental rugs at the next Service League meeting. She indicated that she and Hal would be pleased to get an invitation to the Literary Volunteers' annual fund-raiser.

"I didn't understand why you were doing this," Phoebe said when the two of them were alone in the kitchen. "I thought you were showing off. But I was wrong, and I'm sorry."

The following day she had to go back to Denver. Oliver

363

was insisting on it. "I have to see this live."

"You can have two days," she told him. "I'll come back for two days, but that's it."

The little world of professional skaters was all atwitter about the fact that Amy wasn't training in Colorado, and other coaches started sniffing around, seeing if she was ready to leave Oliver. But she didn't want to leave Oliver. She didn't want to break her close association with Henry and Tommy. She simply wanted to stay in Iowa for a while.

In October, the professional season began. The professional competitions weren't really true competitions. They were television events, designed to run opposite football games. only the most competitive-natured skaters, like Henry, cared very much who won. But the appearance fees were considerable, and the exposure enormous.

The hoped-for triple salchow was not going to happen. Amy knew that technically she was not skating her best. "That's not good," Tommy said when she confided this to him. "Even at your best you're one of the worst skaters here."

But professional competitions weren't about technique. They were about performance, and Amy was still one of the best performers. Her new material was so strong and so unexpected that she started winning by unusually large margins.

Since the competitions were taped for future airings, they were often held during the, week. One Friday afternoon Amy was at home in Upton when Ellie called. "Oh, Aunt Amy, I need a huge, *huge* favor. Can you baby-sit Alex and Claire on Saturday night?"

It was a complicated story, involving a date with someone Ellie adored. "I asked him. Do you believe it?

None of us have ever asked a boy out. And Charles never dates. I used to think it was because he was so smart, but Nick said it might be because he's shy and nervous—"

"Nick? You talk to Nick?"

"Oh, sure. Well, it isn't *talk*. We e-mail each other almost every day, and he told, me that I should go ahead and ask this guy myself. So I did, and I was so nervous that I forgot that I told my mom ages ago that I would sit tomorrow night, and none of my friends can do it, and if I tell my mom I want to go out, then she and Dad will stay home, and I will feel really bad and—"

"Ellie, I can't follow a word that you are saying, but I'm very happy for you. What time do I need to be there?"

When Phoebe heard of this plan, she was horrified and called Amy. "I can't let you do this."

"Dad and Gwen are going out." They had been invited to dinner by one of Gwen's new friends. "Ian is taking his kids to the movies, so I was going to rent a video for myself. You have videos in Iowa City, don't you?"

"Giles can go to this alone." Phoebe was not going to be distracted. "Everyone will understand."

"But that's not the issue," Amy countered. "Look, Phoebe, that afternoon at the lake, you said I never do anything for the family, and—"

"I should not have said that," Phoebe interrupted. She was mortified. She hated being reminded of that.

"Maybe you shouldn't have said it *then*. But you should have said it sometime because you were right. So for the first time in my entire life I've got a chance to do something for you, and you're being a pill if you don't let me. Furthermore, if you change your plans, Ellie will

365

be miserable, and apparently this date is a pretty big deal to her."

"It is that," Phoebe acknowledged.

"Then I'll be there at seven."

Phoebe and Giles had left by the time Amy arrived. Ellie explained all the rules about bedtime and television, and then the doorbell rang and Ellie went pale. So feeling quite the helpful aunt, Amy went to open the door, and then it was young Charles's turn to go pale. He had clearly not expected to be meeting Ellie's famous aunt. He dropped his eyes, snatched his hand away as if hers were burning, and greeted Ellie as if she were a St. Bernard rescuing him from a blinding snowstorm. But he was surprisingly good-looking for the captain of the chess team.

Amy had never baby-sat before in her life, but she proved perfectly able to microwave a bag of popcorn and read some stories. Fortunately, the kids didn't fight and went to bed almost willingly. Amy then watched her own video and looked through reports of charitable foundations until Phoebe and Giles got home.

"Did Ellie get off okay?" Giles asked. "Were the two of them miserably nervous?"

"He was so terrified of me," Amy answered, "that she looked like high ground in a rising river."

Giles put his arm around her and kissed her check. "You do have your uses, dear sister-in-law."

Phoebe walked her out to the car. "I know I'm sounding like a broken record, but I still can't believe what I said to you at the lake. I was so completely out of line."

"Oh, Phoebe . . . don't be so hard on yourself."

Phoebe ignored her. "Do you know the Demeter-Persephone myth?"

"No," Amy answered. There was no point in pretending that she did.

"It's Greek. Demeter is goddess of the earth. Persephone is her daughter. Persephone is abducted by Hades, god of the underworld, and Demeter is so grief-stricken that she stops doing her work. The earth is taken over by perpetual winter. She's like Lot's wife, the woman who looked back and was turned into a pillar of salt; they're both symbols of grieving too much."

Amy no longer believed herself stupid. Phoebe's intelligence was conventionally analytic while hers was intuitive, kinetic, and aesthetic. Amy did not envy Phoebe her intelligence; she did not wish to be other than she was. But Phoebe was better educated, and Amy did envy her that.

"So you feel that you've been grieving too much?"

Phoebe nodded. "There's been times since Mother died that I've felt like a pillar of salt, full of tears yet unable to cry. But Demeter and Lot's wife were grieving for the loss of children; I've been grieving for my mother. Mother did die too early, there's no question about that, but most women lose their mothers. Of course you should mourn your mother, but I cringe at the thought of Ellie or Claire being as paralyzed by my death as I have been for the last . . . it's almost been two years already."

Phoebe was learning. She was learning how to forgive herself for her mistakes.

She was wearing a dramatic necklace, a slab of malachite suspended from links of heavy silver. Amy touched it. "That was Mother's, wasn't it?"

Phoebe nodded.

"What about the lapis lazuli? Do you wear it much?"

"Probably more than anything else."

367

Amy wasn't surprised. The lapis lazuli necklace and bracelet were the simplest of Mother's jewelry. "And the garnets? I did love them when I was a girl."

Phoebe smiled. "Claire does too."

Claire was five; she refused to wear anything that wasn't pink. "Are they a nightmare?" The garnets had been Eleanor's only Victorian jewelry. They were ornate and overwrought, badly set in fading gold.

"I've never figured out what to wear them with," Phoebe admitted. Then her eyes shifted away, and she spoke without looking at Amy. "Why didn't you want any of Mother's jewelry?

"It wasn't that I didn't want it." Amy's words came out in a rush. Phoebe had completely misunderstood why she hadn't taken any of the jewelry. "No, no, it wasn't that. I mean, the opals and the topazes . . . But it did seem to me that you should have everything, that it would mean more to you than to me."

Now, however, she could see how Phoebe had interpreted what she had intended as generosity. "Did it seem like I didn't care about Mother's dying? I did, of course I did, but I knew how devastating it was to you, and somehow that's what that time was about for me, worrying about you more than grieving for her."

"You were worrying about me?" Phoebe didn't like people worrying about her.

Amy went on quickly. "It wasn't that I didn't care about her dying, but in some ways I had already grieved for—well, not really for her—but for her place in my life." She hoped that she wasn't going to make everything worse by saying this. "I had to accept a long time ago that Mother was never going to understand me and would never really value what I did."

Phoebe sighed and shook her head. "My relationship

with Mother was so strong and good, it's hard to understand how yours could be so different."

"You and I are different," Amy said. "And ironically Mother may have been the best possible mother for me. So many kids skated to please their mothers, and I used to envy them, having mothers who cared so much, but now I see how bad that was. From the very beginning I had to skate for myself. Mother made the process work—she wrote all those checks—but she didn't particularly care about the results. I didn't have to succeed for her."

Phoebe was a mother. She understood this perhaps better than Amy herself. "I know your tastes and interests were very different from hers, but in some ways you were more like her than I am. I follow every rule ever made, and she never followed any. I knew that she was disappointed that you had so little interest in books, but secretly I worried that I was disappointing her because I was so unadventuresome I thought I ought to be like her, and I wasn't."

"Is that why you work so hard at everything?"

Phoebe smiled, a tight little half smile. "Giles would say so."

"Phoebe"—Amy had to ask her this—"have you and Giles found a new lake yet?"

Phoebe shook her head. "No. We're working on it, but I know that I am trying too hard to find something exactly like our lake. Giles has sent away for about seventeen thousand sets of house plans, and he's enjoying that . . . You know, Jack offered to come help him build it next summer."

"He did?" Amy was surprised. It seemed odd that Jack was talking to Phoebe and Giles when she wasn't.

"Giles loves the idea," Phoebe said, "although I think

369

we should get someone else to rough it in during the spring. Then the pair of them can wire it and finish it together . . . if we find a site, of course."

But there was a site, a perfect site. Amy had to try again.

"I realize it came out all wrong this summer, this business of the Rim, but I still mean it. It's there for you and Giles if you want it."

Phoebe shook her head. "I'm still baffled by this. It's hard to believe that you, own the Rim. Why did you buy it?"

"Because I'm an idiot who believes a lot of drunks, because I wanted to be the savior of the universe."

"So why didn't you tell any of us?"

"Because it seemed so transparent, that everyone would know that I wanted to be the savior of the universe . . . but that doesn't matter now. For whatever reason, I do own it. Did you talk to Giles about it? Did you tell him?"

"No. That would make it seem like I was trying to do everything my way, that I wasn't willing to leave the lake."

She had a point. "But now that you've looked for other places, maybe it would be different. Why don't you at least mention it to him? At a minimum he ought to know that his sister-in-law is an idiot who believes a lot of drunks."

"No," Phoebe answered. "I said I would move to another lake, and I will."

"Would you think about it?"

"No."

There was clearly no point in saying anything more. Phoebe was not listening to her. So when Amy got home, she sat down with her father and Gwen and told them that she owned the Rim.

Hal was as surprised as Phoebe had been. He shook his head. "Sometimes I think that your mother and I never understood one thing about you."

"Maybe you didn't, but you never tried to change me," Amy answered. "That's the important thing." She had never fully appreciated that before. Her parents had never tried to turn her into Phoebe or Ian. It was a good thing because it would have been hopeless. She would have made a very poor Phoebe, but she was doing a pretty fine job of being Amy.

"Why are you telling us about this property now?" Gwen asked. "Are you hoping to sell it to Phoebe and Giles?"

Amy suspected that Gwen thought it as good an idea as she did. "Sell, give . . . I don't really care. But Phoebe won't even tell him about it." She explained what was happening. "And I'm not going to talk to him behind her back."

"That's very wise," Gwen said.

Hal was drumming his fingers against the arm of his chair. "This really is a good solution, isn't it?"

Neither woman answered. It was obvious to Hal that they thought so.

"Eleanor and I both had grave reservations about Joyce." Clearly he thought that this had some connection with what they were talking about. "We discussed them, and I assumed, I thought it just went without saying, that we would never say anything to him. But Eleanor always spoke her mind about everything. She said something to him, I don't exactly know what, but I think it only made him feel more protective of Joyce and made him marry her that much more quickly."

371

"So that's why you are always so careful not to interfere in our lives?" Amy asked.

"That episode certainly confirmed what was probably a natural inclination. But"—he stood up—"this is a very different case, and I think it is now time for me to interfere. I will talk to Phoebe."

He must have called Phoebe the minute he woke up because Amy was pouring her first cup of coffee, not even ready to think about, what she would wear to church, when the phone rang. Gwen handed it to her. Giles spoke without any greeting. "If I write you a great big check for this piece of property, are you going to rip it up?"

That would be Amy's first impulse. "Not if you really hate the idea."

"I do. I'm utterly incapable of accepting such a generous, gift. At least I hope I am. I want that lot so badly I might even stoop to graciousness in order to get it."

Amy hugged the phone to her ear. She was so happy that this was happening. If anyone on earth deserved her sister, it was this wonderful man.

He admitted that he might not have been so enthusiastic about it in July. "Minnesota claims to have ten thousand lakes, and I suppose we shouldn't have gotten discouraged, having only looked at about nine thousand of them, but fatigue was setting in."

He insisted that they all come to Iowa City for dinner that night to talk about it.

Phoebe's dining room table was covered with house plans and blueprint kits. Giles was full of questions, what were the dimensions of the most likely building sites, what the drainage was like.

Amy was useless. "I don't know. I can't estimate

372

distances unless I'm on my skates. I don't even know what drainage is. Why don't you ask Jack? He went there with me. He might have noticed."

Giles instantly disappeared and came back a few minutes later. Jack had some notion of the lot size. "But he says that even he wouldn't pick plans based on those estimates."

"Take note of the 'even he,' " Gwen said. "No one can accuse Jack of having unnecessarily high standards. If he says something isn't good enough, then everyone needs to run to the nearest bomb shelter."

"Oh, I think in some things Jack has very high standards," Giles said, and pointedly looked at Amy.

That was Sunday, and Monday morning Amy was once again pouring herself a cup of coffee when the phone rang. Gwen was in the shower, so she answered it.

Static crinkled through the line. "I'm in the truck," a voice called out, "and I'm an hour south of Indianapolis. Can you hear me?"

It was Jack. A familiar wash of joy flooded across Amy. "Yes, I can hear. It's me, Amy."

"I can't hear you," he was still shouting, "but tell Giles I am going up to Minnesota to do those measurements for him."

Halfway through the word *Minnesota* the static suddenly disappeared, and Amy had to hold the phone away from her car so that his voice didn't blow out her eardrums. She replied in a normal tone. "The line's clear now. You don't have to shout."

"Amy?" He had thought he was speaking to his mother.

"It's me, and I hear you. You're driving up to Minnesota to measure the lot for Giles. You're driving

373

from Kentucky to Minnesota to measure a building site."

"It's not much more than a thousand miles. It will wreak hell with my pinball game, but I make sacrifices. I assume it's okay with your dad if I spent the night in one of the cabins. He showed me where a key was hidden."

"I'm sure it's—" But the static was back, and a moment later the line went dead.

Wednesday, Jack called with the dimensions Giles needed. A number of trees were going to have to come down, and Jack pointed out that they could probably get better prices on tree work now than in the spring, when everyone was wanting such work done. He was quite willing to stay and arrange for the work if people would tell him what they wanted done. So Giles and Phoebe flew up for the weekend to make some decisions; Amy and Gwen took care of their children.

Amy was amazed, It took her family five years to move a gas light. Now Giles and Phoebe were hopping onto airplanes, intending to have their new cabin roughed in by next July.

"It's so beautiful up there," Phoebe gushed when she and Giles got home. None of them had ever been to the lake in the fall. "The popple and the birch are these wonderful shades of gold and yellow. Everything was so quiet. I didn't want to come home."

Apparently Jack hadn't either. During the two days before Phoebe and Giles arrived, he had prowled around some of the junk shops that people had set up in their garages. He found a couple of propane iceboxes in decent condition. He called Hal. How about if he picked them up and installed them in the big garage? And then as long as he was trenching a gas line out here, why not put in some lights?

And then after Phoebe and Giles returned home, while Jack was waiting for the tree work to start, he found a wood stove that had a fifteen-gallon water cistern. "It's too big for the cabins, but if we sink a well—"

Hal interrupted, laughing. "Jack, stop bothering me. Stop driving into town to call every time you have an idea. Do whatever you want. Send me the bill."

Gwen clasped her hands. "My baby's going to be all right."

## CHAPTER 20

AMY LOVED HER ROUTINE. EVERY MORNING SHE shared a quiet cup of coffee with Gwen, the only other person in the house yet awake. They would talk about the redecorating, about the new people Gwen was meeting, and about Amy's workouts. Gwen admitted that she didn't understand half of what Amy said about her skating, but she hadn't understood submarines either.

On the way to the rink Amy often stopped and bought doughnuts for the rink staff; after practice she picked up sandwiches so Gwen didn't have to make lunch. Her practice schedule was common knowledge, and a couple times a week a few retired people would show up to watch her. She stayed at the rink during the Tuesday-Thursday preschool class, helping the tots put their skates on, chatting with the mothers. Emily had been boasting about her famous aunt so much that her teacher arranged to have the class come to the rink as a field trip. Amy couldn't imagine what a group of first-graders

375

could learn from watching her do the same thing over and over, but Gretchen had some Amy Legend key chains made up, and each kid got one to hang from the zippers of their backpacks, so she was almost as cool as the trip to the fire station.

Travel from Iowa was more difficult than it had been from Denver, but even that was turning into an advantage. She had known for a while that she was involved with some charities that really did not need her. They had so thoroughly developed the potential of their fund-raising base that the presence of a celebrity made little difference in how much money they raised. Amy Legend's presence at their annual banquet was a lovely reward for a job well done, but the job would have been equally well done without her. The long waits for a connecting flight out of Chicago made her think carefully about each trip. She quit hopping on a plane every time someone breathed her name.

Ian's new therapist didn't seem to think much of him living with Hal and Gwen. "It's important to have shelters and safety nets," she said, "but what example are you setting for the children?"

"I never quite know what she means," he said when reporting this conversation to Hal, Gwen, and Amy, "but I'm getting the picture on this one. I need to take responsibility for my children."

So he rented a house for the rest of the school year. A nice lady from the nearby Mennonite community came two mornings a week to clean and do the laundry, but Ian was still at the schoolyard every afternoon at three-thirty to walk Scott and Emily home. The two of them were still fragile, trembling at any disappointment, but Scott was a star on the third-grade soccer team and Emily was getting to pick out another wallpaper border.

376

Amy felt as if she should leave too. The best thing she could probably do for Gwen now was give her time alone with Hal.

"But you don't want to move back to Denver," Gwen said.

That was true. Amy didn't want to live in Denver anymore. She wanted to go on working with Oliver. She wanted to retain all her business ties with Tommy and Henry. But she wanted to live near her family. "But I can't live with you and Dad forever."

"No, I suppose not," Gwen agreed. "But you're gone a lot, and frankly it's easier for me to have you here than it would be to drive across town and pick up your mail and newspapers."

That was true. If she got her own place, she would have to figure out how to take care of things when she was gone. She couldn't recreate her life in Denver; she couldn't buy a condominium in a high-rise with a doorman, a front desk, and a concierge. The tallest building in Lipton had five floors, and the closest thing any establishment had to a doorman was the cheerful mentally disabled man who helped load groceries at the Safeway.

On the other hand, if she got a place of her own, she might have gutters that needed cleaning.

It was time to make Thanksgiving plans. Ian was trying to negotiate with Joyce so that the children could see her, but Holly and Jack were coming, and Amy had accepted no holiday shows, so there would be eleven of them. Gwen said she was perfectly willing to cook; she was also equally willing to go to Phoebe's. Phoebe was saying that she was also willing to have it at either place.

"How shall we resolve this?" Phoebe asked.

"Amy, what do you want to do?" Gwen asked.

Amy blinked. "What do *I* want?" She had not expected that question. "I haven't given it any thought. It seemed easier to let the two of you decide, and then you can be the ones who are wrong."

"Amy, if I didn't love you so much," Gwen said, "I would say that you sometimes have too much in common with my sister and her daughter, both of whom live to have other people be wrong."

Gwen's sister Barbara and her niece Valerie were Nick's family. "Keeping your mouth shut is so safe," Amy replied. "Your sister's smarter than you know. But maybe we should try something completely different." Last year's idea of everyone going to a big hotel no longer sounded appealing. She preferred something homier . . . although in truth as long as Jack was going to be there, she would have gone to Neptune. He was still at the lake, and so they talked to him only when—

"I know." She suddenly had an idea. "What will the weather be at the lake? Would we freeze to death if we went there?"

"Thanksgiving at the lake?" Phoebe asked. She looked surprised.

"Jack is finishing the garage as a communal kitchen," Gwen mused. "It might work if the weather; isn't too awful. What's it like there at Thanksgiving?"

Phoebe didn't know. They had never needed to know. The family had gone only in the summer. "I imagine it's cold."

"But how cold?" Amy asked. "Uncomfortable cold or instant-death cold? How would we find out? If we wait until morning, I could call Gretchen." Amy had already concluded that if she was going to buy a house in Iowa, she should hire some Gretchen-type person as a housekeeper and assistant. That person could run the errands, collect the mail, and cook some meals . . . although she would not clean the gutters. That had to be very clear. Amy's gutters would be far too delicate to be touched anyone but Jack. "She can find out anything."

"So can I," Gwen said. "We'll call the local radio station right now." She was already moving to the phone.

Five minutes later, she had an answer. "Guess what? It's like everywhere else. The weather at Thanksgiving varies. There's no telling. It could be in the mid-forties with no snow; it could be below zero with three feet of snow. But it's been a dry fall so far."

"Which means nothing," Phoebe said.

They were all quiet for a moment, no one wanting to make the decision. A heavy snowfall could trap them at the lake for days. The road would eventually get plowed, but not immediately. And if it was truly cold, biffy trips would be memorable indeed. On the other hand, to be there, with the last few golden leaves clinging to the branches of birches, with the Norway boughs soft and perhaps snow-filled, with the smoke from the fires curling up from the cabin chimneys through the thin autumn air . . .

Phoebe threw up her hands. "Oh, why not? The worst that will happen is that we'll be snowed in for the rest of the winter, but then it will be Amy's turn to be wrong, and that thought will keep us warm."

Everyone loved the idea. Ian told Joyce that she had to commit herself absolutely to spending Thanksgiving with her two younger children or he was taking them to the lake.

"I just don't know why we can't wait and see if Maggie's going on this ski trip," she answered.

"Because Scott and Emily's plans are as important as by hers," he said, "and they're in no shape to cope with uncertainty."

But she was unwilling to make definite plans. "She,s trying to see how much she can get away with," Ian told the rest of the family. "So we're coming to the lake. My kids are going to be with people who think they are important, and I'm not going to have to spend the rest of my life listening to what a great time you all had freezingto death."

The television networks and cable stations had learned that the only programming that could hold its own against holiday-weekend football was figure skating. So throughout November Amy was traveling every week, appearing in the competitions that would be shown over Thanksgiving. Each time she returned, Phoebe and Gwen had done more to plan and prepare for the holiday.

Gwen had decided to fly up the Friday before. "We really don't have any idea what Jack's been up to. He says everything is in great shape, and for the most part I do believe him. But he is a man; he will have forgotten something."

Phoebe clearly wanted to go with her. "But I'm in charge of the Multicultural Thanksgiving feast in Alex's class on Wednesday. I have to be there."

The three of them were at Phoebe's, making pilgrim hats and collars out of black and white construction paper. Gwen and Amy were enjoying the work; Phoebe was grateful for the help.

"I could come," Amy said. "I leave Detroit Friday afternoon. I could meet you in Minneapolis. I won't be much help in the kitchen, but I generate body heat."

"We're going to need that," Gwen agreed.

She was going to see Jack again.

Last summer Thanksgiving had seemed so vague an far away. it had loomed as the problem. She and Jack couldn't remain lovers because of Thanksgiving and Christmas. That's when the family would be together.

But Thanksgiving was finally here, and this time Amy wasn't coming to see the family. She was already with the family. What difference was that going to make?

She skated horribly in Detroit, landing only one of her triples, doubling all the rest. But no one else skated any better, and so her scores were fine. The skaters' hotel was close to an upscale grocery store, and when Amy's luggage was transferred from the Minneapolis-bound flight to the little commuter plane, it included a big cardboard box full of Belgian chocolates, Spanish oranges, and champagne from France. "I've never traveled with provisions before," she said to Gwen when they met in the Minneapolis airport. "But I have brought all of Europe with me. I'm turning into my sister."

Jack was meeting them at the airport in Hibbing. It was too small a facility to have jet ways. Stairs were wheeled up to the side of the plane; the passengers climbed down and crossed the runway. Amy had done it often in the summer but never in November. The sharp chill in the air caught at her lungs, froze the inside of her nose.

Gwen gasped at the cold. "Whose idea was this?"

Amy didn't answer. Jack was waiting.

She and Gwen hurried across the tarmac. The glass of

terminal's windows was tinted against the sun; Amy couldn't see inside. But the airport was warm, and there Jack was, leaning back against the wall, straightening, stepping forward when he saw them.

Gwen called his name. Amy held back so that he could greet his mother first. They embraced, Gwen patting the back of his shoulder. Then Gwen stepped away, and he turned to Amy. He hesitated, she paused, but it really was wonderful. to see him. She had to touch him. She moved forward; his arms closed around her. She felt the soft weave of his shirt against her cheek and the brush of his lips in her hair.

He stepped back. "You're shivering. I thought you would be used to the cold."

If she was shivering, it wasn't from the cold.

He looked great. Once again his thick chestnut hair needed to be cut, but he had on a sage-colored rugby shirt under a plaid wool shirt. The sett of the plaid was shades of green—olive, sage, and moss—while the accent line was rust.

"I love your shirt," Gwen exclaimed. "The colors are wonderful on you. Did you get it up here?"

Amy knew the answer to that. No, Holly had given it to him. There was no way Jack had picked out that shirt himself. He would have bought navy blue.

"Holly sent it to me," he said. "I was telling her how cold it was, so she sent up a couple of shirts. She says that she doesn't care about me being cold, she just can't stand to be seen in public with me because I dress so badly."

"You don't dress *badly*." Gwen wanted to be sure that her children were getting along. "You haven't developed a good sense of color."

"No, Gwen," Amy put in. "He dresses badly."

"I suppose he does." Gwen sighed, then spoke briskly. "We have a ton of luggage. Hal went over to the chemistry department and got the most gorgeous cardboard boxes you have ever seen, and I filled every single one of them."

The Hibbing airport did not have automated baggage service. Luggage was taken off the airplane by hand, wheeled into the airport on a cart, and then transferred to the claim area by the same people who processed the tickets. Gwen's and Amy's suitcases arrived soon enough, but Gwen's boxes were the last items off the plane, perhaps because of the boxes' stern preprinted warnings about the chemicals that had originally been shipped in them.

While they were waiting, several people came over and spoke to Jack. He would introduce them to Gwen and Amy. "This is my mother and her stepdaughter Amy."

"You know a lot of people," Amy said to Jack as they carried the luggage out to the curb.

"Not that many. The lumber yard guys and I are real buddies, and people at the airport, I know them."

"Why?" she asked. As far as she knew, no one had flown up to see him.

"I've been taking flying lessons."

He sprinted across the parking lot to get his truck. Amy urged Gwen to wait inside the warm terminal; Gwen refused. If Amy could wait outside with the luggage, so could she. A minute later Jack's black truck eased up to the curb. He got out of the cab and went around back to lower the tailgate.

Amy handed him the first box. "You're learning to fly a helicopter?"

"Not yet. It turns out that helicopters are hard to fly.

You're better off starting on fixed-wing aircraft . So I'm down here a couple days a week, sometimes more."

Gwen had been listening. She too seemed pleased. "Can I assume that five years from now you are going to be running passenger service to the moon?"

"No. I think I'm out of the business world for a while. I've been talking to the Red Cross. They seem to think that once I learn to fly a helicopter, they could probably use me at disaster sites."

"Jack!" Gwen stared at him, surprised. "The Red Cross? I had no idea you were thinking about anything like that."

"I wasn't. It was Amy here." He jerked his thumb in her direction. "Apparently she can't stand to be seen in public with me because I perform no public service."

"That's true," Amy agreed. "But I also don't like the way you dress."

Gwen was shaking her head, not because she disapproved but because she was surprised.

"I know Dad wanted me to join the navy," Jack said, "but I don't think that would have been such a great idea."

"I know that," Gwen murmured. "I've always known that."

"But I think this should be okay. Since I don't need to worry about money for a while, I can stay a volunteer and keep pretty clear of the bureaucracy while still managing to do some good."

"This might be the thing for you," Gwen said slowly. "It really might be." And Amy felt her hand being squeezed surprisingly hard. It was Gwen, thanking her.

They both understood what had happened. Working up here in these silent woods, Jack had laid a ghost to rest. *I'll be doing something that counts, Dad. You'd be proud. I have not let you down.*

The drive passed quickly. Even though Jack spent it describing in detail what he had been doing, even though he had said he had had a couple of guys come help him, Amy was still amazed when they got to the lake. The big garage, which had once been storage space for Giles's boat and ten-year-old cans of unusable paint, Jack had finished into a pleasant, comfortable living space. He had insulated the walls and paneled them with pine. He had enlarged the windows, tiled the floor, and put in two wood-burning stoves, one sleek and efficient, the other an old, hulking cast-iron beast with burner plates on the top and a water tank at the side.

Installed along one wall were the stove, sink, and counters. "The lady at the lumber yard," Jack said, "laid this out so that two or three people can work at once. She said it will be awful for just one person, but it's ideal for a crowd."

Such was the plan. When Hal and Gwen or any other small party was here alone, they would cook and eat in their cabin. But when everyone was together, they would open the garage. Then the cabins would become private, the garage public.

Hal had told Jack to go ahead and get new furniture, which Jack had done by walking into discount furniture shops and pointing. He had ordered two complete "suites" of living room furniture: one had a sofa, two big chairs, and assorted tables; the other had a sofa, love seat, and assorted tables. One was gray, the other an oatmeal tweed. The gray was a stone gray, and the oatmeal blend had more taupe in it than brown, so the two upholstery fabrics looked almost adequate together. Gwen and Amy believed that was simply luck. They could have been pearl gray and tan, and Jack would have bought them.

"Do you think he's color-blind?" Amy whispered to Gwen.

"No. We had him tested when he was little. He just doesn't care."

How ironic that she, of all people, should fall in love with someone who didn't—

She stopped herself. *Fall in love?* Why had she thought that?

Because it was true. The flood of joy she felt every time she saw him or spoke to him . . . if that was just sex, she would have felt the tingling lower down. This sensation started in her chest, spreading quickly down her arms, up the back of her neck. Every hour she spent with him made it clearer and clearer. There would never be another man more important to her than he was. He would always be the one she thought of first, the one she turned to first. She didn't need to be with him to love him. She only needed to be herself and have him be himself.

So what did this mean? She didn't know. But the holiday weekend would tell them so much. They should share Thanksgiving with the family and then see. On Sunday when the holiday was over, she would speak. On Sunday they would talk.

The family was two strands of beads that had been joined together by the clasp of Hal and Gwen's marriage. As the two youngest of their generation, she and Jack had been the last bead on each strand, and the danger had been that the two of them would slip off and roll together into some dusty hidden corner. Then in the case of her family, the other beads might have fallen off as well, Ian staying in California, forever struggling to hold his marriage together, and Phoebe forcing herself to be content with some other lake.

But a necklace is a circle, and this family would become a circle only if the two loose ends met and joined. Amy and Jack were those two ends.

Amy could not think analytically; she knew truth through metaphors. This metaphor told her the opposite of what everyone had said in the summer. She and Jack were not a threat to the family; the family would be stronger, it would endure more as a circle than as a strand.

Jack had certainly turned the garage into a space that was right for this new family, even though at the moment it looked blank and a bit uninviting. There was nothing on any of the surfaces, and Jack, skilled interior designer that he wasn't, had arranged the furniture precisely as it had been in the discount showroom—gray on one side, oatmeal on the other.

So Gwen and Amy set to work. They moved furniture, blending the two sets. From the upper shelves of the cabin closets, from boxes stored underneath beds, they found lap quilts and extra pillows. From the tops of the bookcases they rescued pretty bits of wood, glittering rocks, and interesting shells that two generations of children had been collecting. They selected the best and arranged them on the tables.

They set up systems, figured out ways of doing things, where people would wash their hands, where they would hang their coats. At night, rather than heat the other cabins, the three of them slept in the garage. Both sofas were sleepers, folding out into queen-size beds, and Amy and Gwen shared one bed while Jack was in the other.

True to her plan, Amy had not told him that she loved

him, but he knew. He had realized it on Friday, the first night they were there.

Gwen was already in bed, and Amy was curled up under a quilt on the love seat in front of the airtight stove. The stove didn't have the romance of an open fireplace, but it put out a comforting heat, and there was a tempered glass door through which she could see the moving flames.

Jack was brushing his teeth at the washstand Amy and Gwen had set up near one of the doors. Amy heard him rinse and spit, followed by some rattling and rustling as he put things away.

Then he came over to the stove and, hooking his foot around the leg of Amy's love seat, inched it back a bit. He lowered himself to the floor, sitting in front of the fire, his legs pulled up, his elbows on his knees, his back resting against the base of the love seat.

His head, his thick, rumpled, curly, sexually symbolic chestnut hair, was near Amy's waist. She pulled her hand out from under the quilt and touched his hair.

He went still. His breath caught and held. He understood.

He didn't move. He was breathless. The floor was disappearing beneath him; he was tumbling, gasping for air and light. Amy knew it as surely as if it were happening to her.

He let his head drop, and his hands made a tent in front of his face. He could have been at prayer.

*I don't deserve this.* Amy could hear his thoughts as clearly as if he were speaking. *She loves me, and I do not deserve it.*

*Yes, you do*, her thoughts answered. *Yes, you do.*

He reached back and took her hand, bringing it around. He opened her fingers and kissed her palm.

"Why aren't you looking at me?" she whispered.

"I'm afraid that I'll find out that it isn't true."

"But it is."

For the moment that was enough. They both knew, they both believed.

No one else was supposed to arrive until late Wednesday, but Tuesday afternoon they heard a car on the trail. They assumed it was someone from one of the other cabins, but then the car slowed and turned into their drive. Amy and Gwen looked at each other. Who could it be?

It was Hal and little Claire. "I couldn't keep away," he said as he hugged Gwen and Amy and took Jack by the shoulder while shaking his hand. "So I taught my eight A.M. class, kidnapped my friend here, and hit the road."

"We brought milk," Claire said proudly. "I remembered."

"That's wonderful," Gwen lied. "We would have been in trouble if you hadn't."

Of course, the problem with milk now was not keeping it cold, but keeping it from freezing.

Phoebe's family was leaving Iowa City on Wednesday noon as soon as the second-grade Multicultural Thanksgiving feast was over, and they arrived in the evening with a station wagon so crammed that it was a good thing Claire had come up with her grandfather. There might not have been room even for her slender little body.

No one had had time to admire the garage, much less unload the station wagon when a third car pulled in. It was Ian. He had stopped at the Hibbing airport to pick up Holly.

389

The lights of his car swept across the garage windows, and everyone dashed outside. Only Gwen had the sense to get her coat, so they all danced up and down, rubbing their hands along their arms, waiting for him to ease into a spot between two Norways. It was dark out, and so they couldn't see inside the car, but Amy moved toward the passenger side, wanting to be among the first to greet Holly.

Then a shout went up. "Nick!"

There were indeed three adult shapes getting the car, Ian, Holly, and—most unexpectedly—Nick of It was fifteen minutes before the clamor cased. Alex wanted to show Scott the hot-water tank. Gwen had to mop up the resulting puddle. Ian was amazed at the garage; he didn't know what to look at first. Phoebe and Giles were dying to explore and get ideas for their new cabin. Holly loved, just loved, the new makeup brushes Amy had suggested she buy. Ellie wanted everyone to know that Nick was completely responsible for how great things were going with her new boyfriend. Thomas was toddling around looking for new, interesting ways to injure himself, and Claire was telling people that it was fine if they hadn't stopped to buy milk because she had remembered to have Grandpa do it.

Eventually those who cared were settled enough to find out why Nick had come.

"Don't get us wrong," Gwen assured him. "We're thrilled, but it is a surprise. I can't believe that your mother and grandmother let you come."

"Well . . ." Nick drawled out the word. "*Letting* me come . . . that's not exactly what happened, but they do know where I am," he added quickly. "I didn't run away."

"Why don't you start at the beginning?" Hal

suggested.

"It started when I was here last summer. I decided that I want to know who my father is. I'm sick of not knowing."

"You don't know who your father is?" Jack grimaced. "I hated not knowing what Dad was doing, where the boats were going and what their mission was, all that. But at least I knew *who* he was."

"So what does this have to do with your being here now?" Giles asked.

"It's been bugging me more and more, the not knowing. Finally I decided to do something about it. I'm boycotting family holidays until they tell me or at least until they tell a lawyer who will tell me when I'm eighteen. At first I thought I'd just stay in my room, but that's what I do all the time anyway, so I called Holly to see if I could hitchhike down to New York to see her. She said you were all coming here, and she sent me a plane ticket. So if you're glad to see me, thank her. It's her dime."

Holly waved her hand. "It was nothing really."

"How long will it take this to work?" Giles asked. "When will they tell you?"

"One Christmas is all it will take." Nick was confident. "They both make a big deal out of Christmas; they like to do all these crafty-type things to decorate. Gold spray paint and hot glue are our version of glad tidings of comfort and joy. They love doing it, but they don't admit that to themselves. They pretend that they are doing, it for me."

Amy couldn't imagine that Nick cared very much about gold pine cones and lace-edged ribbon. "What will you do once you have his name?" she asked.

"I don't know. I don't think showing up on his

391

doorstep is such a cool idea. He may not have any idea I exist. I can't even get Val and Barb to tell me if he knew she was pregnant. Also I don't want anyone thinking I'm after money. Maybe it makes sense to have someone else, a lawyer or something, approach him first."

"That's not a bad idea," Giles said. "And given that you've got three lawyers and one something among your relatives—"

Jack interrupted. "Why do I think I'm the 'one something'?"

"It could be me," Ian pointed out. "I'm not a lawyer."

"What about me?" Amy was determined to be the Afterthought no longer. "I'm not a lawyer either, and if I call this dad of Nick's, he'll call me back."

"That's certainly true," Gwen said. "Trust me. People return Amy's calls. In fact, I'm willing to put money on it. All three of you put in a call at the same time, I'll bet anything that Amy's call is returned first."

"This is my life we're talking about here, not a horse race," Nick said, but he was clearly pleased at people's interest.

"I can't say that I recommend the horse-race approach," Giles said, "but we'll certainly help you figure out the right thing to do."

"And if he's interested in getting to know you," Hal added, "remember we're here to help. There'll always be room at the table for family."

"He might have seven children," Nick said.

Hal clapped him on the shoulder and smiled. "This is the wonderful part of being a man, Nick. You get to say things like 'There'll always be room at the table,' and then the women have to do all the work."

Nick grinned. "I may have been underrating family

392

life."

It was growing late. As reluctant as everyone was to go back out into the cold, Gwen had made it clear that not a single suitcase was to be opened in the garage. People had to sleep in the cabins.

Neither the bunkhouse nor the porch of the log cabin could be heated enough for sleeping, so Amy and Jack had dragged the bunk beds into the main room of the log cabin. Phoebe and Giles were to take one of the bedrooms in the new cabin; Ian was to be in the other. The kids would spread out on the floor of that cabin. Amy and Holly had the bedroom of the log cabin; Ellie was on the sofa, and Nick and Jack were on the bunk beds.

"This will be the last time we have to do all this figuring," Phoebe said as she was collecting the many things her family had already strewn all over the garage. "Our cabin will be done next summer. Then Ian and his family can have the new cabin and Amy, Holly, and Jack the log cabin."

"I don't need the new cabin every year," Ian said immediately.

"We can still trade."

"You haven't seen what a difference Jack's skylights make in the log cabin." Phoebe had seen them when she had been up in October. "You may think the new cabin is the short end of the stick."

Thanksgiving Day dawned cold and dear. Even before they were out of bed, Holly and Ellie were marveling over the skylights. Jack had installed four, one in the bedroom, one in the kitchen, and two in the living room. Bright swaths of light spilled downward, sweeping across the floor, sliding up the log walls. This cabin

393

would never have the convenient layout of the new cabin, but it was unquestionably more beautiful.

"I think I could lie here forever," Holly sighed happily.

"I can't," Amy said, even though she loved lying here in the light, knowing why Jack had installed these rooftop windows. He had hoped that they would tell her that he loved her. "I have to pee."

"I wish you hadn't said that, Aunt Amy," Ellie moaned from the living room sofa. "I was trying so hard not to think about that."

The two of them pulled on their clothes and dashed shrieking to the biffy, the blast of cold air that greeted them when they opened the cabin door making their needs more urgent. But Gwen and Jack had already been up for more than an hour, so the garage was warm and a twenty-cup blue enamel coffeepot, the kind used on the chuck wagons of Western movies, sat in a pan of hot water on top of one of the wood stoves.

Even though it was mind-numbingly cold outside, everything else seemed startlingly easy. Gwen had set out mugs, cream, sugar, and spoons on a little side table so coffee drinkers weren't always trapising through the kitchen, elbowing cooks away from the stove. The tables were picnic tables with benches, so there was no need to hunt up chairs for every meal. Metal dishpans full of soap water were set on the wood stove, and everyone put their dirty dishes directly in the water. Kids then washed dishes on the picnic table, leaving the sink open for adults to tackle the pots and pans.

The women spent the day cooking, and Amy openly admitted that she enjoyed being the one who knew where things were. "I know it's not going to last," she said to Phoebe. "By tomorrow you'll know everything better than me, but today I'm going to gloat."

"You may gloat all you want," Phoebe answered. "But in turn you have to promise not to laugh, because while you've been turning into me, I think I've been turning into you."

Ellie leaned back from where she had been chopping celery and pointedly looked at her mother's rear end. "No, you haven't, Mom. Not by a long shot."

"Ellie!" Laughing, Phoebe swatted her across the arm. "What kind of thing was that to say?"

"The truth," Ellie answered.

"She's spending too much time with Nick," Holly said. "He's not a good influence." Then she looked at Phoebe. "I have dibs on Amy's butt. What other part of her are you taking?"

"The clothes part. You know how we decided not to dress up for Thanksgiving dinner?" The family usually wore black-tie for holiday meals, but no one could quite envision stumbling out to the biffy in satin pumps, so orders had gone out not to bring formal clothes. "I realized Tuesday afternoon that I really was going to miss that."

"I wish you had told me," Holly said. "I didn't bring a thing."

"I know. I thought about calling you, but that would have left Gwen and Amy out."

"We wouldn't have minded," Gwen said.

"I would have," Amy said. She might be struggling to change her role within her family, but no prospect of enduring happiness would make her give up her "Best Dressed" title. A person had to keep her priorities.

"I know," Phoebe said. "So I had this idea, and I know it sounds sort of stupid, but Giles egged me on"— it wasn't like Phoebe to be so hesitant—"and most of

395

the stuff the thrift shop hadn't been able to get rid of, and they gave me a lot of it, and we had extra room in the car."

"I have no idea what you're talking about," Holly said.

"I do." Amy clapped her hands together. "We're going to play dress up."

Indeed they were. Phoebe had gone to the local thrift shops and filled four big trash bags full of gorgeous junk. It was indeed out of character for her.

But it was fun. At first Holly and Ian were merely being cooperative, but within minutes a giddy playfulness captured even them. Only the two younger boys felt incapable of dressing up.

Giles had been warned to bring his tux, and Phoebe had driven over to Upton to get Hal's. So the two of them were conventionally dressed except for their shirts. Giles's was a tied-dyed swirl of yellows and reds, and Hal's was a seventies monstrosity, Alice blue with blackedged ruffles. The shirt's collar points were so elongated that Hal was planning to carve the turkey with them. Jack was in his own jeans and one of the earth-toned shirts that Holly had given him, but he had accessorized himself with a pleated red cummerbund from whose folds dangled little plastic Santa Clauses and reindeer. There was a matching bow tie, but generous soul that he was, he was letting two-year-old Thomas wear it. He instead selected neckware that was silk-screened to resemble a bottle of Glenfiddich scotch whisky. Ian was wearing a red-lined black Dracula. cape, and Nick had donned a metallic silver Hershey's Kiss Halloween costume.

The two little girls were safety-pinned into pastel prom dresses. Ellie and Gwen had on matching fifties-style cocktail ensembles, bumblebee yellow skirts slit up the front to reveal black toredo pants. Holly's gown was trimmed in acid green bugle beads; no one knew exactly what color arsenic was, but the general consensus was that she should be kept away from all food-preparation sites. Phoebe was in a draped, bias-cut oyster satin gown that Hal instantly recognized—or pretended to do so—as a homemade copy of Eleanor Roosevelt's gown from the First Ladies Hall at the Smithsonian. Amy selected a crinoline-lined, ruffled royal purple taffeta skirt with a big watermark on the hem. She ripped a scarlet paisley shawl in half, wrapped one half around her torso in a mock bustier, even managing to fold the shawl into an interesting V at the front. She then used the other half of the shawl as a sash. Everyone instantly told her that she looked too good, that her outfit was too close to something a human being might actually wear. Since she was already cold, she pulled off the shawl, stole Jack's camel-and-tobacco-colored wool shirt, and cinched it at her waist with an elasticized silver sequined belt. All agreed she was now more in keeping with the spirit of the evening.

Then Phoebe brought out a worn velvet jewel case and called the two little girls over to her. Amy went too. She wanted to see what Phoebe had brought. A red, white, and blue rhinestone American flag pin would be the perfect thing to finish off her outfit.

But the jewelry was not from the thrift shop. Lying on a bed of ivory satin, glinting sullenly, were Eleanor's garnets, the ornate, elaborate parure that Amy had admired so much as a child.

They really were ugly.

Claire and Emily squealed. "Oh, can we wear those? Can we? Can we please?"

"If you're careful," Phoebe said.

The set was large enough that each girl had a bracelet and a brooch the size of a Campbell's. soup can lid. Neither had pierced ears, so Phoebe had wired the earrings to barrettes, and they were wearing them in their hair. There was only one necklace, but Phoebe told them that they could trade every half hour.

"Is there any chance I can get in on the necklace rotation?" Amy asked. "I always wanted to wear it."

"They'll get bored with it halfway through dinner," Phoebe answered, "and you can do whatever you want. But in the meantime . . . we need you to sit down and close your eyes."

"Me? Why?" She noticed that Ellie had joined them, her hands behind her back. "Okay." She sat down on one of the picnic benches, her purple taffeta billowing up over three spaces.

She felt something cold at her throat and then warm fingers at the back of her neck. "You can open your eyes now," Ellie said.

Ellie was holding a small hand mirror in front of her. Amy looked at herself. Inside the collar of Jack's wool shirt, hanging just below her collarbone, was her mother's opal necklace, five rectangular-cut opals separated from each other by tiny diamonds. Simple and elegant, it had been given to Eleanor's mother, Amy's grandmother, when she had made her debut in London. Phoebe was holding the matching earrings.

"I also brought the topazes for you," Phoebe said, "but they were too good a match with that shirt."

"Phoebe . . ." Amy was speechless. "You don't have to do this."

"I want to. She was your mother too."

Amy could feel her eyes tingle, her mouth start to

398

tighten. She was going to cry. For the last two years Phoebe had hugged Eleanor's memory to herself as if it were hers and hers alone. She was now sharing the memory, easing her grief.

Hal came over and put one arm around each of his daughters. Apparently Phoebe had told him that she was giving Amy the opals and the topazes. "I'm going to sound like a silly old fool, but the two of you growing closer is a source of tremendous gratification. I always thought of us as a close family because of the lake, that we were close because we had this wonderful place where we spend so much time. Then I got to know Gwen and her children. They didn't have a special place like this, but they're closer to each other than we've ever been. A place, no matter how special, no matter how sacred it is, wasn't going to hold people together. It's the way they feel about each other, and I wish I could say this without sounding like a Hallmark card, but I don't seem to be able to."

Amy liked Hallmark cards. "There's a reason Hallmark sells however many million cards a year; some of them are right. Some of them say things that need to be said."

"Can I have some help?" Gwen called out from the kitchen side of the room. "From someone other than Nick?"

She was trying to take the turkey out of the oven, and her assistant was standing by uselessly, hampered by his complete ignorance and the probable flammability level of his silver metallic Hershey's Kiss costume.

True to their sex, all the men were quite ready to help now that everything was almost done. Until it was time to change clothes, they had been worthless, spending the entire day poring over Giles's blueprints and tramping

399

back and forth between the cabins and the newly cleared site at the Rim.

After dinner they got the plans back out—apparently building plans were almost as satisfying as televised football—and Amy drifted over to look at them. She couldn't tell a thing from them, but that was all right. Looking at the plans was really only an excuse to come sit by Jack.

Giles explained the cabin design to her. It was an A-frame, not big at all, but it had an open kitchen and living space, two little bedrooms in back, and a loft with two more small bedrooms. The lakeside of the cabin would be almost all windows. A broad deck opened out to the beach.

The plans had been professionally drawn, but the table was littered with yellow legal paper that the men had been making notes on. She recognized Jack's hand on one, so she picked it up. It had a rough hand-drawn site plan of the log cabin lot. She could identify three of the buildings, the cabin, the woodshed, the biffy, but there was a fourth square, much smaller than the cabin but larger than the others, drawn into an empty corner of the lot.

"What's this?" she asked, and before anyone answered, she picked up the sheet of paper that had been with it. It was obviously a drawing of a very tiny cabin, really only a bedroom. She could now recognize the architectural symbols. The cabin was to have a door, windows on three sides, a small stove, and three gas fights. "What's this?" she repeated.

Jack glanced over his shoulder. "Mom and Holly don't know about this yet, only Hal does, but I'd like to build this for my sister. She's been a good sport about coming up here, and she'll go on being a good sport, but

I've been trying to think what would make her want to come here, not just because she's humoring Mom and me. She's used to privacy, she's used to quiet. Giles said that he didn't feel like he belonged up here until he started working on his boat. I think if Holly has her own little cottage, she'll come to love the place as much as Mom and I already do."

Amy looked over her shoulder at Holly, who was at the card table playing double solitaire with Nick. The soft gaslight muted the acid glitter of the bugle beads on her gown.

Amy touched her opals. Everyone had changed since the beginning of the summer. Phoebe was gentler, Giles more willing to put himself first. Ian had stopped living with blinders tied to his eyes. Ellie was more confident; Nick was willing to admit that there were things he cared about. Jack had made peace with his father; Amy had learned to live within the heart of the family. And of course she and Jack had fallen in love.

Everyone had changed except Holly, cool, organized, self-contained Holly. Holly might never change; she might always be the elegant, urbane creature whose natural name and warm coloring had nothing to do with what she was like. But if she ever was going to change, the change would start, Amy knew, at the lake.

"And then, of course," Giles said slowly, "the log cabin becomes not Amy, Holly, and Jack's. but Amy and Jack's."

Amy's eyes shot to Jack. But he was folding up his papers, and suddenly he started being very careful about how he was folding them, getting the edges perfectly lined up.

"Do you feel like you need permission?" Giles went on. "You won't get it from Hal or Gwen. They won't

401

interfere like that. You can't have an affair, you know that. In fact, you can't even have much of a courtship. You can't be like normal people. You can't splash around in the shallow end for a year or so. You'll get the rest of us wet. The two of you, you have to jump straight into the deep end. But if you're willing to get married, and if you want permission, for what it's worth, you've got mine." He stood up. "Now, I suppose you have things to talk about." He faced the room and raised his voice so that everyone could hear him. "Let's play charades." And as a parting gesture he poured the rest of his red wine into Jack's beer. The ruby liquid funneled down and then blended into the amber beer.

"He thinks we should get married," Amy whispered.

Jack nodded. "I know."

"It's probably been our only choice all along, marriage or nothing."

Jack nodded. "I know."

"But this summer . . . I wasn't ready to talk about marriage."

Jack nodded. "I know."

On the other side of the room, the kids were shouting. They loved the idea of charades. Emily jumped up so quickly that she kicked the Parcheesi board by mistake and all the pieces slid off.

"Would you stop saying that you know everything?" Amy kept her voice low. "And tell me what you think."

Alex had been winning Parcheesi, and now charades didn't sound so good. He thought they ought to figure out where the pieces had been and finish the game first. "I know where my pieces were."

"They weren't there." His sister Claire snatched them off the board as quickly as he could put them down. "You weren't that far."

"I was too."

"You were not." The brother and sister were fighting.

Jack glanced over his shoulder at them. Then he bent his head close to Amy's "I've always assumed that if I ever got married, I'd do it about three days after meeting her. So by my standards we're been courting nearly forever."

If they weren't in the same family, it would be different. But if they weren't in the same family, they would have never met.

Giles was speaking to the kids. "Emily didn't mean to knock the board over, Alex. I know you don't like what's happened, but you need to accept it and move on. Do you want to play charades or not?"

"I want to play charades," Alex said, "but I want to finish Parcheesi first."

Was this the way other couples decided their futures? Yes, there had been imported champagne, but it turned out that Amy's beloved didn't like champagne and he was drinking beer, beer that was now mixed with red wine. There was candlelight and a fire, but those were physical necessities; without them everyone would be freezing and bumping into the furniture. The kids were on the floor bickering. Gwen and Hal were sitting on the love seat, the bumblebee yellow satin of her skirt spilling over his knee. Giles was tearing up slips of paper for charades; Phoebe was gathering up pencils; unfortunately Eleanor Roosevelt's gown had a little train on it, and people kept stepping on her. Ian was showing Ellie how to use the timing feature on his watch. Holly and Nick had finished their game, and they were doing the last few dishes.

"I'm not going to stop skating until I'm ready," Amy said, "and that means traveling."

"And I can't promise I'll stay in one place or one job for more than a few years."

She didn't care about that. "Our kids certainly won't win any perfect attendance awards."

But they would travel, they would see Europe, they would ride in limousines, they would live at disaster sites.

Amy put her hand out. Jack covered it with his. So what if they didn't know exactly where they would be living, what they would be doing, for every minute of the next fifty years? They would share the adventure.

"I would kiss you if I could," Jack said. "But if anyone saw, Giles would never get this charades game going."

That was true. "I think everyone's going to be pleased."

"I don't know about everyone, my mom, your dad, yes . . . Holly, Phoebe, and Ian, them too . . . but frankly I don't think Alex and Scott will give a damn one way or another, and if we have a wedding and they're forced to dress up, they're going to be pissed off."

That was certainly true, but Emily and Claire would be thrilled to be junior bridesmaids. "What about you?" Amy asked. "Aren't you going to be pissed off if we force you to dress up for a wedding?"

"I'm wearing this." Jack flicked a hand across his cummerbund and set his little plastic Santa Clauses dancing.

Giles had finally succeeded. The kids were dumping the Parcheesi game into the box, ready to play charades. Alex and Scott were shrieking that they wanted to be the captains, they wanted to choose their teams.

"No, no. Jack and Amy will be too humiliated when they are chosen last," Giles said. "We'll divide by sex.

404

Men against women."

People were starting to stand up, the men gathering near Nick, the women near Ellie.

"I'm really bad at charades," Jack said to Amy, "but I don't suppose we have much choice." He got up, took a last swallow of his beer, then grimaced. He had forgotten about the red wine Giles had poured into his glass. "Listen, the ice on the lake is plenty thick. People were out there all day. If I sweep off a patch tomorrow, will you skate for me?"

Since she had come directly from a competition, she had her skates with her. "I'd love to."

Holly was gesturing to them to get with their teams. Amy let her arm brush against Jack's and started toward the women's team. Her royal purple skirt caught against the picnic bench. Jack had to lean down to free her.

They would tell everyone tomorrow. She would skate on the lake, and then they would tell the family that they were getting married.

She wouldn't be able to skate well. The ice would be rough, and the space small. But that didn't matter. She would be skating at the lake. After dreading the place for so many summers because she couldn't skate here, now she was going to be able to.

She sat down with her team. Holly and Phoebe were full of ideas for charade clues; Ellie was scribbling them down as fast as she could. Gwen was helping the two little girls take the garnets out of their hair, but she was still listening, commenting on Holly's and Phoebe's ideas. Amy had nothing to add. Jack's shirt felt warm against her arms, her mother's opals were a cool, delicate weight, and the water-marked royal purple taffeta rustled when she moved.

Tomorrow she would skate at the lake.

405

Dear Reader:

I hope you enjoyed reading this Large Print book. If you are interested in reading other Beeler Large Print titles, ask your librarian or write to me at

Thomas T. Beeler, *Publisher*
Post Office Box 659
Hampton Falls, New Hampshire 03844

You can also call me at 1-800-251-8726 and I will send you my latest catalogue.

Audrey Lesko and I choose the titles I publish in Large Print. Our aim is to provide good books by outstanding authors—books we both enjoyed reading and liked well enough to want to share. We warmly welcome any suggestions for new titles and authors.

Sincerely,